WHISPER OF SUFFERING

Dragon of Eriden Book 1

SAMANTHA JACOBEY

Lavish Publishing LLC

First Edition

Dragon of Eriden Book 1

2018 Lavish Publishing, LLC

All Rights Reserved

Published in the United States by Lavish Publishing, LLC, Midland, TX

Cover Design by: Victor R. Sosa

Cover Images: CanStock

Paperback Edition

ISBN: 9781944985554

www.LavishPublishing.com

Contents

For my family and friends who brought this story to life…
Thank you for being part of this project.

Richard, Christopher, Jonathon and Steven
Life is an adventure – work hard, take the risks, and remember to enjoy the time you
are given.

Lainey, Mady and Savanna
You are a princess, even when life doesn't treat you that way – imagine your
happiness and work to make it come true.

Melinda, Emma and Kathy
You are all beautiful women who understand how precious life is, and that you are
never too old to start a new adventure.

Special thanks to, Carol Harris for our ship name, Kathy for proofreading, Desiree
for formatting, Kristin and the Sassy Bitches for the million things you tirelessly do
to support me.

Foreword

Hello, dear reader. Welcome to Eriden, a magical kingdom of long ago. This story is a light fantasy written to entertain and inspire the young and the young at heart.

Along the way, you will meet my interpretation of several races and many characters, as well as travel across a mystical foreign land.

To aid you on this journey, you will find a set of maps and character profiles in the back of each of the books.

If you ever feel lost or have forgotten who someone is, simply flip to the back and have a look.

Otherwise, thank you for joining us on this magical adventure and I hope you enjoy.

Prologue

ZIRADON'S EMERALD green eyes stared straight ahead. A large ceremonial fire in the pit before him reflected upon their glassy surface. Bound by fierce dark magic and unable to move, he dug his claws into the cracks in the rocks beneath him.

Snorting, a puff of smoke escaped his deep brown muzzle and curled gently around the light brown horns that protruded twelve inches from his forehead to their sharp points. The rounded tips of his ears flicked back and forth as they pivoted to listen, the cuts in his ancient face burning as the cloud floated over them.

Every muscle in his sleek body tense, he waited. For endless hours, he had fought against his attackers; those who sought to overthrow his kingdom and bring an end to his reign as the Supreme Dragon of Eriden. A title he held for over half a millennium, it was more than just a name bestowed upon him. His reign meant balance and peace in the land for all creatures. In the end, outnumbered, he'd been taken, and his bitter fate lay in the flames that flickered in the cool night air.

"What do you wait for?" the ancient sovereign snarled.

"Patience," Gwirwen hissed in return.

Pacing calmly around, then between the circle of dragons that lined the shadows of the cliff, the leader of the renegades lumbered through the darkness. Below them, the rumble of the surf vied with the pop and crack of the embers as waves broke against the rocks. His wide, white body swaying as he moved, the stiff spines that lined his backbone creaked ever so slightly, his long tail dragging the ground as it followed.

Restless, he paused, leaning back on his haunches and spreading his massive ghost-white wings so the breeze caught them and stretched the worn skin taut. The claws of his front legs reaching above him, he pawed into the cool blackness. Breathing a hot blast of crimson into the ebony sky, he roared, then returned to his former pacing.

Behind him, Ziradon heard the beat of a full-sized pair of wings landing on the

1

earth and scattering a few stones. His keen ears detecting the quieter flutter of a smaller pair, he flattened them against his head, growling softly, "Who else will be joining your rebellion?"

From out of the black, a lesser female form emerged with a tiny creature ambling along timidly beneath her as the older dragon forced her forward. "I have brought the child," Ziewen announced to the group. "She was hidden but not well enough," she added, her voice laced with amusement.

The oldest of the few females in their kingdom, Ziewen had laid the eggs of three of Gwirwen's followers, so her treachery did not surprise him. "Your sons will be the destruction of Eriden," Ziradon informed the newcomer. His emerald orbs searched for a glimpse of his precious dragoness, his most recent and only surviving offspring.

"Kaliwyn?" he puffed. He had hoped she would remain concealed, protected by the few completely loyal to him and thereby escape the cruelty of those who stood against him.

The miniature dragon of only a few years measured a mere three feet from nose to tail, about one-seventh of her father's size, and one-fifth that of the other female. Her three male siblings who had preceded her had died two centuries before, leaving her as the sole heir to her father's love and legacy. She had been a welcome surprise to him, a new beginning for an old soul, but it appeared to be a mere fantasy, and their end would come much sooner than either of them could have known.

Wriggling herself free of her captor, Kaliwyn found Ziradon's commanding form and pushed herself against him, attempting to hide beneath his protective wing. However, his binding prevented her from anything more than pressing her shivering golden-brown scales against his as she sobbed. "Father," she beseeched, her golden muzzle pressed against him as she inhaled his scent.

"Be brave, my child," Ziradon soothed with a gravelly tone. "End her suffering quickly," he commanded of his long-time advisor. "She should not be made to wait her fate." He had lost children before; his sons who had died in the Great War. He refused to be broken by those who plotted against them, as groveling would be beneath him. "Let us die together and face the next life side by side."

Gwirwen's laughter erupted from a low rumble; in his eyes, the tiny dragon's fortune had been sealed the moment she drew her first breath. "For many decades have I waited for my turn to sit upon the throne of our kingdom. And with each passing year, you have promised that one day it would be mine. No heir was born to you for two long centuries that I have served, save this one, this one weak dragoness."

Ziradon blinked his large round eyes calmly. "It is not your destiny to wear the dragon's crown. Free me and let us continue as fate has determined our course to stand, and my daughter shall grow into her place as queen of Adiarwen and Supreme Dragon of Eriden, as it should be."

"No!" Gwirwen barked in return, his large body coiling as he faced his prisoner squarely. Flames danced between his teeth, even as he fought the urge to destroy the small heiress. "I choose my destiny. And I determine *your* fate. Bring her," he commanded to the others. "We shall imprison her in the body of a human, and

Ziewen will deliver her to one of their villages across the sea, among the mortals of the rim."

"Kaliwyn, my sweet!" Ziradon gasped as she was torn away and dragged a few feet from his bound form. "Do not do this. Kill her now. Spill her blood upon the soil, that she may remain a part of Adiarwen for eternity. Do not send her bones to turn to dust among the mortals."

"I shall have my revenge," Gwirwen replied, joining his minions as they formed a ring around the smaller dragon. "Two hundred years of waiting and you will feel each one of them as a thorn beneath your scales," he promised. Their eyes glowing brightly, the group focused their magic, their lips snarling as they chanted an ancient curse.

"Please, do not do this!" Ziradon begged as he pushed against his bonds, his plea falling on deaf ears. Before him, he could see her between their massive bodies. Her sleek golden-brown scales curled into a ball, her red spikes followed the line of her back from the top of her head to the tip of her tail. "My beautiful child," he grieved, closing his eyes tightly, as if to shut out the image of her small dragon form as it was replaced by a flimsy human girl.

Still curled tightly, Kaliwyn cried, weeping into her newly formed hands. Shiny, honey-colored locks of hair cascaded over her bare skin, and her shoulders shook with her anguish. Daring to peek, bright green eyes glared up at her father's nemesis. "You monster!" she spat defiantly, managing to stand on her wobbly legs and clamber the few yards to her father's giant form.

Once again attempting to burrow beneath him, his rough scales scratched at her pink flesh, and she dragged her pudgy fingers along the width of his chest as his chin pressed down on the top of her head. "Father," she sobbed once more.

Scarcely able to nuzzle his offspring, Ziradon inhaled the scent of a mortal where a dragon princess had once been. "My sweet Kaliwyn," he choked, his heart broken at the thought of the miles that would isolate her from her home.

"Take her away," Gwirwen commanded. "Fly her to Nalen and drop her there."

"Yes, my lord," Ziewen agreed. Catching her by the hair and roughly dragging her away, the sharp rocks scratched and cut the girl's bare flesh. Driven by the scent of blood, the dragon scooped her prey into the pouch on her belly, where any resistance to the transfer would be rendered pointless.

Spreading her giant, yellow wings, which spanned an equal twenty feet to her body, she dove off the cliff and caught a draft coming up from the pitch-black ocean. Soaring above it, she flew due east, covering the miles that separated the magical realm of Eriden from the distant creatures who infested the rest of their world.

Atop the crags of the dragon cliffs of Adiarwen, Ziradon moaned, unable to hold in the tortured groan. "My child," he huffed. His voice loud, almost shrill, the stones strewn across the cliff reverberated, and the ground shook. Grief poured from his being, deep sorrow at having lost the only possession he had left to cherish.

His eyes smoldering, he thought of Kaliwyn's mother, Kilawon, his most recent queen. A beautiful young dragon, she had filled his heart with hope and his days with renewed life. But she had been killed in an accident soon after their only child had hatched, and he had raised their dragoness alone.

The night's events brought her death into question and the depth of his closest advisor's treachery into focus. He glared at the fire coldly, still hoping for freedom and the chance to right the wrongs that his family had endured.

Amused by his suffering, the group of dragons circled him once more. Marching in a slow line, they used their power to pull the rocks around them into a stone cage, covering the fire and their restrained victim in an unbreakable prison. When they had finished, Gwirwen placed his white muzzle against a split in the stone and blew out the flames before he growled, "A meal will be delivered to you each day, and you will remain here for eternity, a spectacle for all to see. Your daughter will live all the days of her pitiful life in a foreign land, never knowing the feel of the Eriden air beneath her wings."

Lying motionless, Ziradon stared at the intersection of the rock above his head. Their magical binding released, he flung himself against it in hopes that it would shatter. The magic of his prison strong, his tough hide pounded against immovable stone until he had exhausted his last ounce of energy.

Again, stretched on the floor of his cage, he panted; his wounds oozing fresh bright red blood. The combined power of the others would hold the rock firmly; there would be no escape. No end to the long and empty days that lay before him, or to the torture that would eat at him over the centuries to come.

ONE

Child of Woe

"AMICIA!"

The girl heard the deep shout of her name float across the meadow, her family's berry source. She had been there since sunrise, moving along the edge of the woods that ran between the open field and their cottage, and she was almost ready to return home to start the next part of the process.

Ignoring him, she continued to pick the wild berries, the calloused tips of her fingers catching each one and plucking it expertly. *Please, not today*, she mentally pleaded, hoping he would respect the snub and continue on his way.

Shifting to a new shrub, the hot rays beat down upon her thick golden braid, heating her neck and flushing her skin. Stealing a glance, she could see his tall frame weaving through the rows of bushes. *Damn him.* They had been friends once; at least she thought they had, but not now. Now, all she wanted was to escape a future she felt powerless to avoid.

Wiping at the sweat beading on her brow with the back of her arm, she pretended not to notice his approach. *I can't deal with this*, she fumed. She knew he continued, his resolve strong. *He will unhinge me and then where will we be?*

"Amicia," Rupert repeated when he had halved the distance between them.

"I'm still cross with you," she called in retort, hoisting one of her baskets and turning her back on him. Her pace as quick as she could muster with the load, she dove into the line of trees and followed the familiar path.

"Don't be cross," he replied persuasively, taking up her second filled carrier when he reached it and following her through the stand of trees.

The trail well worn, her bare feet pattered on the packed earth, but she could hear his pursuit, even over the rustle of her skirt that floated around her ankles. "How's your mum?" she heard him call when he had all but caught her, causing a moment of rage to well up within her.

Coming out the other side of the small forest, Amicia's anger waned, and her heart felt heavy at the sight of the only home she had ever known; a house at the back of the clearing that stood in severe disrepair. Her father had become ill over two years before and had passed away this last winter, leaving her and her mother alone. Frowning at the thatch, she feared the roof wouldn't last another year, but she hated the thought of asking Rupert, or anyone else, to see to it.

It was a small two room bungalow in which she still slept in a small bed in the larger room. The front area of it housed a small kitchen with a plain wooden table for dining and preparing meals. The other half of the great room consisted of two straight-backed chairs and a fireplace, with her lumpy bed shoved in the corner to the left of the stone hearth. A small box at the foot of it held everything she owned in the world: three dresses and a few trinkets.

In the smaller room, her mother slept through as of late, night and day. "Same as she was." Ami somberly dropped her gathered treasure onto a table in their small yard.

Stomping over to the short stone barrier of the well, she fetched water in the drawing pail and poured it into a large bowl. Sloshing as she carried it, she returned to the workbench, where she began washing the fruit in small handfuls, then spreading them on the flat surface to inspect for quality. "Build a fire," she commanded.

Hiding his scowl, Rupert obeyed, arranging the logs in the pit and skillfully setting them ablaze with the tools from the kindling box. Returning the kit to the shelf, he inquired, "Water to boil?"

"Yes," she replied stiffly. "Use the big pot, half full."

Selecting the largest of the three from their hooks along the front wall, he exhaled loudly as he hauled it over to the well and used the bucket to complete the task. Hanging it above the flames, he waited for his next chore.

When she said nothing, he grew uncomfortable at her silence. "It wasn't a bad idea," he muttered loud enough for her to hear. "I would take care of the two of you. I swear that I would," he groveled.

"I'm not going to marry you, Rupert," she spat, working diligently and not daring to look at him.

"You're a silly girl, Amicia Spicer," he chided. "You think proposals fall in your lap every day? Not in Nalen, princess," he mocked her.

Pausing, she grunted, then cut her eyes over to glare at him. "I've known you since I was a child, Ru. Can I help it you don't feel like a husband to me? We're more like friends, not lovers." Dropping her gaze as she spoke, a wave of fear rocked her before she steadied herself and returned to her work, taking solace in the routine of it.

"Now love," he cooed, stepping towards her. His voice dripping with sweet honey, he plied her with thick, persuasive tones. "It would be the same as it is. We'd be friends of a better sort, that's all. You would grow to love me as a husband, the way a proper wife would do."

The word *proper* grated on her nerves. She had seen many a man's definition of proper, and she wanted no part of it. Holding her tongue, she continued to scrub and sort the berries to dump into the pot to simmer.

Inside the house, the cough of an old woman interrupted their conversation, and

Amicia sighed loudly. "I told you I can't. My mother loved my father. It's his passing that has driven her to the grave so quickly after he left us. I don't feel that for you, and it wouldn't be right to pretend that I did."

His deep brown eyes glaring at her in the afternoon sun, Rupert ground his teeth. "An old man your father was, and your mother is equally aged. Let them go, Amicia. Take up your new life with me, before I'm too old for children of my own."

Her hands shaking, Ami didn't stop. She hoped that he would remain calm at her refusal. If her father's health hadn't failed, she felt certain she would have been married off to the man there with her already, and she was thankful that she had not been.

But he was right about one thing; her parents had been old when she was born, and they had needed her to care for them and to run their business in their waning years. That's the only reason she had remained with them after coming of age. As their only child, it was her place to care for them for as long as they needed.

Not getting a response, he eventually grunted, his voice dense, "I'll be at the mill if you need me."

Turning his back, Rupert exited through the side gate, giving it a slam before he took the road towards town. If her father had promised her hand before his passing, that would have been one thing, but with no such understanding, he had little grounds to force the issue if she continued to refuse. He wanted her but not badly enough to take her by force; at least not yet, it seemed.

Watching him go, Ami pulled her long, braided locks with her hand, twisting them up into a quick bun to allow the air to reach her neck. Securing the knot, she continued her chore until the pot of berries hung over the fire and she could go into the cottage and tend to her mother.

Inside, the air felt heavy, and a musty odor filled her nostrils. Glancing at the door to her mother's quarters, she paused to listen to the ragged breaths. Opening windows in the kitchen and above her bed, she hummed pleasantly, pretending that everything was fine, and her mother would join her at any moment; but she knew that the older woman wouldn't. Time was against Arely Spicer, and soon she would be buried in the ground beside her beloved husband.

"Are you ready for some supper, mum?" Ami called pleasantly.

"Yes," a raspy voice replied.

Placing a small pot on the fire in front of the chairs, Amicia warmed the meal and served it into a bowl. Entering her mother's bedroom, she pushed back the drapes and opened that window as well. Pulling a seat up beside her bed, she cautiously fed the thin, cracked lips one small spoonful at a time.

"You should marry that man," her mother stated abruptly, disturbing their rhythm.

"Why would I want to do such a fool thing?" the young woman bit tartly, softening the retort with a small smile.

"I'm dying, Ami," her mother persisted. "Gus and me will be buried. You'll still be living, and you should take a husband, have a family of your own."

"I'll make do," Amicia snapped, standing and placing the bowl on the small table next to the bed. Her features drawn, she turned away, adjusting the bedding that covered her mother's thin frame. "I've only been of age for a year, and I'm sure there are better suiters to be had."

She could see the deep lines in Arely's face when she glanced at her and fought the urge to rub in the truth. Her mind leaping to her younger self, she recalled how long she had been working, first by their side as she learned and eventually in their place, as they had grown too old to carry out the labor of their small spice farm.

Ami had been running the business on her own for years; almost since she had become strong enough to carry a bushel of berries. She picked and boiled, canned and dried. She even hauled them into town to conduct the sales and down to the docks to make the trades. She might miss her mother, but in the end, her life would be little different after she had passed.

"I don't need a man, mum," Amicia held her resolve. "And I don't feel I'm the sort to be raising young."

"Ami," her mother breathed, her air noisy when she gasped the name. "I have something I must tell you, my child."

"Please, mum," the younger woman begged with a shake of her golden lump of hair, "no more talk of Rupert. I'll decide when it's time to give a man my hand." She grinned at her mother, hoping to appease her.

"No," the old head rocked against her pillow. "No, sweet Amicia. There's something else you must know before I'm gone."

"What, mum," Ami replied, taking her mother's hand between hers and clasping it tightly. The boney fingers cold against her warm flesh, fear seized her gut at the realization that her mother had a few days at most.

"Tell me, mum," she stammered, blinking back tears. She could pretend her life would be the same, but deep down, she knew she wasn't ready to lose her other parent so soon.

Her clear blue eyes clouded, the older woman gasped. "So hard," she wheezed. "After all this time, I always thought you would realize…" Her voice trailed away.

"Realize what?" Ami prodded, lifting the frail digits and pressing them to her lips.

"Me and Gus," she panted, "we found you when you was a little girl. Three, maybe four you was."

"Was I lost?" Amicia smiled through her pain, her mother's words confusing and probably delirium.

Her mother nodded. "Yes, maybe you was. You was lost, and we found you, and we kept you. No one ever came looking, and you became our little girl. Our little miracle, Amicia." Her old set of eyes wide, she glared at her, unblinking as she made her confession.

Staring at her as she spoke, an icy chill crept up Amicia's spine, and the cool evening breeze from the window made her shudder. The words caught in her throat, she could feel hot tears trickle over onto her cheeks. "Are you saying you're not my mother?" she eventually managed faintly.

"Tis true. So many times have I longed to tell you, but it never seemed right. But now the secret's been told, and I can rest my head that it has been set right."

"Set right!" Amicia lost herself for a moment. "Mum, please. You can't mean this. I'm your daughter!"

But as soon as the words tumbled out, she knew her denial could not change what she had suspected most of her years; her parents had not been young when she was born. To the contrary, they had both been grey and wrinkled as long as she could remember. That, and they had always called her their gift from God. *Could this be why?*

"Oh, mum," she said quietly, squeezing her mother's fingers firmly. "It's ok. You think I should marry Rupert?" She changed the subject, the pain in her heart too much to face at that moment. Her only defense, she ignored the situation, pretending it away. Dropping their connection, she picked up the soup and stirred it to continue as if nothing had been said.

"If he is the one," her mother agreed. "Follow your heart, my sweet Amicia. Follow your dreams to the place where you belong."

Pursing her lips, Ami helped her mother finish the meal, then returned to the kitchen to wash the bowl. Her mother's words had stolen her appetite, so she left the small house and went back outside, ostensibly to check on her fruit.

Finding everything in order and the water gently boiling, she gave the kettle a few stirs. Satisfied that her mixture would not stick, she walked around the far end of the structure and followed the path that led down the hill behind the small dwelling. There, the gentle slope gave way to a sharp drop-off that quickly shifted from grassy soil to broken rock and the ocean below.

Staring out across the water, her mother's words churned inside her thoughts. *Follow your dreams to the place where you belong.* More times than she could count, Ami had stood in that very spot, watching the waves and the sun as they met in the distance. The wind whipping around her, she rubbed her arms vigorously, refusing to go back inside.

Closing her eyes and enjoying the rays on her cheeks, the ball of fire sank deeper into the horizon. Rocking gently, she felt as if she could leap from the cliff and soar across the top of the sea. That's what she dreamed of – flying across the water, to the west of their home. Always away from the harshness of life she had come to accept as her existence. Always into the sun, floating and diving, as if she were a gull, free to roam where ever the next gust of wind might take her.

TWO

Dust to Dust

AMICIA AWOKE to the silence of the empty cottage. Lying in the still of the morning, she stared at the ceiling above her, the timbers of the old roof creaking eerily. The thatch thin in places, she could see the discolored patches that glowed slightly from the sun shining upon it. It was much later than she normally slept, but this day she would have no chores to complete, save one.

Her mother had passed away the day before, and they had prepared Arely's body for burial that evening. Then, everyone had gone, leaving her alone in the old house that no longer felt like home; not since her mother had confessed what they had done.

For days, her mother's words had torn at her heart. Retracing her life, the simple and honest work of her years, she could put her finger on no specific moment when the truth had been clear. But in the shadows of her days, she knew her mother's claim to be true. She did not belong in that family, on that farm, or in that life.

Sliding from under the covers, she slipped out of her night clothes and washed herself in a basin of cold water, as she had begun so many of her days before. Then, donning a simple black gown, one she only wore once or twice a year, she went over to the kitchen and made herself a small breakfast of bread and hard cheese. Sitting by the fire in the living area to eat it, she jumped when a knock sounded on the door.

"Who is it?" she called, wiping at the tears that she hadn't realized she had cried.

"It's me," Rupert replied, pushing the wooden covering open a crack. "Are you decent?"

"Yes, I'm dressed." She got to her feet and smoothed her skirt.

"I'm here to see you to the parish," he informed her, removing his hat and holding it in his hand as he shuffled inside.

Quite handsome in his dark suit, Ami managed a smile for him. "She's in a better place, Ru. Father can look after her now."

"It's not Arely that I'm worried about," he confessed, the dark circles under his eyes exposed as he moved nearer. Seeing the pain in her clear green orbs, he closed the distance and swooped her against his chest with his right arm, his left hand still holding the hat as he curled it around her. "I'm so sorry, Ami," he breathed into her thick, blond hair.

"I know," she sniffed, her tears flowing and dripping onto his jacket. "I'm making a mess of you," she teased. They had seldom so much as touched one another, and she felt awkward in his embrace.

"I wash," he replied, holding her firmly.

Standing together in her parents' home, the one that no longer belonged to her, Amicia's heart ached, and she drank in the comfort that he offered. She had insisted she did not need a man, but in that moment, she needed someone; anyone who could keep her grounded, that she might make it through what lay ahead.

"How long before the service?" she whispered, her cheek smashed against the fine cloth that covered his broad chest. Her fingers toying with the lapel, she focused on it, rather than the raw ache that festered within her.

"As long as you need," he soothed, releasing her and holding her arms firmly while she regained her footing.

"We'll go then." She raised her chin defiantly. She had not spoken of her mother's confession and had no intention of doing so. If anyone in the town knew of their deception, they had never given any indication; not to her. She was Arely's daughter in their eyes. She must complete her task before she would be free to decide her course.

Guiding her out of the house, Rupert helped her onto the wooden seat of his carriage, a small two-seat buggy pulled by a single pony. He didn't use it often. His old horse had seen better days and spent most of the remaining ones grazing in a pasture next to the mill.

Giving the girl a firm pat on her leg, he stood up straight and marched around to the other side. Hoisting himself up, he adjusted himself into the driver's side, glancing at her stiff form perched next to him. Lifting the reigns, he gave them a loud crack, which sent the aged mare stumbling along the cobblestone path.

Nalen was a sprawling town, with a few thousand people in and around. Some were new, some were only visiting, but most had lived their entire lives in the area. As the miller, he knew almost everyone, as did most of the tradesmen, such as the Spicers. The small parish would be standing room only for the old woman, her legacy in the township spanning half a dozen decades or more.

Rocking next to him as the wheels turned, Amicia felt disconnected from her body, as if she hung in the air above them; watching as they ambled along. The morning bright, it seemed unfitting to bury her would-be mother on such a fine day. *How could they have kept such a secret?*

To have been adopted would not have pained her so. There were some occasions when a child would need a home. Her parents had not been unkind, after all. Teaching her their trade would be expected of any family, real or contrived.

Opening her palms, she stared down at the lines and thickened hide of her fleshy pads. They had been toughened by years of picking berries, harvesting stalks of dill and leaves of thyme. Her years of service were not what drained her spirit.

Closing her hands into fists and lowering her lids, Ami drew in a deep breath, then blew it out through her nose. She wanted to calm herself and to wipe away the regret that twisted her gut. But she couldn't. It sat there, like a lump of putrid meat in her belly. Aching, gnawing at her innards incessantly.

Jerked back from her thoughts, her eyes fluttered. Rupert's hand clasped around her smaller digits, offering her what comfort he could. She had accepted his hug at his arrival, and she feared that doing so had only encouraged something that could not grow.

Biting her lip, she stared at the appendage, considering her options. Not accepting him by opening her grasp, but not pushing him away either, they rode in an uneasy silence she dared not defile, with his palm pressed against her closed knuckles.

Arriving in front of the long sanctuary, a middle-aged man with a wide girth met the wagon to help Amicia out of the cart. A baker by trade, Ami knew him, as he was a regular client of the Spicers.

Accepting her hand, he held her balance to the ground and once there offered his arm. Her fingers planted in its crook, he walked beside her, leading her down the center aisle to where a place had been reserved for her on the front row.

Taking her seat, Amicia kept her sorrow in check. Her hands curled loosely in her lap, she stared at the floor before her and waited for Ru to join her so the service could begin.

A moment later, a dirty pair of tattered shoes stopped before her. Facing her, the visitor stood perfectly still, and she raised her eyes slowly to take in the young man's equally soiled clothing. Her heart pounding, she reached the face of a stranger with the scruffy beginnings of a beard and shaggy red hair. "Yes?" she squeaked.

"For you, my lady," the boy offered, holding out a single red rose. The stem long, it had been freshly cut and the bud had only just begun to open.

Accepting it carefully so as not to catch one of the sharp barbs, Amicia's mouth twitched. Staring into the clear blue eyes, she pondered where he might have gotten it. Holding her speculation, she whispered, "Thank you. You are new to Nalen?" she asked, certain they had not met before.

"I only visit from time to time," he explained, his smile oddly soothing. "Do you travel?"

"Travel?" she repeated, the idea peculiar. Her gaze dropping to his offering, she absently drew it to her nose and inhaled deeply to breathe in the scent. "No..." she began, lifting her chin to see that he had vanished.

Looking to the left, then right, she pivoted in her seat to find Rupert marching up the center aisle. However, the young man who had presented her with the sweet gift was nowhere to be found.

Arriving at the front, Ru planted himself next to her, and the pastor began to speak. They had waited for him to join her, and she knew in their eyes she already belonged to him. Cursing that fact under her breath, she adjusted herself and put a cushion of air between them. She then focused on the podium and the service as her heart thumped heavily inside her chest.

A few people spoke, offering kind words and condolences, but Ami hardly heard anything they said. Her heart ached with the loss of her mother, but not for the physical body they would soon lay beneath the earth. When she wept, it was not for Arely, who had been her caretaker for as long as she could recall.

No, her tears were for something far deeper; far darker. Her so-called parents had kept their secret and could have taken it to the grave, if her mother's conscience had not gotten the better of her on her deathbed. Smelling her rose again, Ami almost wished that she had.

Flicking her gaze over at the man next to her as she slowly lowered the flower, Amicia caught the smallest of smiles on Rupert's lips. *He thinks I will relent,* she surmised. Now that her parents were gone, why shouldn't she? A miller's wife she could be and bear his children. The idea of it sent the stone in her gut rolling. *Never.*

Returning her gaze to the front of the crowded room, she glared at her mother's wrapped corpse. Laid upon the alter, the mourners would pray for her soul in the hope that she would find peace in the next life. Her jaw growing tight, Ami found herself unable to join them.

Anger and sadness had hardened her heart. For six days, her mother had lived with her admission hanging between them. For seven nights, Amicia had tossed and turned in her tiny bed, unable to sleep; unable to fathom the magnitude of their lie by omission.

The service ended, and Rupert clasped her empty hand to guide her. Out in the front of the parish, they gathered into a sea of moving bodies, as the number who had come out for the ceremony indeed numbered many. Walking in a slow procession, they made their way to the cemetery that lay on the other end of town. They followed the wagon that held Arely's swathed body, and Amicia felt numb as she placed one foot in front of the other. Marching along, the creak of the wagon wheels played as if they were an organ, adding dulcet tones to the songs of the crowd as they sang in low, reverent voices.

Looking around her, she could feel the eyes of many upon them as Rupert provided her a steady arm on which to lean. Twisting the stem of her gift with her agile fingers, she considered the shy gentleman who had presented it to her. She had not seen him among the mourners, but she felt touched by his thoughtfulness as she breathed in its aroma.

Her thoughts jumbled, she briefly wondered what would become of her parents' house and meadow. They would be hers by right of inheritance, but she held no desire to keep them. An old house, a few acres of land filled with gardens and patches of wild berries. It would have made a nice home for a family of her own. A place for her future if she had wanted it.

Glancing up at the man next to her, she pondered how things could have been. If he had been her lover or if her heart had been more receptive to his attempts at courtship. Rupert Miller had not been the kindest of men, but he had been decent enough. *Respectful.* That's a word she could use to describe him. The idea of it brought a small smile to her lips, and she emitted a brief, spastic laugh before tearing her eyes away and placing them once again on the cart before her.

Rupert had been a close family friend when she was a child, and if her father's health had not failed, she felt certain he would have offered him her hand when she came of age. But they had needed tending, and in their selfishness, they had kept her for themselves. Her lips pursed, she felt grateful once more that they had. A respectful man does not a husband make, she felt sure.

Arriving in the field of stones, the mourners waited for Arely to be laid in her resting place, then moved forward to form a large crescent around the open hole. After another brief prayer, they filed past to pay their final respects, each dropping a handful of soil into the grave.

Waiting until all of the others had said their goodbyes and returned to their lives, Amicia came forward, allowing the dirt to sprinkle loosely between her fingers. Watching it fall, she whispered her forgiveness to the woman who had left her behind. *I know you did what you thought was best, mum. But the future is now mine to decide, and I know I will never stand in this place again.*

Ami had not formulated her plan. Her fear of what lay ahead had not allowed her the clarity of thought to do so. She had been caught up in the anger and pain her parents' dishonesty had twisted within her. However, as the earth slipped from her hand, it carried her anguish with it, sprinkling it over the body of the woman who had loved her and cared for her in the only way she knew how.

As the last grains trickled away, a spark ignited deep within Ami's chest, a burning realization that the ending that lay before her was not her own. *Follow your dreams to the place where you belong.* Her mother's words sprang from the depths of her being, and she could hear them as a melody carried on the wind. *Do you travel?* the young man seemed to whisper in her ear.

A stiff breeze catching her hair, she reached to smooth it as a full smile reached her lips. "Goodbye, mum," she said softly as she dropped the gifted rose on top of the pile of dirt. Almost wistfully, she accepted Rupert's hand. Walking next to him, she swung their arms slightly, a sense of joy filling her emptiness and pushing the sadness away. A fire had begun to burn inside her, a deep ache far greater than the angry passion their treachery had spawned.

Purer, hotter, more robust, she could feel the embers scorching her from within. A truth lay among the flicker of flame, an excited understanding in clarity. She had a purpose. She did have a place that she belonged. And if this woman she had buried here today was not her mother, she had a family.

Would they still be looking for her?

Had they *ever* been looking for her?

The idea a parent could have lost their child and not searched for it seemed absurd. She knew that they had and maybe still were on some level. They would be pleased at her return. There could be no other possible response.

Arriving at the parked carriage, Amicia accepted Rupert's help back into her seat.

"You seem at peace," he observed with a smile of his own. "I was afraid you would not take this well."

"I'm fine, yes," she agreed, folding her hands into her lap and waiting for him to join her. He would take her to her house, but it was no longer her home. Her home lay across the ocean. That's what the fire in her heart had told her. A home and a family were waiting for her, and she didn't plan on wasting any time getting there, as her days of living in Nalen had reached their end.

THREE

Ships in the Night

"YOU HAVEN'T SAID MUCH," Rupert informed her in a hushed tone when they had cleared the buildings of the small hamlet.

"There isn't much to say," she replied in monotone. Her tears gone, she rocked along with the sway of the cart, occasionally bumping against his muscular arm. Sensing that he expected something, some hint at what her plans might be, she glanced quickly up at him, licking her lips. "I'm not going to marry you, Rupert. I meant it. I am not a miller's wife."

"Nonsense," he countered evenly, prepared to make his case again. "If you won't come to me, I'll come to you. I can make the repairs on your house, and you can continue to run your family's trade. I can sell the mill or hire an overseer for the day to day of it all…" he rambled, his voice growing quieter with every word.

His tough exterior seemed to crumble, which surprised her. She had expected him to be angrier or to put up more of a fuss. Staring straight ahead, Ami did not reply. Her jaw set, she considered allowing him to believe their betrothal lay ahead just to shut him up. When they arrived at her cottage, she didn't wait for him to come around and instead climbed out of the wagon and stomped through the small iron gate.

Close on her heel, he stopped short when she spun around to face him. "Don't say no, Ami," he begged. "I can't bear the thought of you living here alone."

"Give me a week," she said through gritted teeth. "Do not darken my door for seven days, and I will consider your request."

Dropping his jaw, Rupert gasped, "A week!" He could scarcely recall having gone a day without seeing the girl before him, much less seven. "I'll do my best," he replied, lifting his hat in a small salute before he shuffled back to his horse and buggy.

Watching him go, Amicia waited until he had disappeared around the curve, then hoisted her long skirt with both hands and hurried inside. Changing quickly into something less dainty, she retrieved her pack and began filling it with necessities.

Choosing her second dress, she folded it tightly to conserve space and tucked it inside. A change of undergarments went next, and finally her only pair of boots. They had lasted two years, but she might get a few more if she were lucky. Her thickest wool socks also found a place as she finished emptying her box to locate her hairbrush and a small round mirror. Giving the remnants a final turn, she saw nothing else that would qualify as essential.

Moving to her mother's chamber, she searched for anything of value. Finding only a few pieces of jewelry, she dropped them into a small leather pouch. She also came across a stash of gold pieces and spread them on her hand to count them before placing them in with those she had already collected. She wasn't rich, but it brought her to a fair sum, and she felt more confident that she would have enough to pay for her fare on a ship.

She paused when she discovered a small dagger that fit inside a plain metal sheath beneath her mother's clothes. She had never seen the knife before, and it surprised her that her mother would own such an item. Perhaps she had been better friends with the smithy in her younger years than Arely Spicer had let on.

Deciding to take the weapon, she placed it beside the pouch of gold, along with a pear and the last loaf of bread. Looking around, she saw nothing else that could be bartered, and she knew she was ready to leave.

Reaching the door, she pulled it wide and stepped out onto the path, where she looked towards town and noted a line of smoke that spiraled into the sky. Gazing at it, she thought of Rupert. *He deserves some inkling of what has become of me.*

Returning to her mother's room, she located her small box of stationary and ink. They did not put pen to paper often, but she had at least been instructed as to reading and writing as a matter of course. Placing the materials on the table, she sank into a chair and stared at the blank page.

The words forming in her mind, she opened the small well of ink and gave it a slow stir with the tip of her pen. Then, with a slight tremor in her hand, she scripted her final words to Ru Miller:

My dearest Rupert:

I have said it enough times, so you must know that it is true. You will have a bride one day, but I will not be her. By the time you find this, I will be long gone, as I intend to book passage on a ship and sail to the west on the morrow. Thank you for your friendship and may good tidings ever come your way.

Best Wishes,
Amicia

. . .

Propping the note in the center of the table, she decided to take the small box of writing items and slipped them inside her bag. She then carried her pack over her shoulder as she left the cottage for the last time.

As she made her way into the woods, a sudden shift in the wind caught the fabric of her long skirt, causing it to float slightly, if only for a moment.

Amicia grinned at the thrill of femininity the action stirred within her. Having worked on her parents' farm every day of her life, she sometimes forgot that she was indeed a woman and capable of being delicate if she chose to be.

Coming out into the berry patch, she walked briskly across the meadow and into the trees on the other side. The sun crept across the sky as she picked her way through, shining down on her bare arms. This being her summer dress, the material had been lighter, with less of it to cover her flesh, and a strange distraction entered her mind as she muddled along the path. *I wonder what my new life will be like when I'm settled.*

Amicia Spicer of old had never had time to consider such ramblings. Her life had been a straight line with no chance of straying off course, and it was a luxury she scarcely had time for now. Her skin spotted and freckled from years of hard work in the sun, her hide might have been considered leathery and anything but the soft or smooth of an indulged lady. *Perhaps there will be fine clothes in my future, with less work to be done. Wouldn't that be an amazing alteration?*

Hoisting her skirt as she stepped over a rock, she enjoyed the feel of the material. Not a work dress, but not a dressy dress, she had never considered how such a simple thing could arouse her. *I will have fine dresses in my new life,* she declared. *Fine clothing and fine furnishings to surround me, with servants to tend my bidding. No more leaky roofs and lumpy beds,* she swore to herself, her breath coming on quicker with the excitement the idea brought.

Leaving her musings, she focused on her escape. Avoiding areas where she might be seen until she arrived at the water front, she made her way to a small inlet that allowed ships to dock safely for loading and unloading their cargo. There, she would use what money she had to pay for her passage, and her new life in the West would soon begin.

Pausing at the top of the cove, Ami stared down at the long dock that formed a "V" in the center of the lagoon. Three of the ships appeared to be loading, as the very point of the wedge formed a wide area where boxes were carried down and placed from above by merchants with goods to barter or sell. Crews from the ships would then cart or carry the smaller crates to the waiting ships, taking them over narrow platforms to board the boats. They would use large rope nets to swing bulkier payloads over and lower them into their holds with large pullies and beams as thick as a man's chest.

Only one of the ships seemed to be unloading, and she discerned that it had probably only arrived a few hours prior. That being the case, she knew she wouldn't bother trying to book her passage upon that one, as it might be several days before the vessel left the harbor. She needed to leave as quickly as she could in case her intended departure was discovered before Rupert's assigned seven days had expired.

Locating a tree to lean against, she took a seat on the soft sandy soil, keeping her pack of treasures close at hand. She continued to watch the men as they worked, getting a feel for their moods. They were a brackish lot, and a plethora of curses and foul language floated up to her on the salty air blowing in from the sea. But they laughed a bit too, and that calmed her reservations at approaching them.

She had been to the dock many times over the years, making her first visits with her father when he had been expecting a shipment or sending one out. In time, she had become the merchant and had a few ships that she dealt with regularly for selling her jellies and spices.

If only one of those ships could have been here to take me where I need to go. However, not knowing exactly which way she was headed, there was only one thing she could say for certain. She wanted to go west, as that's the direction her gut insisted upon. *I can't wait for one of them to arrive. I must leave tonight, before my intent is discovered, but how to choose?*

They sailed on an ocean formed by a vast ring of land; continents and islands surrounding a massive sea. She knew the names of towns traders visited; Deernesse, Baycoast, and Newrock were only a few.

Her mind clouded for a moment, the mission before her felt daunting. She would either have to discover the direction of each ship's travel or simply find one that would take her and hope for the best.

While she made her observations, she noticed a large, burly man with dark hair pulled back in a short, stubby puff at the base of his skull. He had a broad chest and muscular build, surely warranted by the hard work of a sailor's life. She decided he was in charge, as he oversaw the cargo as it was brought up for loading and directed the crew as to the processing of it. Squinting at the hull of his vessel, she could make out the name: Sea Serpent. *How horrid!* she thought, instantly put off by the moniker.

The crewman reminded her of Rupert in a way, and her mind wandered. She thought of the long days her suitor had worked in the mill and the evenings he would spend afterward helping her in her fields, never seeming to tire of the toiling that must be done in either location. After a few minutes of daydreams featuring children and a future that would never be theirs, she pulled herself back to the present and her task at hand.

The sun low in the sky, Amicia decided the time had come. Dusting the sand from her skirt, she made her way down the dirt path to the entrance and padded along the wooden planks of the pier. She forced a smile to her lips, hoping to pass as pleasant as she made her way along.

Her hair gathered into a ribbon tied at the back of her neck, it puffed out and curled in a mass of frizz down her back. The golden rays accenting the bright highlights as they lay across her bare shoulders, the workmen and sailors paused as she passed, each giving her a look up and down.

Selecting the ship tied off on the far end, the young woman stopped in front of the tattooed man she had been observing from above and smiled at what the close-up version of him presented. Sweat glistened on his bare skin and he smelled of work. His aroma strong, it prickled her senses. His masculinity did not disappoint, and he appeared to be ignoring her as he continued his sorting of cargo for loading.

Clearing her throat, she waited, her eyes drawn by the broad bare chest and hard muscles that rippled over his back when he moved; sultry enough to make a girl swoon. If he were looking for a woman, she felt certain he would have no difficulty locating one willing to share his company. "Excuse me, sir," she stated confidently, lifting her nose as she addressed him. "Who might I speak to about booking passage on this vessel?"

Bent over a large crate, inspecting its contents, the man froze, then tilted his head to peer at her dirty toes before straightening to his full height and glaring down at her. "Book passage?" he grunted. "This ain't a luxury liner, ma'am," he added in a surly manner. "This here's cargo." He indicated their haul with a flick of his wrist.

"Yes, of course it is." She stood straighter, squaring her frame. "But surely you have room for a passenger, especially one willing to pay."

Grinning, the Mate glanced around at his fellow crewmen, evaluating their response to a woman on board their vessel. "I'm the first officer, and I assure you, we don't take passengers, paying or otherwise." He smirked, then turned his back on her to continue his task.

Unceremoniously dismissed, Ami drew a deep breath and held it for a moment. Her features twisted into an angry pout, she considered what she should do next. She would have liked to tell the man before her what she thought of their policy but decided against it. The sun would set soon, and she had three more ships to investigate before the hour grew too late.

Strolling down the dock, in the direction that she had come, she hoped that she appeared calm. Ready to pay her fare and be boarded, she would secure her escape before anyone discovered she had gone. It would all depend on if Rupert kept his word and if no one else showed up at her parents' home snooping. Either way, she had no time to wait for a proper passenger vessel, or luxury liner as the first mate had put it.

However, luck was not with her, and her lip stuck out in a full pout as the last light disappeared and she had been turned down by all four of the vessels, even the one that had been her last option. *Damn*, she sighed to herself. Dejected, she made her way up the hill and dropped her bag before she sat once more beneath her tree, where she watched the men work into the night.

Leaning her head back against the bark, she clutched her small pack across her lap. Not prepared to give up, she considered how she might sneak aboard one of the ships unseen. "It won't be easy," she muttered to herself, noting that most of the crews appeared to be headed into town, and likely the pub, while a few of the sailors, including the rugged first mate, remained behind.

Her mother had always said that patience was a virtue, and the young blonde found hers being tested as the air rolling off the ocean grew cooler after the sun set. Holding her skirt around her bare legs and feet, the material of it no longer felt fine; it felt inadequate, but at the moment it would have to do.

Below her, a few torches burned on board the ships, and the sound of the town called softly over her shoulder. In between, darkness settled over the water, and the planks of the pier dwindled into flat, empty calm.

Deciding that it was time to take her chances, Ami flung the pack over her shoulder and padded gently down the path once more. Keeping her pace slow to quiet her steps, she reached the hardness of the wood without so much as a hint of another person about. Spurred on by her success, she slunk down the section of timbers to the left, towards the Sea Serpent, the first boat she had tried to board. With the soft sound of water lapping gently at the support poles and the hulls of the ships, her heart pounded within her chest.

Reaching her target, she hesitated for a moment to listen to the sound of the night. Mid-summer, the day had been long, and the small community flourished in the warm days. Glancing up at the ridge, she could see the soft glow that meant the lamps were still lit in the streets, but soon they would be put out, and the crew of the massive vessel would return.

Slowly working her way across the narrow gangway, Ami knew she needed to be in a hiding place before that happened. Arriving at the deck, she quickly identified the hold she had picked out from her seat under the tree and easily climbed down into the pitch black of the deck below.

Pausing, her eyes adjusted to the deeper darkness, and she made her way around the stacks of boxes and crates. Bags of milled grain piled in the far-left corner appeared inviting, and she restacked them, leaving a narrow space between them and the wall. Slipping into her hiding place, she realized she had forgotten something: a blanket.

Riding in the bottom of a ship would be a cold prospect indeed, and her mind raced as she considered how she might obtain one before the crew returned. Deciding to investigate a few of the crates for anything that could serve as bedding before they did, she left her pack in her new residence. Cautiously, she made her way around, weaving in and out of the narrow walkways and trying the lids.

It was then that she discovered the crates were near impossible to open and she would need a tool to do so. Not ready to give up, she continued, only able to peek inside a few in the dim light. However, when she arrived back at the front, her eyes landed on a narrow metal bar hanging at the bottom of the stairs. Immediately, she knew that its purpose was exactly that: opening the boxes.

Snatching it hurriedly, she took on the storage bins with renewed fervor. Moving as quickly and quietly as she could, she discovered a pack of hides, presumably from the tanner, and none too soon as she had heard voices in the air above her.

Selecting one off the top, she closed the lid and returned the iron bar to the hook, then shuffled back to her pack and wiggled into her bunk, such as it was. Wrapping the stiff hide around her the best she could, she tried to ignore the rumbling in her gut as she drifted off to sleep.

FOUR

Stowaway

DESPITE THE LEATHER blanket covering her, Amicia awoke with a freezing chill rattling her body. It took a moment in the near darkness to recognize her location, and she surmised they were no longer tied to the dock; her churning gut told her so. The roll of the ship gave her a violent fit of nausea, and she shot up out of her nest, hoping not to soil her hiding place with vomit.

Clawing her way in desperation, she stretched across the stack of mill. Her head hung on the other side when the contents of her stomach spewed out and splattered in small splotches on the dark wood. Fortunately, she had not eaten since the morning before, so the bile came up thick and sparse.

Once her spasms had subsided, Ami wiped her mouth with the back of her hand and sank slowly into her hiding place. Placing her palm on her cheek, she thought she might be a tad feverish, but she couldn't be sure with the coolness of the air around her.

Twisting onto her side, the bags of mill before her, she thought about Rupert and considered that he might have produced them, the idea of his providing her hiding place bringing a small smile to her pale lips. "He was such a kind friend," she whispered to herself, taken with a moment of sadness in her semi-delirious state.

Closing her eyes, she thought about her choice to leave the only home she had ever known, second-guessing herself in her weakness. The yearning within her had waned, but she could still feel the pull of it, like a small child tugging at the hem of her skirt as she tried to ignore it. *Rupert would have made a decent husband,* she concluded for the second time in as many days. *But is that all that I am?*

Deciding emphatically that it was indeed not all that she was, she shook off the moment of pity. Listening to the sounds of the ship, it occurred to her that her choice to stow away had been ill considered, as she had no idea how many days they would be at sea, nor which direction the ship had sailed. She realized she needed to take charge of her situation, one way or another.

She had no real amount of food and would soon be in need of other necessities. Add to that, she had never considered becoming ill on the journey. Frowning heavily, she hoped that a little sea-sickness would be the worst of it.

Wiping her spittle onto one of the cloth bags, she groaned. *Dear God, make it stop!* Closing her eyes, she swallowed hard in an effort to keep from polluting more of the hold.

After a few minutes, the urge had diminished, and she sat up straighter to look around once more. *Maybe I need to eat,* she theorized, remembering her pear and bread in her bag. Deciding to give them a try, she dug them out before nestling back down behind the wall of flour.

Above her, she could hear footfalls on the deck and briefly felt envious of those who could walk around and enjoy the warm sun. Glaring in the direction of the stairs, she considered if she should simply march up and present herself to the captain. Taking a small bite of the pear, she chewed it slowly while she entertained possible scenarios along those lines but couldn't seem to decide on one with a pleasant outcome.

Finishing the fruit, she moved on to the firm loaf. Nibbling at it, she wished she had thought to bring more. But at least this would get her by for a day or two, and if their voyage lasted longer than that, she would have to risk more drastic measures.

While she enjoyed her meal, savoring each bite as if it could be her last, a loud pair of boots clomped down the stairs on the opposite end of the room. Scrunched down so that only her eyes and the top of her head remained above the line of her make-shift wall, Ami watched as a large man in a sweat-stained shirt lifted the metal bar and opened a few of the crates.

His actions aroused her curiosity, as a simple inspection of the cargo seemed unlikely. To her surprise, he brought out food items, and she quickly deduced that he was the ship's cook. He appeared to know exactly where each item that he wanted was stored, as he opened the boxes, removed a few items, and sealed them back, while collecting his gatherings into a dirty cloth bag.

Thankfully, all the food containing crates appeared to be along the far wall, at the front of the hold. Therefore, he never came close to Ami's hiding place, and she could observe him without being noticed. When he had enough, he returned the bar to its hook and stomped back up the stairs.

Her eyes bright, Amicia forgot all about her queasiness. Licking her lips eagerly, she considered if she dared to investigate the boxes by the light of day. Deciding it would be too risky, she finished the food she had brought with her in a slow pace, only then realizing that eating without water to drink had been a mistake.

Her gut churning, she felt as if she might vomit again, only this time coating the floor with masticated pear and bread, and the idea of it only made her sensation of salty saliva worse. Glaring at one of the casks that she had learned contained water, her thirst became unbearable, and she knew she had to take the risk.

Daring to venture out of her hiding place, she opened the barrel and eagerly used her hand to scoop up mouthfuls of the cool liquid, slurping it noisily in her haste. Pausing mid scoop, her eyes landed on a small, single, metal cup hanging by its crude handle on the wall above the barrels. Snatching it from the hook, she filled it and swallowed the lot in a few large gulps.

Downing a second, she drank more slowly, then wiped her mouth on her bare arm as she returned the mug to its place on the wall. Cutting her eyes over at the stairs and listening intently to the sounds above, she could feel a sense of calm settling over her as her satiated hunger comforted her.

Replacing the cover on the water, she used the bar to open a few of the food boxes for a proper snoop, since she was there. Her lips drawn into a small smile, she felt as if her fortunes had turned. Hastily, she gathered a small portion of cheese, a strip of dried meat, and another biscuit to serve as her dinner later that evening. *If I had a canister for water, this would be perfect, with all the food I could want, right here for the taking.*

Dropping the items off in her sanctuary, she searched more boxes, hoping to find a pot, bowl, or cup of any kind. She needed one for the water and taking the cup off the wall would be plain silly. She also needed a second receptacle to use as a chamber pot, or personal toilet. Finding neither, she swore under her breath.

Frustrated, she skirted the crates one last time. She had checked all that she could access, so digging any further would be pointless. Deciding that the corner on the opposite side of her bedding would have to do, she scrunched down to relieve herself on the wooden planks.

Ami had heard tales of the living conditions on ships, and her sensitive nose had informed her that they had not been exaggerated. She knew that the men of the ship would use the head at the front of the vessel to handle their business, but that was one trip she wouldn't dare attempt, even in the darkness of night.

She could only hope that none of them would notice the odor her markings would leave and that she would remain unseen until they put in at the next port. Then, she could exit quietly in search of a more accommodating vessel with a leisurely amount of time to do the choosing.

Back under her blanket a few minutes later, Amicia curled into a ball and managed to sleep. For how long she couldn't be sure, but it occurred to her when she awoke that the crew didn't come into the hold often, thankfully. She had begun to feel relaxed in the space, as if it belonged to her in a way, or did for as long as she remained undiscovered.

The cook made another appearance later in the day, and she ate her dinner after he had gone. Making another trip to the water barrel, then restocking her food supply for the next morning, she took her time to explore more of the options, finding some dried fruit pieces that would make a nice breakfast.

Ending her first full day on the ship in a pleasant mood, she made another stop in the corner. Then, taking one last look around, she felt ready to turn in for the night, as the light had faded, and she knew the sun had set.

Lying on the rough wood for her second night, she could feel the air getting colder. Deciding she needed a second of the sections of leather, she crept out of her hiding place and opened the crate. The squeak of the nails unnerved her, as the rest of the ship had become silent, and she knew that although darkness meant she had less chance of being interrupted, it also meant that her odds of being heard were greater.

Retrieving the section of hide, she closed the box and returned to her corner. Folding the new piece, she placed it over the planks to form a more cushioned and insulated resting place. Curling onto it once more, she placed her original over her, with her pack under her head, and drifted off to sleep.

Amicia could feel something was wrong. They had been at sea for ten days, and everything had settled into a monotonous routine of sorts, much like the first day she had been on board: cook, food, water, toilet, nap. Then the cycle would repeat in the evening, and she would sleep through the night. But not this night.

Above her, the boots stomped well into the darkness; the sun had set, but the men had not settled into their beds. The boards creaked, and torchlight filtered through the cracks. She could hear the voices, but not the words, and it frightened her to not know what had them in an uproar.

Her mind running away with her, she could imagine all sorts of perils with pirates and sea monsters both high on the list.

Unable to bear the not knowing, Ami crept from her secret spot and moved towards the stairs. Placing her bare right foot on the first rung, she hesitated, holding her breath and listening. Then, summoning her courage, she placed the left on the next step and then the right again.

Panting, she fought to control the sound of her panic. Slow, step after step, she made it within three of the top when a clear voice could be made out. "I'm telling you, the cup's been used. One of the barrels has been tapped, I tell you. If it ain't one of the crew –"

Cut off, she didn't hear the rest.

Her eyes wide, her brow furrowed in terror. Turning, she slithered back down the steps. Looking around wildly, she knew it would be minutes at most before they were in the hold searching for her.

Staring back to the left, into her corner, she could see the boxes that hid most of her stack of mill bags. They couldn't pick her out immediately, but eventually, they would discover her haven.

Taking a few steps, her gaze floated over the myriad of crates that filled the hold. *Could I hide inside one of those?* Even if she could find one with enough room, she wouldn't be able to open it, get in, close it, and return the bar to its hook.

She stamped her foot in disgust. *Damn.*

She needed to get to another part of the ship; that was all there was to it. *If I can get out of the hold, maybe I have a chance.*

Snatching the bar from the hook, she took it with her as she slipped down the row of food boxes. Finding one she could squeeze behind, she pushed her way in and scrunched down, still holding the piece of metal. *I could use this like a club, if I have to fight them*, she rationalized.

That wouldn't work, they're men and far stronger than you! she debated with herself. *At least they'll think I'm in a crate*, she panted. *While they're searching, I can sneak out and try for the stairs.*

The trap-door above opened with a bang as it dropped back against the deck. Her eyes wide, beads of perspiration formed on her brow as the herd of boots and bare feet thundered down the stairs in pairs. Their torches bright, the room instantly filled with dancing shadows as they spread out through the maze of cargo.

Her mind racing, Ami thought about her hiding place; her blankets and her pack. *My pack!* She suddenly remembered her belongings. *I have money, I could offer to buy my way aboard.* Although, the idea of facing the first mate again did not please her.

She could see a pair of legs through the crack where she had squeezed in. Whoever he was, he appeared to be guarding the stairs. *Damn!* Her heart racing, she could only see this ending one way: as their prisoner. Deciding she had to at least try to escape, she crept out to the edge of the boxes and looked up.

Above her, a young man stood next to the beam that supported the hole above and stairs that connected it to the floor. Watching as the men scoured the room, he didn't see her, if only for the moment. Gripping her metal bar with both hands, she prepared herself to attack him.

But what if I hurt him? Would they be any less angry if she killed one of them trying to escape?

"Looky what we have here," a voice grunted as a hand seized her wrist and pulled her to her feet, then freed her of her weapon. She had been so focused on the cabin boy, she hadn't seen the other man approach.

"Unhand me!" she squealed, fighting to pull her arm free.

Dropping the tool, the crewman struggled to find a second hold, only succeeding in tearing at her dress and exposing more of her flesh. His grip on her firm, he swung at her as she fought for her freedom, landing punches to her ribs and arms.

Screaming, Ami pulled the hand squeezing her arm up and sank her teeth into his dark flesh, shrieking when he pushed the appendage into the bite and forced her to stop. Pulling at her hair with his free hand, he yanked her head back and she stared at the ceiling as he studied her terrified expression.

Others had become aware of the scuffle, and one of them landed a solid blow to her face with a fist, knocking her to the floor in the open area where the stairs entered the vast room. Crawling on all fours, she inched towards the exit, but a line of boots formed, blocking her escape.

Rolling onto her back, panting, she could feel the burn and licked gingerly at the salty blood as her lip swelled. Leaning on her elbows to hold her back off the rough surface, she stared up at them as the circle of men tightened around her.

"It's a woman!" one of them gasped.

"Aye," a second agreed, his features masked by the shadow of the torches.

"Damned stowaway!" another snarled.

"Welcome aboard, missy," a deeper voice chimed in as the man knelt over her and forced her down to lie flat, tearing further at her clothing as he sprawled across her. His eyes dark, he pulled at her skirt, ripping it as he worked the material up her body.

Striking him with the sides of her fists, Amicia struggled but had no hope of pushing him off. A second man dropped down, catching her arms and pinning them above her head. Looking up at him, his teeth were clenched as he growled at her struggle.

"Stop, please!" she pleaded, then screamed. Still squirming as cold air covered her naked legs, her vision blurred with tears of angry fear. "I beg you, please don't do this," she cried, certain they would all have a turn at her. Managing to pull her foot free, she kicked wildly, making contact with unseen body parts and earning another solid punch before she lost consciousness.

FIVE

Dark Discovery

"UNHAND HER, YOU FOOLS," Piers Massheby's voice boomed in disgust. Seizing his crewman by the shoulder, the burly first mate tossed him aside and glared down at the unconscious female. Recognizing her, he muttered, "For fuck's sake," under his breath.

"Find her things and bring them to my quarters," he commanded, while he knelt beside her and inspected her wounds. Seeing the large gash on her temple and the blood smeared on her bared torso, he grimaced. Scooping her up, he tossed her over his shoulder as if she were one of the packs of mill and began the ascent to the deck above.

Careful not to drop his load, he made it to the top and climbed out onto the wooden planks. Shifting her into his arms, he glared down at the woman he had explicitly dismissed before they left Nalen.

"It's a girl," Baldwin Carter observed breathlessly as he joined the ship's first officer, bringing a lantern to light his way. He hadn't been part of the search, and it shocked him to discover their stowaway had been of the female gender. "Hey, Rey!" he bellowed, turning towards the stern and calling to his buddy. "The stowaway's a girl!"

"Forget that," Piers snapped. "Go get a change of your clothes and bring them to my bunk," he instructed, taking the small lamp from him.

"My clothes?" The younger man faltered. "What you want with them?"

"Well, mine won't fit her, now will they?" The first mate chuckled as he stomped down the narrow ledge that would take him to his quarters under the wheel house. Making the sharp right through the door, he sat the lamp on his table to the right of it. He kicked a wooden chair obstructing his path to the bed aside and laid the young woman on his bunk.

Her breast exposed, he used a scrap of the cloth that had once been a dress to cover it, then pulled the blanket over it as well. Locating a small rag, he placed it over the cut on her head and held it there to catch the blood while he inspected the split in her lip.

A set of knuckles rapped sharply on the doorframe, and the captain announced sternly, "I hear our vagabond is a woman."

"Aye," Piers replied, "and before you come down on me, no, I didn't let them have her."

"You think you can keep them off her?" the older man asked doubtfully. "We're another week from Newrock at best, and it won't be any better when we get there."

"I'll handle it," his first mate grumbled, still focused on his charge.

"Sorry." Baldwin arrived and excused himself with a nervous snicker. "You asked for these?" He offered the pants and shirt to Piers.

"Aye, just drop them on the table," came his short reply.

Doing as instructed, Baldwin laid the items next to the lamp and grinned at his friend, who had come to join them. "See, Rey? A girl!"

Reynard Daye craned his neck for a glimpse but caught the dark gaze of the captain instead. "Sorry, sir," he clipped, standing up straighter and considering bolting.

"What do you two know about this?" the captain asked warily, squinting at two of the youngest members of their crew.

"N-nothing," Rey stammered with a shrug. "Bally just said it was a girl." He half grinned, his face flushed.

Suppressing a smile, the captain clamped the one closest to him on the shoulder. "Bally, you and Rey are in charge of helping look after her. Get Piers whatever he needs, and I don't want that girl left alone at any time until we get her back to Nalen."

"You don't think she's headed to Newrock?" Rey questioned as the captain pushed past him and headed up the stairs to check the wheel.

"Pfft, no." He laughed out loud and glanced down at his crewman from the top step. "I doubt she stowed away on a cargo boat so she could go join a brothel."

"A brothel," Baldwin repeated, looking over at his best mate. "You mean…?"

"He means, you two are going to help me look after her," Piers replied, shoving the smaller man towards the door and handing him his lantern. "Go get some sleep and be back here in the morning so we can work out that schedule for sitting with her. Bring breakfast when you come," he ordered.

Lighting a lamp on the wall and setting the glass cover in place, the windowless room took on a soft glow. He looked over at the young woman ruefully as he began gathering a few items to treat her wounds before he bedded down for the night. He knew her presence on the ship would be a hassle he really would rather have avoided.

The following morning, the three men sat in the cramped space, eating breakfast and drinking coffee when Amicia awoke. "Just lay still," Piers commanded as soon as her eyes fluttered open.

Hearing the voice to her left, the girl stared at the dark wood of the roof above her. *Definitely not the hold.* Her mind clouded, she recalled the hunt for her and the scuffle that followed. Looking down at her body, all she could see was a coarse blanket over the top of her.

"I said relax," the man stated more gruffly, standing as he leaned over her and inspected a wound on the right side of her head. "You've got a nasty cut. I stitched it, and we don't wanna get that bleeding again."

"Where am I?" she asked with a huff of air, noting the sting of her lower lip when she spoke. Laying her fingers over it, she could feel a few stitches in it as well. Her body ached, and it frightened her what might have happened while she was unconscious.

"You're safe. You're in my cabin on my bunk." He relaxed against the side of the bed, glaring at her. "Didn't I tell you this wasn't a luxury liner?"

"Yes." She sniffed, her bottom lip pulsing as it quivered, her chin puckered with little dimples.

Rey stared at her, watching the exchange. "Don't make her cry, Mate."

"I'm not making her do anything," his commander informed him tartly, cutting him a sideways glare. "This is Rey Daye, crewman. And Bally, cabin boy." He flicked a finger to indicate the pair. "One of us will remain with you in this cabin for the duration of your journey."

"Are we far?" she asked excitedly, her spirits instantly raised at the thought of finishing the voyage.

"We make port in Newrock in a few days," he supplied. "We'll have you back in Nalen in a few weeks."

"Nalen!" she screamed, sitting straight up, then catching the fallen blanket to recover herself. *Oh, my God, I'm naked,* she observed before she stated aloud, "I can't go back to Nalen!"

"Then you can get off at Newrock, if you like. I'm sure they'd love to have a pretty young wench like you," he snapped. "New girls are hard to come by there."

"What's that supposed to mean?" Her eyes narrowed with anger at his derogatory term.

Glancing over his shoulder, Piers looked coolly at the two men still seated at his small table. "One of you care to enlighten her?"

When neither of them made a sound, he muttered, "Figures," then continued at normal volume for her benefit. "Newrock is a mining town. It's the only thing on the whole island, a bunch of men digging in the dirt for treasure. The only women there… are in the brothel," he ended flatly, allowing her to make the connection.

"Oh, no," she breathed, her chest rising and falling quickly as she fought for air. "Shit!" she blurted, her face growing bright red.

"Aye." He eyeballed her, unable to hide the smile that suddenly sprang to his lips.

"Why are you grinning?" she growled, adjusting her cover and shifting her angry glare between the three of them.

"Nothing." He laughed out loud as he turned to the exit. "Baldwin, you got chores, young man. Best get to them," he announced as he stomped through the portal.

"Yes sir," the cabin boy replied, following and closing the door behind him.

"What's going on?" she sputtered after they had left. Shifting her gaze between the remaining man and the door, she raised her voice, "Answer me!"

His eyes wide, Rey managed to find his voice, "It's like he said. We're putting in at Newrock, then we head back to Nalen."

"This boat doesn't go anywhere else?"

"No... ma'am," he stammered. "This ship only makes one run. Every six weeks, we put in at either end, Nalen and Newrock. Till the snow comes on Newrock, that is," he stated more confidently.

"What happens then?"

"I don't rightly know." He shrugged. "This's my first year on this route. I was cabin boy on another vessel before this, and I only hired on this one about six months back when we made the first run of the year."

Glaring at him, Ami could feel her anger burning in her chest as she fumed. "You mean I risked my life to hide on a boat... that only makes one stop... and I can't even get off there?"

"Ship. Yes ma'am, one stop." He corrected and confirmed at the same time. "Would you like any help getting dressed?" he offered casually.

Her face taking on another bright red flush, tears streaked down her cheeks, and her voice squeaked, "No, I don't want any help!"

"They banged you up pretty good." Getting to his feet, he moved closer with the bundle of clothes. "Good thing the Mate was there to stop them from doing anything serious," he continued, laying the shirt and pants on the bed next to her and giving them a pat.

Resting her hand on the material, she scowled. "What's this?"

"Some of Bally's clothes. The Mate says they'll fit you best on the ship." He smiled encouragingly. "Bally didn't like it much, hearing he's the same size as a girl."

Ami chuckled nervously in spite of herself. "They didn't..." Her voice trailed away. "They didn't force themselves on me?" she managed meekly, her eyes avoiding his.

"I reckon not." Rey stood up straighter. "Piers's in charge, and he told them they wasn't allowed."

"Then why are you three sitting with me?"

"Captain's orders. In case you need anything, I suppose." He laughed out loud, growing confident in the presence of the small blonde.

"I doubt that." She squirmed, glancing around the room. "Do you mind waiting outside while I get dressed?"

"Sure, I can do that. We brought your bag up, too, in case you need it." He indicated her pack hanging on the back of the door as he took the exit and closed it behind him.

Staring at her belongings, she considered putting on her other dress. Glancing at the shirt and pants, she wasn't even sure they would fit her. Sliding her legs from beneath the warm blanket, the air of the cabin felt cool against her bruised flesh. Inspecting the dark purple splotches that decorated them, she recalled the struggle she had put up when the crewman had pulled her out of her hiding place.

Her tattered dress hanging off her, she ran her fingers over a few of the fragments, then noted the other cuts and bruises that had been treated by the first mate while she had been out. A tear escaped, and she cried a few more, wiping at them angrily, then recalled that Rey had informed her she had not been violated. *Thank God for that.*

Opting for Bally's clothes, she fished her change in undergarments out of her bag and slipped into them. Pulling on the man's pants, she laughed to find that they did indeed fit. *He is the same size as a girl.*

Donning his shirt and the sweater that went with her winter dress, she ran her hands over the material, as if ironing it onto her flesh. She didn't like the idea of being surrounded by men who would, or could, hurt her if given the chance. *At least the captain has given me some protection,* she mused.

Remembering her wool socks, she knew the weather was a bit warm for them, but she wanted to wear the boots as well, in case she needed to kick anyone any time soon. Shoving her feet in, she sighed. "Nalen," she mumbled to herself. "When we get back there, I'm getting on another boat, only this time I'm going to find out where they're headed before I do!"

Finally decent, she cracked the door and peeked out. His back to her, Rey stood at the railing watching the ocean glide by beneath them. "I'm dressed," she announced, stepping back to allow him to enter.

Back inside, Rey rubbed his palms against his shirt as he studied her. Her hair a frizzy mess, he could see the dried blood matted in places. "I should fetch some water to clean you up a bit," he offered.

Glancing down at her new wardrobe, then at her bare arms, she nodded. "Yes, I could definitely use a bath. Will I be safe alone?"

"Of course," he agreed with a firm nod. "Or, you can come and visit the head. It'll only take us a few minutes. The bathing water and soap are nearby, on the lower deck."

Looking both ways to find the walk empty as they exited, Rey took the girl's hand and led her along the side of the ship. Glancing out at the wide expanse of water on the right as they passed the hold on the left, Ami gasped, "There's no land!"

"Why would there be?" He laughed, tugging at her to keep up. He had begun forming second thoughts the moment they left the first mate's quarters and wanted to make the trip as short as possible if he could help it.

They made it to the head without being noticed, and he instructed, "Take a piss, or whatever you need, and I'll fetch the rest." Leaving her to do her business, he went down the steps to their bathing area. The sailors each got one bucket a week for their bath, but at the moment the area was deserted.

Glancing around anxiously, he filled a pail with water and slipped a cake of soap into his pocket. Waiting a few minutes, he scanned the deck, feeling foolish at having brought her and nervously considered what would happen if any of the crew noticed them before he could get her safely back under cover.

Adjusting her clothing back into place, Ami joined him a few minutes later. Sliding her fingers into his free left hand, she followed obediently as he led her to the Mate's quarters, the container of fresh water gripped tightly in his right.

"You seem tense," she observed as they reached the center of the ship once more.

"Aye. I'm going to smack anyone who approaches with this bucket, so be ready," he informed her with a small laugh.

Smiling herself, she felt safe in his care. "Thanks, Rey," she replied, squeezing his digits as they entered the narrow passage to arrive at the door.

Inside the small space, the young man helped her use the water to remove the blood from her hair and to clean the streaks from her face and arms. Sensing her discomfort when she moved, he commanded, "Here, sit and let me do it."

Placing her in one of the chairs in the center of the room, he moved about her, tending to her needs. Using her brush, his strokes were gentle as he removed the knots and tamed her wild curls.

"I think you've done this before," she observed with a small giggle.

"Sisters," he replied with a grin. "Is that cut bothering you?" he inquired, indicating the way she patted her lip with trembling fingers.

"A little," she confessed, on the verge of tears.

"The Mate thought that it might," he soothed with a sigh. "He left some witch-hazel for it." Opening the small pouch of medical supplies that the first officer kept on hand, he pulled out the tiny bottle and a small clean square of cloth. Demonstrating, he instructed, "Place the material over it and tilt it, like this, so it gets a little wet, but not too much." Handing it to her, he watched as she repeated the process. "Good, now dab it on your lip."

"What does it do?" she asked as she applied the treatment, wincing at the sting of it.

"Cleans, disinfects, and even numbs it a little," he said with a nod. "Getting an infection is dangerous, and around here, it's really easy to lose a hand or a foot even to a small cut."

"Oh yeah?" She folded the cloth and gave it another tilt on the bottle before applying it again. It burned like hell, but a moment later it felt better. "We have stuff similar to this at home. I never thought to bring any of it, though."

"Well, you only have the one bag, you couldn't bring everything," he agreed with a chuckle. Leaving her to her lip, he returned to her hair, finishing the cleansing and brushing. Deciding she would be more comfortable with it up and away from her cuts, he used a ribbon from her bag to tie it into a knot.

"Did my mirror survive?" she asked timidly, not sure if she really wanted to look.

"Uh, yeah," he agreed, fishing it out. Handing it to her, he waited, a bit anxious at how she would react to the abuse her delicate features had suffered at the hands of his crewmates.

Staring at the small round circle, Ami thought about the year she had been given the device; the last gift Gus had presented to her before he died. Blinking back tears, she held it up and examined her reflection briefly before her hand dropped back into her lap.

"It's ok," Rey soothed, his fingers tracing the back of her smoothed hair as he knelt beside her. "You'll heal, I promise."

Holding it up, the glass felt cold against her skin as she studied herself more closely. Her lip had been split right down the center, and a tight group of stitches held it together. Both of her eyes were blacked, but the right had seen the worst of it with the cut on her temple. The stitches there felt tender when she touched them, and she put the tool aside. Using the medication, she applied the small cloth there as well with a sigh.

"Are you ready to eat?" Rey asked, hoping to distract her. "We saved you some of the breakfast."

"Yes," she agreed quietly.

"Ok, climb onto the bed and sit with your feet up," he suggested. "I'll get your food and scoot in there beside you, if that's all right with you."

Smiling up at him as he cared for her, Amicia felt relieved; at least some of the men on the boat weren't out to hurt her. "Thanks, Rey. That would be agreeable," she replied as she moved to do as he had asked.

SIX

Newrock

ARRIVING AT MESS THAT EVENING, Baldwin rubbed his hands on his shirt anxiously. Rey had spent the entire day with the girl, while he had taken on his usual chores about the ship, leaving him at a disadvantage.

But he would get his chance to meet her shortly, and he wanted to make a good impression on their young stowaway. Running his fingers through his hair, he straightened the black cloth cap that he always wore, and then marched to the end of the line.

Gathering a tray of food for the four of them, he hurried to the first mate's quarters. Giving a sharp knock, he cracked the door and pushed his way inside, where he placed the lot on the table next to Rey. "Part of that's for you and her." He pointed at the girl, adding, "and save some for the Mate."

"What's this?" Reynard scowled. "I've been locked up in here all day, and I don't even get to fetch my own dinner?"

"Sorry, Mate's orders," Bally groveled as he dropped into a chair and began picking out his portion while stealing anxious glances at their blond passenger.

Rey parted his lips to say more, but the door opened, cutting him off, so he directed his displeasure at the older man. "What's with the grub? I don't even get to go out for the evening?"

"You can make a trip to the head if you like." Piers laughed, glancing at the young woman sitting sideways on his bed, with her back against the wall. "Do you have a name yet, love?" His sultry tone obviously changed when he addressed her rather than the young men.

"Her name's Ami," Rey grunted, "Amicia Spicer." Selecting a few morsels, he laid them on a handkerchief, then stood and handed them to her. "She's from Nalen," he tacked on for good measure. Gathering his own food, he climbed onto the bunk next to her, also with his back against the far wall and his feet sticking off the side beside hers.

"Spicer," Piers ciphered, connecting her to her family's trade. Watching the pair, his jaw rocking side to side in a grinding fashion, he scowled. "Well, the two of you got a bit cozy, don't you think?"

"We've been locked in here all day." Rey shrugged his right shoulder and then continued to eat, spitting out between bites, "We had to talk about something."

Amicia grinned slightly at his candor, tense again with the arrival of the other two men. She had found Rey easy to talk to and had answered most of his questions honestly. There were still a few points of contention she would rather not discuss with outsiders, but for the most part, she would describe the young man as harmless, if not friendly.

Taking a seat in the vacated chair, Piers took the remainder of the food and began to eat eagerly. When he had finished half, he announced, "You two need to get your gear. We'll all be bunking in here tonight."

"Why?" Bally asked innocently. "There's not enough room, is there?" The cabin a mere ten feet squared, the bunk took up at least three to four of it from the far wall, and that left little room for anything else besides the table and three chairs.

"There's plenty," his commander replied. "Rey and Ami can share the bed and we either get the chairs or the floor, take your pick."

"Why are we all staying in here?" Rey repeated, lowering his hand from his mouth slowly. "Has something happened?"

"No, and I want to keep it that way." Piers cut his eyes over at him, giving him a stern glare, his unspoken *shut up* clear.

"What are you afraid of?" Amicia asked quietly.

Giving her the look for a moment, he shook his head. "Just a precaution, love. If they know they have to get through three of us, you'll make a less tempting target."

Her eyes wide, her heart began to pound. With the friendly conversations with Rey Daye, she had almost forgotten about the reason he was protecting her. "You don't really think they would do that, do you? I mean, I thought maybe last night it was just because they were upset that I was hiding on their boat." She smiled as much as her lip would allow, trying to sound unworried with the situation.

"No." the Mate shook his head slowly. "This crew's at sea for weeks and months on end. Chance comes to have a woman, well…" He cut his eyes over to the man seated next to her. "Most of them aren't too particular about the screams."

"You're making that up." Bally laughed, then snorted, before he fell silent at the cold stares of the others. "Seriously?"

"Seriously," Piers stated flatly, still eating in small bites. "Go down and get what you need for the night. Hit the head and then come back here."

"Do you need to go again?" Rey asked Amicia as he cleared the bunk. He had walked her to the bow earlier in the day before Piers brought her a small black pot that now sat in the corner behind the door.

"No," Piers interrupted, answering for her. "She uses the murphy," he stated, pointing at the receptacle. "After Newrock, maybe she can come out onto the deck for a bit, but for now I think it's best if she stays inside." He didn't give a reason, and he didn't have to. Piers Massheby was in charge, and his word was final.

Ami could feel the tension in the air, so thick it nearly smothered her. *Something's wrong. He knows they're going to come after me.* It surprised her that he and the younger two men would stand up for her against the whole of the others. *I guess that's why the captain put them in charge of me.*

Sulking slightly, Ami used her pot while Rey and Bally went for their gear and Piers waited outside. She had never worn pants before, and it felt odd to her, having her legs bound so tightly. She had to work the material down to cop a proper squat, with getting them back up again another chore.

Stretching afterward, she bent over at the waist to touch her toes, then pushed herself up on them and reached for the ceiling above her, exploring the feel of the material against her skin. She had sore spots after her beating, and it felt good to regain some of her movement, even in the restrictive clothing.

When her overseer came back in, she quipped, "I'm going to go crazy if you keep me in here. The hold was bad enough. I'm used to working on a spice farm, with air all around me."

"Oh yeah? I figured as much, given your name. So, why'd you leave it in such a way you can't go back?"

Her injured lip sticking out in a perfect pout, she glared at him. "My mum died."

He had been picking at the scraps of the meal and paused, then continued for a moment. "And your pop?"

"He passed last winter." She sighed, drawing her sweater around her. "It's just me now. I don't have anyone, not even the farm," she embellished, not wanting to share the details of her decision with the stranger.

"Huh," Piers grunted, his presence filling the room and chipping at her nerve. When she said nothing else, he left it at that and pulled the table out of the corner. He shoved a chair into its place, giving him a wall to lean against. "I reckon I'll sleep here," he announced when the others had returned. "Bally on the floor, or against the door. If anyone needs a piss, use the pot."

Looking down at the girl on the bed, Rey's Adam's apple bobbed. Sitting on the pliable surface having a chat had seemed fine, after a bit of getting to know her. Stretching out on it next to her while she slept was something different.

Seeing his unease, Ami grinned to herself. Kicking off her boots, she stacked them at the foot of the bed and scooted over next to the wall. She faced it to hide her amusement over his discomfort, and a small smile painted her lips has she closed her eyes and breathed deeply.

Rupert had been rather forward with his advances as soon as she had come of age, so the younger man's shyness seemed somehow refreshing. She felt safe there, in the midst of the three men, and so grateful they had come to her aid.

Taking his place next to her, Rey faced the room so that they lay back to back. Leaving her the blanket, he slept in his clothes, staring at the door and ready to defend her honor if the need should arise.

Eight days later, the ship docked at Newrock. No one more thankful than the girl, Amicia was allowed to leave the Mate's quarters and visit the wheel house above. Climbing the steps with quick thuds in her boots, she beamed at her view of the ship and the town they were tied off next to.

Rey stood watch at the end of the narrow passage that connected the area to the rest of the deck to ensure she didn't go anywhere else, and that no one else paid her a visit. Watching her with a small grin, he enjoyed her eagerness as if he were living part of her wonder, as she had never been anywhere but Nalen. Pacing back and forth, up to the top of the steps, then back to the mouth of the access, he surveyed coolly, keeping tabs on her and an eye out for trouble.

Up on top, Ami was surprised to discover that the "wheel house" was hardly a house at all. It had three high walls around the sides and back, but the front lay open, so that she could see the full expanse of the ship before her, as well as the sea beyond the bow.

"This is amazing," she breathed, speaking to Baldwin, who kept her company while the rest of the crew unloaded the cargo and paid a visit to the brothel. Placing her hands on the wheel tentatively at first, she then grasped the spokes more firmly and giggled with child-like glee.

"Yeah, I like ships." He grinned sheepishly, joining her at the helm. "It's not much of a life for a family man, but for someone young like me, it ain't bad. I've got a few friends, like Rey, and they're really all that I need."

"What, you don't dream of taking a bride and learning a trade, or something like that?" she teased. She had come to like Bally and Rey very much, as if they were the brothers she had never had. *A family I never had.* She sighed, still bitter at her mother and father's betrayal. The thought darkened her mood, but only for an instant before she pushed it away.

"Nah." He chuckled, his face flushed. "I'm more of a free spirit. Besides, Rey started as a cabin boy on another ship, same as me, and now he's crew. In a few years, I can do the same."

At the top of the step at that moment, Rey snickered. Being cabin boy on the other vessel had been a challenge; one he thankfully survived and hoped never to repeat. Turning, he began the next round of his loop.

"Is being a cabin boy bad?" She frowned, seeing the other man appear briefly and then disappear again.

"I don't get paid," Bally grumbled. "I get room and board, fed, and I get to clean the head. It's not really a good job." He snickered, wrinkling his nose and shaking his head, which caused her to laugh.

"It's honest work," she replied, lifting her chin and noticing the clouds as they floated over. "Does it get very cold here? Rey said you guys won't deliver to them during the winter."

"Yeah, it gets ice locked for a couple of months," he informed her, squinting at the horizon. "We got two more trips, and then they're on their own until spring."

"We must be far north of Nalen, then," she surmised.

"Yes, north and west." He pointed at the map of the ocean that lay spread on the chart table. "See." He indicated the tiny island where they were anchored. "This is Newrock and this is Nalen." He placed a stiff digit on each one, then scooted them across to where they met in the top east corner of the central ring.

"I've never seen a map of the world before," she stated in awe. "I've heard about it, but I never imagined it was so big."

"Why would you?" Rey cut in, having lengthened his steps onto the wheel house deck so he could catch their conversation. Dropping the line, but not waiting for the reply, he turned his back and started the next loop.

"I guess I wouldn't have any need," she agreed, watching his back vanish. "Why does he keep coming up here and leaving?" she demanded once he had left earshot.

"The Mate told him to keep look out, so he's watching the entrance to the wheel house here, and he's keeping an eye on us. I'm not normally allowed up here, either."

"Oh," she gasped in surprise. "But you like all of this. The steering, and the map, and knowledge about the world."

"Definitely." He nodded vigorously, his enthusiasm bubbling within his words. "The world is huge, and I want to see it all, or most of it. There's more world than we will ever need. I think there's a few who live out in the netherlands." He indicated the area outside the circle of land with a wave of his hand. "But most of us stay along the coast or the continents of the ring, and that's good enough for me."

"The ring," she repeated, tracing the loop with her own finger. "That's funny how all this is almost a perfect basket of sorts. A big ocean with so many islands in the center of a rim, like a bowl of soup."

"Yeah. And it's filled with land and fish of all kinds, everything we need. Only those crazy adventurous types go out close to the edge."

"To the edge?" She laughed, unsure if he teased her. "You mean the edge of the world?"

"Sure, out here." He waved his hand off the side of the table, where the map ended. "If you go out too far, you fall off. I'm staying clear of the edge, for sure."

"Yes, I'm glad we won't be going too far out, then. When we get back to Nalen, I'll need to get another boat and find where I'm going to live."

"You mean you don't know?" His features grew serious.

"No, I haven't figured that out yet." She slid the tips of her fingers lightly over the long string of islands that formed the west side of the ring, south of their current position. "Maybe over here."

"Not many people live over there," Bally informed her. "There's stories about them that do. Cannibals and such."

"Cannibals?"

"You know, people who eat other people."

"I thought they were just a myth, like fairies and dragons."

"Dragons?" Rey chimed in, even closer to them on this pass. Ending his pacing, he crossed the rest of the deck with a few loud stomps. "Who said anything about dragons?"

"No one," Ami stammered, gazing up at him with wide green eyes. "We were just talking about the western rim, and that dragons and fairies... and stuff like that... they're just something people tell their children to scare them at bed time." His demeanor made her anxious and she found herself tongue tied by his angry scowl.

"Oh no, those things are real. If you go too far west, you'll find them," Bally boasted as if he already had. "But don't worry, Ami. Rey and me'll help you find a nice place to live... without the cannibals or the dragons."

Giving the younger man a dark stare, Rey growled, "Yeah, we'll make sure you steer clear of the west and all of those things. And better yet, let's not even talk about them. Ok?"

Her brow furrowed, Ami could feel a wave of confusion overtake her, and she clipped, "Rey, what is wrong with you?"

"Nothing." He cut his gaze over to her. "Sailors just have a respect for certain things and talking about them is considered bad luck. So, take my advice and don't even so much as breathe the word *dragon* again for the rest of this trip," he instructed. Turning his back and marching back to the stairs, he fully expected them to heed his warning.

Watching him go, Ami sighed. "Men can be so unpredictable!"

"I guess so," Bally laughed, having heard many a story about sea creatures and sunken ships, but apparently Rey Daye had been far more affected by them than he had been. "I could tell you some stories if you ever want to hear. We should do it when he won't be interrupting us, though."

"Thanks, Bally." She giggled, not wanting the other man to be upset by them. "I'll keep that in mind next time I need a good scare."

SEVEN

Stormy Seas

SEEING that the last of the empty water casks had been stowed and fresh ones brought out, Piers surveyed the contents of the hold. Except for the food stores for their return voyage, every crate and barrel had been removed and replaced with an empty one, which would be traded once again when they arrived back in Nalen.

Inhaling deeply, he blew the breath out through his nose in a slow and deliberate manner. Then, turning on his heel, he squared his shoulders, as if preparing to face some dark demon, and stomped his way to the deck above. Looking up at the wheel house, he could see Bally showing the girl the navigational charts and pointing at the horizon.

"Amicia," he whispered, "where were you twenty years ago?" In his younger days, he had sported a few regrets, but as of late, he didn't look back too often. There wasn't much point in wallowing in things that he couldn't change, and he liked to stay focused on the here and now.

Tearing his eyes away from her, he announced loudly, "Let's get these hatches sealed," indicating the pullies that raised and lowered the large set of coverings centered above the hold.

Some of the crew seized the ropes and hoisted the load. A few minutes later, the access had been closed and locked, ready to set sail on the morrow. "Fair enough. Everyone is dismissed for the evening," he bellowed.

Gazing up at the girl once more, he admired her simple features, now that her body was on the mend. He had removed the stitches from her lip and temple the day before and couldn't help but notice the natural beauty she possessed, especially with the dark rings all but gone from around her eyes.

Amicia Spicer would make a fine conquest, and he pursed his lips as he considered his chances of getting next to her for the evening, or even a few if he were lucky. The other men would visit the brothel, but for Piers, there was no greater thrill than the feel of flesh that had been given freely and not paid for. He wanted that from her if he could have it. Nodding to himself, he considered what it might take to get it.

Crossing the planks with a clip in his step, he greeted Reynard warmly. "How was our guest today?" The younger man had been playing chaperone for her and Bally since dawn and had done a right fine job of it, or so it would appear.

"She was good, actually." Rey laughed, turning to follow him up to the top level. "A perfect angel, she was." His head bobbed as he spoke, not making any mention of their wayward conversation.

"Wonderful to hear," the Mate said with a wave of his hand over his shoulder. "We'll need you to deliver our dinner this evening."

"Aye, sir."

Skirting the side via the narrow path, the pair climbed the stairs, and Piers announced loudly, "Baldwin, take care of our lady's murphy. She'll be needing it this evening, I'm sure. Then, you lads have earned a night off. See yourselves into town, but don't get into any trouble. We make sail at first light, don't forget." His voice robust, he winked at her when he had finished speaking, and he noted the glow his attention gave her, bolstering his nerve.

Laughing loudly, the duo didn't hesitate, as they each had work to do before they could leave the ship. Watching them go, Piers briefly thought about the brothel and the women they would find there. They would have exactly what they wanted, bought and paid. He, on the other hand, would earn his conquest if he were to have one. The promise of his prize made his heart skip a beat, inwardly excited at the thrill of the hunt that lay in store for the evening.

Turning to her, he spoke to Ami in a different, lighter tone. "Did you enjoy your day out?"

"I did!" she replied, her smile broad. "Bally showed me the map of the world." She sounded extraordinarily happy, her fingers tracing the line of islands on the west, the ones she had been warned against. "It was a nice day," she said more quietly, with a small nod.

Joining her, he fished, "You like him." That could put a crimp in his plans if it were true.

"As a brother, I suppose," she said wistfully. Looking up, her gaze caught his, and she demanded, "You mean as something more?"

Relieved, Piers swallowed and modulated his tone. "He's a nice kid. He or Rey either one would make a suitable husband one day, if you could get them off this ship!" He laughed, breaking their connection to indicate the map. "I've sailed most of these waters," he stalled, bragging a little at his experience as a seaman.

"And what about you?" she challenged, raising her chin and sticking to the point. "Will you make a suitable husband one day?"

"I'm afraid not, love," he said in a quieter voice. "Not much in it for a salty old sea dog like me."

Meeting her stare, he held the smile, imagining her bare skin the night he had dressed her wounds. He would like to see her again by the soft glow of his cabin's flame now that she had healed. But, unlike his crew, he did mind the screams. If he were to have her, she would need to volunteer. "Dinner?" he asked, offering her his arm.

Ami had enjoyed the Mate's company. Something about him felt different from the others, and she wished she could draw out their time together. Parting him with his beloved boat would be unlikely, but they could enjoy the return trip to Nalen, nonetheless. She accepted the appendage, and they retired to his quarters, where Bally and Rey had already been and gone. Her pot clean, their dinner sat on the table, and the light on the wall burned, casting its soft glow across the chamber. Only tonight, the flicker seemed sad, as if something hung over them, ready to smother their budding relationship.

Ignoring the shadow that the small flame produced, Ami sat in one of the chairs and began selecting her share of the meal. "You don't fancy a trip into town with the others?" Somehow, it pleased her that he had chosen to forgo the tradition and spend his night with her. "I'm sure I would be fine for a few hours without you," she coaxed.

"Oh, no," he replied.

He shook his dark hair as he joined her, and she noticed that his customary knot had been removed to reveal long dark waves that hung a few inches past his shoulders. "I didn't realize your hair was so long!" she observed in surprise, not accustomed to seeing it on the men from town.

"Of course, all sailors grow out their hair. It's a tradition." A bottle of wine in his hand, he presented it to her to view, placing it on the table as he observed, "This is the first meal we've had alone. We might as well enjoy it." Lifting the beverage, he extracted the cork and poured a bit in her small metal cup.

"Where did you get that?" she asked airily, surprised by the gesture.

"I've had it." He grinned, offering hers. "I've been saving it, in a manner of speaking."

"Don't tell me you're wasting your special bottle on me," she gasped, her face taking on a soft flush.

"Oh, no!" He laughed loudly, admiring her stained cheeks. His confidence strong, he felt certain she would be willing when the time came, if he were patient enough to continue his stroking of her desire. "I have a whole crate of them, actually. I break one out every time I get a beautiful young woman into my cabin," he boasted.

"I suppose you get one every trip." She grinned, suspecting the contrary and nibbling at her bread and cheese as she watched him covertly. He had been her favorite of the three men since she had moved into his cabin, and his showering of attention had unnerved her, to say the least.

Shrugging slightly, he confessed, "Not as often as a man might like." Gulping his cup of wine, he beamed, his brown eyes shining with desire.

"So, what happened to you?" she persisted. "How'd you end up sailing back and forth across the ocean, instead of having a wife and a brood of young ones?"

Helping himself to another cup of the wine, he sighed. "That's a long story, Ami my dear, and not necessarily a good one."

"Good is in the eye of the beholder," she pushed eagerly, yearning to know him more deeply.

Stopping his movements, he stared at her, then asked, "Why do you want to know? In a few weeks, we'll have you back in Nalen, and you'll be off on another ship, in search of that place where you belong." Resuming serving himself, he could sense her mood as it changed, and he lifted his gaze to meet hers. "What did I say?"

"I don't know," she panted, on the verge of tears. "It's not you, I swear it." She tried to smile, failing in the cause. "My mum said that to me, before she passed."

"Said what to you?" he asked as he sat up straighter, forgetting his loins for a moment and genuinely concerned that he had upset her. "Ami, I'm sorry –"

She held up her hand, cutting him off. "*Follow your dreams to the place where you belong*, that's what she said. I'm not sure what she meant, but I feel like I'm being drawn... somewhere." A tear trickled over and she swiped at it quickly. "That's why I left Nalen. To search for it," she whispered, her heart vulnerable in a way it had never been.

She had never made plans with Rupert. Perhaps knowing him all her life had taken some of the mystery out of it and had stolen the magic between them. Being close to Piers, excitement roiled within her, like the flame she had felt when she realized she must travel to a new world that would be her home. Something about him suited her, and by his actions that evening, she suspected he might actually feel the same; if she didn't frighten him away.

"Oh, Ami," he breathed, pulling at her and enjoying the feel of her against his broad chest. "Amicia Spicer, I knew I could see it in you. When I saw you coming up the dock before you ever got to me, I knew." He pictured her strut, with her long skirt swishing about her ankles, and could hardly contain his desire. Kneading her arms and back with his palms, he groaned.

"What did you see?" she simpered, comforted by the strength of his hold on her.

"That fire, that burning from within. Bright as the sun, you are, or as a star shooting across the sky," he whispered into her hair.

"I'm not the sun or a star." She chuckled, amused by his seemingly sensitive demeanor. "You surprise me, Mate," she informed him softly, her hand toying with his shirt as he held her. Her resolve felt paper-thin, and forgetting that he was a sailor, she could imagine having him to comfort her all the days of her life.

Releasing her, he stammered, leaning back into his chair. "I surprised you? What, with this?" He opened his palms. "You needn't be surprised by any of this. I thought you might be in the mood for a bit of wooing, that's all."

"Wooing." She giggled, thinking of Rupert and his repeated proposals for a moment. "Wooing is good, I suppose."

Somehow, her expression didn't convince him, and he could feel his opportunity to get more familiar with her slipping away. Lifting his cup, he made a toast to her. "To Ami. May she find the place where she belongs."

Lifting her own, she seconded the toast, but an awkwardness settled over the couple. They each had wants and desires from the other, but neither of them had expressly stated them. That left a lot of room for doubt on both sides of the table.

They ate in utter silence until all the food had been devoured and the wine bottle half emptied. Then, the girl stood and went over to the bed she had been enjoying since her discovery on board. "I never thanked you," she said, turning to sit on the shelf and face him. "I should have. Thank you for all that you have done for me."

"You don't have to thank me, Ami," he replied, whispering her name. "I started out as a crewman," he shifted the topic purposefully as he moved to take a seat next to her, as Rey had. Keeping their conversation light, as if he had intended to answer her questions all along, he would sit with her into the wee hours of the mourn as they shared.

"Well, I actually started out as a blacksmith, but I'm terrible at working with my hands. By the time I had served my apprenticeship, it was quite clear that metallurgy was not my calling."

"Your calling was the sea," she teased, the sparkle returning to her eyes as she leaned closer to him, which pleased him as he laid an arm across her shoulders and snuggled her against the side of his chest.

"Not exactly." He also grinned. "I took the job until I found something better. Ten years later, I earned the rank of first mate. That's when I became comfortable, and I've been on this ship ever since." He stroked her hair, his heart beating faster with anticipation.

"Commanding the crew." She saluted him, her face turned up to his. She could not have appeared more provocative if she had tried.

"Yes, commanding the crew and seeing to the cargo." He shrugged. "So, what about you? You're a strong, capable young woman. Where do you see your calling taking you?"

"I didn't think you had noticed," she murmured with flushed cheeks. "I mean, I had begun to think you were too old for a young woman, such as myself," she added deviously, "beautiful or otherwise."

"Oh, I noticed." He grinned, his finger extended to trace the line of her jaw. His thumb brushing her lips, he whispered, "I assure you I've had my share of tumbles, both beautiful and otherwise." He taunted, his mouth close enough to taste her. "But, I'm a bit old for taking on a new career, a wife, or a family," he finished flatly, leaving her hanging. "I want to be clear about that. We have three weeks until we get you back to Nalen, and I would certainly love to spend that time with you, but that is all that I can offer, my sweet, for I myself am married to the sea."

He could see her eyes glaze over, perhaps in anger, so he soothed, "If you're really looking for a traveling companion, or…" His tongue flicked over his lips. "If you want something more permanent, I'm sure Rey or Bally either one would be happy to accommodate you. If you're looking for more of a tumble or two, well…" He leaned against her more firmly, as if he were finally going to kiss her.

"Is that what the wine was about, then?" she demanded, raw rage glaring at him as she placed both palms against his chest and pushed.

"It was about sharing a bit of company!" he scoffed, not releasing his hold on her as she struggled against him.

"Fine, we shared a bit of company!" She hid her tears with her hair as she pulled away from him to stand in the center of the room. Removing her boots, she dropped each on the floor with a thud. "Are you going to move, or do I get the chair tonight?"

His jaw hanging open, he relinquished the bed, then demanded, "You didn't really think we were going to set a wedding date –"

"No, I didn't think anything, Piers." She bit his name like a curse, tearing at his pride. "Good night," she spat, sliding into the covers still fully dressed. Facing the wall, she fumed, angry at him for thinking he could part her from her clothing so easily, and at herself for thinking he could be anything other than a sailor, married to the sea as he put it.

"Good night," he replied, the bottle of wine in one hand and a chair in the other. Placing the seat next to the door on the narrow deck outside, he took a large swig straight from the bottle. Staring out across the bay, he laughed to himself. *I guess my luck with women is slipping*. Normally they would have been finished, and he'd have been asleep by then.

EIGHT

Golden Sun

REYNARD DAYE COULD SMELL trouble the moment he entered the first mate's quarters the following morning. He had enjoyed his night in town, drinking at the bar, and had almost worked up the courage to visit the brothel. When he joined this crew, he had promised himself that he would, at least once before the year was out, but he hadn't made it yet.

Instead, he had sat with a pint, nursing it and contemplating how thoughtful it had been for Piers to take on sitting with the girl so they could have the night off; the whole night in fact. *What if it had been a ruse?*

"Did he hurt you?" Dropping the tray of food on the table, his hands doubled into fists, he made no attempt to hide his rage. "Last night, while he had you alone, did he behave himself?"

Looking up into his beautiful hazel orbs, Ami could feel her gut twist at the depth of his protectiveness. "No, he didn't hurt me," she bit back, wiping at her red eyes. No, she had caused whatever pain she suffered for believing Piers Massheby could be anything other than a salty sea dog and a scoundrel at heart.

She had let his shielding her from the others fool her into thinking that he might care. To the contrary, it only meant he was selfish and that he didn't want to share. "Seriously, I'm unharmed," she said again, forcing a faint smile.

"Good." He nodded, indicating the tray, his demeanor still tense. "I've brought food for us, and this is my day with you."

"Good," she repeated, grinning more fully and relaxing easily in his company. "Thank you, Rey. At least there is one of you I can count on." Taking her seat, she let the statement fall flat across the room, not offering any explanation as to her meaning.

Instead, she picked up their conversation from the day before as she served herself. There had been talk of dragons, but Rey had insisted quite adamantly that they should not be discussed. So, instead, she inquired, "You've been a sailor for some time. Where all have you been? Are there really cannibals along the western shores?"

"I hardly find that a tasteful subject for a young lady." He chuckled, sitting beside her and selecting his own food. "But I've heard that story myself many times about the wilds of the west. I can't verify the claim though. No ship I've ever been on has dared to sail further west than Newrock, much less put to port there."

He glanced over at her a few times, hoping she would leave it at that. Bally's morbid fascination with dragons had bothered him, and he felt no desire to enlighten the girl. What he did know of such fire-breathing monsters didn't come from second-hand tales. He had lived the nightmare, and he had no intention of poisoning her thoughts with his past.

"Are there ports there, west of Newrock?" she asked in surprise. "If ships don't go so far, then why would there be people there?"

"I guess because they want to be." He laughed out loud at her persistence. "And yes, there are ports there. Some vessels surely brave the unfriendly waters, just none that I have ever sailed on."

"We should go there, then, just to explore it." Her eyes shone as she suggested it. "You could go with me, you know," she offered, smiling sweetly. She had spent half the night crying over the Mate. The other half she had thought about what he had said; that Bally or Rey either one would be a good traveling companion. In the end, she had decided that he was at least right about that.

Slowing his movements, Rey avoided looking at her while he considered the proposal. "I'm bound by contract to this vessel until winter comes and we can no longer make the run to Newrock," he reminded her. "Would you be willing to wait for me until then?" Peeking at her between his long dark locks, his gaze smoldered.

Damn, she was pretty. He had been overwhelmed when she had been discovered, this delicate creature he had sworn to protect. Now, he had gotten to know her and the idea that she might contemplate a future with him had him considering the possibilities; ones that didn't involve being a crewman.

Her lip taking on a small pout, she sighed. "But it's only mid-summer, and winter is still some months away. I can't stay in Nalen that long…" Her voice trailed away. "You can't break your contract?"

"I don't get paid if I break it," he supplied, continuing with his meal. "They don't pay the bulk of my share until we finish the last run."

Outwardly, he remained calm, although his heart raced beneath his thin white shirt. He had considered the girl next to him out of reach, but she appeared to be receptive. Whatever the Mate had done had surely pushed her in his direction, and he would take it. But, could he convince her to hold her fervor until he would be ready to begin their quest?

"Maybe we could hide you somewhere," he offered.

"Hide me? You know I can't stay here!"

"Not here!" He laughed aloud. "You could take a ship to another town. I've been to many, and some are rather decent. You could wait there, and I would meet up with you." His gaze flicked down at her lips, admiring their pink fullness and how they might taste if he dared to kiss them. "Would you wait for me, Ami?" His voice soft, his eyes grew wide with the unspoken promise his words held.

"And we would sail to the west and explore it?" She sounded genuinely excited. Sitting up straighter in her chair, her face glowed with the possibilities. Her journey seemed far less daunting if she were to have someone, a man in fact, along to look after her, and Rey would be the perfect choice.

"We could, I guess," he faltered, thinking fast. "But there are other places I would want to show you first." He realized she had missed his meaning; he would have to be clearer at some point.

"Well, the west is what I want to see," she replied more stiffly, clutching his arm. "Please, Rey. Promise me you'll take me there."

"I promise," he agreed with a gurgle, caught up in her whimsical state. He wouldn't, of course; only a fool would purposely go to a place no one ever came back from. But if she believed that he would, he had time to change her mind. "It's settled. When we get back to Nalen, I'll help you find a ship to a safe waiting place, and I'll join you there when my contract is fulfilled."

"Agreed." She offered him her hand, beaming at her cunningness.

He shook the appendage, certain in her plans to travel with him. He would have time to convince her that he was as good a man as any, even the Mate, and of a better age for her at that. If he were able, he would have her hand, and it would be a new life for both of them that they found in that place she was searching for.

After finishing the meal, the pair moved to the bed and continued to visit, but as the afternoon wore on, Ami grew restless. "Let's go up to the wheel house and look at the map," she suggested, climbing off the bunk. "We can make our plans for my place of waiting and all those we wish to visit."

"We can't do that," he replied, feeling a bit of panic. "Mate's orders were clear. You remain here for the duration of the voyage," he said sternly, rising next to her.

"I'm sure he won't mind," she insisted, fishing her hairbrush out of her bag and brushing out her long blond strands.

Ami's hair had always been wild, with a frizz of curls when she didn't keep it bound. Forcing it down, she wound the long locks into a braid to keep them in place and tied it off so that it hung down her back in a heavy lump. "I promise, I won't go anywhere else. No one will even notice that I'm there."

A knot formed in Rey's gut, as he knew full well that anyone who looked up at the wheel house would know that she was there. "Ami, please," he breathed. Stepping towards her and catching her hand, he toyed with her fingers. "I haven't asked you to do much. Please stay inside and don't get us into trouble."

"Are you afraid of the first mate?" she asked, her clear green orbs cutting through him like warm butter. "You're a man, the same as he is. You are perfectly capable of watching over me there as easily as here," she argued.

Swallowing, his Adam's apple bobbed, and he bit his bottom lip as he turned her words for a moment. He might be a man, but the Mate had more than twenty years on him. Twenty years of muscle and sweat, as well as experience with other men and the world. If anything happened to her, the Mate would beat him to a pulp.

He wanted desperately to follow the other man's advice, but doing so might make him appear smaller, weaker in the girl's eyes. If she were going to save herself for him, he needed to appear capable of being the only man she needed, and his ego took control. "All right then, at dusk I'll take you up. We'll watch the sun set, and then return for our dinner."

"But that's still hours from now," she persisted.

"It's the best I can do," he maintained, towering over her smaller frame. "I've grown quite fond of you, Amicia Spicer. If you truly wish to be my companion, then you understand I would never place you in harm's way. I said I would take you up, and I will, but you have to trust me on the rest."

Ami glared at him, his forcefulness unlike the boy she had been getting to know. "All right, Rey," she acquiesced, "I'll do as you ask." She felt as if she were toying with him, that he had greater desires for their future than simple travel-mates would imply, and she should set him straight. However, honesty hadn't worked well for her so far. Perhaps allowing him to believe so would serve her better.

Returning to her seat, she picked up one of the books the first mate had located and presented to her, probably from the captain's collection. Opening it, she read the pages to him slowly, turning them one by one as she distracted herself until it was time for them to go outside and get some air.

Three hours later, Piers came down from the upper deck and a visit to the head, facing towards the stern. Stomping over the wooden slats, the sun setting to his left as they headed south before turning east for Nalen, he caught the glimpse of a female form standing at the chart table. *Shit*, he grunted, increasing his pace.

Skirting the cargo hold, he looked around to see who else might have noticed her. His heart thumping loudly in his ears, he entered the narrow passage that ran along the west railing, glancing into his quarters as he passed by.

The lamp had not been lit, and it would be dark in the small room when they returned. *Stupid girl*, he fumed, reaching the stairs and clomping up to the wheel house. *And Rey let her do it.*

Reaching the top, he exploded, "What the bloody hell is going on here?" Shoving a finger in her face when he reached her, he bellowed, "You are supposed to remain below!" With a quick pivot, he addressed the younger man, "And you are supposed to keep her there! What the fuck are you thinking, bringing her out like this?"

Holding his resolve, Rey stood his ground. "Relax, Mate. She isn't harmed. We came for the view of the sunset and to spend a bit of time with the charts. I'll take her back below in a few minutes, and none will be the wiser."

"None will be the wiser?" Piers poked him in the chest, forcing him to take a step back. "These are dangerous waters and having a woman up on deck is just asking for trouble," he growled.

"The sun's almost gone," the girl laughed, defending her right to enjoy it. "What harm could come of it?"

Glaring at her, the first mate considered his options. Their argument had made a much larger scene than if he had simply allowed her to enjoy the view. "Tonight. That's it. After that, you stay below, and you don't set foot outside that cabin until we put in at Nalen."

"And you!" He turned on the other man once more in his biting tone. "Clear your things out of my cabin. Bally and I will take it from here."

"Piers, please!" Ami leapt to his defense. "This was my idea, I swear it! Please don't punish Rey for my choice," she begged, her bottom lip trembling at his dismissal.

"Enjoy the view," the Mate clipped, ignoring her plea. Instead, he stomped over to the side and glared out at the golden sun as it set. His eyes danced along the western horizon, in search of what he wasn't sure.

"Fool kids," he muttered under his breath.

Men weren't the only dangerous things out on the ocean, and not the deadliest. There were other creatures who would tear the ship apart if they caught the scent of a woman on board. He had never seen one, but he had heard the stories and been close enough to the danger. He hoped that he never would.

Sulking, Ami moved to stand beside him, watching the sinking ball of fire. "It's beautiful," she gasped. "I think I've never seen a sunset so large."

His anger softened, Piers found it difficult holding onto his rage. "Yes, the sun in the west is a magical thing."

"Magical?" she repeated with a small smile. "Have you ever sailed beyond the western horizon, Mate? Past the coast of the great ring?"

He nodded, pursing his lips. "Only once. The crew had been terrified. We got caught in a great storm, or we wouldn't have gone there at all. We were lucky to survive," he said in a quieter tone, gazing down at her. "I want to protect you, love. I'm sorry that I hurt you last night."

"It was my fault." She sighed as the last bit of light disappeared, and the darkness pressed down upon them fully. Drawing her sweater around her, she grinned. "I had a friend about your age, back in Nalen. You remind me of him sometimes. There, he was the one always pressing me to marry him and have a family. I know how it can feel when you don't really want that, but someone else does," she confessed, the air between them crackling with an attraction she had no desire to resist.

Catching movement over her shoulder, she glanced at Rey, having forgotten that he was there. Turning to him, she said more loudly, "Maybe someday I'll meet the right man and we'll both feel the same way at the same time."

Rey smiled at the suggestion, then asked, "Are we ready for the meal?"

"Yes." Piers didn't hesitate. "Go below and get our platter. I'll light the lamp and get our lady settled in," he said to her with a wink.

Back inside his cabin, they discovered that Bally had delivered their dinner and the lamp already burned. "I thought she wasn't allowed outside," he stated crossly. Realizing that he had missed out, he had taken to fuming in the cabin while he waited for them to come down and join him.

"She isn't," the Mate agreed, "but fortunately, it would appear no harm has come of it." Taking his seat, he served himself, as did the others, and they ate in near silence.

Half way through the meal, the wind began to howl, and thunder could be heard rumbling in the distance. A firm thud shook the ship from port to starboard, causing it to rock in an unusual fashion. The others looked surprised, but the older man's eyes held pure terror. Leaping from his seat, he threw open the door and stepped out onto the ledge, where he could hold on to the railing and peer into the darkness.

Lining up beside him, the four of them surveyed the churning water below them, not seeing anything but the flashes of lightning in the clouds rolling in low overhead.

"Perhaps it was the wind," the girl offered with a small laugh. "You said this was a strange part of the sea," she said to Bally with a small punch to the arm.

"No, it's not the wind," Piers informed her, hearing the distinct sound of wings flapping beyond their view. His heart pounding, he knew the beast was upon them, and it was too late to run. Catching her by the arm, he pulled her closer and commanded, "We have to get off this ship, now! It's our only chance!"

"Off the ship!" Rey demanded, "Have you gone mad? It's a little storm. We go back inside and wait it out."

His eyes wide, the first mate shook his head. He had never seen one, but he had heard that sound before. "No, Rey, it's not a storm. It's a dragon. It has come for her, and if we don't get off this ship, it will kill us all."

NINE

Dragon's Fire

AMI STOOD STUNNED by the Mate's words. "What do you mean a dragon?" Sure, they had talked about them only yesterday, with Bally telling her they were real, but she still couldn't believe it. *Cannibals, maybe, but not dragons!*

"We don't have time to argue," the Mate shouted back. Dodging inside his quarters, with the girl close behind, he claimed her bag from its place on the back of the door and dumped it out on the bed. Giving it a shake, he announced, "We can use this. Let's go!"

Grabbing her small sack of coins and shoving it in her pocket, the girl followed him, still grumbling, "I don't understand why we would leave a perfectly good boat, in the middle of a storm, no less."

Catching her around the waist, Rey urged her along, calling over the howling wind, "The Mate's a good man, Ami! A good leader. If he says we have to go, we go!" Glancing over at his friend at the same time, Bally appeared a pasty, ghost-white when a flash of light lit up his features, tightening Rey's gut with fear. "I hope," he added under his breath as they crossed the deck towards the entrance to the hold.

Reaching the mid deck, Piers shoved the bag at Ami. "Take this and go below. Fill it with as much of the dried meat, cheese, and bread as you can. And try to keep it dry. It's no good to us if it gets wet and spoils."

Turning to Baldwin, he gave his next order. "Rey, you and Bally go find us some rope, all that you can get, and take it below. Use or cut some smaller pieces to form handles inside the lids to four of the empty water casks."

"Inside the lids?" Bally asked, his brow furrowed.

"Yes, inside, so a person can hide within and pull the lid shut on top of him."

"Aye, sir," Bally replied, pushing through his fear. He had complete faith in the first mate and no desire to let him down.

Finally, seizing the lines to the pullies, Piers shouted over the rising wind, "Grab ho, men. We need to get the hold open!" He knew if the doors were damaged before they did, they would not be able to get their raft out once they had built it, and that would be the end.

Heaving on the pullies with all his strength, he groaned loudly with his effort. Confused, but obedient, the crew joined in to help. The wind gusted against him, and Piers struggled to hold his feet as he strained, hoping they would have enough time to complete their task before the real attack began. A few seconds later, the great doors were open, and he headed below.

Down in the hold, Amicia dug through the crates of food with trembling hands. She had located a few strips of the leather from the tanner, similar to the large sheets she had used as bedding when she first came on board. Lining her bag with them, she anticipated that they would hold the water out and preserve their food, as the first mate had requested.

Snatching up handfuls of the dried meats, she shoved those in first, followed by a few rounds of cheese. "Oh, my God!" she gasped. *I need the dagger. The one that belonged to mother.* Would she have time to retrieve it?

Topping off the pack with some loaves of flatbread, she forced it closed and tied the strings to hold it shut. Then, throwing it over her shoulder, she mounted the stairs. Climbing quickly, she wanted to make it to the Mate's quarters and back before anyone noticed that she was gone.

The storm had increased exponentially, and the ship tossed around like a cork in a bottle. Cold rain slapped her in the face when she entered the narrow tunnel that led to the wheel house. Squinting her eyes against it, she made it to the door and grasped the frame firmly as the ship rolled on a giant wave, her body trembling with adrenaline only exaggerated by the frigid downpour.

Once it had crested, she was able to step inside and dug hurriedly through the contents of her bag that had been strewn upon the bed. Locating the small knife, she shoved it inside the top of the pack. Realizing anything left behind would be lost forever, she made another sift through the mess.

Spying her hairbrush and mirror, she claimed those as well. Finally, opening her mother's box of stationary, she rolled it around the pen and shoved it and the ink down into her pack before declaring the rest to be worthless.

Throwing the bag onto her back once more, Ami fought the continued heave of the deck as she returned to the center. Lightning flashed and thunder rolled as she clamored back down the stairs, where she found that Piers and the others were building a raft. Just as she reached them, a fierce scream from a large, unseen beast filled the air.

Ami froze in place, anchored by fright.

Piers could see the terror in her eyes. "Ami, help us," he commanded, hoping to distract her from the creature circling above them. "We need to work quickly." The raft taking shape, they had lashed a group of four empty barrels onto a pallet with a single filled water cask in the center, the lid on it tightly closed.

"This is madness!" Rey shouted, indicating the full barrel in the middle. "It will sink us for sure."

"No, it will float," the Mate insisted. "I'm going up top. You secure the net so we can hoist our raft over the side." Seeing that Ami still had not moved, Piers grabbed her by the arms, giving her a shake. "Amicia! Listen to me! I know that you are frightened, but you have to trust me. I've faced a dragon before, on that ship I told you about. I've seen the fire inside of you, Ami. I know that you can do this, but you have to be strong. You can't give up!"

Moving only her eyes, she looked at him, his face shoved down close to hers as he spoke. "I'm scared," she managed.

"I know that you're scared," he repeated, pulling her against him into a full embrace as water dripped down their faces. "We can do this, love. I swear it. You just have to believe."

"I believe," she parroted, nodding against him.

"Good. Get the ropes and nets in place," he called to the others as he released her. Taking her hand, he led her to the stairs. "You have our food?" he asked, inspecting the lump on her back.

"Yes." She nodded, her teeth chattering. "And my mum's knife. I got the knife," she stammered, her thoughts jumbled. Blinking against the spray, she willed herself to focus on him.

"Good, come with me," he implored, tugging on her arm as they climbed.

Up top, he dropped the ropes for the hoist down into the hold and shouted, "Secure the lines! I'm going to need a hand!"

Doing as they were told, the pair quickly had the large net put in place. Once Rey and Bally made the final connections, they climbed for the top. Above them, the Mate and a couple of the crewmen gave the taut ropes a firm pull, hoisting their contraption to the deck and setting it down, allowing it to rest there.

Staring at the rigging above them, Ami could see shapes and shadows in the flashes of light above them. "Dear God, this is real," she sobbed, her hair plastered against the side of her face as water dripped from her chin and ran down her neck.

"Ami! Get in," Piers screamed, indicating one of the empty barrels. Pushing her towards it, he placed their small bag of provisions in the bottom and then helped her climb over the side.

"How do you know it will float?" she begged. "How is it going to keep out the sea?"

"It's made to hold water, love," he explained calmly, soothing her as the others clamored to their own casks. "It will keep the sea out. Scrunch down and put the lid on. You can push it off when you are away from the ship, so you can stay dryer until then. Use the handle Bally built inside to pull it into place."

Obeying, she knelt in her tube, sitting on her bag and holding her knees to her chest, then pulled the rope to be sure the lid had sealed above her. Shivering, she waited while he attached the lid to the handle on the side of the barrel with a small section of rope, so it wouldn't be lost when she pushed it off later.

Rey and Bally each secured their lids to their barrels as well, and then climbed inside the empty casks. The older of the two shouted, "Aren't you coming with us?"

"I'll have to swim out to you," Piers bellowed back, tying his covering on last. "Put your lids on and get clear of the ship. I'll get you out into the water and then swim out to meet you."

"Ok," Rey agreed with more conviction than he felt. In truth, he could have sworn he had just said goodbye to the other man for the last time.

Placing the lid over the last barrel, the one intended to be his, Piers smacked it firmly, then shouted, "We have to get this over the side, now!"

A small group of the crew had gathered around as the trio prepared to leave. Staring at the first mate, it wasn't hard to figure out they were abandoning the ship. Ordinarily, they might not have agreed with the course of action, but with the beast flying overhead and tearing down the masts, they were inclined to agree with getting rid of the girl. The dragon was after her, and the sooner they got her off their boat, the better, and before it had been completely destroyed preferably.

Pulling on the ropes, the raft was hoisted and swung wide. Letting it down a little less gently than Piers would have liked, he swore loudly, but what was done was done. Cutting the lines from the pullies, the makeshift sanctuary bobbed across the water, bouncing wildly on the waves, but it floated.

Piers stood stock-still, watching as the three were carried away from the ship. As the distance between them expanded, he knew his odds of reaching them to get aboard the smaller craft grew slimmer with each foot. Grinding his teeth, he had no doubt he had made the right choice; if he couldn't reach them, at least they would survive.

A blast of hot air caught his attention, and he snarled, "So, the fire comes!" Leaping into action, he crossed the deck and pulled a sword from the rack at the end of it. Then he turned on his heel and waved it into the air. "Fight me then!"

In the darkness of her barrel, Ami could feel the churning of the water and hear it beating against the wooden slats. They no longer sat on the deck of the ship. Pushing up on her lid, she worked her fingers under the edge and held it firmly against her head, as if it were a large, flat hat. The droplets stung her fingers as they pelted the covering, but she gripped it tightly to keep it in place.

Holding the gap at about six inches and tilting it so that the rain landed and dripped off the back, outside the barrel, she watched the silhouette of the ship burning in the growing distance as the current carried them away. "Piers!" she shouted when she recognized his form, fighting and slashing at the giant beast as it swooped in and clawed at him with its hind legs.

Lifting their lids in a similar fashion, Rey and Bally joined her, awestruck by the scene before them. "I can't believe this is really happening!" Rey called to the other man, his eyes wide with a mixture of fear and rage. "We shouldn't have left the ship!"

"We had to," Bally replied, indicating the girl with a raised chin. "The Mate trusts us to look out for her!"

Shaking his head, Rey wasn't so sure. Glancing at the young woman, she appeared in shock, with bits of water still hitting her in the face and dripping from her chin. "Don't watch, Ami," he begged. "Please, love. Close your lid and stay inside." He didn't want her to watch the other man die.

But Amicia couldn't tear her eyes away. "Dear God, please save him," her blue lips whispering into the biting wind.

A moment later, the entire vessel rolled, spilling the remainder of the crew and cargo into the sea as it broke into smaller pieces. Screams floated on the wind, with the smell of blood and charred flesh. The light of the blazing remnants cast an eerie, glowing shadow across the water, a bright orange, with wedges of black where the waves crested and obstructed the view.

"My God," Rey breathed in utter disbelief.

Tears on his face, Bally stared, speechless, as the trio had a great view of the slaughter. The dragon, whose wings spanned more than twenty feet, rolled and dove at the water time and again, grasping at the floundering hoard with massive talons. Lifting the men out of the surf, it squeezed the life out of them, one at a time. Alternating, the beast spewed flames, burning those who clung to the remaining timbers of the vessel.

Bawling uncontrollably, Ami called to Piers a few times before Rey caught her and pulled her up to face him, ignoring the rain that drenched him as he did so. "Be quiet! The longer the dragon spends over there, the better our chances of surviving over here!"

"Exactly," Piers agreed, shoving his sword between the barrels and wedging it into place before using the rope to hoist himself up. Not pushing the lid off of his barrel, he clung to it for a long moment by lying over the covering to catch his breath after the treacherous plunge. The fight had stolen his wind, and the swim had been a struggle, but he had made it, and for a moment, he was simply thankful to be alive.

"Mate!" she squealed, tears of relief streaming down her face.

"I'm here, love," he soothed, pushing the cover off his cask and shoving his right foot in, followed by the left. Once he had gotten himself into the bobbing barrel, he placed his lid over his head like the others. "I strongly suggest we all close up and hide. We'll talk when the sun comes up and decide what we're going to do next." *If we survive the night*, he added mentally as he squirmed his way into the narrow tube and pulled his lid into place above him.

TEN

The Drift

CRAMPED INSIDE HIS CANISTER, Piers awoke to the sound of Ami coughing, most likely sick and vomiting. Leaning his head against the wooden slats behind him, he breathed deeply to clear his mind. The events of the night before seemed jumbled, landing on top of each other, and confusing him at the moment.

It had been a squeeze getting in, and the round walls had prevented any real movement as he slept. He felt stiff, and his body ached. He remembered the swim… and the dragon. *The ship is lost. The crew is lost. We are lost.* The reality of it crushed in around him, tighter than the slats that held him in place.

Opening his eyes, he could see streams of light with tiny particles sparkling and floating in them; thin rays shooting in one side of the container and landing on the opposite side. Forcing his left shoulder firmly against the curved wall, he managed to get his right hand up to touch them, reflecting them off his fingers. He smiled at the simple beauty of the light, as if he were a small child toying with a candle for the first time before being burnt.

As his head cleared, he realized that they were beams of sunlight, allowed in through holes that had been punched in a ring a couple of inches from the top of the barrel, just below the line of the lid from the outside. *Airholes.* He hadn't thought of that; fortunately for them, someone had.

Pushing up on the lid, he slid it off and let it fall. The tether to the side held, and it banged around noisily as it landed and bounced against the wall of the cask and splashed into the water. Judging from the sound, they sat at least two feet above the water line, maybe more, but the flat had floated just as he said it would.

Pushing his arms above his head, he narrowed his broad shoulders and worked his way out. Standing, he huffed noisily, gripping the edge. On the opposite corner from him, Amicia's back was to him. He couldn't reach her, but he could tell that the young woman had been ill, as she leaned over the side, her face hidden by her own barrel.

"Ami," he said sharply. "Look at me, love!"

Holding up her hand, she signaled to him but didn't lift her head. "I'm ok," she stammered. "I just need a few minutes. Maybe some food." Spitting, she vomited again, then whined.

The two lids on the containers that flanked her slid off almost in unison, and the two other men appeared. Closer, Rey laid his hand on her back, offering comfort. "Steady, girl."

"I'm fine," Ami managed tartly, wiping at her spittle. "I was sick in the hold, too, the first morning I woke up there. It'll pass."

To the east, the bright sun had cracked the sky, the ball of fire sitting almost clear of the water. The ocean between them shone like glass, with the rays reflecting off the smooth surface. A beautiful dawn, on any other morning they might have missed it, but not this morning. This morning, it was all that they had.

"There's holes in my barrel," Piers pointed out, giving them a distraction so the girl could have some peace and recover. "Who do I have to thank for them?" he stated gruffly.

"Yeah, I put them there," Rey replied sternly. "You didn't ask for them, but if Bally were putting on handles inside the lid, I thought we might like some air."

"Thanks." The first mate nodded with a grin of approval. "I missed that. I guess that makes you my new first mate."

"First mate," Bally interjected, still frowning in concern at the blonde as she turned to face them, leaning her rear end against the edge of the barrel for balance as she moved. "I guess you get to be captain, then? And I get to be crew!" He laughed at the prospect, certain his situation had not really improved.

Pausing for a moment, they all considered the outcome of the ship's sinking and then began to giggle uncontrollably for several minutes. Caught up in the jovial spirit, even Amicia laughed while holding her belly. They were alive, and for at least a moment, pure jubilation ran through them.

Soon, the boisterous mood ebbed, and they looked out at their surroundings at the wide-open sea on all sides. No waves crested, no ripples formed, and on every side the sky met the water on the horizon. Taking it in, the group grew somber.

"Where are we?" Amicia finally asked. When no one replied, she summed up their situation in a single sentence. "So, the ship is gone, the rest of the crew is dead, and unless we have a bit of luck, our corpses will rot in these barrels."

"Well, that puts a pretty fine point on it, now doesn't it," Piers sneered. She looked up at him with sullen eyes, and he continued. "Wallowing won't help us, love. Aye, I'm in charge. The Captain went down with the ship, and we're all that's left. So, I say no sulking allowed!" he boomed.

His loud voice startled the others, as he had intended. They needed to get square with reality if they were to survive. The three of his remaining crew stared at him, not about to argue his position among them. They would already be corpses, rotting in the sea, if it had not been for him and his quick thinking. They would go far under his leadership, or at least they each hoped that they would.

"We're all agreed then," he said more calmly, cracking the faintest of grins. "We'll all keep a positive attitude here, no matter what comes of us. We need to assess our situation without letting it tear us down. If we do it well enough, we just might make it out of this. Or to the next step. I'll take even that at this point, as one step leads to another, until there are no more steps to take."

Nodding, the others voiced small forms of affirmation, and Ami asked timidly, "Does our new ship have a name, Captain?" The ill-fated Sea Serpent had not been a grand vessel, but this was certainly a step down in her estimation, positive attitude or not.

Her question amusing, he smiled more fully. "Of course it does! This here is The Bobber!"

The group laughed once more at his frivolity, and he held the smile. "We're alive, Ami. Let's keep it that way."

"Aye, Mate." Rey nodded, then faltered, "Or Captain. That will take some getting used to."

"Then leave it alone." Piers shook his head. "I was only joking. Mate works for me. We four are going to get through this, whatever our titles."

Anxiously, they chuckled again, each deciding that they would get through it, no matter what came at them, but all secretly hoping it wouldn't be the dragon.

Looking around more aggressively, Ami sighed. "Well, on the ship, in the hold, eating seemed to help. If you don't mind, I'd like to get a snack."

"Sure," Piers agreed. "Pull our bag up and let's see what you packed us."

Bringing the sack out of her tube, Ami placed it in the center of their raft, on top of the water barrel. It appeared smaller than when she had carried it around before with the clothing in it. It seemed to hold less, now that it held all they would have for food for who knew how long.

"It will be enough," Piers reassured, as if reading their thoughts. Opening the bag, the outside had gotten wet, but her leather lining had kept their supply dry. "Nice work," he praised, indicating her packing skills with sincerity. "We'll leave it in the sun to dry the outside later today, and it will be good as new."

A few of the bread pods had been crushed, so he divvied those up for their breakfast. "We'll stick to small meals and ration what we have. The longer we can make this last, the better off we will be."

Closing the bag, he pushed it back towards the girl. "I think you require the least amount of room, so put it back in yours for now. But please be careful. If we lose that, we're in trouble," he warned with a wink.

"Don't worry," she reassured as she positioned it back in the bottom of her cask. "I won't let anything happen to it."

"Right." Rey opened the lid to the water, ready to reveal his second surprise. He had put the little metal cup inside it, and it floated on the surface. "Is anyone thirsty?"

Grinning broadly, the first mate clamped him on the shoulder, praising him even more loudly than he had about the air holes. "That is a magnificent contribution. We'll be able to drink without dribbling any through our hands and to ration our supply of fresh water as well."

"It wasn't that big of a deal." Rey beamed despite his denials. "I saw the cup on the wall when I chose the barrel, and so I grabbed it."

"I'm glad that you did." Ami grinned, accepting her cup to drink. Piers was still ranked highest among the men in her eyes, but Rey had definitely moved up in her estimation of him in the last few minutes.

"We'll have to refill the barrel when it rains," Bally pointed out, also accepting a cup full of the precious liquid. They were all well aware that the water around them would be poison if they were to drink it; even a little might be enough to kill them.

"Yes," Piers agreed. "The water is more valuable than the food. We won't last more than a few days if it runs out."

Shuddering, Ami nibbled at her hunk of bread, her eyes trailing over the glassy surface. "I never expected it to be this calm," she admitted in a meek tone.

"No, it's rarely this smooth," Piers informed her. "It's as if the wind has completely died away." Facing Rey, he too surveyed their surroundings, noticing a patch of land far off to the south, beyond his companion's head.

Seeing the other man's expression, Rey turned and saw the island as well. "Is that land?" he demanded, his voice catching a hint of excitement.

"I'm afraid that it is," the older man replied somberly.

"Why the long face?" Ami asked eagerly. "If that's land, then we can be saved. All we have to do is get there." Thinking of her mirror, she squealed, "Or we can use my glass to signal for rescue!"

"Right," their new leader agreed, "but that is a long way from us, so a signal would be useless at this point. And, unless my senses deceive me, we are not headed towards it."

"We're moving west, aren't we," Bally observed while squinting at the small mass on the horizon.

"Aye, I believe that we are," Rey seconded.

Crossing her arms, Ami assumed a small pout, the most she dared with their positive attitude motto. "Ok, so what lies to the west of us then?" She had been eager to get there since her mother died, but suddenly the idea of it filled her with dread.

Silence fell over the group as they each considered what they knew about the path they appeared to be taking. When no one voiced a reply, she pushed, "You've been there, Mate. You said that you were on a ship that visited the west, so what's out there, beyond the coast of the ring?"

"We saw land," he informed her quietly. "Like that in the distance, and we never got close to it. We were attacked by a dragon, same as we were last night, only this time I didn't see what actually happened. I was a kid then. The cabin boy, so that tells you how long ago it's been."

His eyes wide, Bally gaped at him. "You never told us this before, Mate. You actually met a dragon, and you never said!"

"Aye, I never said," Piers snapped. "You think most people want to hear about such things? Believe in such things? I'd be branded a mad man for sure!"

"So, what happened?" Ami soothed, steering them back to the story at hand.

"The storm came," he replied, "the same as it did last night. Only our captain, he seemed to know something about them. He turned the ship due east at the first sign of it and raised the top sail. We began throwing our cargo over the sides, increasing our speed every way we knew how. Even our cannons we tossed."

"Did the dragon not sink your ship?" Rey asked in amazement.

"No." Piers shook his head thoughtfully. "No, we seemed to pacify it with our course change and the haste of our retreat. As if we had gotten too close to something, and all it really wanted was to turn us away. It let us go, and we got the hell out of there, in a hurry."

"Then what happened?" Ami breathed, mesmerized by his escape.

"We stayed at top speed until we could make port. Three days we went, until we met a small island that a group of villagers occupied. We put in there and replenished our stores. From that day on, that was our line. The island of Myrth, and we never sailed past its shores again. Not in all the years I remained on that vessel."

"Wow," Rey agreed. "So, you're saying there's an island of dragons out here, and they'll be watching for us so we don't get too close."

"I'm not saying anything of the sort," Piers bit back angrily. "I never saw any island, and I never actually saw the dragon. Some of the men described it, fair enough, and from what I fought last night, their accounts were true. What it means, I can't say. Sailors don't speak of the flying devil. It's bad luck, as you all well know," he growled.

"It means we have to be careful," Ami whispered.

"It doesn't matter," Baldwin observed. "An island or no island, it's the edge of the world we have to watch out for. If we're moving west, and there's no wind to blow us there, then we're caught in the current. That's where we are."

"What current?" Piers clipped, giving him a scowl.

"*The* current. The water is moving fast, flowing to the edge where it drops off into oblivion."

"That's rubbish," Rey chortled. "You're saying the world is flat, when any man with half a brain knows that it isn't. It's round, like an orange, and that's why the sun goes around us every day," he described, holding up his hand and his portion of bread to demonstrate the piece of fruit with the sun making its trek around it.

"You two," Ami intervened. "The map is flat, but only because the table is flat, and it has an edge all around our ring of land called the netherlands, so someone has seen it. What matters is that we are alive, and we won't be if we panic about falling off the edge!"

"That means it's unexplored, the netherlands does, that's all," Reynard retorted.

"Quiet, all of you," Piers commanded sternly, holding his temples at their bickering. "Flat or round, it makes no difference. We'll either fall off the edge, or we'll come out on the east side of the eastern lands when we come around the other side. We'll find out soon enough if we don't figure out how to get out of this current." *Or starve to death before we get there,* he thought to himself angrily.

Presented with a real problem they could address, they began pondering ideas for beating the pull of the water as it sucked them along. Leaning over to tap the smooth water, Rey sent a small set of ripples across it, then sighed. "I wish we had a paddle for a dinghy," he confessed, thinking of the smaller boats that some ships carried upon them. "That would have been nice."

"Yes, it would have. Unfortunately, we didn't have any on our ship, or we wouldn't have needed to build the raft," Piers pointed out, running his hand through his hair and over his brow. Sweat smeared on his forehead, he had been wiping at it at more frequent intervals. "It's getting rather warm," he observed, looking around at the others and seeing that Amicia's fair skin appeared flushed. "Ami, use your lid as a shade and hide beneath it," he commanded, demonstrating with his own, which put him in an awkward position. "Like this."

For the girl, it was easier, as she had the pack of goods to sit on. Holding the flat surface above her, she smiled. "Am I covered?"

"Yes, it'll keep the sun off of you. We're out in it more, I guess, so we won't burn as easily as you."

"All right," she agreed, adjusting her arms to produce the widest patch of shelter.

Returning to their discussion about steering, they searched for a method that seemed at least plausible. "How about if we get out and swim?" Rey suggested. "We can push the flat along for Ami, and even take turns if we have to."

"Even if we could, we couldn't keep it up indefinitely." Piers shrugged, indicating the patch of land that had clearly moved to the east. "As soon as we stop, we would be moving in the wrong direction again, and that's assuming we could overcome it at all. Even the three of us might not be strong enough to beat it."

Observing the land as well, Bally gasped, "We're moving so fast, why can't we feel it? That land is going to be gone before the sun sets. Do you think we're already past the ring of the western coast?"

"Maybe, at this speed," Piers agreed. "Without our charts and the stars to go by, it's hard to say where we are."

"So, we stay in the flow and hope it takes us to land," Rey observed. "And hope we find it before the dragon finds us." Having grown warmer than he could stand, he reached over and splashed himself with a few handfuls of the salty water and then scrunched down in his barrel, holding his lid over his head as well. "At least this is cooler," he announced after he had gotten settled.

By late afternoon, they all sat huddling beneath their tiny patches of shade. They bobbed along in semi-consciousness as the four of them slept off and on until Bally finally stood, turning his back on the girl. Hanging over the side of his accommodations, he relieved his bladder into the water below. As soon as he did, the other two males stood and urinated, Rey adding a groan of satisfaction to the process.

"Hey, that's not fair!" Amicia complained, a tear forming in her eye. She had been thinking of just how she could work out taking a piss for what seemed like hours, and here they had taken their own right in front of her.

"Get up and hang it over the side," Piers informed her bluntly. "It's only the four of us here, so it's not like anyone else will see."

"You'll see!" she snapped. "This isn't a dress," she reminded him, "I can't hide anything under these… things!" The very thought of it brought a hot flush to her cheeks.

Sulking, she sat in her tube and waited, the pressure inside her building. When she couldn't stand it any longer, she unfastened the pants and began jerking them down her legs. Her bladder aching, she hoped that she could get them off before she fouled the inside of her barrel.

Hopping up onto the side and fighting for her balance, her pee dribbled, then squirted in a solid stream, loudly hitting the smooth water below. When she dared to look over at the men she felt sure were watching her, she discovered their lids all sitting on top of their barrels. They had each sunken inside and sealed themselves in to give her all the privacy they could.

When she had finished, she managed to get her pants back into place and secured them. "Thank you," she announced loudly. "I'm decent again."

Pushing their lids up, the trio of men rejoined her, pretending as if nothing had happened.

"Hand me the bag, and we'll set it up here to dry now," the Mate commanded. Pulling it out for him, she plunked it onto the center barrel once more, then balanced her personal shade above her head. Returning to their discussion of the west, the world, and how they might steer the flat, they whiled away the minutes until the sun had made its journey across the sky and it was time to break out their dinner, such as it was.

ELEVEN

Dragon Tales

LYING IN HIS BARREL, Rey used his lid for shade to protect himself from the glaring sun. It had been seven days since the ship sank, and they were doing their best to make their food stretch. Outside, he could hear the splashing as Baldwin surfaced next to their small craft.

"You see anything?" he called, not bothering to stand.

"Naw," Bally replied, hoisting himself up. Once inside his own cask, he placed his lid over his head and grunted. "This is a damn dead sea, for sure."

"Don't say dead," Piers corrected from inside his tank. "I'll go next," he informed them. Climbing out of the tube, he located the end of the rope his crewman had left coiled over the others that held the barrels together. Tying it around his waist, he gave it a tug to ensure it was secure, then dove into the clear blue water from the front side.

They had been using the setup for days, searching the bottom below for anything they could use or eat. The rope kept them connected to the raft, so it didn't float too far ahead and strand them while they were submerged. Leaving by the front, the flat would pass overhead while he searched, and he would surface behind it when he caught up, as their pace had slowed, but they still moved towards the west.

On the bottom, he scoured over jagged rocks. Only about three or four fathoms down, the sun shone brightly through the shallow depths, illuminating the barren bottom. That had been about all he had seen each time that he went down; stretches of rock or sand with little or no vegetation growing in it. He kept telling the others that eventually they would find something, but he had begun to wonder if that were true.

When his lungs grew tired, he swam for the surface, clinging to The Bobber for a minute on the back side. Refreshed, he dove under to return to his empty cask and climbed out to sit on the narrow edge of the platform that served as the base to their craft. It floated about two feet below the surface of the water, so small waves lapped at his chest as he breathed.

"Guys, I hate to admit it," he said wearily, "but if there could be a desert in the middle of the ocean, I think we've found it. The water is so shallow here, like we should be near land, and yet there's nothing…" His voice trailed away.

"Great," Bally replied, tapping the side of his tank with his knuckles out of boredom. "Now what do we do?"

"We take a nap and conserve our energy," the Mate replied, standing to get back over into his space. "We'll eat when the sun gets low and talk about our options."

Listening to the exchange, Rey thought about the young woman in the barrel next to him. "How you doing over there, Amicia?"

When she failed to reply, he got to his feet and leaned over the opening, shoving her lid aside to peer down at her. She sat on their dwindling sack of food, her head resting against the wall of the container with her eyes closed. Studying her, he detected the movement of her chest that signaled she was napping, and probably had been the entire time.

"I don't like how much she sleeps," he announced to the other two.

"It's better that she does," Piers countered. "With nothing to do but worry, at least she's keeping her sanity."

"I think she's sick," Bally chimed in, tapping again.

"Maybe," Rey agreed, taking a seat and covering himself once more. Drifting off into a fitful slumber, he was awakened by wild screams to find the sun had all but set. "What's happening!" he shouted, standing up in his tube.

Looking around, he discovered that everyone was up, but it had been the girl crying out. "Are you ok?" he demanded, seizing her by the arm to pull her over for inspection.

"I'm fine," she snapped, yanking the appendage away. "A nightmare, that's all."

"Another one," Bally clipped, cutting his eyes over at her. She had awoken with screams and tears half a dozen times by then, but so far had refused to divulge the details of her visions.

"Leave her alone," Rey instructed, still attempting to stroke her arms and comfort her. "She'll tell us when she's ready," he said softly, his hazel orbs filled with concern.

Looking up at him dolefully, Ami didn't reply. Instead, she shifted the gaze over to Piers. "Is it time for the meal?"

"Aye," he agreed, offering his hands to receive their bag of rations. After two days, they had counted their food supply, only to discover it would last a short two weeks, provided they all continued to eat, and it would be exhausted in a few days.

There had been a bit of discussion about how to make it last longer, but eating less than one small meal a day each seemed counterproductive. Instead, they had grouped it into small bundles, which they broke open one per evening and shared. During the day, they enjoyed water, but that too was running low.

Following his nightly routine, Piers unrolled the scroll of paper and made a note of the day, the depth of the water, and the terrain along the bottom. He also penned that they were going to consume their dinner and that they still had not seen any signs of life in the water below them. Rolling it up, he returned it to the pack and retrieved their bundle of food.

The others might have thought his recordkeeping silly, but none said so if they did. Everything they could do to normalize their existence strengthened their chances of surviving, and they would never take that away from him. Of course, if they died, the log would serve as their epitaph; the details of their final days upon the earth.

"Rey, I believe it's your turn for the story, mate," he informed the younger man when he handed him his hunk of meat and sliver of cheese.

They had been taking turns, each of them sharing something from their child-hood, or some other interesting event. Nothing too deep; just something to pass the time and keep them sane while they bobbed along.

"I'm running out of stories," he grunted in reply.

"Well, it's your turn, so come up with something," the other man stated more gruffly, refusing to let him bow out.

"Fine." Rey scowled, nibbling a few bites off his meat and chewing them with quick, small motions that twitched his nose as if he were a rabbit. Feeling an anxious twist in his gut, he glared at the woman next to him. She had grown temperamental and had little to say to any of them. "Want to hear another dragon story? I don't have much else left."

"Another one?" she groaned. All three of the men had taken to telling dragon tales, and she had heard at least a dozen by that point. Part of her considered they might have been the cause of her disturbed sleep, but she wasn't about to admit it. "Ok, let's hear it." She sighed while rolling her eyes.

Ami doubted that any of the stories had been true, except maybe the first one, which had been the Mate's explanation of when he had first encountered one of the beasts. Come to think of it, it had been his only one, as well. The rest had come from Rey and Bally, as if the pair were each trying to outdo the other in the grandeur and sheer stupidity of their exploits.

"All right." Rey grinned wryly. "If you recall from my last adventure, I grew up on a fairly large island called Domania."

"Yes, on a farm," Bally sneered.

"Hey, there is nothing wrong with a farm," Rey shot back, glancing at the girl and noting her pallor as she picked at her food. "Anyway, we had eight of us kids there. Eight living anyways. Mum had three that didn't survive, and they were buried out in the field."

"In the field?" Ami asked in surprise, cutting her eyes over to glare at him. "You didn't have a graveyard or cemetery on your little island?"

"It was a family plot," he offered, turning his hand up to the sky. "So, I had seven siblings, only I was almost the last one born. Only one other boy came after me."

"Where's the island?" Piers interrupted.

"What difference does that make?" Rey demanded.

"It just does," the Mate scoffed. "I'm trying to get a good picture on this, and you have to tell us all you can. It's the story and keeping our minds busy so we don't go crazy out here, so tell it right, Reynard."

"Ok, the farm was built on a new settlement on one of the western isles, on the edge of the ring. Domania, like I said."

Bally grinned. "I know that place. They have a lot of cattle and stuff there."

"Yeah, we milked the cows and made cheese for trading," Rey agreed, studying the lump still in his hand as he worked to make it last. "Anyway, late at night, while everyone was asleep, these creatures would come flying in. Most of the time, they stole our cows, but every once in a while, they would leave one all burnt up, like a smoking pile of wood that smelled like –"

"That's disgusting," Ami cut him off. "Are you trying to make me sick?"

Rey glared at her, his mouth hanging open, before he managed to reply, "No. Why would I try to make you sick?" His voice rippled with anger, and his teeth clamped shut in a near snarl.

"All right, I think that's enough story time," Piers took charge before the two of them came to blows.

"But I'm not finished," the other man shouted, waving his arms at the two of them. "You said you wanted a story, damn it!"

"Well, finish, but you don't have to be so explicit," Ami said with a small pout.

Frowning, Rey pushed on. "So, sometimes, during the night our farm would be visited by creatures. Flying monsters who stole our cows or burned their bodies. I could lay in bed at night and listen to them screeching like they were talking to each other, too. The village in the middle of our community was terrified of them, and they called them dragons."

Bally rolled his eyes, emitting a small snicker. "Wow, wonder where they got that."

"Well, these dragons were really vile, and they tormented us. They let us rebuild our barns, our crops, or our herds. Whatever they destroyed. But, they only did it so they could come back later and tear it all down again," he insisted. "I think they could have totally wiped us out if they wanted to, but they didn't, like it was a sick game of some kind."

"Is that why you were so adamant about them that day in the wheel house?" Ami cut in with the connection, suddenly suspecting at least this story was true.

Locking his jaw, Rey glared at her. "Ok, yeah. Only, I was a kid, so I didn't understand what was going on, and the grownups didn't talk about it in front of us. It was all dark and mysterious. All I heard were the whispers and half conversations. And the dragons when they were tearing up the place." He envisioned his secret attempts to get a look at them when he was young and how the flying shadows he had discovered had haunted him beyond words.

Staring at him, a slight breeze rustled her hair. Catching the long strands, she smoothed it as she considered how the fear had stayed with him, even as he had become a man. "I'm sorry, I thought you guys were just making up all these stories you've been telling. I didn't think any of them were real."

"Well, not all of them." He flushed in the failing light, noticing a row of clouds forming on the thin line between the sky and the sea. Glaring at it, he pointed. "Is that a storm?"

Turning to follow his gaze, the others studied the dark patch on the horizon. The stars and moon provided light during the night, but the thick clouds blocked them out, and a flash of light arched within it.

"I think it might be!" Piers said with a smidge of excitement. "Hopefully it will come this way, and we can at least replenish the water. Better leave the top open when we turn in tonight."

His vigor renewed at the prospect of at least something going their way, Rey grinned. "Anyway, back to my story. I didn't know much the dragons at the time. All I knew was that I was at the bottom of the line as far as inheriting my parents' farm, so when I got old enough, I lit out of there and have never been back. I joined up on a ship as the cabin boy and did that for a few years, until I got the spot on the crew…" His voice trailed away as he realized none of them were listening.

They were all transfixed, staring into the distance. The stars disappeared as the rolling darkness approached, and the flashes of lightning danced through the thunderheads. "That's going to be one hell of a squall," he observed more quietly. "You don't suppose that's the dragon's storm, do you?"

"I doubt it," the Mate informed him with a shake of his head. "Was that it? On your story?"

"Yeah, I guess. I heard lots of sailors talk about the dragons on the ship, though, even if it was considered bad luck. They say they are woman haters. They never bring a woman on board because that makes them angry and that's why they sink ships." He finished in a quiet voice as he studied the girl next to him, considering if it were true. "At least the ones along the western rim," he clarified.

"I heard the same thing," Bally agreed with a firm nod. "I don't recall ever having a woman on the ship before, so I don't really know. Of course, our ship never sank before, either."

"You two." Piers shushed them with a shake of his head. "Can't you leave the girl alone for at least one night?" He tried to play it off, as if the pair had been having more fun at Ami's expense, but deep down, he had to wonder. He had heard many a story of the like, and he feared that it had been exactly that which had cost his crew their lives.

He did know one thing for certain, and that gave him a sick feeling in the pit of his gut about the approaching storm. No captain in his right mind would ever allow a woman aboard his ship as part of the crew while he sailed the western seas. Call it an old sailor's tale or not, having a female on board was always considered bad luck for the ship, as much or more so than talking about the dragons, and this time it had certainly turned out that way.

TWELVE

Not Amused

SITTING ON THEIR BAG, Ami rested her lid on top of her head and balanced it with the back of her barrel. Her fingers gripping the rim, she leaned her nose against her knuckles and glared at the approaching tempest. Part of her felt relief at the coming storm. It was new and different, and they had not had anything new or different since the first morning after the ship sank.

However, the idea of being rocked by the waves and wind horrified her. She had been aboard one ship in her entire life, and it now lay in pieces on the bottom of the sea. This vessel, if she used the term loosely, hardly qualified as sound. "I think we're going to sink," she stated quietly.

Standing in his empty cask, Piers took charge. "See that the ropes are secure," he ordered, rechecking those within his reach.

Almost certain the chore was a ploy to calm the woman among them, Rey leaned over the side of his barrel as well, fidgeting with the knots and giving them a shake. A loud crack of thunder boomed behind him, and he pivoted and dropped back into his slot simultaneously, pulling his lid slowly into place to cover him. Cutting his eyes over at the girl, he could see her green orbs as wide as a pair of full moons in the dim glow.

"Relax, Amicia," he soothed, his voice trembling even as he tried to sound brave. Diagonally across from him, Baldwin closed his lid completely, hiding inside the barrel from what could be nothing other than pure terror. Looking back at Amicia, he wished that they had that dinghy, or anything really, that he could hold her through the storm.

"Ami," he repeated more calmly.

"I'm fine," she snapped, her white knuckles gripping the edge as the rain pelted their lids in a sudden explosive downpour.

Watching the barrel in the center, Rey sighed. *At least the water will fill up at this rate,* or he hoped that it would. They had no real collector, other than the barrel itself; no way to gather run off and funnel it in, so it would have to do.

Eventually growing tired of the spectacle, he noted that Piers and Ami had both closed their lids and were presumably snuggled inside. Pulling his shut, he gave the rope handle in the center a firm tug, ensuring that it had seated and sealed completely before closing his eyes and drifting off to sleep.

Or at least he thought he had been asleep. When he opened his eyes some time later, no rays of sun greeted him from his air holes. Instead, he felt damp, chilled, and cramped in the small space.

Closing his eyes, he tried to wish it away by sleeping a bit longer, but the pitch and roll of their craft indicated actual waves crested outside, another new development they had not encountered before. His eyes adjusting to the darkness, he knew at least some light had to be filtering in, and he decided that the sun had risen, even if he couldn't see or feel it.

Pushing up on his lid, he peeked out to see his three companions all stayed in. "Hey, guys!" he called loudly.

"What?" the Mate shouted back, not bothering to open his.

"I think the sun's up," he hollered. "Should we get up?"

"Well, it may be up, but it ain't out," Bally replied in a muffled voice. "It's fucking freezing in here."

In her bucket, Ami began to laugh in spite of herself. "That's what you get for trying to scare me with all your dragon tales!" she taunted through their thin walls.

Piers joined in the chuckle for a few minutes before he settled down, thinking more clearly. "We should just stay put," he informed them. "Stay dry the best you can, and don't open your lids unless you have to."

"Aye, sir," Rey agreed, closing his and pulling it into place.

In her barrel, Ami had the food, and she suddenly wished they had each gotten a share before they closed up for the storm. She felt guilty that the others wouldn't be able to eat. After considering the issue, her nausea pushed her, and she realized that she really didn't have a choice. If she didn't put a little something in her belly she was going to be sick.

Opening the pack and finding a ration of meat, she called, "Does anyone else want a bit to eat? I'll have to eat something, or I'll vomit."

"No, I don't need anything, but you're going to need this cup," Piers informed her from across the way. "You can't eat without getting a drink. Rey, here, pass this over to her." Poking the metal vessel out through a thin slot, he waited for the other man to take it.

"Got it," Rey replied, accepting the offering. "Ami, I'll take a chunk," he announced, since his arm would be wet from passing the cup anyways.

Making the trade, Ami stood, quickly scooping a drink from down in the barrel and sitting again in a matter of seconds, but long enough to be soaked in the downpour. "Wow, it's really coming down!" she updated them over the sound of the water hitting her lid.

"How full is the water barrel?" Piers inquired.

"About half," she replied with a smile. "If this keeps up, we'll get a full barrel back out of it for sure."

"Well, that's some good news." He grimaced, shifting the best he could but unable to stretch. At some point, he knew he was going to have to stand, and then he would be wet and miserable until the sun came out and pardoned them from the deluge. One thing was for certain; he had discovered that being on the ocean without the minimal comfort of a ship was no fun at all.

After she had eaten, Ami passed the cup back to Rey, so he could also have his fill. His belly satisfied, he tried to make the best of it, rationalizing that his wet shirt was worth getting each of them the drink and the snack. He managed to fall asleep and dozed through the drum of water on his small round roof. The first thing he noticed when he awoke for the second time was the silence.

Pushing his lid open once more, the heavy downpour had waned, but a slow drizzle had taken its place. "Well, it's not raining. But it's not dry," he muttered, removing the cover and standing for a stretch and a piss over the side.

Hearing his friend moving around, Bally joined him, followed by the first mate. When Ami didn't stir, he knocked on her barrel, calling loudly, "You all right in there?"

"I'm fine." She sighed, having already been up and balanced on the edge for a pee herself as soon as the rain had stopped, more or less. Opening only a crack, she peeked out. "You guys want your share now?"

"I'll take mine." Baldwin accepted it eagerly.

Handing Piers his, Ami came out into the moist air, which added extra frizz to her wild mane. "How long do you think the fog will last?"

"No idea." The Mate chuckled. "It's pretty thick. I've only seen it this heavy a few times, myself."

"Wonderful." She sighed, sitting back down and covering her head with the lid, as if it were going to help.

"Are you ready for a story?" he asked, seeing her worn spirits getting the better of her.

"Are you telling it?" She was prepared to say no if she had to hear anything else about fire-breathing monsters and scorched cattle.

He grinned at her playfully. "Aye, I'll tell one. You wanted to know about me becoming a sailor, didn't you?"

She snickered. "You said it was your only option after you couldn't make it as a blacksmith."

"Aye, that part is true," he agreed, lowering his chin to give her a twisted glare as he smiled enticingly. "But I didn't really tell you about my family. It's a sad story, really, and I think this weather suits it." His mood shifted, and the grin disappeared as a grave expression replaced it, giving the impression whatever he would divulge held great importance; at least to him.

"Sounds sensational," she sneered. "By all means, tell us your dreary tale," she encouraged jokingly. The look on his face caused her breath to grow shallow, and she hid her discomfort behind a small giggle.

"Well," he began, glancing at the other two men as he leaned against the edge of his barrel and ignored the drizzle. Rubbing his hands together quickly, he crossed his arms and stated calmly, "Let me start at the beginning, since they haven't heard any of it. I grew up in Palmeto, which I'm fairly certain you've heard of."

"I have," Rey agreed, equally conscious of the tale's importance to the man before him, if his demeanor were any indication. "That's one of the largest trade towns on the eastern coast."

"Sure is!" Bally perked up, as usual oblivious to the somber mood of his entertainer or the apprehension of the others. "Super rich from what I hear –"

"Yes," Piers cut him off, nodding firmly. "It is a wealthy township. Tens of thousands of people live there, and many more gather there to sell their wares. My family was what you might call... aristocratic." He allowed the word to hang in the air. When it had sunk in sufficiently, he cut his eyes over at the girl and added, "I'm the governor's son."

"The governor's son!" the other three gasped in unison.

Holding up his palm, he calmed them. "Yes, only I haven't admitted it in over twenty years. Not to anyone." Staring at Ami across from him, his brown orbs bore into her clear green eyes. Regret swimming in the windows to his soul, he wondered again if his life would have been any different if he had met someone like her as a younger man.

"So, as you can imagine, I never wanted for anything," he continued with a loud exhale of air. "I had servants and chambermaids at my beck and call, and I was rather popular among them, if you understand my meaning." He grinned deviously, giving Rey a wink.

"Yeah, I get it," Reynard agreed with a smirk, followed by a peek at the girl who had turned the storyteller down and had more or less promised to save herself for him before the ship sank and spoiled their plans.

"Aye, so I had it made. I'm the oldest, and I was groomed from the time I was born to take my father's place when the time came. Only, I wasn't happy with that. I was bored and angry, and pretty much made an ass of myself every chance that I got. Anything that my parents wanted, I made sure I did the opposite. Over time, they grew tired of my insolence. To put it mildly, they were not amused with me and my wayward mindset. That's when I informed them I wanted to be a blacksmith," he said with a chuckle.

Ami sat up straighter, recalling what he had said about his apprenticeship. "They let you?" she asked quietly, conflicted by what he had shared.

"Let is hardly the word." He laughed, wafting a hand through the air. "They paid for my place at a local shop, and I was apprenticed to the smithy there for three years. The work was brutal, and needless to say, my lesson was learned. At the end of my term, I went to my father, hat in hand so to speak. I was ready to take my place as his successor," he said quietly, his face drawn in obvious pain.

"Oh, Piers," Ami consoled, leaning forward as if she could reach him. Gripping the side of her barrel, she waited for the rest.

He nodded slowly. "Aye. He turned me away. Said I had made my choice, and that I was a blacksmith. Of course, I had only done it to spite them, but it was too late for that. They had disowned me, and my younger brother will be his successor any time now from what I hear."

"You haven't been back?" Bally demanded, still in shock that the Mate held real power.

"No, I've never returned," Piers continued quietly, slowly shaking his head side to side. "When they cast me out, all I had was the shop, but I hated the work. I hated the fire and sweat, and so I simply left. I took a post on board a vessel as a cabin boy, and away I went." His hands waved in the air, as if they were a ship taking sail, and he ended with a loud laugh.

"You're right. The weather does suit this story." Amicia sighed, glancing around at the three men. "What a horrible way to end up as a sailor!"

"Aw, it wasn't so bad," he added, continuing to grin. "I've enjoyed it for the most part. It gets a bit lonely now and then, but I've lived my own life. One that I'm happy with in the grander scheme of things."

Glaring at him, Ami wasn't so sure. She heard remorse in his voice, no matter how much he wanted to cover it. "I'm so sorry, Piers," she sympathized with a furrowed brow.

"Really, love, I wouldn't have it any other way," he insisted, adjusting himself in his tube anxiously as he was not ready to sit. "But as I said, I have never shared that story with anyone, so I would appreciate it if you kept it between us... if and when we make it back to civilization," he requested, glancing at each in turn.

Swallowing, Ami thought about her own parents, or would be parents, such as they were, and how her life had turned out. She could fully agree, there were things from her past she would rather remained private. *And Rey, with his burned cows and no inheritance*, she considered wearily. "We make a fine lot, don't we," she said aloud.

"Hey, it could be worse," Bally defended. "We have each other. All of us here, like we were all meant to be. Don't worry, Mate. Your lordship is safe with us." He laughed, and the older man grinned back, shaking his head slightly.

"We do have each other," Amicia agreed. His words tickled in the back of her mind, strumming the familiar chord she had come to accept. "The place where we belong," she translated, her gaze meeting the older man's as she did.

"Exactly," Piers agreed with a nod. "Maybe we're all headed to that place, together. On The Bobber!" he shouted, spreading his arms wide as his laughter echoed through the fog.

Shaking her head, the girl smiled as she slunk down into her tube and called, "Well, I hope we get there before we all starve to death. For now, I'm going back to sleep."

Watching her pull the top on over her, Piers glanced at the other two men. "I think she's right. A bit more rest would be in order."

"We're marooned in the middle of the ocean," Rey laughed, ready to secure his lid, "all we do is lay around and rest."

"Fair enough." Their leader sighed, working his way into his barrel and wishing it were just a few inches larger at any rate. "But I'm sure all this rest will come in handy once we get on shore," he added, certain any place they landed would have its own obstacles to be faced.

THIRTEEN

Endless Water

CLINGING TO AMI'S BARREL, Piers stood thigh high in water, his feet supporting him on the edge of their base beneath their floating shelter. Sitting inside, her legs tucked beneath her, her head rested against her arm and hand as she gripped the edge. "Breathe, love," he instructed, stroking her mass of hair.

"I'm breathing," she retorted, not moving as she spoke.

"Come on," he coaxed. "Let's brush out your hair and tie it up for you." He had watched Rey do this for her several times, and she always felt better afterwards.

"No."

Her flat response a punch in the gut, he felt it to his core. Glancing at the other two men, they watched him as he fawned over her, their eyes sullen as they glared at the spectacle.

"It's your turn to tell the story," the first mate insisted, pushing at her shoulder. "Sit up and tell us about your spice farm."

"It's a lie," she sobbed, her body trembling as she cried.

Stunned, he glanced again at the others, lowering his face so he could hear her better. "What's a lie?"

"The farm," she sniveled, shifting so she could peer up at him with her clear green eyes.

Her cheeks sunken, her gaze appeared hollow, taking his breath away. They had eaten the last of their food ten days prior, and he had taken to clinging to her tube that morning out of fear she would perish if they allowed her to sleep. Her end was near, and he knew it.

"Ami, please tell us the story," he begged, his voice cracking as he grazed her cheek with the back of his fingers. "Have some water," he urged, indicating for Rey to open their supply. "We have plenty of water, love," he soothed, his tone soft as he addressed her.

Fishing out a cup of the precious liquid for him, Rey handed it to the other man and placed the lid back over the center cask. It had rained on them enough to refill the barrel. If they had found any food in the ocean below them, they would have been fine. It broke his heart that this was where and how they would lose her.

Accepting the metal cup from him, Ami sipped the liquid. It burned her cracked lips, and she struggled to get it past her swollen tongue. Coughing at the last drop, she pushed the empty vessel back at him. "That's enough."

"Ok." He smiled, happy she had something in her belly. "Now, tell us about this imaginary farm of yours."

Cutting her eyes over at him, she squinted. "It's not imaginary," she informed him tartly. "It just wasn't mine."

Relief painted his features. Down to his undergarments, the salty water lapped at his legs, scorching them in hot sun, but he didn't care. He would remain there, hanging from her keg as long as she needed him; as long as he could keep her talking. "But it belonged to your parents, right?"

Stretching, the girl stood, stirred by her anger. Hoisting her lid, she raised it over her head, beads of water dripping from the edge where it had been floating in the water. Under her shade, she grimaced. "I don't know the whole story. Not really. I only know what my mother told me before she died."

Encouraged, Rey joined in the prodding. "What did she tell you?" He feigned great interest in the tale as he leaned closer and rested on the edge of his own container.

"Well, apparently they found me. I wasn't born to them," she admitted quietly. Licking her dry lips, she nodded. "Yes, I was about four, or so they thought from my size. And they found me somewhere on or close to their farm."

"My parents were old, you see," she informed them, looking at Bally and considering his age. "I think you and me are about the same in years, but I can't say for sure. They found me and took me in, and no one came looking for me. No one knows where I really came from, so I have no past and no idea where I'm going."

"Didn't they search for your parents or where you came from?" Baldwin united with the others in their effort. Shifting to her side of his container, he scrunched down as he leaned on it so he stood right next to her and shared her shade. The weight all on her corner, the raft tilted slightly, but stayed upright.

"If they did, they didn't really try very hard. In fact, I would think not, as no one in town ever mentioned my being adopted. Either they assumed that I knew, or they themselves had been fooled by my parents' pretending." She sniffed, their lie twisting her empty gut in agony.

"And when did you discover this exactly?" Piers nudged gently, placing his hand on her shoulder to give it a squeeze.

"Mum told me a few days before she passed."

"Oh," he consoled, massaging her bony back firmly. "But what about the farm? Was it a nice place to grow up? I mean, surely they were kind to you, taking you in and treating you as their own." He couldn't let her stop there. He had to keep her talking until they came to the end of the endless sea. That, or she could no longer speak. The thought of her in that condition troubled him, and he swallowed the knot in his throat as he focused on her words.

"The spice farm was wonderful, or so I thought. We had a meadow filled with wild berries. We would pick them and turn them into jellies for trade. And the orchard of fruit trees that my father tended." She smiled, forgetting for a moment that he had deceived her. "He gave me the mirror, you know," she faltered. "The one in my bag. Gave it before he died," she said quietly, blinking back tears as she thought of the old man who had been so kind to her.

Shaking her fingers, as if to calm herself, she cut back to the farm, which was less painful to talk about. "We also had a cliff behind the house, that over looked the ocean –" She stopped in mid-sentence, and her eyes glazed. Standing on the bobbing raft, she thought of the place she had whiled away so many hours. "The ocean," she breathed.

"Ami?" Rey asked softly, concerned with her changed behavior. "Ami, what are you thinking about?"

"The ocean," she repeated. "It called to me, all the days of my life. I stood on the cliff, listening to the waves, imagining that I was a bird, able to float and soar and coast above it, with the wind in my face and the splash of the surf beneath my wings."

"That's beautiful," the Mate agreed, managing a weak smile as he continued to caress her firmly.

"No." She shook her head, her brow furrowed, and her eyes still staring into some distant memory. "It was calling to me. Beckoning me to the place where I will die."

Frowning, the older man grasped her arm. "Ami!" He gave her a shake. "Ami, you are not going to die. Listen to me!"

But the girl appeared to be in a trance. Dropping her cover, it fell onto Bally and he caught it, placing it back into the water as she collapsed against their leader. Easing her down into the barrel, he stroked her hair and sobbed, repeating, "Don't leave us, Ami. We're going to be saved. I swear it."

Kneeling, he clung to her cask, refusing to relinquish his spot despite the instability in their craft. Murmuring to her intermittently, he touched her hair and face, longing for another day, or even another hour, if he could have it.

Watching him, the other two males suspected he had been overcome with delirium. They were all susceptible at that point, as the air seemed to swim, and the horizon danced with mysterious shapes beyond comprehension. Objects that moved with them, never closer or farther as they floated along.

Bally, unable to watch, also took his seat and closed his cover above him. Pressing his palms over his ears, he muttered to himself, trying to drown out the other man's voice as he spoke to the girl.

"Amicia," Piers whispered. "Amicia!" he screamed more loudly. She didn't stir, and he began to cry in earnest, his saliva thick and sticking to his lips as he blubbered. "I love you," he confessed. "Please, stay with me, my sweet Ami."

Blinking back salty tears, Rey only stared, drinking in the words of the other man. "We all love her, Mate," he consoled, wishing that there was something, anything, any of them could do about it.

"Mate!" Rey shouted, slapping him on the arm. When he didn't respond, he closed his fist and punched him; that got his attention.

"What the hell is the matter with you?" the older man bellowed. "Can't you see I'm grieving here?" It had been hours since Ami fainted, and he had spent the time pining over her, lost in his sorrow. Glancing around, he noted that the sun had moved to set, and it would be dark soon, which twisted his gut with fear she would not see another dawn.

"She's not dead," Bally informed him smugly, touching her face from the other side. "She's unconscious, that's all."

"So?" Piers squealed, tortured tears staining his stubble covered cheek. "We've spent weeks here with her. All of us fighting for our lives. We should be looking out for each other, you heartless bastards," he grumbled, his voice dropping to a hoarse whisper.

"We are looking out for each other, Mate." Rey pointed to the north west. "We found some land."

Standing, Piers gasped, "Fuck me, it is land!"

"Yeah, so what are we going to do about it?" the younger man clipped.

"Well, it's to the west of us, which is good," the first mate breathed, his pulse quickened and his mind clearing. Wiping his face, he sorted out their options. "But it's north of us, as well, so the current won't take us there. We need a push."

"Like we talked about?" Bally suggested. "We swim and push the raft for her?"

"Yes," Piers shouted. "We push it for Ami! Everyone into the water. Let's go!"

Clumsily climbing out of his barrel, Rey slipped into the salty sea. It had been eating at their flesh for weeks, and it burned when it made contact, but he did his best to ignore it. They had a goal, a concrete reason for their next breath, and he would give his last to push the flat if it meant that Ami might be saved.

On the other side, Bally also entered the cold abyss. Grasping the rope and the barrel before him, he kicked wildly, pushing against the craft. "We can do this, guys," he informed them through gritted teeth. He might be the smallest and youngest of the three, but he cared no less for the girl and would give his best effort to save her.

With all three of them pushing, the raft turned so that Piers's empty barrel became the bow, parting the water and sending ripples off to the sides. Ami's trailed behind, where the Mate pushed against it. Between the three of them, they fought against the current, at first not feeling as if they made any headway. Soon, however, the shape of the land began to fill in, and they could tell they were moving towards it.

"That's it, mates," Piers praised. "Think of Ami. Think of saving our girl."

Rey wasn't sure if his first mate was talking to him or himself, but it spurred him on either way. Thrashing his legs, his fingers cracked and dribbled blood into the water as he fought to keep his hold on the course rope. "AAAAAyaaaa," he screamed against his desire to stop and simply sink to the bottom of the sea.

"Don't give up, Rey," Bally called from his corner. "I can see trees!"

"I see them, too," Reynard replied, peeking around the side and then refocusing on his stride. A moment later, he paused, then shouted, "Be still. Everyone stop moving!"

As soon as their feet grew motionless, the sound of voices carried over the flat calm of the water. "Shit, are those sirens?" he sputtered. They had all heard the tales of singing maids of the sea, vile creatures who lured sailors to their deaths.

Bobbing in the water next to him, Piers scowled. "I think they are. But, dying on dry land would be preferable to this, I say we keep paddling."

"Agreed," Bally chimed in, glaring at them from around the barrels. "Grab on and let's go!"

Shaking his head, Rey seized the rope and resumed his position, striking the water firmly once more. Muttering to himself, he wasn't sure that he would agree, but at this point, they had little choice. Ami's time was up, and if they didn't get her on land soon, sirens or no sirens, she would be lost to them all forever.

FOURTEEN

Land of the Sirens

COMING TO, Rey could feel the warm sand beneath him. Rough against his face, the granules dug into his salt-sore flesh. Huffing air and blowing it out through his nose, he puffed a few times, pushing the grains away from his sensitive nostrils.

Hearing the sound of water lapping, he lifted his head, flopping it side to side as his eyes combed the shore. Next to him, the flat they had been pushing sat on the land almost completely, perhaps forced up by the small waves that gently licked the beach.

"We made it," he breathed, overcome with joy. Resting his head against the ground, he called more loudly, "We made it!"

When no one replied, he pushed himself up again, this time rolling over and sitting to discover his feet still in the water. Pulling them out, they were bare, and his toes bled from the smallest of scrapes created by the rough sand.

Fighting tears at the agony the cuts and brine produced, he grabbed the ropes on the side of the raft and hoisted himself up. "Ami!" he shouted, seeing that her barrel was empty.

Stumbling around the side, neither Piers nor Baldwin were to be found. "Where is everyone?" he gasped, afraid he had been the only one to survive. *But Amicia had been on the raft,* he rationalized. "We made it, I know we did!" Falling onto his knees, he collapsed into an unconscious lump in the hot sun.

Minutes. Hours. Days. Weeks. *How long have I been here?*

Rey stared at the canopy of trees above him. His mouth dry, he couldn't swallow. Blinking, his eyes burned. *Darkness.* Yes, darkness surrounded him, only held at bay by dancing light. *A fire.*

A shadow moved. Turning his head, he saw a tiny woman standing beside his prone body. *Gibberish*. She spoke to him, but her words were meaningless. She offered him a drink from a small vessel; not a cup, but more like a shallow bowl.

Lifting his head, he accepted the swallows, slurping at them eagerly. Her hand landed on his chest. *Tiny*. Her fingers short, it could fit entirely within his palm. *What the hell?*

Withdrawing her appendage, she stared at him with wide blue eyes. *Blue as the sea.* "Where am I?" he croaked.

Lifting his head, he tried to see more, but his temples ached. Resting the back of it against the ground beneath him, he felt as if small insects covered his body, crawling over his flesh and tickling it beneath their miniscule feet. Bright lights flashed around him, as if stars exploded in the night before he fell back into the darkness.

Sunlight. Bright crisp sunlight. His eyes closed, they glowed red, confirming the sensation. *Open*, he commanded his hazel orbs. Squinting, he forced the lids apart, then blinked. They did not burn as they had before.

The beach. He had been there last. No, he had been under trees last. Someone had moved him.

Looking around while only elevating his throbbing head ever so slightly, he saw the creature again next to him. *She's tiny.* He hadn't imagined it. A woman, smaller than he had ever seen, with large blue eyes and hands half the size of his, at best.

Shifting his gaze, he could see more of them. Hundreds of them. They clung to the branches of the tree above him. They sat on the sand of the beach at his feet. Their words carried on the air, like a song. *Fuck.*

"Where are my friends?" he demanded angrily.

"Shh," Ami implored, squatting next to him, opposite the tiny creature. Taking his hand, she pressed it into hers, a shell of some kind sandwiched between them.

"Rest," the siren commanded.

"No shit," he gasped. "I've lost my mind!"

"No, Rey." Amicia giggled, waiving his caregiver away. "They're mermaids," she informed him quietly, laying his hand on his chest and toying with the shell between her fingers.

"And they speak to us in our own tongue," he insisted, confident he was delusional.

"No, they have their own language," she informed him, smiling as she smoothed his dark ringlets of hair. "They gave me this, so I could hear them." She showed him the shell more clearly. Turning it slowly, she presented the rough, chalky-white outside and then the rainbow-colored inner piece. "It's magical," she said softly, a tear slipping over and streaking her cheek in the warm light.

"Magical," he repeated, still dazed.

Wiping at her face, she sniffed loudly, nodding. "This whole place is magical. I can't even promise that we're still alive," she sobbed.

"We're still alive," Piers informed him, taking the spot vacated by the mermaid.

"This is the most... incredible," he searched for the right words. "Yes, incredible, most amazing place I have ever seen!"

"We made it," Rey stammered.

"Yes, we made it," Piers agreed. "Get some sleep, and we'll talk again when you're stronger."

Closing his eyes, Reynard didn't argue.

Cold. Rey shivered violently. His body ached, and the air felt chill.

Opening his eyes, darkness surrounded him once more. No fire danced. No song could be heard. Sitting up gingerly, so he could lean on his elbow, he saw tiny bodies littering the ground. Moving slowly, he reached out with trembling digits, touching the pudgy arm of his caregiver, who lay in the damp sand next to him.

Instantly awake, she leapt to her feet, squatting on the soft earth. She blinked at him with her large blue pools that seemed to glow in the moonlight.

Using his hand, he imitated drinking from a cup, and she scurried away, up and running between her miniature comrades on two legs. Returning a moment later, she offered him the drink from the shell he recognized as the odd shaped bowl from before.

Sipping the sweet water, he drank it all in a few swallows. Then, pushing himself up to sitting upright, he found that he could look her in the eye squarely, even as she stood at her full height. "You're a mermaid," he whispered.

She smiled, cocking her head as she blinked at him. If she understood him, she gave no reply.

"Where's Ami and Piers? They were here... before."

Nodding at him, she held the grin.

"You understand me," he said more loudly, causing a few of the others to stir.

Getting to his feet sluggishly, he picked his way through the cluttered shore. Down at the edge of the water, he realized they were in a lagoon, with the water in the center protected on three sides. Behind him, large trees stood at the edge of the beach, and two sides held a thin line of shrubs and greenery as they jutted out into the ocean.

Before him, the water spread in a sparkling sheet a hundred yards out and another hundred yards across at the widest point. "This is incredible," he breathed, hearing the Mate's voice instead. "Piers. Amicia." He knew they were alive. "I have to find them," he said to his mermaid, who stared up at him with wide bright eyes.

Beside him, the creature followed, observing as he explored. Her feet bare, they made tiny prints in the sand, the little pads of them making soft thumps as they struck the moist earth. Her body covered in a dark, lacy dress, of a fine material he had never seen before, it fitted and yet flowed around her. He smiled at her plump form, her perfection obvious.

"You're not scary," he offered, thinking of the stories he had heard of sirens in the past. They had cleared the lagoon and were on an open stretch of sand no longer littered with slumbering forms. "Why don't you speak to me?"

Smiling up at him, she offered her hand in reply, opening her small fingers to him. He accepted it, and she curled the digits around one of his. Pattering along, the water splashed at his toes, but they no longer burned. Kneeling, he inspected them in the bright glow of the biggest, fullest moon he had ever seen and discovered their injuries had healed.

"Well, that's a relief," he muttered, setting off again. Holding her tiny hand, she was just tall enough to wrap her diminutive fingers around his. Reaching a bend in the shore, he looked back to where they had come from.

In the dark shadow behind him, he could see the outline of the entrance to the lagoon. A peaceful place, hidden on the open beach, it occurred to him that it was her home, the alcove of the sirens.

But they weren't the vile, deceptive creatures he had heard stories of. *Not at all.* She had nursed him, protected him, and provided for him. Looking down at her, he considered offering to carry her, as her short legs pumped at a heavy clip to keep up with him. He decided that might be offensive, as she clearly was not a child, even with her childlike size and features. He pursed his lips, considering the options.

Finally, he repeated more sternly, "I need to find my friends. Can you show me where they are?"

Smiling, she took a few steps in the direction they had been headed, tugging gently on his hand. Following, he kept his pace down, allowing her to lead him around the curve so that the lagoon disappeared behind them.

There, on the new stretch of sand before them, sat the flat only a few dozen yards ahead of them. Dropping their connection, he ran towards it, overjoyed as adrenaline pulsed through his veins. "Ami!" he screamed, looking down into each of their barrels, finding all of them empty.

"Even her bag is gone," he observed aloud, lifting the lids and searching in between the casks. "The Mate's sword isn't here, either."

Arriving next to him, the siren grasped the material that covered his legs, tugging at it firmly. Looking up at him, she appeared frightened, as she shivered in the cool air around them.

"What is it?" he asked, forgetting she had yet to speak to him.

"Rey, is that you?" Baldwin stepped out of the thick brush beneath the trees that lined the shore.

"Hell yeah, it's me," Rey shouted, tearing across the sand and catching his friend around the chest with both arms, swinging the smaller man into a hug before dropping him.

Grinning up at him, Bally laughed, then admonished, "We should keep the noise down. Not all the creatures who come out at night are friendly."

"Ok." Reynard turned to call his new friend over, discovering she had fled. Looking down the beach, towards the turn they had made between there and the lagoon, he wondered if she had gone back to the others. Not able to see her, he felt sure that she had.

"Where's Piers and Ami," he demanded, turning his attention back to his long-lost pal.

"They're sleeping," Bally informed him, slapping him on the arm and guiding him into the brush. "Come on, and I'll take you to our camp. And you're not going to believe this," he chortled as he led the way.

Stomping after him through the thicket, Rey's heart pounded with joy, as utter relief welled within him. *We made it.* They were on dry land, all of them alive and well, or so it would seem.

Coming into a clearing, he paused, grinning as he took in the scene before him. The walls of their area were made of thick trees that had been chopped away and cut into slats that acted as a partition or fence for their camp. Cleared to form six sides, if he could call them that, it would be far roomier than their floating accommodations of late. The canopy above made a nice roof, and although it wouldn't keep out all the rain, it would probably keep them fairly dry if it did.

In the center, a fire burned, illuminating the space with warm, swaying light. Stepping towards it, he offered his hands, toasting them in the heat the small blaze produced.

On the side to the right, a rough table had been constructed, with four chairs formed by a flat seat like a short bench, but no back. Apparently, they had fully expected him to join them; that or they had picked up a stray he had yet to meet.

On the left side, pallets covered the ground. Strung together from thatch material similar to that he had seen growing under the trees, he knew they were their beds. His grin fading, Ami lay in the center of one of them. Piers had spooned up behind her, with his arm draped protectively across her waist.

"Hey, guy –"

"Don't," Rey commanded. "Don't wake them, ok."

"Why not? They're going to be so thrilled you're back," Bally whispered loudly, staring at him in disbelief.

"They can be happy in the morning." Rey turned to the table and shuffled over to the chairs. Taking a seat on one, he noticed the girl's bag hanging on the far fence, and a shelf that had been carved into the tree of that wall, which held her hairbrush and mirror, her dagger, and a few other curious items.

Taking a seat next to him, Baldwin scowled. "What's wrong with you, man?"

"Nothing." Rey shoved his face into his hands and stared at the couple covertly between his fingers. His heart heavy, he couldn't believe his own eyes. "How long have they been so cozy?" he asked bluntly after he had calmed down, aware that their understanding had never been fully declared, and she had broken no vow to him.

Frowning, the younger man got to his feet, sneering, "You'll have to ask her about that," over his shoulder as he sauntered over to one of the mats, where he stretched out and drifted off to sleep.

Glaring at his friend and his surly response, Rey didn't bother with a retort. Instead, he scooted closer to the center, warming himself as he considered exactly how he was going to act when the light came and he had to face the others. *You're going to smile*, he told himself sternly as he watched them slumber. *Ami has no idea how you feel about her, and for once in your pitiful life, you're going to keep it that way.*

FIFTEEN

The Kingdom of Eriden

"OH, MY GOD - REY!" Amicia squealed, waking him from his troubled dreams.

After brooding over his discovery for close to an hour, he had succumbed to his exhaustion and taken one of the empty thatch mats to sleep on. "Ami," he breathed, overjoyed to see her before his head returned to him. The girl lay over the top of him, her golden mane cascading around him.

Reaching up, he touched her cheek with a gentle caress. Her lips parted in a wide grin, she was indeed the most beautiful creature he had ever encountered. Her hand resting over the back of his, she slid his palm to her lips, where she kissed it gently, then stood, using the appendage to pull him to his feet.

Once standing, the surrounding camp, as Bally had called it, appeared somewhat ordinary by daylight. The fire burned low in the center, and the trees hung over it, protecting it from the heat of the day. "Good morning," he bade the girl, stepping back from her and glancing over at Piers, who seemed oblivious to her forward behavior.

"Well," Ami sputtered, "good morning!" She bowed slightly to him, awkward at his formality, but still openly joyous to have him there. "Would you like something to eat?" she offered, wafting her hand at their table and the meal that had been placed upon it.

His hair hanging loose, Reynard used it to hide his face. He had promised himself he would not make a scene over their obvious betrothal and intended to do so. Instead, he forced his voice into a light tone. "Is this from the mermaids?"

"Yes, some of it." Amicia took a seat on one of the backless chairs. Pushing a bowl of fruit towards him, she smiled. "They have shown us where to find the patches of wild berries and trees laden with sweet offerings. It reminds me of home, only different," she said with a flush as she glanced at Piers.

Standing abruptly, the older man commanded, "Let's go, Baldwin. We have work to do." Laying his hand on her head briefly, he pushed her wild locks away from her face and kissed the girl's forehead. "We'll be back before sunset, love," he said more softly.

"Ok." She nodded, her cheeks flushed for a moment as he left her.

Picking at the basket of mixed berries, Rey avoided the intimate connection between the couple. He selected a few, then noted a platter that held a small amount of roasted fish. Taking a pair of the strips, he asked, "Is this from here? I thought these waters were dead."

"Yes, it's from here," she supplied, scooting up to the table and resting her elbows upon it to lean on. "The sea here around the land is filled with life. Only that which lies between is barren, like a barrier. I think it's intended to keep us away."

"And where is here, exactly?" He continued to probe as he chewed, not really looking at her as he spoke. His stomach grumbled, and he felt ravenous, eating more quickly as the sensation grew.

"This is the Kingdom of Eriden," she said more quietly. She had noticed his standoffish demeanor, and it troubled her that he appeared to be hiding from her behind his long locks. "Is something wrong, Rey?"

"No," he clipped quickly, still not catching her gaze. "Everything is fine. I just want to know all that I can, which you seem to have gleaned a great deal about this place." Flicking his hazel orbs over at her, she glared at him, but he didn't return the connection, breaking it in an instant.

"You seem to know a lot about where we are," he continued, keeping his tone as even as he could muster. "How long was I unconscious?"

Her green orbs darting around her, Ami blinked rapidly. Rising from her seat, she moved closer to the smoldering fire. Her back to him, she could tell something had altered his perception of her. Perhaps he could sense the change in her, the one that had happened almost upon their arrival.

"Seventeen days," she said softly, inhaling deeply and pushing the air out slowly through her nose. "You were sick the longest," she continued without prompting, ready to give him what he needed to rejoin their group. "When we landed, we were all ill. I don't know how... maybe they carried us, maybe they transported us by some kind of magic, but the sirens took us to their city."

"They have a city?" He had missed that.

"Yes, you were there. It isn't like the towns and homes that we think of." She offered a smile while warming her palms. "They live in the trees and on the sand, there in the harbor."

"Ok, then I did see it," he agreed, recalling his awakening the night before. "So, when did you build this place?"

"Piers constructed it after his health returned. I was only ill for a few days."

"A few days!" he snapped. She had been the worst out of all of them, and she had recovered the quickest? This bit of news didn't make sense, and he rocked his jaw side to side as he considered its validity before he continued to stuff himself on the delicious fish and fruit.

Turning to face him, Amicia returned to her chair. Sitting up, her back stiff, she folded her hands and laid them on the table before her. "Something happened to me, Rey," she confessed. "Almost as soon as we reached the island. It was almost... magical. A feeling from deep within me, surrounding me. In the air as I breathe it. In the ground beneath my feet." It was hard for her to put the sensation into words. It had moved her so deeply, as if it had reached the very core of her soul.

Looking up at her, he met her gaze, and his heart thumped rapidly inside his chest. He could see it, too; almost a glow that emanated from her. "How long were you sick?"

"Three days," she whispered. "They brought me the nectar, and it healed me right away. Bally also recovered fairly quickly, and the Mate was back with us at six. You took the longest, and we were so afraid you wouldn't make it," her voice trailed away, heavy with anguish as a tear spilled over and streaked her cheek.

Wiping it away, she forced a smile to her lush lips. "I'll show you the garden when you've eaten. It's magical. This whole place is, really."

"Magical," he repeated, almost to himself. "I saw you. You and Piers were there in the lagoon, talking to me. You had a shell –" He stopped short when she leapt up from her seat and turned her back on him, then marched across their small dwelling. "Hello?"

"I hear you." She giggled, selecting a few items off her shelf. Returning to the table, she placed the object he had seen before him on the flat surface. "They call it a *merdoe*. It's for listening, and when I hold it, I can hear them. I can understand their song." Turning away, she began brushing out her long hair, preparing it to be braided.

Lifting the merdoe, he inspected the rough, chalky white outside, observing the pits and imperfections of it. Turning it over, the inside was flawlessly smooth, iridescent as it reflected the bits of sun that peeked through the leaves above them. "It's beautiful," he muttered, running his thumb over the perfection of the inside.

"It only works for me." She sighed, twisting her hair into a bun and pinning it.

"How do you mean?"

"I have to be holding it with you. The Mate and Bally have both tried it, and they can only hear the mermaid's song, or understand it, if I'm holding it with them."

"Interesting." He chuckled, flipping it a few times before returning it to the wooden surface. Retrieving it, Ami shoved it into the pocket on her pants. Watching her, Rey recalled how much he loved her hair when it hung wild around her and framed her face. "You should leave it down," he commented, before he had even realized he was going to.

"Leave what down?"

"Your hair," he stammered. "I mean, it looks nice when it's down."

"It looks like a mess when it's down." She laughed, her eyes catching a sparkle and her smile lingering on her pretty pink lips, the bottom split by the faintest of scars from where her cut had healed. "Are you ready to see more?" she said more softly.

He agreed by getting to his feet to follow her outside.

Close behind, he picked his way through the tree roots and stalks of wild plants that covered the floor of the jungle. It surprised him how quickly the landscape had gone from beach to heavy forest when Bally had led him to the camp.

"So, why were they still holding me at the city?" he asked, fighting for his footing. "Why didn't you take me to the camp after it was built?" His mind filled with questions, he tried to bring out the essential ones first, but this one hurt him deeper than any other. *Why had they practically cast me aside so soon?*

The girl did not reply and instead stood in a clearing when the trees gave way. Stomping up beside her, he glowered at her profile, until his eye caught movement next to his head. Turning to swipe at the floating insect, he realized it was a butterfly unlike any he had ever seen.

Large, each wing measured greater than his palm. Bright yellow for the most part, blue streaks spread from the body out to the edges, as if an artist had added them with the finest of brushes. Frozen, he watched as the girl held up her hand, her fingers folded into a shelf, where the insect landed, opening and closing its wings gently.

Ami giggled as if the two of them had shared a private joke before the creature fluttered away, soaring up into the sweet-scented air above them. Following its winding path, Rey took in the rest of the opening, his ears detecting the sound of the massive waterfall almost at the same moment that his gaze fell upon it.

"Oh my God," he breathed, the splendor of the pond before him stealing his breath for a moment. The surface flat calm as it reached them, the water glistened with sunlight that shone from above. On all sides, the jungle closed in, like a safe protective cocoon.

"The mermaid city is that way." Ami pointed, indicating the narrow brook that exited the pond on the south end. "The stream flows from here, through the center of the sirens' land, and into the harbor there, where it meets the ocean."

"So, the lagoon is fresh water," he observed, moving closer to the edge. "May we drink it?" He knelt, not daring to touch it before he asked. The air around him felt sacred, as if he had entered an ancient temple he did not wish to defile.

"Yes, have all that you like." She laughed, taking a knee next to him.

Using his hands, he formed a shallow bowl and scooped up a mouthful of the deliciously clear liquid. Having a second and then a third, he gurgled, "It's amazing! Is this what she was giving me, in the shell?"

"Yes, mixed with the nectar. That is why they kept you at Riran, so they could care for you with their special healing," she finally supplied, indicating the large pink and purple flowers that grew next to the waterfall, on the west side. Grass grew beneath and around them, and they could be reached through the pond or by the long walk around. On the east side, tall cliffs formed a sheer rock face that could not be climbed without the greatest of risk.

"The nectar is their medicine," he surmised, happy to know he had not been abandoned after all.

"Yeah, it's magical —"

He cut her off, saying the word *magical* on top of her, then following it with a nervous laugh. "You keep saying that about this place, and I have to agree, it does have a different feel than home. But is it really? I mean, how do you know that magic really exists here?"

"Some things cannot be proven, or shown, or seen, Rey. Some things can only be felt. I feel the power here. In the air, in the rocks and soil, in the water as it flows," she replied, her eyes dancing with light.

"This is it then." He nodded somberly, finding it hard to hold the smile.

"It?"

"That place where you belong." His head bobbed again, recalling their stories from their time on the flat. "You really were meant to come to the west."

Her jaw dropping, she stared at him in surprise. "I hadn't thought of that," she gasped, ashamed that he had read her so easily. "I mean, it felt so comfortable. It's like a worn pair of shoes when you really need a new pair. Something you love so much, you hate to give it up, and hang onto it because it's familiar…"

"And you just can't bring yourself to say goodbye," he finished for her. "Exactly. I think you're home, Ami," he said with a grin he didn't feel. If this were the place where she belonged, where did that leave him?

SIXTEEN

To Walk in Moonlight

PIERS SAT on the ground a few feet from the gentle lap of the waves. The sun hung heavy in the sky to his right, where it would soon disappear behind the land of the western coast. To his left sat what remained of their flat, his clothing draped over the sides. The air warm around him, he lay back against the rough sand and stretched, the breeze drying his flesh and leaving a salty film.

"Is it time for supper?" Baldwin asked, dropping down onto a section of sand a few feet away.

"Are the tools hidden?"

"Aye, sir." Bally covered his face with his hands and drank in the golden rays.

"Then supper it is," the older man agreed. Rolling over to his knees, he knelt in the soft earth for a moment before pushing up to stand. "My old bones." He chuckled, retrieving his shirt and pants before following, as Bally had already disappeared into the trees.

Arriving at their camp a few minutes later, the smell of stew greeted him. "Aye, lassie." He laughed, spying the girl in the center of the circle, stirring the pot he had provided her a few nights before. "Decided to give it a try then?"

Smiling as she bounced over to him, obviously happy at his return, she turned her face up to him and waited. Grasping her arms firmly, he held her, lowering his lips to brush softly against hers. "Sweet Ami," he breathed, catching her hair with his left hand as bits of it floated around her. Tugging it gently out of her face before releasing her, he greeted the other man. "So, did you enjoy your tour?"

"It was magical," Rey replied, laughing at his use of what appeared to be the word of the day. "I can't believe we found this place."

Piers studied him, his dark eyes squinted slightly, as if he wished to look inside his very thoughts. "Well, I'm glad you found it so," he stated calmly, taking a seat at the table on the far end so that he faced the opening in their perimeter and the majority of the room lay at his right hand. "Thank you, love," he sang, accepting the bowl as Amicia placed it before him.

"Yes, Ami says you've found an old settlement that you've been raiding." Rey indicated the caldron that hung over the fire and the setting for the table. "It's nice to have a few comforts here in the wilderness."

"Aye," Bally chimed in. "We go every day and see what else we can dig up."

"What about the people?" Reynard asked between bites. "If there was a settlement, there had to be people."

"They've been gone for some time," the Mate countered evenly. "It's deserted now, so we take whatever we want."

In her seat, Ami sipped at her broth, then picked out a few of the vegetables to eat. "Isn't it beautiful here?" she said airily.

"Heavenly, love," Piers replied, earning a surprised stare from the newcomer. Giving him a quick scowl, as if to silence the words before he spoke them, his face instantly morphed into a wide grin.

"I shall be in the village this evening," the girl continued. "I wish to know more of Riran, and Olirassa has agreed to share it with me."

Piers held the smile. "Oh. To walk in the moonlight, then?"

"Yes," she agreed, finishing her last few bites in haste. "You will miss me?"

"With all my heart," Piers replied, laying his right hand against his chest and providing his happiest face yet.

"Good." She put on her sweater and kissed him quickly on the cheek as he ate. "I'll be back before the dawn," she called over her shoulder as she disappeared through the narrow path that served as their entrance.

As soon as she had gone, the Mate's grin disappeared, and he used the back of his hand to remove the feel of her lips from his face. "Get the tools. We only have a few hours," he commanded to Bally.

Quickly finishing off his meal, the youngest male exited by the same path as the girl. An adequate amount of time had passed for her to have reached the beach herself and be gone, and it would be safe for him to do so.

"What the hell is going on?" Rey snapped, keenly aware of the instant shift in his leader's mood.

"We have to talk," Piers replied, standing and leaving his meal unfinished. Fishing a long stick out of the tree limbs above him, he set to work on it, assessing his progress and then laying it across the table. "And we have to work fast. Everything must be hidden before she returns."

"Ok, so what's going on?" the younger man repeated.

"Ami is spending the night in the siren's city, with the queen."

"I gathered that," Rey growled, growing weary with repeating himself. "But what are we doing?"

Piers finished gathering his supplies, placing remnants of a sword and a machete on the table alongside the handle he'd been constructing. Turning abruptly, he sat down with an iron file in his hand and stared the other man in the eye. "I need your word, Rey. I need to know you've got my back. Bally's just a kid. He follows orders, but he isn't a warrior. I need to know when things come to blows, you'll stand with me in the fight."

Glaring at him with wide eyes, his mouth hung open for a minute before he stammered, "Of course I've got your back! You're my captain, or as good as, so just tell me what this is all about."

"She showed you around, correct?" Piers picked up the machete, inspecting it before he used the file against the blade, removing the thick black corrosion that covered it with heavy scrapes.

"Yeah, she took me around. We saw the waterfall and the pool, along with their sacred healing flowers. And Riran, only there weren't any mermaids that I saw."

"They stay out in the water during the day," Piers stated confidently. "They come on shore as the sun sets, for the most part, and hang out on land during the night. What else?"

Rey shrugged. "I don't know. A bit of the forest, and along the beach there in the lagoon, where the brook empties. It's really beautiful, like a paradise."

"Paradise is a prison, Rey," the Mate put it bluntly. "All this…" He wafted his file around at the trees above him. "None of this is real."

His brow furrowed, Reynard prepared to argue, but Bally returned with his arms full of old tarnished bits of metal and dropped them on the ground next to the fire. "What are you doing about it, then?" he asked instead.

"I have the sword, but it's only one. I'm going to build us another, a few spears, and an axe, if I can manage it."

Moving over to inspect their haul, the crewman recognized barnacles when he saw them. "These aren't from a settlement," he accused. "Where the hell did they come from?"

Bally pointed in the general direction of the beach. "There's a ship about half a mile from shore and six or eight fathoms deep. We passed over it when we came in, and the Mate saw it on the bottom."

"You're scavenging from a sunken vessel," he surmised. "You take the flat out and fill it up?"

"No," Piers clipped, still scraping the metal. "The raft won't leave the shore. The current's too strong. You can't pull it out more than a few feet. As soon as you let go, it floats right back up onto the land. We tried."

"Could you just stop what you're doing and talk to me?" Rey demanded, shaking his dark ringlets in anger.

Pausing his hands, his commander stared at him. "What do you want to know?"

"Why is this place a prison?"

"Because there's no crew left from that ship!" Piers shouted, smacking his fist against the table. Ratcheting his voice down, he continued, "The queen is all sweet as honey, as far as Ami is concerned. All the sirens are."

"Yeah, they rescued us," Rey pointed out, reclaiming his seat.

"They didn't rescue us, they rescued Amicia. They only helped us because she desired it. The queen will barely even speak to me, even with that little trinket she gave to Ami. It's no wonder it only works for her," he bit angrily.

"You're saying they would have let us die."

"Aye, they have no need of us. And when I asked about the ship, they pretended not to know anything about it."

"And how do you know that they do?"

"There's no bodies," Bally cut in, taking the file and the machete so he could continue the work over by the fire.

"Nope, not a single one," the Mate informed him, leaning onto his knees with his arms folded. "We've made five trips out so far, gathering these few things that we could carry. Not a single set of bones to be found among the rubble."

"And you're going to do what, attack the mermaids?" Rey asked quietly, confused by their plans and suppositions.

"No, we're getting out of here. As soon as we have some weapons, we're going to move down the coast and look for a better place to build a shelter until we can construct a boat and get off this rock," Piers stipulated, lifting a few of their latest finds to inspect them. "If we can get Ami to go with us."

"Why wouldn't she go?" Rey asked with wide eyes. "She's your wife or as good as, shouldn't she do as you say?"

Cutting his eyes over at him, Piers stared at him in surprise. "She isn't my wife. I have taken no vow with her, and I don't plan to."

"Oh, man," Rey whined, hunching over and placing his hands over his face. "I saw the two of you when I came in last night. You can't tell me you haven't consummated your marriage."

"I haven't touched that girl," the Mate hissed. "She's consumed by something, some power. She sees me as her lover, and I allow it, but I assure you I have consummated nothing and would never as long as she is under this dark spell."

"So what's with all the 'heavenly, love,' and all that shit?" Rey hollered back, angry that Ami appeared to be his toy.

"I have to keep up appearances," Piers confessed. "As long as she's happy, we can work on our plans, out of sight, mind you. When the time comes, we'll figure out how to get her away."

"So you're saying you two aren't really together?" Peeking out of his hands, Rey caught the small grin on the first mate's face, a feeling of relief washing over him. "Oh my God, I thought you two were really in love or something!" He laughed anxiously, recalling the other man had professed exactly that just before they swam for shore.

"No," Piers stated flatly. "The long and the short of it is, that ship sailed for me long ago. I'm old enough to be the father of every one of you, and with Ami not knowing her parentage, don't think that thought hasn't crossed my mind," he added with a chuckle.

Listening to the conversation, but having stayed out for the most part, Bally began to cackle, "Wouldn't that be awful to discover, Mate."

"To say the least," he agreed, grinning himself. "She will be yours one day, Rey, if you desire it. I'm almost certain of it. But that could be many months, or even years from now, so you must be patient if that is ever to be."

"I understand." Rey nodded firmly, his features stoic. Setting his jaw, he dared one last question. "What are we going to do if she won't leave? She believes this is the place in the west, the one her heart has been drawing her towards."

Piers sighed. "I know she does, but it isn't. This is a wilderness full of magical creatures, not meant for the likes of man. If we don't get away from here, we will all die."

"Ok," Rey agreed, finally lifting one of the broken swords to give it a once over, now that he understood their purpose. "I'll help with whatever I can, but I don't see how we're going to make useful weapons out of any of this."

"I'm a blacksmith, remember?" The Mate grinned deviously. "We've gotten enough from the ship. Now we hunt for a place to build our forge and these can be remade."

Smiling, Rey nodded. "All right. I'll get to work knocking these barnacles off, and we'll get it all put away before we get some sleep. We can hunt for that tomorrow."

"Me and Bally will take care of the forge. Ami's been wrapped up in you since we landed, worried over whether or not you would survive. I think if you can keep her occupied during the day, we'll do the rest."

"Fine by me." Elated at the prospect, Rey had already spent days with her on the ship when he was her protector, so a few more walking through the forest and talking to butterflies would be easy as plum pie.

SEVENTEEN

Sleepless Nights

"HERE," Ami instructed, offering Rey a small shell.

Accepting it, he studied the inside. "Aye, I think this one is nice." Placing it on the end of his finger, it covered just the tip. The outside a bright, bleached white, the inside held the colorful rainbow of her merdoe. "But this one isn't magic?"

"No." She grinned, taking it back and placing it in the pouch, along with the rest of her collection. She had been picking out pieces for over a week and intended to build a necklace for Olirassa. Her ninety-first birthday celebration would take place in a few days, and the girl wanted very much to be a part of the sirens and share in their traditions through the event.

"My shell is enchanted. The magic was added," she explained. Over her shoulder, she heard the splash of small feet as they approached. "That's Oldrilin, isn't it?" she speculated without turning around.

"Aye." He snickered at his tiny admirer stopping behind her.

Pulling the merdoe from her pocket, she placed it in her right palm and held the hand up. Laying his left over it, his fingers curled around the back of her warm skin, sandwiching the small device between them. They had become practiced at the procedure, as it allowed the tiny siren to communicate with him through the stone.

"Rey," her small voice sang joyously.

"Oldrilin," he replied, grinning down at her.

"I've been given permission to ask you your presence at the celebration," she announced, bouncing in place while rocking side to side with anticipation.

"And I would be happy to attend," he said with a firm nod.

Splashing into the water, she offered him her hand, and he took it with his right, so they could amble down the beach with him between them. "What shall I wear to the occasion?" he teased.

"What you always wear is fine," Oldrilin replied with a giggle.

"Good." He didn't anything else to put on anyway. "You know, Oldrilin, I'm surprised that you would ask me to the party, though. I would have thought after a couple of moons, you would have gotten tired of me by now."

"Oh, no, Reynard!" she squealed. "Love Rey Daye. Keep him always be my friend."

He swung the small fingers, his heart warmed by the sentiment, despite the Mate's dark warning about the mermaids. In the two months since he had been well enough to rejoin the others, things had been rather uneventful on that front, and he had come to consider if the other man had been flat wrong about their intentions.

Nonetheless, he spent most of his days being paraded around by Amicia. She treated him as a brother, which he didn't mind, and he served as her protector, not that she had needed any. The forest and lagoon were a paradise, regardless of what the Mate said about them.

They visited the pool and the waterfall almost every morning, where they drank the delicious water and strolled through the grass. The flowers in the back provided the sweetest nectar, and they enjoyed the company of the butterflies on a regular basis.

In addition, they had regular moonlight strolls with Olirassa, their queen. He had to admit, she seemed harmless enough. She shared bits and pieces of the history of Eriden, and in return, they provided news about the east and the mortals of the rim, as their species was referred to. Even Rey was permitted to speak, and the queen seemed quite taken with his tales. He could hardly see her as a threat to them, now or in the days to come.

Stroking Lin's fingers gently with his thumb, they reached the part of the beach where the flat had once stood. After the Mate and Bally had finished searching the scuttled ship, it had been dismantled to prevent drawing attention to the path that led to their sanctuary in the woods. Passing at their slow pace, he realized one must know exactly which tree to look for if you were to locate the trail at all.

Arriving at the far end, before the peninsula that jutted out abruptly and formed the western borders of their space, Ami spied another collection of shells in the shallow surf.

"Here," she commanded gleefully. "Let's see if we can find a few more to add to the necklace." Dropping Rey's hand, he would no longer be able to speak to Lin, but they would manage. They had learned to get along pretty well with or without her help.

As soon as they had added a few more to the pouch, the trio sloshed up to the edge of the water and took seats in the moist sand, where the sun shone down upon them from straight above. "It will be afternoon and eve soon," Rey observed, glancing at his siren as she played with the bubbles in the water next to him, a long stick in her hand as she poked them.

Offering his hand to Ami, he waited for her to place the shell between them so he could converse with their small friend. "Is that the only reason you forgo the sea today, to invite me to the ball?"

"Always love the sea." She still toyed with her find.

"Yes, but not today," he pushed, slightly bothered that she had come to him at midday rather than the early light of morn before returning to it, or the late hour, just before the sunset when they left the salty waters. "Lin, look at me," he insisted, grasping at the fine material that covered her body. Pulling at it, he encouraged her to pivot, and she looked woeful when his eyes met hers. "What is the trouble, Oldrilin?"

Lin shrugged. "Her majesty is pleased you wish to attend."

"And when is the event?" he asked more calmly, sure he could puzzle it out if he had enough clues.

"The quarter moon of the waning crescent," she said with a bright smile. Pulling free, she splashed through the shallows a moment before running out and disappearing into the ocean. Her tail flipped, that of a large black fish as a parting salute before she vanished without a trace.

Releasing his hand, Ami returned her merdoe to her pocket. "Does it matter when she asked you? At least the invitation is given, and I will not attend the event alone."

"Aye." He nodded, still staring at the spot where she had turned to bid him farewell.

However, he knew that it mattered a great deal, as Piers had been right on that detail. The mermaids almost never came out of the water during midday and preferred the hours of the night, so much so that they expressed time and date by the phases of their giant, magical moon. Each night's moon had a specific name, and twelve cycles of the moon constituted their year. From what he could tell, it had always been so for the sirens, for as long as they had existed.

Looking up at the sun once more, he cackled, "I guess it really doesn't, and I am invited to the dance. We should find a few more shells so we can put the necklace together tomorrow, as the waning crescent starts tonight, and quarter will be in three days."

Arriving at their camp in late afternoon, the pair prepared their pot for the evening's stew. Using her dagger to clean the crab he pulled from the rocks earlier that afternoon, Rey marveled at the amount of meat the creature held. "I don't think crabs at home are this large," he boasted.

"I've never eaten them before," Ami replied, selecting vegetables from one of their repurposed casks and chopping them into smaller bits.

They had taken the raft apart and brought the materials into their camp, where their water barrel now collected and stored the water they needed throughout the day and night. Located beneath the trees, the Mate had set up the perfect collection system, so even the smallest rain ensured their stores were replenished.

The other casks held various items. Once Rey had returned from Riran in good health, Bally and Piers had reclaimed salt from the ocean and killed a few small game animals, which they dried and stored in another of the casks, calling it their emergency reserves. Ami had seen little need of it, though, as the land of the sirens was rich with wild game and vegetation, enough to sustain the four of them and then some.

The stew prepared and bubbling over the fire, Rey and Ami each stretched out on one of their thatched mattresses. Looking up at the canopy of trees above him, he asked quietly, "How long do you suppose we will stay here?"

"Why forever, of course!" the girl replied in surprise, as if the thought of ever leaving had never occurred to her.

Rolling onto his side, he stared at her profile, as she still lay on her back. "Does the Mate make you happy?" he asked absently.

This time, she did not give a response and rolled onto her side as well, so that her back was to him. "Sleep well, Rey," she called to him quietly.

Closing his eyes, he dozed until late evening, when Bally and Piers returned from their new forge. They had obviously paid a visit to one of the pools of water that collected in the forest, as their hair was wet, and their skin was clean when they arrived.

"I found some more roots for you, girl," the Mate announced, dropping them on the ground next to her storage cask.

"Ah, lovely. I'll clean them on the morrow and put them away until we are ready for them." She appeared quite happy with their arrangement, and if Rey's questions had given her any pause, it did not show.

"What time will you return from Riran?" Piers was anticipating her nightly trip, as she had scarcely missed a visit in the two moons since Reynard was healed.

"I shall return early, as I will be going alone for the evening." She sighed sweetly, her thoughts distant with the plans for the ball. "We are preparing for the celebration festival, and the queen will be too busy for our usual conversation," she informed him, offering him her hand.

"Then I will await your return, love," he cooed, pressing her fingers to his lips and bidding her farewell.

After she had gone, Rey asked in complete surprise, "Surely she does not see this as a normal relationship between a husband and wife."

The Mate chuckled. "She thinks I am courting her. She is aware that we are not wed, but our date is set, and she is my intended."

"Oh really." The younger man stroked this thin, but progressing beard. "When are the nuptials planned to take place, then?"

"Olirassa has granted us a wedding on the half waxing moon, three moons from now. About three months." His shoulders sagged a little at the thought of the date looming in the future. "We must be gone before then."

"Well, you look rather clean for a blacksmith. Any luck with the forge?"

"Aye," Bally vouched, joining them from his trek through the forest. Laying a long, curved sword on the table, the black handle of it had been fashioned with leather and gems for the grip.

"That's for you." Piers pointed at the magnificent blade and smiled behind his cup.

"For me," Rey breathed, lifting the weapon and inspecting the fine edge. "It's remarkable, Piers, thank you."

"Bah. It's a sword," the other man denied modestly. "Bally also has an axe, so we are, in the least, no longer defenseless. I will make the blades for spears over the next few weeks, and we will be ready to travel."

On the walls hung the ropes that had once held their flat together. Eyeing them, he scowled, "There will not be much that we can carry. We must fashion packs to haul upon our backs. Can you convince Ami we are in need of blankets or cloth?"

"I can try." Rey shrugged at the possibility, relinquishing his sword to Bally, who would hide it for him until they were ready to depart.

"Good. We will wrap them around our food, and fashion bags similar to hers. That will make our load easier to carry."

"Have you decided where we will go? Oldrilin says that there are other creatures to the west and north of here. Elves and nymphs, as well as wild creatures who would eat our flesh if they happened upon us," he informed him in a low tone. "This is an untamed land, not at all like the villages of the rim."

"Aye, this place is filled with savages," Piers agreed, helping himself to another bowl of the stew. "We will go west and avoid the mountains. We have explored the lower face of the cliffs, and I am certain that place belongs to the elves. Once we clear the peninsula to the west of us, I'm sure the mermaids will let us go, and we will be free of them."

"And if they do not wish to let us have Amicia?"

Gripping his spoon more tightly for a moment, Piers scowled. "We will not ask their permission. One of the nights, she will go for her visit, and on the morrow, we will take her away. They will not know she is gone or to where until there are many miles between us. And, if we stay to the land and avoid the coast, they will not see and certainly not try to follow."

Rey grinned wryly. "So be it. I have one of them I will miss, though. Oldrilin has become quite dear to me."

"She would live as your servant," the Mate suggested.

"Perhaps," Rey agreed, cleaning his bowl with a piece of bread Ami had baked from more of the island's unusual plants. Chewing it thoughtfully, he observed, "In a way, I suppose she has always served me. As my nursemaid, she brought me the nectar and saw to it that I was healed. I feel that she cares for me. To what ends I cannot say."

"You cannot bring her," Piers stated calmly, shaking his head for effect. "Her loyalty would always be unclear, and she would not last long so far from the sea."

"But, they have legs. They can walk upon the land. And even today, she paid me a visit at the top of the day, with the sun straight above our heads," he insisted.

"Did she, now." The Mate appeared pensive, considering the news. "What was her reason for the visit?" He cut his eyes over to gauge Rey's response.

"To invite me to the festival, the queen's birthday party."

"And when is that?" Bally spoke up, then hid his face at having blurted out of turn, always silently listening to the proceedings of his elders.

"In three days, at the quarter moon of the waning crescent," Reynard supplied without argument.

"I'll think on this." Piers dropped his spoon in his bowl and rested his arms on the table to lean on. "I'm getting old," he groaned. "The forge is a great deal of work for a man my age, especially one so out of practice."

"Out of practice," Rey scoffed, recalling the beauty and perfection of his new blade. "Your work is exquisite. I can't believe you told Amicia you had failed as a blacksmith."

"I failed within my heart, and that is all that matters," the older man replied, getting to his feet and taking his dish to wash. "We should sleep. Ami won't return for a few hours, and we have done all that we can here for now, but soon sleepless nights will be upon us as we prepare for our departure."

EIGHTEEN

Fire and Fury

SITTING IN THE COLD, damp sand, Rey's heart raced. Flashbacks of being ill, frightened and alone on that beach a few short months ago filled his head, and his body trembled with dread. Rubbing his arms briskly, he fought for control. *Come on, you can do this.*

Out on the beach before him, Ami ran through the edge of the water in her bare feet. She had insisted on taking her boots off for the event, and they were waiting for them at the entrance to the lagoon. Her feet had been toughened from years of summers without shoes, and she hardly noticed the rough sand beneath them as she ran and played with her siren friends.

Caught in the memory, he recalled the time he had spent with the girl on the ship, locked in the first mate's quarters as she hid, and he protected her. She had been so different then; focused and confident. Watching her now, she seemed almost child-like in her joy, and he wondered if the sirens had something to do with her altered persona, as all of them seemed to possess those same basic qualities. Free spirits, blowing on a whim and splashing around in the waves without a real care in the world. He could see the beauty in that, even if it weren't very practical.

His teeth chattering, Rey hadn't dared set foot near the cool water. If they had lit a fire, it might have been different, but he had learned since becoming Ami's companion that the sirens detested fire, which was probably one reason why the others had moved to their camp before he could join them. The sirens had only agreed to lighting one, which had occurred while he had been ill and had probably saved his life. Other than that, flames inside the borders of their lagoon were strictly forbidden.

Watching the girl as she mingled with the smaller females, he smiled. *At least Amicia's having a good time.* Her face glowed, even without the conflagration, and the quarter moon put off an extraordinary amount of light with the ocean there to reflect it. Giving the bottoms of each leg a few rolls, he rose from his spot and dusted the grains off his pants. He made his way over to join her and to brave the liquid up to his ankles.

"May I?" He offered her his arm and held a smile, even as the frigid waves lapped at his toes.

"Of course."

She accepted the appendage graciously, her fingers toying with the material that covered his warm flesh beneath. Strolling along the beach, they made their way over to pay their respects to the queen.

The siren leader sat on a large rock, which reminded him of a throne, or what he imagined one would look like since he was not accustomed to spending time with royalty before coming to Eriden. Red and green moss grew across the top and down the sides, as if it were covered in a fine silk cloth. Softening the harshness of the stone, the vegetation brought color to the subtle greys and browns of the shore and accented the queen's iridescent gown.

Her feet dangling, they almost touched the earth below as she kicked them merrily. Her head pivoting from side to side, Olirassa seemed quite spry for a girl of ninety-one. Watching her subjects as they frolicked at the event in her honor, she looked as if the celebration pleased her, and she blissfully received any who wished to bid her a happy birthday.

Before leaving the camp, Ami had wrapped the necklace in a large green leaf. Giving it to Rey to hold, he carried it in his pocket. Pulling it out, he uncovered it, and they both respectfully knelt before her. Amicia placed her merdoe in her left hand, and Rey grasped it with his right, still holding the broad leaf in his other hand so he could offer it to the guest of honor.

"Your majesty." Rey presented their gift by pushing it towards her. "We have something special for you. We collected the shells ourselves and barely finished putting it together yesterday." Holding it out to her, his hand shook slightly, so Amicia added her free appendage underneath to steady him.

"Sorry," he mumbled. "I'm a bit cold tonight." When he first joined Amicia for her nightly visit to the queen, he had not been permitted to even speak to her. It had taken time to build her trust, and even now he felt the trepidation at her power.

Before him, her tiny fingers caressed the string of shells. Her golden-brown hair stuck out around her head with wild red highlights he could easily detect, even in the dim light of the evening. Her green eyes shone, reminding him of the siren who had become a dear friend. "Olirassa," he breathed, "do you like it?"

"It is beautiful," she replied. "Every day I shall wear it and think of you," she promised, smiling at him fully in a way she had never done. "How curious about you I am, Rey Daye. You came into our midst, and you have brightness brought upon us. I have enjoyed your tales of the rim and the mortals to the east." She bowed slightly to him as she spoke, her purple dress shimmering as she moved.

"Thank you, my lady." He bowed to her, a sense of relief flooding his trembling body. "I have most enjoyed the telling. May we share many more sweet occasions in the days... err nights, to come."

Accepting the gift, Olirassa handed it to another mermaid, who would put it away for safekeeping. Standing and moving to the side, the pair still held the stone between their hands, so the song of the sirens remained clear to him; all the laughter and joy that they shared in their festivities.

Arriving at the east bank, they waded out a short distance in the shallow water and sat upon the sand. Watching the creatures before him swim, Rey whispered, "How do they change so quickly?" He spoke of the flips and flops of the mermaids, who were so small when they walked on the shore like miniature people, and yet so large when they swam as fish in the sea. "Do you think it is the water that somehow triggers it?"

"I don't think so," Ami replied, also quiet so as not to offend their hosts. "I believe it is part of their magic, that they are able to transform when they desire it. Or perhaps their legs are merely an illusion, that or their fins are," she laughed, also watching the rainbow of bodies roll and spin in the shallow pool before them.

Turning in the water, Oldrilin appeared in her black and shiny form; a fish to the best that he could tell. A moment later, she walked out of the lagoon, her hair wet and dripping as she splashed merrily, running towards him.

"Rey Daye enjoy the dance." She giggled, twirling before him as if she were a mini ballerina performing for him beneath the bright end-of-summer moon.

"It's lovely," he replied, observing that many of the others swayed and spun along the shore and up in the trees. If the queen had thought sharing stories with him had been interesting, it had been doubly so for him, as such unique beings he had never encountered. Their voices filled the air around them with music, and he felt a peace beyond compare. *Perhaps I have fallen under their spell as well,* he mused.

As the song faded and the night grew long, the hour approached when all the mermaids would find a spot to curl up for a few hours of sleep. They would rest until the sun woke them in the morn, and then be off into the lagoon for another day in the wide sea, splashing and playing, as if that were all life must ever be.

"Amazing creatures," Rey remarked aloud as he tugged on Ami's hand, ready to guide her back to their bunks in the camp. Stopping to retrieve her footwear, she leaned against a large tree at the beachside entrance to the lagoon. Pulling on her socks, she lost her balance and sat with a heavy thud and a peal of laughter. "You should carry them."

"I'll sit to put them on," she replied, continuing to smile. "While my feet are sturdy enough for the sand, I'm afraid our path to the camp is rougher than I prefer."

Leaning against the branches, he waited, and that is where he was when the first firebolt smashed into the branches opposite him before the trunk exploded into flames. Knocked to the ground, Rey felt dazed, shaking his head to clear it as he stared at the massive blaze.

Remembering the girl and event simultaneously, he screamed, "Ami!" reaching her with a quick roll. She sat on the sand, having regained her upright position from being knocked flat by the blast, and she worked desperately to get her foot in the second boot.

Shoving it in, she got to her feet as more shoots of fire scorched the waterline and set the entire front line of trees ablaze. Screaming, Oldrilin ran towards them, falling just before she reached them. Without a second thought, Rey scooped her up, intending to place her in the water on the other side so that she might swim away, as many of the others appeared to be doing.

However, when they reached their own beach, they made two discoveries. The first, Bally and Piers had heard the chaos and gathered their supplies, intending to come after them if they had not shown up when they did. The other, mermaids cannot transform or swim when they are injured.

Sitting to lower her into the water, Rey forgot all about staying dry, as tears trickled over his cheeks and beard. Her small arms and legs pocked by burns, she simply lay in the water and cried. "What's wrong with her?" he sniveled, wiping at his nose. "Why doesn't she swim away?"

Fishing the shell out of her pocket, Ami only needed a moment to discover the truth. "She can't," she wailed, her green eyes full of tears of their own. "They are being slaughtered. They cannot escape into the ocean if they have been burned." No wonder they detested fire.

"We have to help them," Bally determined firmly with a smack of his fist into an open palm, confident the others would agree.

"Not a chance," Piers replied. "We barely escaped the dragon last time, and this time I count three flying around. We need to get into the tree line and head west, now!"

Pulling off her sweater, Ami prepared to wrap it around the tiny creature. "Rey, carry her!" she commanded. "We cannot leave her here."

"Of course not," he agreed, having already made that determination for himself, and he scooped Lin out of the water without needing to be told twice. Accepting the garment to protect her, he wrapped her gently and held her against his chest.

Throwing their gear over their shoulders, Piers and Bally took the lion's share, while Ami managed her bag, which had been stuffed once again with whatever food they had on hand. Stomping along the edge of the forest, they kept to the shadows just inside the tree line. Following the beach, they made it all the way to the peninsula before they turned inland, hoping to leave the water and the dragons behind.

"We have to stop," Ami whined, catching the Mate's arm from behind and pulling firmly upon it.

"We keep moving," he growled. "The farther away we get, the safer we will be."

"But we're exhausted," Rey seconded her opinion. "Please, Piers. Let us rest and tend to the injured."

Glancing down at the siren Reynard carried in his arms, the first mate felt little pity for the creature. However, he had a great deal of respect for the man before him, and he could tell he was in pain, torn by her injury. "All right, we rest, but everyone stays close. I'll find the best place."

Tromping ahead, he located a small clearing that would suffice and directed the others to it. Taking up spots on the bare earth, each of the men dropped their loads and inspected their bundles. Bally had the sword and axe that had been forged, along with the one that the Mate had made off with from the ship the night of its sinking.

"You have weapons," Ami observed, and her features brightened as she realized she carried the food that would preserve them, at least for a few days. She figured at some point they would double back to the lagoon and return to Riran. The smile faded when she made the larger connection. "You intended to leave all along."

Not looking at her, Rey saw to Lin, who appeared to be sleeping in her sweater-nest. Adjusting it so she would be more comfortable, he observed, "We'll need some dressings for these wounds soon enough, or she'll get an infection."

He had ignored her observation, but Ami knew it was true. He had asked her only a few days before how long she thought they would stay, and now she knew why. Standing, she towered over Piers as he slumped against a tree. "You never meant to make a home with the sirens," she accused, her hands planted on her hips in the form of fists.

Looking up at her, she was a beauty to behold, even with strands of hair escaping her braid and floating wildly about her head. The light shining through them from the setting moon accented them, and he felt his heart ache with the wish he could have been the man she wanted him to be. "No," he stated flatly, waiting for the rain of fury.

"Ami," Rey cut in, satisfied his charge had all he could do for her at the moment. Leaving her bundle, he also stood. "Amicia, listen to me. The sirens are a magical and wonderful people, but they are not us. We might have stayed a while longer, but eventually we had to leave."

"So, you were in on it too!" A tear streaking her dirty cheek to drip from her quivering chin.

"Of course I was." He sighed, stepping closer and seizing her arms, holding them firmly. "We have worked together to ensure our survival. Don't you see?" He indicated their packs of preparations.

Staring down at their meager belongings, she wiped at her drops of angry sadness. She had been under a magical enchantment for weeks and could feel it slipping away. "Why did the dragons come?" she asked, her voice quieter as her thoughts cleared.

"I don't know," the Mate replied, digging into the ground with the heel of his boot. "But whatever the reason, I'm sure it's a bad omen for us."

A silence settled over the group as each considered that sentiment. Finally, Rey breathed in loudly and announced, "Well, what's done is done. But I think we can all agree on one thing… the dragons know we're here, and that means our safest route is to watch for our chance. At some point, we have to get off this land and try to make it home if we ever hope to escape them."

Looking up at him with doleful green eyes, Amicia heard the words and on some level understood the truth behind them. But, they did not change the fact that she was home. She felt it in her gut, and if the group of men ever did flee, they would do it without her.

NINETEEN

Jerranyth

WIND WHISTLED in the trees above her head, distracting her thoughts as Amicia tromped along behind Piers. The other two men close behind her, they carried packs made from the blankets she had acquired for them, which gave her an angry pout that she had unwittingly aided in their plan.

A bird, singing noisily, brought a small smile to her lips before it faded, and her dark scowl retook its place on her delicate features. They had been hiking through the wilderness for two days. If she had been weary of the raft, she was even more so of this.

However, there would be little point in complaining. It wasn't as if they had seen anything or anyone worthy of commentary since they left Riran the night of the fiery dragon attack. They simply marched along, resting now and then and keeping their own company along the way.

At least last night they had come upon a clear pool of water fed by a small spring, she recalled, tracing the memory of the evening in full. They had been climbing, as the trees grew up the side of a mountain, so their progress had been slow. From the sweet taste of it, she suspected that this bit of fresh water was fed by the same source as the waterfall and sacred pond in the siren lands, and she pondered what had become of her miniature friends.

Stopping beside it, they had made actual camp, and Rey had bathed his tiny mermaid in the cool water. Her wounds had festered into small pustules, and she drifted in and out of consciousness while he tended to her. He cleaned the wounds the best that he could and bandaged them with strips torn from his own shirt.

If they had the witch hazel, things would have been better. As they were, Ami feared she wouldn't last more than a few days, at best. But Lin had opened her eyes and fed upon a bit of water and nectar that he had gathered for her. That gave him hope, and she dared not take it away from him by voicing her concerns.

During their respite, she had also found a few of her personal things, such as her mother's dagger and father's mirror, in the bottom of their food bag, meaning they had been shoved into the pack first. Waving her hairbrush at Piers, she had accused, "It seems odd that your first thought was to bring this for me."

"I picked up your belongings, thinking you might like to have them," he replied with a shrug. "Your hair requires tending. A bit more than most, I might add. Did you not want your brush to keep it under control? Perhaps we should shave your head and be done with it," he taunted.

Her green eyes narrowed as she glared at him. "You claim you're not in love with me, but you care for me as if you are. I find it hard to believe we would not have wed if we had been able to remain with the sirens."

"Can't a man simply do something nice for a woman he is fond of without having some deeper meaning cast upon it?" the Mate grumbled, turning his back on her and putting an end to the conversation.

His attempts to make less of his feelings for her made her smile again, and she stared at the back of him as he moved ahead of her, choosing their path with his stubby collection of hair scrunched at the base of his skull. A moment later, the woods fell silent as the bird's song ended abruptly. A loud shout froze the group of wayward humans in their tracks.

Bally still carried the bundle of armaments, as they had seen no sign of danger since exiting the beach, leaving them defenseless to the unknown parties now in their path. Gathering in a small circle, the group exchanged tense glances with one another as they considered their options.

From out of the trees, tall, slender creatures surrounded them, brandishing weapons all pointed at them. One with a bow set the nock and pulled the string, keeping Bally under guard. A second held a long sword over his head, ready to strike at anyone who dared to move.

With the distinctive cat-like slant of their eyes and point of their pierced and decorated ears, Rey recognized them from the descriptions the mermaids had given and appeared happy with their arrival. "You're the elves!"

A male with long dark hair made a surly sounding reply, and Ami slipped her hand into her pocket, fishing out her merdoe so that she could at least understand his rude remarks.

Stepping forward to inspect what appeared to be an infant Reynard kept wrapped in her sweater, he pulled back the material from the small face and gasped, "Why have you stolen this creature?"

Amicia frowned, then translated, "He wants to know why you have stolen 'this creature,' Rey."

"I haven't stolen anything," the man in question denied, instantly angry at the use of the word "creature" to describe the mermaid. "This is Oldrilin and she's injured. We were at the queen's festival two nights ago when Riran was attacked by dragons."

"We barely escaped with our lives," Piers interceded, hoping to calm his companion by waving an upturned hand at him in a stopping motion. "This siren was burned and couldn't swim away with the others. She is Rey's friend, and we brought her to care for. We didn't mean her any harm."

Studying him for a long moment, the elf glanced around at each one, then faced the girl. "Queen Olirassa invited *you* to her celebration?"

"Why wouldn't she invite us?" Amicia demanded, standing taller. "We're her friends and have been since we landed here over two moons ago," she announced confidently.

Extending a long slender finger, the elven leader grazed her cheek as he stared into her clear green orbs. "I see." Glancing down at her hand that clasped the magical shell, he lifted it and nudged the fingers to spread them, inspecting the trinket but allowing her to keep it.

Spinning, his long robe flowed around him. "Come, then. I will present you to my queen and discern what is to be done with you."

"He wants us to go with them," Amicia interpreted once more, looking around anxiously at the others.

"My friend needs help," Rey interjected, stepping towards him. "Please," he said more quietly when the elf turned, glaring at him. "She said elf medicine was the best in all the land," he practically whispered.

"The water creature spoke well of us," the leader grinned, directing his comment to Amicia. The gesture added a twisted appearance to his features, not altering her confidence in him. "Bring her, and we will see if her life can be spared."

"They're going to help her," Ami informed Rey, urging him to follow.

Instantly eager, he fell into step behind the elf, cradling Lin all the more tightly in his excitement. Help lay before them and hope beyond any they could have held had they not been found.

Piers appeared less enthusiastic, giving each of his captors a cold stare in turn before moving to follow his comrade and the head elf. Amicia marched after him, and Baldwin brought up the rear, with their guards behind to ensure no one tried to escape.

The company arrived a short time later on the edge of a vast city snuggled within the trees and rocks. Tall spires peeked from the tops of the branches, and Amicia gasped in wonder as she lifted her chin, laying her head back to admire them.

"This place is incredible," Bally declared, putting the girl on edge with how easily he had been drawn to them.

"We don't know anything about them," she warned in a hushed voice. They had already visited one enchanted kingdom only to have it destroyed by the dragons that seemed to be hunting them. What would become of the elves if they were to take them in?

Hearing her comment, the elf in charge plied her with another eerie grin. "I am Anerion, lead huntsman to our queen, Lady Cilithrand. Welcome to Jerranyth," he announced coolly. The introduction made, he waited.

Pursing her lips, she repeated, pointing at him with an open palm, "Anerion, this is Rey, Bally, and Piers," she stated calmly, presenting the men and then herself. "I'm Amicia, but most call me Ami."

"Well, that was not so difficult." Her host nodded firmly, turning once more to lead them into the elf kingdom.

Approaching a wide gate, large stone pillars stood to either side, each topped with a statue of an elf maid with open arms. The iron covering for it split in the middle and lay swung open, creating a transparent tunnel about ten feet long. Passing through it, they could still see the wooded area that grew right up to the stone walls that surrounded the city of Jerranyth and marked its boundary.

Upon entering, they came into a courtyard that occupied the middle of the path. Cobbled stones formed the floor of the plaza, which appeared square at near a hundred feet side to side and front to back. In the center, an ornate fountain spouted water into a shallow pool surrounded by a bench for sitting to enjoy the view.

From this central gathering place, the walkway broke up and wound back into the dwellings that lined the cliffs and slopes of the mountain via steep paths and magnificent sets of steps and stairs. Stopping them, Anerion parceled out the group to various elves, who would see to their needs while they were there in the city.

"This is Rey," he announced to a young maid who joined them. "His siren needs attention as quickly as you can manage it."

"His siren," she replied, her surprise evident. Peeking inside his make-shift blanket, she shook her head at Lin's condition. Taking Rey's arm, she guided him towards a set of stairs to the right of the great fountain, where a tall hedge hid what lay beyond.

Ami watched him climb up and out of sight when they met a turn and asked, "Where does she take him?"

"The siren will be mended," the leader of the hunting party assured. "You will follow me to the queen's chamber, and the other two of your friends will visit with a few of my kinsman while they await your return."

As Anerion led her to a more exquisite staircase directly across from the gate, Piers attempted to follow but was stopped by a pair of stout elves who guarded the palace entrance. They each held long spears and crossed them before him, denying him access. "Ami, wait!" he called after her, alerting her that he had not been permitted to join her.

"Wait for us here," she commanded, squeezing the merdoe anxiously.

"I don't like this," he growled. They were being separated from each other, and he would not be able to protect her.

"There is no cause for alarm," Anerion replied to his concern.

Glancing between them, Ami smiled anxiously. "I'll be ok, Piers. Go and wait by the fountain, and I'll be back once I've been presented to the queen."

His jaw dropped at that development, as her being presented to anyone only troubled him more, not less, especially since he was in charge of their company and not her. However, he had no grounds to argue. Outmanned and unarmed, he knew the elves could do whatever they liked, and they would be powerless to stop them.

Returning to Bally as she had requested, he stomped back to the fountain, glaring at it as it spewed water into the shallow pond that surrounded the half-naked statues of more elven maids. Standing beside it, he looked down into the clear water that made it difficult to assess how deep it actually was. The bottom decorated with softly tinted green and yellow tile, a bright gold grout held them in place, which caught the overhead light of the sun and brightened the water to a warm glow.

Swimming in the depths, large orange and blue fish the size of his arm moved in slow, oscillating motion. He counted seven of them, each moving in random, elegant curves around the small tank. Feeling calmed by the peaceful creatures, he glanced around to see what the remaining elves were up to.

Next to him, one of those they had first encountered in the woods had opened Baldwin's pack and had taken to inspecting his craftsmanship. When he held up the sword he had presented to Rey, the question formed in the air, and he bit, "I made it from salvaged metal from the sunken ship next to the mermaid's lagoon."

Satisfied, the elf continued to go through the contents while Bally laughed, "You don't think he could understand you, do you?"

"Aye, he understands," the Mate grimaced. "This place is quite a mystery, but I've gotten that much figured out." When the young man didn't reply, he sighed, "The beings here are magical. They can all talk to each other, and they all understand our words, even if we can't understand theirs."

"How fortunate for them." The younger man laughed as a new elf, perhaps his age, joined them. Lifting Bally's axe, his slender fingers gripped the handle, and he tested the weight of it with a few swings. "That's mine," Baldwin bragged. "The Mate made it for me." He pointed to Piers as he explained, then back to himself, adding, "I'm Bally."

Nodding, the elf indicated his understanding, patting himself across his chest and announcing, "Animir."

Baldwin broke into a wide grin at the introduction and followed when Animir beckoned for him to do so. This time, they departed to the left and back down the slope, leaving Piers alone with the other elves and the rest of their gear. Looking around anxiously, he scowled, muttering at having been treated as a prisoner while the others were shown the curtesy of guests.

Smiling at each other, two of the elves who remained with him called to a third, and a moment later a small barrel of wine was produced with glasses for all. As soon as it appeared, the square filled with a dozen tall elves, all dressed in various styles of robes and drapes of fine, shimmering, silky material. Serving themselves from the supply, they chattered about him, holding up toasts and smiling.

Accepting a glass for himself, Piers could no longer hold his frown at the rich aroma and succulent taste of the beverage. After a few glasses, he found himself claimed by three of the young maids, who seemed quite interested in his rugged appearance as they fawned over him openly.

"I'm Piers," he informed them with a twisted grin, "but most of my friends call me The Mate."

The girls giggled, offering their names. Matching his height, Tirith, the tallest and blond, had clear blue eyes and a thin build. Poldur, who had to be the shortest elf he had met so far, was rather portly, with ebony locks that hung just past the small of her back, and she glared at him with misty grey orbs.

Cothiel might have been the most average of the trio, and of the elves, both in her build and plain brown hair with mahogany-colored eyes. But, she had spirit, latching onto his arm and refusing to be parted from him for the rest of the afternoon.

His defenses dissolving rapidly, Piers enjoyed the wine and the company, not understanding a word that they said to him but languishing in their attention just the same.

TWENTY

Queen Cilithrand

FOLLOWING THE LEAD HUNTER ANXIOUSLY, Amicia gazed around her with wide eyes. If the sirens had been the simplest of creatures, with a lust for life itself and the honesty of the sea, the elves were the purest of opposites. Everything around them had been finely crafted from exquisite materials. Hard woods, gold, and silver were their favorites, with jewels and gems accenting the walls and furniture.

Leading her down a long and winding corridor, the elf did not falter, keeping his gaze straight ahead. In front of them, a pair of doors that arched to a point twice the height of the elves opened, and she was shown into a long, wide chamber. Walking slowly down the center of smooth hard stone, a thick carpet covered the floor on either side, where tables and shelves filled with unfamiliar objects lined the walls.

Along the right side of the room as she entered, vast windows brought in the natural light as the entire wall was practically made of glass, while the left held none, being a wall formed from the rock of the mountain itself. The inner wall had been polished, and the stone held a crisp, smooth appearance; mostly deep grey, but streaked with bright red and orange rivulets of color.

Anxious at the sound of her boots thumping on the hard floor, Ami grew tense in the formal air of the great hall. Her breath quickened when she arrived at the far end to stand before the queen, and she squeezed her merdoe anxiously as she waited to see what happened next.

Anerion presented her with only a bow, then turned on his heel to exit the way he had come. Standing before the raised platform, Ami's hands trembled as she fidgeted with her precious translator. Swallowing, she kept her eyes on the queen's gown, as she felt certain it would be presumptuous of her to stare at the sovereign or to look her in the eye. When the silent stillness grew long, she raised her chin and met the older woman's gaze.

Cilithrand was a slender, delicate woman. Her features were accented by paint that only the richest of society could afford at home. A luxury beyond the reach of all but the elite, her lips were stained a deep purple, which matched the accents in her green and gold gown. Her simple brown hair drawn into a braid at the front of her head, it parted to expose the jewel crested tips of her ears. Many of the elves Ami had seen were pierced, but this was indeed the most splendid of displays.

"Your majesty," Amicia breathed, bowing before her as she resumed staring at her feet.

"What is your name, child?"

"Amicia Spicer," she declared in a shaky voice.

"And how did you arrive in the Kingdom of Eriden?"

"Our ship was scuttled by a dragon," the girl explained. "We survived on a small raft and crashed upon the shore here three moons ago." Daring to look up, she glimpsed the queen's face before lowering her gaze once more.

"Are you afraid of me, child?" The queen had seen the fire within the girl as soon as she entered her chamber, but after speaking with her, she sensed that Ami was unaware of its existence.

"Very much," the young woman whispered hoarsely, dropping to a single knee. Leaning upon it, she waited, half expecting to have her shoulders separated from her head at any moment by one of the two guards with heavy spears that stood on either side of the throne.

But the blow did not fall, and a tinkle of laughter filled the chamber. "Rise, Amicia Spicer. No harm will come to you within my walls." Standing, the monarch descended the few steps and joined her on the main floor of the room. Her gown long, it trailed behind her in a heavy train, the sound a soft rustle as it slithered over the stones.

Getting to her feet, Ami stood next to her. At least a foot taller, the elf appeared to be a giant, as did all of those they had encountered. Raising her hand, the older woman indicated for her to walk with her as they strolled through the room. Her movements small, she kept herself rigid as she stepped onto the soft carpet and glided along the inner wall.

Arriving at a small table, a pedestal in the center of it had thin, shimmering material flowing down the sides, landing on the flat surface six inches below its crest. There, at the top, sat a small round ball; opaque, which glittered in the bright light of a window that angled and focused light upon it from across the room.

Lifting the small round orb, the queen stared into it for a moment, then smiled. "Tis true. You have come to us from the rim of the mortals."

"Yes, of course I have," Ami defended, surprised the woman had doubted her.

"You were fortunate to have fled the sirens," she went on, unaffected by the girl's comment. "Three men serve you, correct?"

"I have three male companions, yes," Amicia bit a little more angrily. To imply that any of them were servants to her grated on her nerves and put her on edge.

"Olirassa will be disappointed that you have removed them. They would have made a fine feast upon them, to be certain."

"Olirassa is our friend!"

Her words sharp, the queen looked up from her gazing in surprise. "Are you a fool, child? Surely you noticed that there are no men in the land of Riran."

"Yes, I –" Ami stammered, cutting herself off and trying to regroup her thoughts.

Seeing her anguish, the elf reached out to her, grasping her arm and holding it firmly. "You are not the first to be marooned upon these shores. There have been several ships to make it past our barriers and to settle in the waters that surround our coast."

Nodding, Ami recalled Piers asking Olirassa about a ship that had sunk near the entrance to their hidden camp. "Yes," she breathed, the memory growing clearer. "What became of the crew of the ship that my companions found?"

Holding out the ball, the queen indicated it with her long, painted nails. "Look inside, girl. For this crystal will show you the truth that you seek."

Inside the glittering surface, a cloud swirled then parted, and Ami could see a ship caught in a storm. Dragon wings and fire fluttered across the scene, and men abandoned the ship, swimming for the land that lay near to them. Arriving on their beach, they were greeted by the mermaids, who welcomed them to the woods.

A moment later, the scene changed. A large ceremonial fire burned, and the men screamed in agony. Their flesh shriveled over their bones, turning to dust as the life-force was drawn from their bodies, until even their skeletons had been wasted and blew away on the breeze.

"There, you see?" The queen appeared confident, lowering the ball as the scene disappeared. "Your friends would have been dealt with in the same fashion, I assure you."

"What about me?" Ami gasped, unsure if the sphere of truth could be trusted. Olirassa had been nothing but kind to her and she could not fathom her betrayal; especially one involving a fire of any kind, as she knew firsthand the mermaids were against them.

"Perhaps you too would have been devoured, or perhaps she had other plans for you," the queen replied, extending a finger to caress her cheek lightly, with her thumb lightly tracing the faint scar that split her lower lip. "Who is to say when one speaks of such vile creatures?"

Looking up at the tall brunette, Ami felt a chill slide over her body, as if the woman were a serpent, slithering over her skin. "I understand," she whispered softly, not wishing to give away her doubt. "We are your guests then?" she asked more self-assuredly.

"Yes, of course! For as long as you have need," Cilithrand replied, gliding her arm across the girl's shoulder and drawing her near as she turned her to walk along the wall once more. "We will have a suite prepared for you and your companions. Dinner will be served in a few hours, so you will have until then to rest and freshen yourself." With a wave of her hand, a small elf maid appeared, surprising Ami that any existed that weren't taller than herself. "This is Sadrir. She will tend you during your stay," the queen informed her while releasing her. Turning, she floated back towards her throne, dismissing the two smaller females abruptly.

"This way, my lady." The girl presented her new mistress with a small curtsy.

Her eyes wide, Ami felt odd to be presented with a servant. As they exited the palace, a breathless feeling of panic overwhelmed her. Walking along the cobble-stone path, they passed entrances to the spires that sprouted from the tops of the trees. They also met several elves as they went about their business, each giving Ami a nod or bow as they strolled by, which only added to her feeling of dread.

Fighting to control her emotions, she followed her maid until they arrived at a large garden filled with luscious flowers. Separated by a large hedge, it formed a quiet haven, away from prying eyes. Crossing the grass to the far side, a wall of shrubs divided the garden further, into smaller chambers which housed small pools of steaming water.

"What is this?" Her mouth gaped in surprise upon entering.

"It's a natural spring for bathing," the girl replied, wafting at her to enter while she spoke to one of the bath maids who stood near the door. After sending her to fetch clothing for their charge, she returned her attention to Amicia. "Please, my lady. I have lavender soaps and a fluffy robe for when you have completed your soak." Her hand open to the blue sky above, she indicated the water.

"You want me to bathe... in there," Amicia asked incredulously. Never in her life had she imagined such a thing.

"Yes." Sadrir smiled sweetly. "Please, my lady." She again curtsied, giving Ami another twist in her gut.

Walking over to the edge, Amicia knelt on the soft earth, resting back on her haunches as she considered the situation. Her hand trembling, she dipped the tips of her fingers into the water. The warmth exquisite, she had heard of such things but had never dreamed she would lay her eyes upon them. "Is it magical?" she asked quietly, afraid to spoil the splendor of the place.

"It is heated by the springs from within the earth. It is why our people settled here thousands of years ago," the maid explained, accepting a few items from her cohort, who had returned with a fluffy cloth and a long gown.

A large tree stood in the corner of her cubicle, and the elf used the branches to hold her necessities as she continued, "We have many such baths here in Jerranyth." Raising her hands, she indicated the walls around them that probably hid similar chambers on the other side.

Looking down at her dirty pants and shirt, Ami sighed. *Bally's clothes.* They had been given to her when she first hid in the Mate's quarters. *It seems so long ago,* she recalled. But it had scarcely been a few months, hardly any time at all in the grand scheme of things.

Glancing at the dress, she scowled. Then she stood and began removing her clothing. "I need these laundered and returned to me," she commanded.

Her eyes wide with surprise, Sadrir bit back her reply and swallowed. Then she said in a soft tone, "If my lady wishes it, it shall be so."

Naked, with only her merdoe in her left hand, Ami stepped into the warm swirls. The stones at the near end provided the perfect entrance and exit, and the pool itself came to her waist when she had reached the flat, smooth bottom. On the far side and end, a bench ran the length of them, providing a place to sit or stretch that brought the water to her neck.

Pulling her hair out of her braid, she released her mass of curls. Dunking beneath the surface, she stood once more, water dripping down her naked curves from her wet hair. Squeezing it out, she laughed, remembering not to drop her special shell.

Over the course of her life, a warm pan of water to wash herself had been a luxury; a bath that covered her entire body unheard of. Taking a seat on the bench, she rested against the side and looked at the girl there to tend her. "Where is this lavender soap that I was promised?"

Smiling, Sadrir presented a small plate, which held different sized bars, bowls and textures of the sweet-smelling cleanser. "Would you like to be washed?"

"Washed?" Amicia coughed, dumbstruck at the thought of having the other woman's hands on her, lathering her body and then rinsing the bubbles away. "No," she choked, "I am quite capable of taking care of that part."

Remaining below the surface, Ami glided over to select her soap. She lay her merdoe on the edge while she lathered, applying the bar to her sticky flesh. Dipping her finger in the cream, she looked up at the girl, laying her hand over the trinket to await her response.

Sadrir giggled. "This is for your hair," she offered, indicating the watery version of the soap. "While you bathe, let me take your shell and have it put upon a string, that you may wear it around your neck. That way, you will never be without it."

"You know what this is for?" Ami asked in surprise.

The maid nodded. "Oh, yes! Magical siren shells are a rare gift. You must have been very dear to them."

"You know the sirens," Amicia observed more quietly, astonished that she would be familiar with them after what the queen had shown her.

Her eyes wide, Sadrir appeared frightened for a moment before she forced her lips into another small grin. "If it pleases my lady, I will tend to the stone."

"Yes, it pleases me," Ami replied with her nose in the air. Removing her hand from the shell, she turned her attention to her hair. Lathering it, she focused on grooming herself, her thoughts turning to Piers and how he had thought to bring her brush for her.

Glancing at the gown that awaited her, she could tell the fine material matched that of the other maids of the elven city. She had toyed with the idea of being so well dressed when she had first contemplated running away from Nalen. Catching a fit of happy giggles, she chuckled to herself as she finished her bath and rinsed the soap away.

Climbing out, she dried with a long piece of fuzzy cloth that felt soft against her skin. Thinking she would be spoiled in such a palace, her laughter faded away as she considered the farm where she had grown up and the life she had always lived. *Damn them,* she cursed her almost parents and their lies. She had grown weary of the hurt their actions had brought her.

Once she had dried, she wrapped her hair in the absorbent material and set about putting on the layers of her clothing. A fine, silky set of undergarments went first, followed by a plain white under gown, and finally, the shimmering, colorful top one.

Staring down at herself, she felt amazed at the fit and the feel of her dream coming true. *I am a lady,* she sighed, with tears in her eyes. Hearing her maid return, she quickly wiped them away before she faced her. "Was he able to complete the task?" she asked, forgetting she would not be able to understand the response without the device.

When she turned to the girl, Sadrir held it out towards her. A small hole had been drilled into the edge, where the shell would have hinged against another, and a silver strand of ribbon had been placed through it. Tied in a simple knot, it would fit over her head, and she hid it beneath the front of her blouse, so that the merdoe nestled between her breasts.

"How is it?"

Understanding her clearly, Ami gasped, "I love it. It's perfect. I will never take it off." Laying her hand over it through the material that covered her body, the necklace made her think of Olirassa, and she sighed. Cilithrand may have tried to poison her against her aged friend, but she could not believe that such deception lay in the tiny woman who had saved their lives when they washed upon the shore.

Pushing the sad thought away, Amicia turned her back to her maid, presenting her next need to her. The back had a section of laces that would adjust the fit, and she explained, "I wasn't able to draw the string very well." Waiting, she could feel the small elf's hands as she tugged them with a firm pull and then tied the knot. Admiring herself once more, Ami sighed with contentment.

"Shall I show you to your suite then?" the girl asked, presenting her with a satin pair of slippers.

"Yes." Ami nodded, smiling genuinely. The thought of getting some rest overcame her, and she felt utterly exhausted, as if she hadn't really slept in months. Not since her mum had passed and her world had turned upside down the night she left Nalen in a ship full of men.

TWENTY-ONE

Elvish Desires

FREEING her hair from the soft towel, Ami's damp waves hung on her shoulders. She gave the curls a tussle, shaking them out as they dripped fine circles of moisture onto her new gown. A strong sense of wellbeing settled over her, and she sighed heavily, as if relaxing into the pleasant state.

Following her petite elven maid, Amicia left her secluded bath house with an air of confidence about her. Crossing the rock pathway, they entered a structure built from large stones via a tall arch. From there, a narrow case of stairs followed the wall immediately to her left, winding around the inside of the tower as it climbed.

Straight in front, a small door sat nestled beneath the case of steps. Offering no explanation for the room at the base of the tower, the elf maid led Amicia to the left, and they began their ascent towards the peak above them.

They wound around the inside of the tower in a tight circle, the left side made of wall and the right open to the floor below. The idea of it caused her heart to pound, and she kept to the inside and away from the edge for fear of toppling off and plummeting to her death.

As they climbed, step by step, Ami's dress floated around her. The sensation of air on her legs felt odd after wearing Bally's pants for so many days. The material made a swooshing noise as she moved, and she became caught up in the rhythm of it. Her heart fluttered as she pranced, her mood improved despite her reservations about their hosts.

Completing a round, they encountered a second door on the mountain side of the spiral. "What's in here?" Amicia paused to catch her breath on the small landing that belonged to the mysterious portal.

"Servant's quarters." Sadrir swished her fingers dismissively, obviously prepared to move on.

"Oh, we have neighbors." Ami raised her hand to knock on the flat surface. "I wish to meet them."

"My lady!" the small elf gasped, her brow furrowed by deep lines of horror. "The chambermaid and her husband care for the tower and your suite. Their station is beneath you! It would be best if we resumed our climb and you ignored their presence as any other noble-woman would do."

Her knuckles frozen with indecision, Amicia cut her eyes over at the shorter girl. "You suggest I should pretend they don't exist?"

"Yes, my lady," Sadrir replied, standing up straighter. Her chin slightly raised, she informed her guest, "Our towers are reserved for the highest of our nobility. To speak to the servants of your spire would be most frowned upon. If ever you have need of their services, you need simply ask, and I will direct them to your desires."

Puckering her lips, Ami considered the news, then slowly lowered her appendage. Lifting her skirt, she returned to her climbing while considering her options. She refused to give up on the idea of meeting those who lived in the tower, but she fully realized it would have to wait until the elf assigned to her had finished her task of delivering her to the suite above and gone on her way.

Making another full turn, they arrived at yet a third door, and Amicia sighed, seeing that the stairs continued, and they had not yet reached the top. "More servants?" she asked with a small scowl.

"Each level holds a single room designed for the upkeep of the tower. Your suite awaits us at the pinnacle," Sadrir finished, as if her words held a prodding to keep the girl moving.

"Fascinating." Ami resumed the steps with a small, satisfied smile.

Taking the next round of the staircase, her dress shimmered in warm light. The sun shone in through small windows in the outer wall, lighting the narrow flight of stairs. Watching as it moved with her, in waves of colored elegance, she felt pretty; almost beautiful. However, she was not accustomed to this type of physical demand and again became winded by the end of the turn.

Pausing on the landing of the next door, she could see the frustration on the smaller girl's face at her repeated stops. "I only need a moment," she assured, then indicated the newest room. "What's in here?"

"Supplies for your quarters, my lady." Sadrir uttered a small, anxious laugh at her curiosity. "It would be impractical to haul everything that you need at the top all the way up the stairs."

"You have a better way?" Ami asked in surprise.

"We have a pully and rope system inside." Freeing the latch, she opened the portal and allowed her mistress inside, confident she would be asked fewer questions if she got them all out of the way at once.

Stepping into the small chamber, Ami's jaw dropped in wonder. One wall housed a small box about three feet square and tall enough to stand on. Next to it, a tunnel that ran the height of the tower provided access to the ropes that could be used to raise and lower the small platform. It reminded her of the large hoist used on the boat to load the cargo into the hold but on a much smaller scale.

"This is genius," she observed. "You can bring up anything that you like?"

"Yes, food, clothing, furniture. We store the wood for your fire in the room below your suite, and rooms like this are for the other essentials," she assured, wafting her hand at the shelves stacked neatly with the aforementioned supplies.

"And all of the towers are arranged so," Amicia surmised.

The word noble-woman swam in the back of her mind, and a small ache formed in her gut that she had been referred to as such. She was a tradeswoman in truth, and no blood of nobility flowed in her veins as she was aware. The dishes and linens on the wall before her more lavish than she had ever laid eyes on, she felt the fear again that they did not belong within those walls, but only for a moment before she was overtaken by a renewed sense of peace and deep wellbeing.

"The towers are reserved for our most honored members of Jerranyth." Catching her skirt with her nimble fingers, the girl bobbed in a small curtsy.

Nodding, her curiosity satiated for the moment, Ami sighed. "Well then, let us view this suite."

Finishing the long climb, her heart beat faster with each round that they made. Passing the uppermost door, the one she had learned held wood for their fire, her thoughts filled with her refreshed state. The warmth of her activity made her head light, and she giggled aloud with a mild euphoric delirium overtaking her. She did make a more presentable young woman, she had to admit, and she briefly wondered if it would finally be enough to turn the Mate's head.

She had wanted to garner the attention of Piers Massheby since she met him and not the false courtship he had presented while they were with the sirens. Ami wanted to be with him; to know his love and the tenderness of his touch. By the time she reached the top, she felt confident her upgraded appearance would be her best chance yet to find her way into his heart.

She exited the case into a wide room, her cheeks flushed with anticipation. On the far wall, a fireplace sat inside the rock of the cliff, with a small log burning inside. To the left and right of it, narrow doors stood, two per side, each opening out into the room rather than in as a proper portal should. *The hinges are on the wrong side*, she observed.

In front of the fireplace, a heap of bags had been placed, and she recognized hers had been brought up as well. The others held less important items, at least for the moment, but she was grateful their belongings had been respected and returned to them at any rate.

Around the walls, small lamps burned, bathing the large area in light. In the center, a rug covered the floor, and a large round table filled the space. It held a grand appearance, with a crystal decoration hanging above it. She had heard of such opulent chandeliers, formed by many small clear gems strung together by fine thread, but like so many things she had discovered in the land of the elves, they had been far above her personal experience.

Observing the beauty of the crystal structure, she noted that small flames burned within the intricate design, casting dancing light on the hard wood of the shiny flat surface. The furniture appeared elegant, and a small cushion on the seat of each chair added the idea of comfort if she were to sit on one of them. "Oh my," she gasped, unable to hide the depth of her awe.

Still standing on the landing, she looked to her right, discovering a small balcony. Flanked on both sides by thick, dark green colored drapes, it had scarcely enough space for a single person to stand and peer out at the valley below. Turning towards it, she gripped the edge of the frame tightly with her right hand and slid her foot out to test the wooden flooring.

"I assure you it's quite sound," Sadrir informed her.

"Well, I want to be sure, don't I," Ami replied with a nervous giggle. Sidling out onto the ledge, she shifted her hold to the stone barrier that enclosed the small space. "Oh my God."

Below her, Amicia could see the whole of the land. They had been given one of the tallest spires, which towered above the trees below. Recalling looking up at them as they had approached, she smiled, not having anticipated being treated to such luxuries while in the house of the elves. "It's beautiful," she informed her hostess.

"Yes," Sadrir agreed with a small giggle at her trepidation. "Each of you has a bed chamber," she added, indicating the doors with an outstretched hand.

Turning, Ami looked at the three open portals again and then left the balcony to examine them further. The fourth door shut, she realized someone had arrived in their suite before her. "I hope that Oldrilin is well," she whispered, thinking of Rey and his mermaid friend.

Sounds echoed through the door for an instant, then vanished. Horrified, she instantly realized it had not been Rey who had arrived first, nor was the Mate alone in his new bed. Glancing at the girl next to her, Amicia knew she had guessed this fact as well.

"So, which one is mine?" Amicia grimaced, her voice loud as if she were announcing their presence to the couple they had discovered.

"You may have your choice of the three," her maid replied.

Leaving her, Ami marched across the common room to claim her bag, then chose the room that fell directly across from Piers's, as he had taken the first chamber on the left. With her on the right-hand wall, on the opposite side of the room, it was the farthest she could get from him and exactly where she wanted to be at the moment.

"I'll take this one," she announced, standing in the door frame to have a look inside. Straight in front of her, a small table with a single chair occupied the corner, each a simpler version of the large one that held the center of the common room. To the right, a full-length mirror stood on slender yet intricately adorned legs, and a bed filled the rest of the chamber.

She recalled the small, lumpy mattress she had slept upon every night of her life, or at least all of them before she left Nalen. This one, topped with a thick blanket and half a dozen small pillows, was no doubt made up with the fine linens she had seen in the rooms below and would be nothing like that which she was accustomed to.

"This will do fine." She tried to dismiss the girl, who had entered while she examined her new compartment.

Instead of leaving, Sadrir lit a small lamp on the wall to the right of the door and placed the striking stone back in its box on the shelf beneath the flame. Turning to the bed, she lifted the blanket and shook it, then laid it open and ready to be climbed into by exposing the luxurious sheets. Lastly, she fluffed a pillow, which sounded heavy when she dropped it back into place, as it was probably filled with feathers.

"Thank you," Ami said more quietly, while placing her pack on the table and wishing she had left the room in darkness. Waiting for her to leave, she felt torn.

Part of her wanted to present her clean, comely self to Piers, but the rest of her wanted to remove the gown and toss it aside in favor of the bed for at least a few days.

Across the suite, the door opened, and an elf maid pranced out. Her smile wide, she appeared more than satisfied with her visit to the Mate's quarters. However, she also seemed to be done with him, as she did not pause in the common room and made straight for the stairs and the exit below.

Stepping out of his room, Piers leaned against the rock wall next to his bedroom. His shirt off, his broad chest bare as it had been the first time she saw him, Amicia scowled when he grinned at her. "I guess you found your own elvish desires to while away the afternoon," he drawled, indicating her altered appearance with a few extended digits.

Ami could tell he was not impressed with her attire or her efforts to please him. "I was shown to the bath," she spat, lifting her chin as she spoke to him. "I see you didn't waste any time persuading one of them to join you for a tumble," she rebuked. "Quite a feat considering you don't speak elf."

He laughed loudly. "Persuaded, hardly. She practically dragged me up here. She had a couple of friends that seemed equally as eager, so I'm sure I won't be spending many nights alone here." His grin appeared almost evil as he twisted the knife in her fresh wound.

Clenching her jaw, Ami fought to maintain her control and to keep her lip from quivering. Her room empty and inviting, she reached for the handle to close the wooden covering just as Reynard and another maiden, the one who had led him away earlier, appeared on the landing. "Rey!" she squealed, momentarily distracted from her nap.

Crossing the short distance, she caught him by the arm, and he stared at her with wide eyes, taking in her elegant form. "Ami, you look so different," he whispered.

"Never mind that. How's Lin?" Her words sprinkled with excitement she did not feel, she seemed to have forgotten all about Piers and his mistress.

"She's resting." He smiled back at her, his exhaustion evident. "The sirens were not exaggerating the depth of the elvish powers of magical healing. I'll check on her again after dinner, but for now, I've been told to get some rest." Glancing at the other man, still half naked, he scowled.

He had passed a young brunette going down as he was being led up, and it didn't take much imagination to figure out what she had been doing there. Turning his attention back to Ami, he smiled broadly. "You look amazing, Amicia Spicer. Don't pretend like it's nothing. You deserve the compliment. A beautiful gown for a beautiful young woman."

Touching her long blond strands, the girl grinned shyly. "My hair's already out of control, but it felt good to wash it. I'll put it up before I lay down for a bit of sleep." Cutting her eyes over, she threw daggers at the older man as she walked to her chamber and closed her door behind her.

As soon as he heard the click of the latch, Rey crossed the three steps to stand before Piers with angry stomps. The two elves who had shown him and Ami up had departed, and the two men had the common room to themselves.

"Why the fuck are you so mean to her?" he demanded through clenched teeth.

His hands forming fists at his sides, he didn't care how big the older man was at the moment. He wanted to beat him just the same, or take a beating trying.

"I have no idea what you're talking about." The Mate bent over calmly, picking his shirt up off the floor and pulling it over his head to cover his tanned skin.

Rey refused to be ignored. "The hell you don't. You know how she feels about you!"

"Yeah, I know." Piers laughed, sauntering over to the balcony to have a peek outside.

"So, what's your problem?"

"My problem," the Mate repeated, puckering his lips as he scoured the terrain below. "The problem is, I'm twice her age, and I've done all that I could to make that clear. I'm not interested in becoming a husband, hers or anyone else's. I'm not going to change my mind, and she is wasting her time wishing for such a thing. And besides, if I take her up on her offer, she won't ever notice the way *you* look at her." He glanced at the other man, nodding. "I should think you would like for me to turn her away."

"I want her to be happy, Mate." Rey frowned, his voice dripping with sorrow. "I hate to see the way it hurts her when you make it clear you don't care."

Turning his back squarely, Piers gripped the stone railing before him tightly. Rage flowed through him, but the last thing he wanted was to set it against the younger man. Inhaling deeply, he breathed out in a calming breath.

"You think having some young elf for a night is better than her?" Reynard pushed.

The Mate laughed. "Aye. I've been here what, a few hours, and I already have one conquest to my name? I assure you, I intend to have my fill of lovely elven maids while we are here, and if you and the princess don't like it, I suggest you ask for different quarters," he sneered, pushing past the other man and stomping down the stairs.

Watching the back of his head disappear, Rey sighed heavily. Glancing around the large room, it didn't take much to figure out they each had a room for themselves. Assuming the one the first mate had been in would be his, and Ami had hers, he and Bally would each get one that flanked the fireplace.

Deciding to take the one on the right and next to her, he paused at Amicia's door. Standing before it, he raised his hand, placing his fingers gently against the smooth surface. On the other side, he could hear her noises; sniffles and a soft whine.

He wished that he could open the portal and offer his comfort, but she clearly wanted to be alone. Besides, the Mate had told him his first night in their camp that one day she would be his. Piers probably meant it, as he obviously didn't mind torturing their companion with his insolence.

Lowering his hand, he had intended to have a nap before dinner, but instead he could hear Baldwin coming up the stairs, laughing loudly. "Bally," he snapped, meeting him at the top. "Ami is getting some rest, so shh!"

"Aye, sorry." The younger man chortled, presenting his new friend. "Rey, this is Animir."

"Hello," Rey greeted, then remembered the language barrier. "How have you been talking to him?"

"We've been making do," Bally said with a grin, looking around and inspecting their suite with wide eyes. "This place is great!" he announced his approval as he arrived at the door on the right of the fireplace.

"That's my room," Rey snapped, pointing to the other one. "That's yours. Where have you been?"

"We visited the armory." Bally shrugged, still inspecting their accommodations. "Animir is one of the caretakers. They have lots of weapons, bows and swords. All sizes, too."

Studying the young elf, Rey scowled. "So why is he still here?"

"Friends," Animir offered with a firm nod, placing his hand flat against his chest to indicate himself.

His mouth dropping open, Rey gasped, "You've been teaching him to speak our tongue?"

"Aye, he wanted to learn." Baldwin trotted out of his room and took a seat in one of the chairs, turning it so that it faced the fire and trying out the cushion. "This place is nice. Did you see how high up we are? Higher than the tallest mast!"

"I know how high up we are," Rey agreed, still staring at the elf. "What else did you teach him?"

"Just some words," Bally mumbled, indicating for his new friend to take a seat. "Sit down," he enunciated, pointing at a chair.

"Sit down," Animir parroted, doing as he had been instructed.

Shaking his head, Rey laughed out loud, then recalled that Amicia was still in her room, presumably sulking. "I'm going to get a nap. You guys hold it down and do not disturb her," he commanded, pointing at her door before closing his own.

Kicking off his boots, he stretched out on his bed and admired the softness of it. He had never slept in such a comfortable place, or at least he couldn't remember it if he ever had. The room pitch black, he sighed.

The Mate was a cruel man, toying with Amicia the way that he did, but in the end, he was right. In time, he would get a chance to court her, and if Piers had to break her heart before that happened, at least he could be the man to help her mend the pieces.

TWENTY-TWO

Magical Lands

THE SUNLIGHT SHINING from the balcony and into the room had all but disappeared when Reynard left his chamber. Stretching, he groaned loudly at the pleasure it gave him. Days and weeks and months had it been since he had slept well, or so it seemed.

Looking round the expanse of the room, the air felt damp and cool in the fading light. *No wonder they keep a fire*, he observed. Drawing the heavy drapes that hung at the sides of the narrow opening, he blocked out the remaining sun and the cool air at the same time. No one else stirred, and from the two open doors on the opposite wall, he deduced that the other men were already below.

Facing the one that shared his side of the tower, he approached on silent steps, knocking faintly. Waiting, he listened. When she did not reply, he knocked a little more firmly and twisted the handle. The latch clicked as he opened it, inching it towards him and peeking into the blackness.

"Amicia," he whispered hoarsely.

Nothing.

Pulling the door open, he stepped in and waited for his eyes to adjust to the dim stream that barely illuminated the room. On the table before him, he could make out her personal items, and her bag hung from the back of the chair. "Ami," he said more firmly.

"What do you want?" She lay on her side beneath the covers, holding a pillow to her chest and resting her face against it.

Creeping forward, the shadows hid her features. Seeing that he had room to sit, he took part of the mattress. "It's time for dinner. We haven't had a good meal in days," he reminded her.

"I'm not hungry."

"Yes, you are!" he laughed in retort. "Your body is, anyway."

Cutting her soft green eyes up at him, she only stared.

"Come on. I'll help you dress," he offered, pulling at her blanket.

"I really don't want to go down." She sniffed, hiding her tears in the shadows.

"I know," he agreed, fully understanding why. "But sometimes we have to do things we don't want to do, and this is one of those times, Amicia."

Growling, she sat up, pulling herself to the edge of the bed and sitting beside him. "Piers is really an ass."

"I know," he said again, nodding. "But it's ok, love." He paused, rubbing her back firmly through her undergarments and noticing the hair she had dutifully pulled into a braid before she lay down. "You are going to go down and have a very good time with our new friends."

"I'm not so sure about that." She grimaced, getting to her feet.

"Well, you'll have a good time if I have any say in the matter," he joked.

"That's not the part I doubt," she replied, her voice not changing as she spoke. "It's the elves. I have my doubts about their intentions."

Standing to help her slip the first layer on, Reynard ignored the comment. He knew that she hurt; her heart and spirit had taken a beating. Her attitude would improve after she had some time to heal, and a good meal wouldn't hurt either.

Lifting the gown, he held it above her head, and she raised her arms, slipping them in and then adjusting the material into place. His fingers agile, he pulled the laces in the back and tied them, then stepped back to admire her slender form. "You really are beautiful," he breathed.

"You can't even see me." She chuckled in the dim light.

"I see you," he insisted, absently brushing the side of her head with the backs of his fingers.

Catching her braid, she bit her lip. "You like it down, don't you?"

"Aye, like a golden halo," he assured her.

Pulling the tie loose, she unwound the braid. Picking up her brush from the table, she informed him, "I can smooth it all out, but it will be all over the place before dinner is over."

He grinned at the thought of it. "I know, I love it that way."

Shaking her head, she finished the chore and pronounced herself ready to go. Pausing at one of the chairs in the common room, she slipped her feet into the cloth slippers and then followed as he led her down the stairs.

On the ground a few minutes later, the couple exited the tower and looked around at the streets and paths lit by small lamps scattered along the way. They could hear the noise of people, and followed the sound towards the palace, where the queen had greeted the girl earlier that day.

When they arrived at the fountain at the center of the square, the maid who had tended to her before met them and announced, "Oh, my lady, I was coming to see to you!"

"I have been seen to," Ami replied, reaching for Rey's arm.

Allowing her to take it, the man next to her inquired, "Does she know how Oldrilin is doing?"

Sadrir smiled. "The siren is resting. I am to take you to the great hall for the dinner."

"She said she's ok, and we are going to some banquet, I think."

"A banquet." His stomach growled at the thought of a fine meal. "They really have welcomed us here."

"I know." Ami frowned. "That's what has me so concerned."

Following the elf maid, they took the left set of stairs into the palace area and arrived a moment later at a great hall that had no roof. There, three tables sat facing the doors in a great "U" with the floor between wide open; enchanting with the stars above it. The one at the far end obviously the head table, the queen sat at the center of it, and servants passed in and out from the doors on that end of the structure.

Joining them at that moment, Piers growled, "Is this fancy enough for you?"

"It's exquisite," Amicia breathed. "I've never even dreamed of such an occasion as this."

"And I've seen far too many of them," the older man bit tartly. Turning around, he swore under his breath and then walked away, appearing to be in a hurry. Pursuing him, a tall slender elf with long brown hair caught him as he made the turn to walk behind the left side table.

Laughing, Rey observed, "How do you like that?"

"Like what?" Ami frowned, noticing the chummy way that the Mate and the elf seemed to interact.

"That's the girl he had in our suite today," he informed her.

"Is it? I hadn't noticed," she lied flatly.

"Come on. You know what this means?"

"I have no idea."

"It means, he got her into bed, and now he wants to move on to the next conquest. Only, she's not letting him get away that easy!"

Watching the pair, she could see that he did seem to be making an effort to remove himself from her grasp. Giggling spastically, Ami agreed, "It looks that way, doesn't it." The Mate had stated he intended to make as many new female friends as possible while they were there. The fact he had run into a snag amused her, and she laughed a little more fully.

Rey chuckled with her and the couple were still at it when Anerion joined them, presenting his elbow for her to take. "My lady," he announced. "I'm here to see you to your seat."

"Oh, thank you." She beamed up at him, clinging to Rey and snubbing the offer. "He's going to show us to our seats, love."

Glaring at her, Anerion did not lower the appendage. Instead, he indicated the head table. "Your seat is next to my queen, Lady Cilithrand."

"Oh! We are at the head table!" she gasped in surprise.

"Only you, my lady," he said, his meaning clear as he glared at the other man.

Picking up on his dismissal, Rey removed her fingers from his flesh. "Go sit with the queen, love," he whispered in her ear. "I'll sit at a side table and enjoy the view."

"What view?" she clipped, angry that he would abandon her.

"You, of course!" He laughed, pushing her towards the elf. "I wouldn't be able to see you if you were next to me, now would I?"

Rolling her eyes, she accepted her new guide. Walking slowly beside him with her beautiful gown flowing around her ankles, the room grew quiet as they passed through the center of the wide floor between the tables. Making their way around the end, she was taken to the center and given the seat to the queen's left hand.

Glancing around the room anxiously, she could see that Rey had been true to his word and sat between two elf maids not far from the close end of the left side table; twenty yards away at most. Accepting her chair, she sank down next to Cilithrand, who greeted her warmly.

"And how was your bath?"

Her royal voice dripped with honey, but it grated on the girl's nerves, sending chills up her spine. "It was splendid," Ami replied, forcing a large, fake smile.

"I am pleased to hear it," the queen said softly. Waving her hand to a servant, the elves began carrying out food and placing the platters on the tables. Serving the plates, those who sat at the banquet feasted happily.

Looking up and down the long, flat surfaces, Ami's eyes grew wide. It almost appeared that the elves were in fact two different races of beings. Tall and slender sat at the tables, being waited upon. *And smaller versions do the serving.*

Working up her nerve, she finally asked, "Are all of you elves?"

"Yes, of course we are," the queen replied stiffly. Taking a sip from her wine, her smile did not reach her eyes. Glancing around, she appeared to be considering her response before she explained, "We of the ruling house have a certain look about us, I guess you could say."

"Your size," Amicia supplied.

"Yes, that is part of it," Cilithrand agreed. "You are in a magical land now, Amicia Spicer. Forget the rim of mortals and open yourself to that which is yours."

"That which is mine," the girl breathed, the air hanging in her chest as if it refused to come out. Her brow furrowed, she said quietly, "I assure you, I have no magic." Instantly, her hand shot up and lay over the merdoe that hung within her cleavage. "Are you talking about the shell?"

"To use magic requires a certain degree of ability, that is all." The queen smiled faintly, confident her suspicions about the young woman were sound. The frail being next to her would be no match in combat, and she would easily be molded as Cilithrand saw fit.

Turning her attention to her meal, the older woman dropped the conversation, instead plying the girl with interesting and trivial facts about her home, the forest, and the mountain on which they had built their realm. Then, when most of the diners had completed the meal, she called loudly, "Bring in the dancers," clapping her hands twice as she did so.

"Dancers?" Amicia asked, a hint of curiosity tickling her from within.

Leaning back in her high-backed chair, the queen raised her hands. Her robes hanging from her arms, the light shone through the thin layers of material that covered them. "These are our entertainment." Cilithrand indicated the two streams of the miniature elves pouring out from the side doors that lay at the ends of the head table.

Guessing none of the new group to be more than four feet tall, Ami gasped, "They're so tiny!"

"Yes, they come from a long line of performers. We all have our place here in Jerranyth." A smile twisted her lips as the queen explained her minions.

In the center of the room, the two lines flowed around the room, one group all wearing pure white gowns and robes, while the other wore black. Forming a moving circle, the two groups bobbed over and under, around and through, in a spectacular display of twirls and spins that sent their gowns swirling and flowing around them.

"It must have taken them days to learn to do that!"

"Years," the queen corrected, leaning closer to her guest. "This is their task. They are born to be a dancer, and work for many years before they are old enough and skilled enough to take the floor of the great hall."

Before them, the dance had changed. Some of the elves had removed their gowns and wore next to nothing as they pranced around in the cool, evening air. Running, leaping, and twisting, they performed stunts like none of the four humans had ever witnessed. The strength in their arms and legs impressive, their need to train for years appeared obvious.

"They're amazing," Ami agreed, watching with a slack jaw. Glancing over at Rey, she coughed. He sat at his table, leaning on it with his elbows and stroking his beard, his clear hazel eyes not on the entertainment at all. True to his word, he was watching her. Smiling, she offered a small wave, which he returned, his bony wrist exposed as his shirt only covered about two-thirds of his arm.

Turning her attention back to the queen and her minions, Ami tried not to think about Rey and his apparent infatuation with her. Why was it she never felt drawn to men who were drawn to her? Thinking of Rupert, she giggled for a moment, then realized it might be considered rude to laugh during the elves' display.

Her eyes darting to the right, she caught sight of Piers, his new female friend sitting beside him. *I guess he wasn't able to get away, yet*, she surmised. Her eyes skimming over the crowd, she finally located Bally, only he had not been seated at a table during the feast.

Standing against the far wall with a small group of males, he appeared happy, chatting away with them. Shaking her head, she wondered what he could possibly be saying to a group of people who had no way to reply to him.

The thought made her laugh again, but she kept it to herself. If there was anything she had learned about Baldwin Carter, it was that. The man could carry on a conversation with a rock if that were all that were available to listen and getting a reply did not seem high on his list of priorities.

The group of dancers performed for what seemed like hours, but in reality, it had not been nearly so long. When they had finished, the party broke up with elves separating into their smaller groups and heading for their beds.

"You will visit me tomorrow, in my palace," Cilithrand decreed as she stood. "I will send my maid, Sadrir, for you early."

"Yes, your majesty," Ami replied, bowing her head respectfully. Getting to her feet, she scurried over to Rey, who had not seemed to take his eyes off of her for a single second.

"You could have at least watched the show," she informed him. "Or pretended that you were."

"I was." He laughed at being caught, taking her hand and guiding her through the crowd. "Since we both had a nap, I was hoping you might accompany me for a visit with Oldrilin before we turn in."

"Oh, I would love to!"

"Good, then let's go back to the fountain. I know the way from there," he supplied, tugging her along as they left the rest of their party behind to fend for themselves.

However, once they had made the turn and climbed the stairs, a tall elf blocked their path. "What are you doing here?" he demanded, looking them up and down.

"We've come to visit the siren," Amicia informed him curtly, not liking the sound of his attitude. "We won't stay long, we promise."

"You are not permitted," he clipped, shifting to block their path more fully.

"I am the queen's guest," she huffed. "Lin is our friend, and we demand to see her!"

Pulling at her arm, Rey whispered, "Perhaps there is another way around."

"There is no other entrance," the guard spat. "Would you like an escort to your quarters?"

"We know the way," Ami replied with less bravado than she had previously managed. Turning her back, she slipped her hand into Rey's. "I'm not sure what to do," she confessed.

Arriving back at the fountain, they found Bally standing there with his new friends. "Hey, guys!" he called, trotting over to greet them warmly. "Why the long faces?"

"We wanted to visit with Oldrilin, but a guard wouldn't let us in," Rey informed his young companion. Glancing over at Ami, he could feel the anger radiating from her.

"Well, I'll get Animir to get us in tomorrow," Bally told them confidently.

"Do you think he will?" the girl asked doubtfully, noticing the elves had not followed and had disappeared instead.

"Sure he will! He's shown me all over this place." The boy proudly puffed out his chest as he spoke. "And he's teaching me elf!"

"Teaching you elf." Rey laughed, not really sure what to make of the odd pair the two younger men made. "Ok, tomorrow we'll go and see her at first light."

"I can't." Ami sighed, ambling towards their building and the long climb to their suite. "I have to meet with the queen early."

"Meet with the queen, what for?" Bally asked in surprise.

"I don't know," she groaned. "I only spent a few minutes with her today. And during dinner, it felt more like she was evaluating me than anything else. Like I was being tested for something." Arriving at the entrance, the three mounted the stairs.

"Anyway," she continued when they had reached the top, "I'm going to bed. And you should do the same," she stated firmly, pulling her door behind her. *If this turns out like I feel that it might, we are all going to need to be rested and ready*, she thought as she removed her dress and prepared to slip back into her bed. For what they should be ready for, she wasn't sure.

TWENTY-THREE

Shadows of Doubt

LIGHT CREPT into Rey's room when he awoke the following morning, seeping in from around the cracks in his door. Watching the dust floating for a long moment, he decided he'd better get moving and see if Animir were as good a friend as Bally made him out to be. Pulling on his pants, he carried his boots and shirt out into the common room, where Piers sat slumped in one of the chairs, holding his head.

"What the hell happened to you?" he demanded, when the older man didn't move.

"Elven wine, and plenty of it," the Mate sneered, looking up at him while still holding his forehead.

"Aye, I saw you still had your elf girlfriend at dinner last night." Rey chuckled at the recollection. Pulling his shirt on, he glanced at Ami's door.

"She's already gone," Piers informed him. "That little elf maid came at first light to get her. As far as the girl, I couldn't shake her, so I made the best of it. Wasn't near as good the second time. I'm sure I won't see her again."

"Oh." Rey's lips scrunched as he pulled on the boots. "What about Bally?"

"Haven't seen him yet. You might check his bed. He's either still in it, or he left before the ass crack of dawn."

"Boy, you're in a foul mood," Rey bit angrily, standing to check their youngest member's quarters. Spying the dark shocks of hair peeking from under his blanket, he called, "Hey! We've got places to go!"

The other man didn't move, so he went in and smacked the hair playfully. "Hey, princess! You're the last one still in bed. Let's get a move on, will ya?"

"Ok," Bally whined, "ok." Pushing himself up on stiff arms, he growled, "First time in forever I've got no chores and nothing to do, and you're dragging me out anyway."

"I need to see Oldrilin. After that, you can go lay around wherever you like," Rey replied softly.

Not arguing, Bally climbed out of the bed and searched for his clothes. A few minutes later, they exited the suite, Piers still sitting in front of the fire with his face in his hands.

"What's with him?" Baldwin asked once they were out of earshot.

Rey chuckled. "Woman troubles. They like him for some odd reason."

Walking down the path, they crossed the square and took the stairs that led to the armory. Animir had taken him there the day before, as he helped see to their supply of swords and bows, and he hoped to find the young elf and discern if he could get them in to see the siren.

Entering a long, narrow corridor, Rey stopped dead in his tracks. "This is the armory?" he gasped, staring at the two long walls lined with weapons. Swords and spears along his left shown brightly in the morning sun. On the right, hundreds of bows with thousands of arrows.

"Yeah. Animir helps make the arrows." Bally beamed at his friend smugly. "He's probably this way." He continued along the path, waving for him to follow.

Exiting the other end, Animir was indeed in the next section, where a small group of elves were stoking a fire and preparing their forge.

"Don't they have enough weapons?" Rey growled.

"I guess not." Bally laughed off the observation, waving at his new friend when they made eye contact.

Joining them, Animir smiled pleasantly, despite the comment about their level of armament. "Hello," he said as clearly as any mortal of the rim would have.

"Hi," Bally replied cheerfully, indicating the taller man with his thumb. "We were hoping you could help us visit Rey's mermaid friend today."

Nodding, the elf smiled. "Yes, for Bally." Waving his hand for them to follow, they headed back through the tunnel of death and arrived a few minutes later at the stairs where they were blocked the last time.

Following behind, a knot formed in Reynard's gut as he approached the chamber where his small friend lay in their care. The guard from the night before had been replaced with another equally menacing looking elf, who glowered at them as they approached.

This time, however, they had a friend, and Animir set in right away, waving a hand around as he explained their situation. After a few exchanges, he smiled, and the guard stepped aside. Beckoning them to follow, he led them into the small structure where the elven nurse greeted him, her eyes wide with surprise.

After another brief exchange, they were taken into a small room where the siren lay in a bed, covered up to her chest with a thin blanket. Her arms lying on top of it, she appeared peaceful as she slept, and tears stung Rey's eyes as he made his way around to the far side of the bed. He knelt beside her, lifting her tiny hand and folding it between his.

Looking at each other in wonder, the pair of elves had been surprised by his demeanor. Poking Bally in the arm, Animir indicated him with an open palm.

"Oldrilin saved his life," Baldwin explained, smiling down at his best friend. "They saved us all, really, when we arrived here, only he was the worst. Lin nursed him back to health."

Rey had formed a bond with the siren who had followed him around after he had healed. It might have seemed odd or even wrong to the outsiders, but it would never be so to him. She was a small, defenseless creature in his eyes, childlike in so many ways. Innocent, and he would do all that he could to protect her if the need should ever arise.

"Is she going to be ok?" Rey asked quietly, wiping at his cheeks before he looked up at her nurse.

Swallowing, the girl nodded.

Grinning, Rey lifted the miniature hand, kissing the back of it gently. "You hear that, Lin?" He laughed, realizing as soon as he said it that no words had actually been spoken. But that didn't matter, the meaning had been clear. "You're going to be ok," he whispered, folding her arm across her chest and patting it gently before sitting back flat on the floor to watch her sleep.

Sadrir had arrived early and helped Amicia put on her dress. Frowning at the process and tired of the fancy attire, she asked, "When do I get my other clothes back?"

Staring at her with wide eyes, the maid stammered, "I will see if they have been washed."

Holding the dark expression, Ami doubted that they had and suspected she would never see them again, much to her dismay. As unhappy as she had been the day she put them on, they were a part of her now, and wearing the gown had lost its luster, no matter how beautiful it was.

Following her down the stairs, the morning air felt cool against her skin, and she realized that summer was coming to an end. Figuring they were farther north than Nalen, she pondered exactly how cold it would get here, especially up on the side of the mountain, as they were.

Strolling into the main stairs of the palace, the guards allowed them passage without a second glance. Only this time, they did not follow the corridors to the great hall. Instead, they made a right turn and ended up in a small private dining room that displayed the rising sun through its wall of windows.

"Good morning." The queen greeted her guest with the always present warmth her eyes never reflected.

Watching her, Ami didn't bother with her own fake smile. The other woman held a plate and selected fruits from a long table filled with options. "You're serving yourself this morning, I see."

Cilithrand laughed. "Of course. I'm not helpless. Besides, it's the best way to ensure I get exactly the ones that I want." She picked out a few grapes and added the to her pile. "Come. Join me," she commanded, indicating the second plate intended for her.

Doing as she had been instructed, Amicia felt tired of whatever game they were playing. The queen was up to something; she felt it in her gut. What was worse, none of her companions seemed to notice anything was wrong with their being there, or with the reception they had received.

Placing a few items on her dish, she carried it over to her seat at the round table the queen occupied by a window. Sitting, she glanced out at the streets below and could see the length of forest beyond the city walls. "You chose a beautiful place to build your palace," she observed.

"Thank you, but I didn't choose it. My father built this realm. I only inherited it after he was killed in the great war," the older woman supplied.

"Oh, that's too bad," Ami replied, feeling awkward. She had never known her parents, not her real ones, and those that had raised her had lied to her for her entire life. "How long have you been the queen?" she asked, hoping to change the flow of the conversation.

"Almost two hundred years." The number caused the girl to choke.

Two glasses sat on the table before her, one of sweet juice and one of water. Opting for the water, she hoisted it, gulping it before she wiped her mouth on her arm. "You're talking actual years, or per twelve moons?"

"They are almost the same, are they not?"

"Almost," Ami agreed, discerning that they did have knowledge of the outside world and the rim of mortals as they were called by those of Eriden. Pausing, her heart skipped a beat. *Mortals.* What if the people of this kingdom really did live forever?

Sipping her beverage more slowly, the girl considered how she might find out without bluntly asking. Deciding to leave it alone, she asked instead, "Do you like running the kingdom?"

"Oh, I don't head the kingdom." Cilithrand chuckled at her innocence. "The Supreme Dragon, King Gwirwen oversees Eriden. I am the queen of the elves. Jerranyth is our realm, and I see to its wellbeing."

"As Olirassa is the queen of the sirens, of Riran," Amicia construed, her nerves raw at the mention of the dragons. *In charge, no less.* "How many realms are there, then? I guess you would all be like townships, and you are perhaps the sheriff or maybe the lordship."

"I am the queen," her host corrected. "There are three realms here in the south, all led by queens. But we rule by the dragon's approval. When Gwirwen came to the throne some years ago, he torched the third southern realm. I'm sure they have suffered greatly since his rise to power."

Amicia stared at her, almost certain the news she had shared held some deeper meaning, but exactly what she could not say, at least not at the moment. "Perhaps we will meet them, then. Which way is it to their realm?"

The elf queen cackled. "The nymphs and satyrs! Silly girl, why would you ever wish to leave the comfort of Jerranyth? Stay with us, and I will crown you my princess," she offered, her smile in place as she did so.

Her skin tingling, Ami did her best to hold the feeling of dread from leaking onto her features. "Of course, your highness," she offered. Diverting the conversation, she asked, "Who were you fighting then, in the great war. The one that took your father." She swallowed visibly, an odd taste forming in her mouth, as if something from the queen's table had not agreed with her.

"Well, the whole of the land, really. That is why it is called the great war. Some of the realms had wanted to overthrow the dragons while others wanted to keep them in power."

Her heart racing, Amicia wanted to ask about the dragons directly but feared the other woman's response to the news that they had been hunted by them long before they got anywhere close to Eriden. Her mind drawn to the ship and the night it went down in fiery flames, she shuddered uncontrollably.

"My child, what is wrong with you?"

"I was just thinking about the dragon," she confessed.

"You have seen one," the matron supplied.

Her eyes wide, Ami nodded. "Yes, I have. The ones that tore apart Riran. The reason we are cowering here instead of still there with the sirens." She thought of the orb of truth and what she had been shown the day before, when they first arrived there. Folding her hands into her lap, she waited for whatever else the queen might divulge.

However, the other woman did not offer any tidbit of information and instead focused on her meal. After a few minutes, she said quietly, "Do finish, my sweet. It is many hours until dinner."

Nodding, Ami selected a few slices of something resembling an apple and nibbled at them obediently, her mind turning all the while. The queen seemed content, but the girl felt certain it was an act for her benefit. *What if she can read my thoughts? What if she already knows all that I know?*

At that moment, Cilithrand looked up at her, dabbing her mouth with a napkin. "Let us be honest with one another," she implored.

Ami's heart raced. *Shit.* Aloud, she asked, getting to the point, "Can you read my mind?"

The queen burst into a boisterous giggle. "Don't be silly, my child." Cutting her eyes over at the girl, she lowered her voice. "We are not connected in such a way. However, in time, I believe that we could be."

Ami's hand instinctively covered her breast and the merdoe hidden beneath it. "Tell me about the magic," she breathed.

"It's quite simple, really," the older woman supplied, sitting up straighter in her chair. "There are those in the Kingdom of Eriden who have the power to use it. We can store it in objects, such as the gift Olirassa saw fit to bestow upon you. And those who can use and release that power."

"A wielder of magic," Ami whispered, her pulse thumping loudly in her ears. "But not everyone."

"No, not everyone." The queen cut her eyes over to observe her guest's reaction.

Amicia's thoughts cleared, but she could not bring herself to speak the words. *I am a wielder of magic.* How and why, she did not know, but her use of the enchanted shell had exposed her to the queen.

"Do not fear me, my sweet," Cilithrand implored. "I will not harm you. You are welcome in my home and my realm for as long as you desire it."

"What about my friends? Are they equally as welcome?"

"Of course!" The queen held up her hands, her sleeves falling and exposing her smooth, pale flesh. "They may stay within our walls and fulfil their every desire."

Her heart thumping, Ami twisted her words, searching for the truth within them.

The queen had offered her protection for as long as they wanted to stay, but what if they wanted to leave?

Calming her features, Amicia forced her lips into a small grin, holding it in place as she acquiesced to the matron, "Thank you, your majesty. You have made us all welcome here, and we humbly accept your hospitality."

TWENTY-FOUR

Enemy of Time

WALKING BACK TO THEIR SUITE, Amicia searched her discoveries slowly in her mind. Each step of the tower a torture, she ached with the knowledge that she and her friends were not safe in Jerranyth, but at the moment they had no way to escape and nowhere to run. That fact clear in her mind, she knew she could not share too much with the others.

Arriving at the top, the common room opened before her. To her right, the drapes to the balcony were tied back out of the way. His back to her, Rey stood upon it, staring out across the realm.

"Hello." He greeted her simply, without turning around.

"What's going on?" she demanded, terror instantly sending her heart racing.

"Nothing," he replied as he pivoted to face her. "I spent the morning with Oldrilin." His face placid, his demeanor only added to her fear.

"How is she?" she asked, the air caught in her lungs as she waited for the words she dreaded to hear.

"She hasn't awoken yet, but her wounds are looking better," he stated calmly, placing his hands in his pockets. He blinked at her a few times, but said nothing else, which only added to his confusing manner.

"Then why the gloom?" She laughed, gasping for her breath. "You scared the hell out of me, as if something had happened to one of us!"

The word *us* brought a hint of a smile to his tired features. No matter what lay ahead, the four of them had formed a bond, and they would be there for each other; he was confident of that. If all went well, they would number five soon enough, the thought bringing a sigh of relief.

"No, we are all fine, as far as I know. And she will be fine as well. All she needs is time," he supplied.

Time. The word had Amicia's thoughts swirling once more. *That's what we don't have. Time.* "She'll get better then," she verbally agreed with a firm nod.

"Who'll get better?" Piers asked, appearing at the top of the stairs and pausing to stand with the couple. "The siren?"

His contempt for the creature clear, he had never accepted the mermaids, even after they had done what they could for them when the group had been washed up on their shore. That is why he had insisted on building their camp in the woods; to get out of Riran and away from them as much as he was able. It was unlikely he would ever trust the one that traveled with them now.

"I know you don't approve, so don't even bother." Rey calmly held up a palm to stop him there. However, grateful for the interruption and the chance to poke a little fun, he grinned. "What's going on with you? Your elf still following you around?" The older man looked better than he did that morning, he had to admit.

"Why no, she isn't." The Mate beamed, leaving them to head into his room. There, he announced, "Good. That servant girl brought my water." Pouring it from the pitcher into a basin that had been placed on his table, he washed his face and wet his hair, then pulled it into its customary knot and secured it at the nape of his neck. Wiping his hands over his jaw to smooth his long stubble, he held the perfect combination of gentleman and rogue in his appearance.

"Why don't you go down and have a bath?" Ami wrinkled her nose at his choice. "The pools are lovely," she added persuasively.

"I asked for a bath, and the girl said she would bring this," he stated flatly, indicating the bowl of soiled liquid. "Apparently, the pools aren't for everyone." Scowling, his eyes flicking up and down her fancy attire, he grunted, "Besides, I don't have time. I haven't seen Cothiel all morning, and it appears that I'm again a free man. Therefore, I'm going to move on to the next one."

"Are you sure you're rid of her?" Reynard raised his eyebrow doubtfully.

"Pfft. She thinks I'm a drunkard, so I'm pretty sure she won't be back. I guess all that wine I drank was good for something."

Shaking her head and hiding a faint smile, Ami left the two men and crossed to her room. There on her table sat Bally's clothes, neatly folded. Relieved to see them, she lifted the shirt to ensure it was in good condition, then touched her sweater fondly. Recalling the small siren Rey had carried wrapped within it, her heart ached. What would they do if she didn't make it?

Taking a deep breath, she pushed the dark mood aside. Lin had to get better. There was no other option she could accept, and she would make the best of their situation until the newest member of their party was well enough to travel and they could flee.

Looking down at her dress, she knew she would continue to wear it, despite the return of her other garments. She didn't want to create an issue with the elves by disrespecting their customs, but at least she had the outfit she would don when they left that beautifully wretched place.

Refolding the items, she left them on her table. Returning to the central location, she discovered that the Mate had exited in pursuit of a fresh conquest, and Rey sat alone in one of the chairs, looking forlorn. Standing next to him, she ran her fingers lightly over his hair to toy with the loose ringlets that hung down to cover his face. "We should go for a walk," she announced quietly.

"Thanks." He peeked up at her, his cheeks flushed at her casual caress. "I know you're trying to cheer me up."

"Absolutely, I am," she replied, kneeling beside him and leaning against the armrest. "We're friends, aren't we?" Staring into his hazel eyes, she could see a darkness within them, almost brooding. Something troubled him deeply, and it would take a bit of cunning to discern what.

"Always," he agreed, patting the back of her hands and producing a smile. Standing, his motions stiff, he indicated the exit with a wave of his hand. "After you."

Smiling up at him, she led the way, but at the top of the stone passage, she paused, the hesitation clear on her delicate features. "You go first. I insist," she stated breathily, wafting a hand at them as casually as she could muster.

"Are you afraid of the stairs?" He laughed at the prospect, taking a few steps ahead of her.

"No, just the fall," she replied with a giggle as he led the way down and she followed, trailing the wall with the tips of her fingers to keep it close.

Descending single file with Reynard in front, Ami watched the back of the man before her. He slouched, dragging his feet, and she could see the tiredness in his thin frame. *Perhaps he is aware of our precarious position and equally unwilling to speak of it,* she mused. If he were her ally, convincing the others would be considerably easier when the time came, and that thought pleased her.

Reaching the bottom, her resolve to cheer him doubled. Slipping her fingers into his, she grasped him firmly. Guiding him down the path, away from the palace, her long gown floated around her ankles as she walked beside him, lightening her mood. A small grin reached her lips, and she felt genuinely at peace in his company.

Elves came and went, but no words passed between them as they sauntered along. Swinging their hands gently, Amicia enjoyed the comfortable silence, and a large smile covered her face when they made the last turn and entered a magical garden attached to the one containing the bath springs.

"What is this place?" Rey inhaled deeply, sensing a change in the air as they entered through a gap between two large hedges. About ten feet in height, the wall of greenery shielded the plot from the path, effectively ensuring their visit there would be private to all but those in the towers looking down.

"This is part of the Sacred Gardens of Jerranyth," she explained, releasing him as he pulled ahead of her. His eager excitement visible, he skipped from plant to plant, inspecting the various blooms.

"They're like the flowers near the sirens' waterfall," he observed.

"Yes, very similar. They hold an ethereal quality, and their nectar is precious to the elves."

"Sounds ominous." Reynard laughed anxiously. "Ghost flowers. Haunted… or cursed."

"Are you afraid of the queen?" Eyeing him warily, Ami dared to ask at his interpretation of her meaning.

Turning to look at her, Rey's lips puckered as he formulated a response. However, before he could speak, their moment was interrupted by the maid who cared for Oldrilin, who burst through the opening in the shrubs and jogged towards them.

"My lady," the girl gasped, out of breath from her quickened pace to get there. "The siren, Oldrilin. She is awake and has asked for you to visit her bedside."

"Oh my God!" Amicia squealed, grasping Rey's arm and squeezing it with joy, "we'll discuss it later, love! Lin is awake and asking for us!"

The announcement scattered his thoughts, and he fell into step beside her as they left the enchanted space. Their pace much faster on the return trip, they passed their tower and then the fountain on the way to the infirmary, but no elf stood guard to block them from entering.

Instead, they were shown to the small room that the mermaid had been assigned without any kind of hassle. Her bed was empty when they entered, giving them pause until they noticed that the tiny creature sat in a large chair, a cup of warm liquid surrounded by her hands as she sipped it.

"Oldrilin!" Rey shouted, then remembered his manners and lowered his voice, "I'm so happy you're looking so well!"

"Rey Daye," she sang, smiling up at him.

Flanking her, the couple each took a side and knelt next to her, placing her slightly above them on the high-backed seat. Lifting her merdoe out of its hiding place, Ami pulled on the string at the back of her neck to free it. Holding it out to Rey in her open left palm, she waited for him to place his right across it, as they had done many times before.

"Rey Daye," the siren repeated once he could understand her. "How good of you to see me here."

"Aye," he nodded vigorously, "you said the elvish medicine was excellent, and indeed it has proven so."

Her wide blue orbs staring at him, the mermaid's expression remained tense, causing Ami's heart to beat faster. "Lin, is something wrong?" she asked, placing her free right hand on her tiny shoulder.

Gazing past them, Oldrilin did not reply, instead taking a moment to assess their surroundings. Then, in a much quieter voice, she said, "Their power to heal is great, but no strangers are welcomed in the halls of the elves. No visitors darken their great galleries."

"But we *were* welcomed," Rey countered, matching her whisper. "They have given us food, clothes." He indicated his companion's fine gown with a flat palm as evidence. "We even have a suite to share while we are here."

Glaring at him, the mermaid did not reply. Instead, she drank from her bowl of broth. Finishing it off, she pushed it towards Ami, who took it from her, breaking the connection with Rey as she stood. Tentatively placing the dish on a small table, she once again offered the man her palm when he had risen beside her.

"Take me to your suite," Oldrilin commanded once he had accepted the appendage. "Words we must share, but only for our ears."

Nodding, he didn't argue. Instead, he dropped the connection and pulled the blanket from the bed and offered it to her. "You need to stay warm, and it's a long way for your little weak legs. I'll carry you."

Her mouth open, Lin prepared to argue her ability, but Ami cut her off, "Oldrilin, Rey has carried you for days, when you were wrapped in his arms as safely as he could keep you. Trust him to spirit you to our rooms, and we will prepare a place there for you to rest."

"You cannot take her out so soon!" the maid interjected, presenting herself at the door, where she had been listening from the other side of the portal.

"Nonsense," Amicia replied. "She is on her way to recovery, and we wish to take her as she belongs with us," she stated firmly, glaring at the girl while lowering her chin angrily. "Do not trouble yourself. She will be well cared for."

Her face a pasty white, the girl stammered, "I have been charged with her care and healing. Please, do not remove her from me."

"I'm afraid I must," Ami insisted, glancing around to ensure they would leave nothing of importance behind.

Rey had already wrapped the tiny body in the bedding and hoisted her to rest against his chest. Bulkier than Ami's sweater had been, he maneuvered to get the right hold before he announced, "We're ready. Thank you for seeing to her," he said to the maid with a curt nod before he marched out of the room with Ami close behind.

Out on the path, the couple scurried along. The siren remained hidden inside his comforting arms, but those that they passed turned and stared after them, as if well aware of what he carried.

"Rey," Ami gasped once they had reached the stairs. Looking up at them, she scowled. "I'm growing rather tired of this climb."

"Aye, me too," he agreed, mounting them at the same time, "but we can't leave, and this is where we must stay."

Following, she felt relieved that at least one of her companions seemed to be aware of their plight. "Bally and the Mate seem perfectly happy here," she informed him when they had reached the top. "They aren't going to want to leave."

Unwrapped, Oldrilin acquired her balance as Rey knelt before her. "Leave we must," she asserted once the couple had again joined hands across the magical shell.

Nodding, Rey agreed, "We understand. But it will take time to convince the others."

Smiling, Ami added, "Yes, a few days I'm sure. We should keep this between the three of us until we are ready to make our claim and try for our escape." Hearing noises echo up the tower, her pleasant expression disappeared. "I hope that isn't Piers back with another girl already."

Noting the noise as well, Rey whispered, "Aye, we're not alone. Perhaps it is the caretaker in the rooms below."

"No," Lin informed him, her crystal blue orbs roving around, taking in the walls and furnishings of their lavish suite. "Someone climbs, I am certain."

Dropping their connection and moving farther into the room, Ami and Oldrilin took seats before the small fire as Rey added a few logs from the stack next to the hearth. Evening had fallen upon them in their travels back and forth, here and there, and it would be time for dinner soon; another long journey if they could not find a way to avoid it.

When Sadrir appeared at the landing, they pretended surprise at her arrival. "Good evening," Amicia cooed sweetly, offering Rey her customary hand to include him in the conversation. "Thank you for the return of my clothing."

"As you wished, my lady," the elf maid replied with a small curtsy. Seeing the siren relaxing in one of the chairs, her jaw dropped in surprise. "It is time soon for this evening's feast," she announced, her voice quavering.

"We would like to be served here tonight," Ami informed her in an authoritative tone. "And we will need accommodations for our small friend here. Is there perhaps something that can be done for her?"

"Yes, my mistress." Sadrir bowed again. "I will have dinner brought up and a table set for you here. And a bed can be added to your quarters if you should like."

"Put it in mine," Rey corrected. "You can trade it for my table instead."

Glancing between them, her features puzzled, the girl nodded. "Yes, of course. We will return shortly with all that you require."

As soon as she disappeared, he began to laugh. "Did you see the look on her face?"

"This whole place gives me chills," Ami retorted, wiping her brow with her free hand. "No smile is genuine, and every word must be measured."

"The tongue of the elf is practiced with lies," Oldrilin informed her.

Rey noted the droop of her small body, its cause unmistakable. "I'm going to put you up in my bed, Lin. And don't argue. You need a bit of rest, and we will wake you for the meal when it arrives." Holding up his hand, he indicated the portal to his room, fully expecting her to enter on her own. When she failed to move, he added, "I can carry you if you would rather."

Her face drawn into a heavy pout, Oldrilin appeared more childlike than ever as she stomped past him and entered the small chamber, pulling the door closed behind her.

Giggling at her coerced departure, Ami observed, "She will be back swimming in the sea in short order, I believe."

"Aye, if we ever get close to it," Rey agreed, dropping Ami's hand and taking to the balcony while they waited for their dinner to be served.

TWENTY-FIVE

A Queen's Gift

CLOMPING up the last few steps to their suite, Bally could hear loud voices, as a debate seemed to be taking place in the common room. Reaching the top, he called loudly, "Is it safe to come up?"

He joked of course, but his three companions understood his trepidation, and Ami replied, "Yes, it is. Don't be silly."

"Ah, good." He laughed, daring to venture in farther with exaggerated steps. "From below, it sounded as if you were having a fight."

Looking guiltily between the other two, Piers shook his head to rid his dark mood. "We're eating here tonight," the older man informed him. "Oldrilin has been carried up from the hospital. She's asleep in Rey's room."

"Oh, I doubt she's sleeping," Baldwin quipped, "not with the way you three were carrying on. But, I'm glad she was well enough to be moved so she could join us."

"Aye." Piers's scowl didn't match the sentiment, instantly enlightening even the youngest of the group to the reason behind the argument.

"You didn't want them bringing her here," he suggested, glancing between the three of them.

"No," Ami supplied with a click of her tongue. "He doesn't trust her," she clipped. She didn't trust the elves, so they were even on that front, but she hadn't bothered to mention it at the moment.

"Well, she's Rey's friend, and we brought her here," Bally pointed out with an open palm. "Where else is she going to go?"

Having stated the obvious, the younger man had essentially ended the discussion. Lin had become a part of their group, whether the Mate liked it or not.

"That's right," Rey agreed forcefully, "so she's here and here she will remain until we depart." His words hung in the air and no one disputed them. After a long silence, they each fell about their business of preparing for their evening meal.

If Sadrir had reservations about providing the group with a dinner in that evening, they were not evident when she arrived to see that their needs were tended to. To the contrary, the couple who managed their tower made a brief appearance, while avoiding all the pleasantries any of them would have expected from polite society. The elf maid gave them orders, and they saw that the group received the utmost care.

A bit stocky, even for a short elf, the man brought in extra wood and stacked it next to the hearth, ensuring the room would be a comfortable temperature. Next, he delivered a service tray filled with dishes, which he placed on the table so that each could dine in comfort. Then he carried in pitchers of water and basins for each of their rooms, as had been provided for Piers previously.

An equally plain specimen, the woman saw to their meal, which consisted of freshly-cooked game meat served with a thick sauce. Bread and slightly boiled vegetables were provided as sides, and a collection of cheeses the group had never before savored were all placed in the center of their large, round table. Finally, an oversized cup of warm broth was provided for the siren.

The meal being ready to be served, two bottles of elvish wine were presented, with gem-encrusted goblets to drink from. The places set, the couple disappeared, and Sadrir inquired, "Will there be anything else, my lady?"

"No, I believe this is everything," Amicia replied, happy with the arrangement. "Thank you, Sadrir. It looks lovely."

"You are welcome, my lady." The girl bowed as she turned to leave by way of the stairs.

Alone, the group glanced around at one another before Rey excused himself to retrieve their newest member. The other three each selected a comfortable, cushioned chair and began serving their plates. When he returned with the mermaid, Reynard folded a blanket and placed it in the seat so that the smaller woman could reach the table and sit with the others properly, then helped her by lifting her and placing her upon it.

Turning her plate before her, Ami caught a fit of giggles, then laughed out loud. Noticing the glares of the others, she fought to stifle her rude behavior to no avail. "Sorry," she murmured while trying to catch her breath.

"What's so funny?" Piers snapped, still angry that he had lost when it came to the siren.

"Nothing," Ami replied, calmer as she inhaled deeply and blew the air out through her nose. "I was just thinking about being on the ship, cramped in your quarters. Especially that first night, after sitting with Rey the entire day. I didn't realize then how dear you would all become to me." She finished in a quiet voice, a tear glistening in her eye.

Her sentiment took the edge off of his rage a bit, and the Mate stared at her flushed cheeks. He glanced at their smallest member, who sat sipping her broth from a spoon. "I'm sorry," he huffed, directing the comment to the latter. "I didn't mean to offend you."

Oldrilin waved her hand, brushing away the apology and smiling at him across the huge feast. If she held any hard feelings, they were not visible on her small features.

Attempting to lighten the mood, Bally announced, "I'll have Animir join us for dinner tomorrow if that suits everyone. I would love to introduce him to our siren."

"Our siren," Rey scoffed. "She isn't a piece of furniture, Baldwin," he snapped. "You don't simply present her to people without asking if it's all right with her."

"Aye, that's what I meant," the younger man back-paddled anxiously. "If it's acceptable to her, I'd like to introduce her to my friend."

The siren, always aware of the conversation even if she didn't take part, nodded in a single firm motion at him. Raising her goblet, she toasted him before tasting of her elvish wine, as if to seal the agreement.

"There, you see? She has accepted the invitation," Ami declared. "Now that it's settled, will you be presenting a guest tomorrow evening?" she asked, grinning behind her own drink as she cut her eyes over at Piers.

"I'm afraid not," he admitted with a shake of his head. "I enjoy their company to an extent, when speaking isn't required, but spending an entire meal with them is, well… exhausting."

His three companions laughed at his declaration, and the conversation shifted in tone. A peaceful calm settled over them, and they shared bits about their days since having arrived in the City of Jerranyth. They had not had a discussion amongst the four of them as such since their arrival, and it felt good to catch up on their experiences and impressions of the elves' realm.

To her surprise, Bally and Piers did not seem hard set upon staying there for any length of time. To the contrary, she noted that they both spoke of when time came for them to leave. "Where do you think we will go?" she dared to ask when the meal had been finished.

"I don't know," the Mate stated with a deep sigh. "Let's get a bit more comfortable, and we can discuss it."

Moving their chairs to form an arch in front of the fire, the group relaxed before the dancing flames. Opting to use the blanket as a shorter seat, the siren pulled it out of hers and sat upon it on the floor next to Rey's feet.

Smiling down at her, Ami observed, "You seem to be feeling much better, Oldrilin."

"Oh yes." She grinned up at the girl, speaking for the first time since coming out of the bedroom. "You will hear my words, Amicia? I shall speak of the elves, if your time has come to listen."

"Yes." The blonde signaled to the others with her hands to calm them. "What is it you wish to share?"

"The elves are not our friends," the mermaid informed her. "We have lived here in Eriden under the rule of the dragons, but only as an enemy would allow his adversary to occupy an adjacent land."

"Did they do something to you? Did they hurt your people somehow?" she asked, shifting her gaze nervously between the men. "She says that the sirens and the elves are not friends, and that the dragons are the rulers of Eriden." Ami had already known that last bit of news but had yet to share it with the others. Knowing now that they would be receptive to moving on, she felt at ease to be more open with them about their situation.

"Is there a way we can share that magic shell of yours?" Piers asked, indicating her necklace by rubbing his hand over his own chest.

"I'm afraid not," she sighed in reply. "I can share with one, but all three of you would prove difficult."

"All right, just continue and translate what you can," he instructed with a grimace.

Nodding, she wafted her hand at the siren, who dove into her story. "You see, a great war divided our kingdom. Two, perhaps three centuries ago," the creature began.

"I've heard of the great war," Ami said with a shake of her long blond strands. "Cilithrand told me about it and about her father's passing, which gave way to her reign."

"Yes," Oldrilin agreed. "The particulars are unclear, perhaps lost over time, but her inheritance of the elven realm has wrought the discourse between our peoples. Galiodien was a mighty king, and he is sorely missed by the southern continent. Cilithrand has been loved less and despised more by those who share this part of the kingdom."

Considering her words, Ami translated them for the others. Placing her hand on her chin, she leaned against the arm of her chair, then shifted the digits to chew upon a finger. "I'm not sure why the king being killed or Lady Cilithrand's coming to power would cause the conflict," she admitted with a sigh.

"Nor am I, sweet Amicia," the mermaid agreed, shaking her head slowly. "I am young among the sirens and only know it has been so for many moons."

"Wait," Bally interceded. He had given what they had been told of the circumstances some thought but could not reconcile the discord. "You're telling us you've been fighting with them over something that happened over two hundred years ago, and you don't even know why?"

Lin nodded firmly, confirming his suspicions.

"Well, that's just silly," Piers stated crossly. "In all that time, have you even tried to make peace between your peoples?"

Again, Lin indicated her response with a firm shake of her head, only this time side to side.

"No," Rey translated, a small pout forming on his lips. "Oldrilin, you must understand that things may have changed a great deal after all this time. It could be that the elves are no longer your enemy," he proposed, reaching to place his hand on her tiny shoulder. "We can't hold a grudge for something so far in the past or even judge them because of it."

Blinking at his reaction, Amicia held her tongue. She feared that their friend's description of the elves had been spot on, but in the end, what proof did she have? A bad omen in the pit of her gut hardly qualified as strong evidence that the elves held anything against them.

"Perhaps you're right," she finally agreed. "We'll stay until Lin is fully ready to travel and leave when she is able. I've been anxious to visit these nymphs and satyrs that the queen spoke of since she first mentioned them," Ami announced with a wide smile. "What do you know of them, Oldrilin?"

Taking on the new topic with a happy grin, the siren eagerly shared what she knew of the third southern group, secretly relieved to be finished speaking of the seditious queen and what she feared would happen if and when the travelers finally decided to flee her realm.

Talking until the fire grew dim, the group eventually made their way to their beds. His table had not been replaced for the siren, so Rey, having given his mattress away, spread a blanket upon the floor. There he slept until the following morn when the light from around the cracks in his door awakened him.

This time, he found that the common room had been cleaned, with the remnants of their dinner removed, and in its place sat a hearty breakfast of fruits, dried meats, and bread. Knocking on Bally's door, he called, "Food's here. You might as well get up and have some." Piers opened his door when he did, and Rey grinned. "Good morning, Mate."

"What's good about it?" the older man grumbled, ambling over to the table and helping himself to part of the spread.

Smiling at their leader's half-naked and typically grumpy demeanor, Reynard made a similar announcement to their girl. He turned back to the food to have his own as Sadrir appeared at the top of their stairs.

Beaming at the group, she declared cheerfully, "I'm pleased to see so many of you awake. Our Lady Cilithrand has announced a visit to you within the hour."

"A visit!" Piers gasped, clenching his jaw tightly shut.

"The queen is coming here?" Bally questioned, scratching at his wild morning hair. "What's she coming here for? I thought she stayed in her palace all the time."

"Why no, my lady visits many parts of her realm," the elf informed him with a smile, noting that Amicia had joined them. "Enjoy your breakfast and have a wash. She will arrive soon."

"For what purpose does she call?" Ami asked, smoothing her dress after a good stretch.

"To meet the siren, Oldrilin," Sadrir enlightened her readily. "She is healing, and it would be improper to ask her to make the trip to the queen's chamber."

Somehow, the girl doubted that, but let the matter fall to the wayside. Selecting a plate, she served herself from the delicious fare and took a seat at the table across from Piers. The others joined them, and even Lin enjoyed a bit of the fruit before they adjourned to their quarters to wash for the royal visit.

While they did so, the housemaid made quick work of cleaning the common room, and everything appeared neat and tidy by the time Lady Cilithrand appeared at the top of their stairs. "Is anyone at home?" she called upon her arrival.

"Your majesty," Ami replied, plying her with her best forced smile. Offering a small bow, she indicated the ring of chairs that had been moved in front of the fire once more. "Please, would you like a seat?"

"No, I shan't be long," the queen informed her with a devious grin. "I've only come to pay my respects to the siren and to offer a small gift."

"A gift?" Oldrilin questioned in a weak voice. Joining the other two women, she stood slightly behind Amicia, perhaps out of fear of the towering matriarch.

"Why yes." Cilithrand smiled as she knelt and waited for the smaller creature to come forward. Holding out her hand, she offered a large white gem, the likes of which Amicia had never seen. "I wish to impart a token of friendship. Many moons has our two realms lain in distrust. Let us mark the beginning of a new age between us."

Holding out the over-sized crystal, she waited for the smaller hands to accept the gift. Her smile broad, for an instant it twisted into an evil grin before it disappeared. "Oldrilin," she breathed, standing once more. "Welcome to Jerranyth. May your stay with us be long and most enjoyable." Glancing over at the girl, she gave her a firm nod and then turned to descend without so much as a parting goodbye.

"Well, that was quick," Rey observed, a little miffed that they had not been properly introduced to her ladyship. "They aren't big on manners around here, are they."

"They stand high on ceremony here," Ami corrected him. "Stations above and below do not mingle."

"Are you saying she thinks she's too good for us?" Baldwin bit angrily, having joined them only as the queen had prepared to leave.

"She is too good for us," Piers corrected. He might have been the governor's son, but that was another life and one he left long ago. "Aristocrats live very different lives than what we do, and not necessarily better by any means. Forget it, guys. We're better off not being noticed by the likes of her," he spat, jerking his head towards the vacated entrance.

Standing in the front part of the room where the queen had left her, the siren still held the large gem. Turning it with a look of awe as she studied its rare beauty, the facets caught the light of the sun that shone in from the balcony. The queen had offered it as a symbol of peace between them, and it would appear that Rey had been right; it was a new age between the sirens and elves.

Placing the stone in a hidden pocket, she turned to the girl and smiled. "When shall we go down to visit the sacred gardens? I've heard they are impressive."

"They are quite lovely," Ami agreed. "Allow Rey to carry you, and we will take you out for the fresh air as soon as everyone is ready."

TWENTY-SIX

A Bad Omen

GATHERING NEXT TO THE STAIRS, the five members of the household made their plans for the day, but Oldrilin was less receptive to the idea of being carried than Ami would have liked. "It's for your own good," she insisted.

Stomping her tiny foot, her arms crossed her chest, and her face formed an angry scowl. "Tis not dignified to be carted about," the siren growled, obviously feeling well enough to put up a fuss.

"I can put you on my shoulders," Rey suggested, not understanding her words, but her meaning clear. Scooping her up despite her protest, he swung her above his head. Her legs straddling his neck, he commanded, "Be sure to hold on."

Grabbing two small fists of hair, Oldrilin did precisely that, her eyes wide with fright as she looked down at the floor below. "Please do not drop me," she begged in a shaky voice.

"Rey, you're scaring her," Ami informed him, stepping forward and placing a calming palm on the siren's leg. "Lin, you're fine," she soothed, giving her a pat.

Uncomforted by the girl's smile, the mermaid squirmed while holding firmly to the dark ringlets, her features twisted in terror.

"Eh ah," Rey squawked, grasping her hands to free his shaggy mane. "Well she's hurting me!" he blurted.

Behind them, Bally began to laugh hysterically. He had been suppressing the snicker from the moment Rey had hoisted Oldrilin up, but his admission of pain had been too much to control.

Amicia could see the humor in it and giggled sporadically as she tried to help the pair find the right position. "Baldwin, stop laughing and help us!"

The younger man doubled over instead, hooting as Rey exclaimed, "Seriously, Lin, that's my scalp you're ripping away!"

"You told her to hold on," Ami reminded him.

"Yeah, but not to my hair!" he snapped.

"I think you should let her walk," Piers suggested, pushing up on the small rear end to get her in a more stable seat. "There, Lin. I think you can ride," he growled.

Leaning over the top of Reynard's head, she released one fist full of ebony strands, her palm landing on his face. Laying his over the back of it, he soothed, "Is she better now?"

"Yes," Ami smirked, "I think we have it under control." Looking at the Mate, she grinned, "Thank you. Are you coming with us to the garden?"

"Uh, no," he confessed, smoothing his freshly washed beard. "I'm going for a walk. And if I'm late back for dinner… don't wait for me," he instructed as he pranced down the stairs on light feet to the tune of a merry whistle.

Watching his scrunch of hair disappear, Amicia sighed, her mood lost for the moment. "That's really who he is, isn't it. A womanizer."

"Aye," Rey agreed, his voice equally subdued. "Don't take it so hard, love. At least he's honest about it."

Shifting her gaze, she stared up into his clear hazel orbs. "Thank you, Rey. I'm sure being honest about our vices makes them perfectly acceptable. It's fine to be a drunkard, as long as one is honest about it." Her green eyes clouded, the sarcasm landed thickly between them, keeping Rey from commenting further.

"I'm afraid I'm not going either," Bally stated calmly, his fit of laughter confined. "However, I will return for dinner, and with all hope, Animir will be with me to meet Lin," he added with a grin and a nod at the siren, who appeared calmer in her perch. "Enjoy your garden!" he called over his shoulder as he followed the first mate down the stone steps.

Feeling less jovial about the outing, Ami retrieved her sweater and placed it on over her gown. The colors weren't a good match, and it clearly removed some of her elegance, but at the moment, she had greater concern for warmth than appearances. "The gardens are this way," she said quietly, leading them down to the ground level and holding the wall as she descended.

Letting her have the walk down to gather her thoughts, Rey stayed close to the wall as well. The sheer drop of the outer edge turned his stomach, and with Lin on his shoulders, he didn't dare risk a misstep. Placing his hand over the back of hers, which she had refused to remove from his face, he grinned. And then he felt it. "Oh my God!"

"What?" Amicia sniffed as they reached the ground level.

Rubbing the small appendage between his thumb and fingers, Rey grinned down at her, "She spoke to me! I swear I heard it! It was in my head, as plain as day light," he declared.

Scowling up at the siren, Oldrilin held a wide smile and nodded firmly to confirm his supposition.

"Is that possible?" Ami gasped, addressing the mermaid who had done the talking. Getting no reply, she frowned. "Well, she isn't talking to me," she snapped, turning and marching out onto the path.

Catching up to her with a few quick strides, Rey felt more comfortable with his load on the even ground. "This isn't so bad," he informed her cheerfully, his fingers gently holding a miniature leg as they bounced along. Sensing Amicia's dark mood, he chided, "Listen. You should forget about the Mate. Honestly, it's a waste of your time brooding over him."

"I'm trying," she declared angrily, clenching her fists so that her nails scarred her palms. "You think it's easy? I love him, after all. I hate the thought that I wasted my only chance to be with him."

Turning through the hedge, she dabbed at her eyes. Noting her distress, Rey carefully lowered his friend to the ground. Her bare feet made contact with the soft grass, and she giggled loudly as she ran across the clearing to the large flowers on the far side. "Be careful, Lin," he called after her, again feeling as if he cared for a small child rather than a woman near twice his age.

Facing the girl next to him, he squared his shoulders, then grasped hers to pivot her towards him. "And then where would you be?" He searched her tear-filled eyes for understanding. "You would have been another conquest to him, no different than Cothiel had been that first day we were here. Following him around, expecting or at least hoping for more. How embarrassing for her to be treated as such before her own people," he pointed out in a quiet voice.

"That's true." Her head bobbled with a small nod, sniffing quietly as she tried to hide her tears by pulling away. Blinking rapidly as she watched the siren play, she longed to be so carefree.

"And worse, you would have been stuck with him still in our group, knowing it had not meant the same to him," he pushed, ready to speak his mind openly. "He's a scoundrel, only caring for himself."

She sighed. "That's also true. How'd you get so wise, Rey Daye?" she asked with a small pout, meeting his tender gaze with her clear green orbs.

Swallowing hard, he held his reply. Anything else he might have said would have revealed more than he was willing to share. Instead, he gave her his best smile and offered his hand. "Walk with me, Amicia Spicer. Enjoy our day and show me the garden. Have comfort knowing I would never hurt you, this I can promise."

Unclasping her shell from around her neck, she placed her merdoe between them as she accepted his firm grasp. "I appreciate your friendship," she informed him when they reached the end of the row. Large butterflies danced atop the blooms and she sighed. "I think we may be stuck here for the winter. The air is cool, even with my sweater, and I fear it will be too cold to travel."

"It will be better once we are down off the mountain," he countered, laughing as Oldrilin rolled in the grass. "I wonder if she misses being a mermaid," he observed, changing the subject abruptly as a distraction. "Or, if she will ever be able to transform again."

"I'm sure that she will once she is completely healed," Ami agreed to the new topic. "If she needs the saltwater, we can take her back to the ocean when we leave. Perhaps she will swim back to Riran, even if we don't go that way ourselves."

Blinking rapidly, Rey fought his own tears. "I would hate to see her go," he admitted in a quiet voice.

"Yeah, me too," Amicia echoed. "For now, let's go and play with her. Forget about being grown up for a while and chase some butterflies," she suggested with a giggle.

"I can do that." He chuckled, dropping her hand and jogging after their diminutive friend. Catching up to her, he sank to his knees beside her. Lin had her hands clasped in front of her, as if she had captured something.

Joining them, Amicia squatted, careful not to dig her own knees into the grass and stain the fine material of her dress. "What have you found?" She offered Rey her hand so he could hear.

"Tis a dragon worm," the mermaid whispered, parting her hands and exposing the small caterpillar. Its body a bright green with yellow spots, two horns protruded from the wide head that moved slowly from side to side as it explored her pudgy palm.

"Oh my," Amicia gasped, her breath light as the excitement filled her. "Will it become a butterfly... or a dragon?"

"In the spring, a most beautiful butterfly." Lin smiled brightly at the thought of the transformation. "He will eat until the first snow and then cocoon himself for winter. When spring comes, his wings will spread so he can fly."

"That's amazing!" Rey held out his hand so the squirming creature could crawl over to him, briefly wondering if they would still be there in the spring to see it. Unsure, he sighed deeply at the prospect of being trapped in Jerranyth once the weather turned bad.

"Don't worry," Amicia comforted, confident what he was thinking. Taking her turn to hold the dragon worm, she stood to place it among the giant blooms. "We will be long gone before he emerges in the spring."

"Hello, Bally," Animir greeted his human friend when he arrived in the armory. "What of this day?"

"Hey, Animir." Baldwin grinned. "Another beautiful day in Jerranyth. I've come to spend it with you here in the forge, if you don't mind. And to have you up for dinner in our suite, later. I want to introduce you to our friend, the siren Oldrilin," he announced proudly.

"She is well?" Animir asked, his command of the language after only a few days impressive.

"Almost," Bally agreed with a shrug. "She's with us in the tower now, so we're having our meals there if you care to join us."

"Yes, sharing is pleasant," Animir agreed. "For this, let us make arrows," he suggested, indicating his collection of parts he intended to assemble.

"Sure, show me how," the shorter man suggested as he straightened his stocking cap. He always wore it, but that day in particular he felt glad to have it, as a cool nip could be felt in the air, especially in the shadow of the forge.

Taking a few pieces of feather, the elf selected a shaft and began to demonstrate how to attach them. Following his instructions, Bally did his best to add some to his own thin slivers of wood, but it proved more difficult than he anticipated. Eventually, he simply played with the parts while Animir got to work on completing the task.

Once they had finished, the pair left the forge and scurried along the path, smacking each other playfully and laughing along the way. Arriving at a garden that ran along the lower edge of the town, they spent the rest of the afternoon using the shrubs as cover as they spied on beautiful elf maids who wandered among the flowers. After about an hour of the spectacle, Bally recognized the Mate, lying in the grass with a portly brunette.

"I'll be damned," he muttered, pointing him out to his friend.

Watching the couple, he could see Piers as he used a plucked flower to tickle her creamy skin. Then leaning in closer, he whispered something into her ear, which elicited a loud giggle from her perfect pink lips that floated across to Bally on the cool afternoon air. Squinting as he smiled at her, the man's age crinkled his skin, but his spirit appeared unmistakably young when he pressed his forehead to hers and laughed in his deep, robust tones.

"He's so lucky," Baldwin breathed, observing as he stood and helped the female elf to her feet. "I so wish I could have his charm. The girls fall at his feet with desire for him, I swear it," he confessed.

"He is your friend, yes?" Animir asked, watching as the couple exited the area hand in hand, presumably to return to the spire.

"Aye." Bally nodded, then laughed. "Only he's way better with the ladies than me, for sure. Maybe we should talk to some of them," he suggested, forgetting for a moment he couldn't understand anything they had to say to him.

"Ok." Animir moved to lead his companion out of their hiding place and onto one of the paths.

"Wait," Bally interjected, getting cold feet as soon as they entered the clearing. "Let's go play with the swords, instead. Sword fights are way more fun than girls anyway."

Laughing at his young friend, the elf agreed. Baldwin was his guest, and he was more than happy to oblige him, whatever his choice might be. "Come then," he called, waving a hand for him to follow as he led him back to the forge and storage hall to select their weapons.

Picking out a small group of swords, the two young men each took one and clanged them against one another noisily beneath the overcast sky. Laughing, Bally used both hands to swing his massive weapon, then spun to avoid being struck by a skilled blow from the elf. "You're too good," he hooted, turning to face him once more. "I need practice," he confessed, lowering the weapon that felt heavy in his grasp.

"You need better blade," Animir corrected. Stopping the fight by holding up his hand, he marched over to the pile they had brought out for their dueling. Trying a few of them with one hand, he finally found the one he wanted and held it out to the other man. "For you," he grunted.

"Ok, I'll try this one." Bally had no real knowledge of swords, so any advice would be useful. Balancing it on two fingers where the handle met the steel of the blade, it felt lighter than the one he had been using, and he looked at it doubtfully. "It's not too wimpy, is it?" he asked, then shrugged. "It's ok, I'll give it a try."

"No." Animir shook his head, placing his hand on the grip and pushing it firmly towards his friend. "Give for you."

"Give for me," Baldwin repeated. "You mean for me to keep it?" he asked, his mouth wide in surprise, "Oh, wow!"

"Yes, for you!" Animir grinned.

Admiring the shiny metal, Bally beamed. "Thanks! I've never had a sword before," he confessed, stepping back and giving it a few swings. Pivoting the blade and twirling it so that it whisked past his body, first left and then right, over and over again, he laughed. "This feels good!"

"Yes, good. Bally keep."

"Aye, I'll keep," he agreed, his face flushed with joy. "Thanks, man. I don't know what to say," he said more calmly, with a deep inhale and exhale to slow his trembling. "Thank you," he repeated, overcome with gratitude.

"Bally friend of Animir," the elf announced, his hand flat on his chest as he said his own name.

"Yes, always." Baldwin again admired the sword. Running his finger over the sharp edge, it caught and made a long cut in his finger, "Ow, shit." Placing the digit in his mouth, he sucked the flow, then pulled it out and flicked it in the air. "That hurts!"

"Ow," Animir repeated, grinning at Bally's foolishness.

"Aye," his friend agreed with a laugh. "Is it a bad omen to cut yourself on your new sword?"

"You fine, Baldwin Carter," Animir replied. "Now, is time for dinner," he suggested, ready to join the others in the suite for the evening meal.

TWENTY-SEVEN

A Hasty Retreat

SEEING the Mate's door closed when they arrived, Ami chose to look the other way. Removing her sweater, she carried it into her room and hung it over the back of her chair. Resting her hand fondly on Bally's clothing, she sighed, longing to put them on and leave the realm of the elves for good.

In the common room, she could hear Rey adding logs and stoking their fire. "We should close the drapes to the balcony, as well," she suggested, moving to do so. "It doesn't provide enough light to be worth the loss in heat."

"Aye," he agreed, glancing around to see that their lamps were lit. "I assume they will deliver our dinner without having to be asked?"

"Well, if you doubt it, you could always go down and ask the chambermaid," she suggested evenly. "Their quarters are the second door up, on the first landing."

"Is that so," he replied. "I didn't know what was behind all those doors. How do you know?"

"I asked." She laughed, still peeking between the drawn drapes at the dark clouds forming on the horizon and realizing she never had made her way down for a proper introduction to the couple. Watching the grey sky, she sighed. "Remember when we were on the raft and could see the rain coming?"

"Aye." Placing his hand on her shoulder, he joined her. "We needed that rain. I can't believe how close we came to not making it."

Nodding, she closed the material and turned away. "Where's Lin?"

"She climbed into my bed for a nap." He laughed, cutting it short when Piers's door swung open and a young female elf made her exit. Stepping aside, he looked her up and down as she passed and began her descent. The Mate's grin wide, he followed her, watching until she disappeared into the abyss below.

Rubbing the hairs on his chest, their leader coughed noisily, cutting his eyes over at the young woman who did her best to pretend not to see. "When's dinner?"

"When it arrives," she replied, still not looking at him. Instead, she fiddled with her merdoe, positioning it back into its place between her breasts.

Grunting, Piers returned to his quarters to wash himself and prepare for the meal that hopefully would arrive soon. On the stairs, Bally and Animir made a fair bit of racket as they climbed the final ascent. Reaching the top, Baldwin announced, "I'm bleeding!" followed by fits of laughter.

His shirt spotted with blood, Ami gasped, "Whatever happened to you?" Her mouth open wide, her heart raced. "Here, get your shirt off, and we'll use it to stop the flow," she commanded.

Pulling it over his head while still giggling, he presented it and the injury to her. "It's only a little cut," he amended, taking his new prize from his friend. "Look what Animir gave me!" Offering the blade to Rey, he beamed with pride.

"And you cut yourself on it," the Mate stated gruffly, joining the group while shaking his head in disgust. Taking over the nursing, he pulled the injured appendage towards him and scowled. "We need to wash this really well. Aye, not a large cut, but it can become infected easily and take your whole hand."

Instantly sober, the younger man clenched his jaw. "Surely not."

"Let him tend to you," Rey seconded the opinion while inspecting the sword. "Wow, this is a really nice one," he observed, nodding at Animir, who grinned at him. "Did you make it?"

"No, I make arrows," the elf corrected.

"Ah, well, it's still a great sword. Almost as good as the one the Mate made for me," Rey laughed, moving away from the others to give it a few swings.

Placing a basin of water on the table for them, Amicia frowned. "You boys should be more careful. The last thing we want is for one of us to delay our chances of departure any further."

"Aye." The Mate pulled the crewman over and used the cool liquid to clean the wound and inspect it.

"What's happened?" Sadrir squealed from the top of the stairs. Walking slowly towards the group gathered around the table, she glanced at the elf who hovered near the fire.

"It's nothing." Piers addressed her obvious concern while tending to the wound. I'd like a needle and some clean thread, though, if you can get it for me. And I'm sure you are aware that we need our dinner," he tacked on, cutting his eyes over at her briefly to emphasize the command.

"Yes, I'm aware of your need of a meal," the girl replied tartly with a nod, her face pale at the sight of the blood. Seeing the boy's bare chest, she scowled. "The blood will never come out of that shirt. Would you like a new one?"

"She's offering a replacement," Amicia translated, her face still drawn with concern as she indicated the stained article.

"Hey, that goes for me too, if I may." Rey showed off his torn edges where he had removed strips to bandage the siren after they left Riran.

"All right, dinner, a needle with thread, and a couple of new shirts," Sadrir detailed with a curtsy before leaving them to their mending.

Staring at the basin of blood-stained water, Bally sniveled, "You weren't serious about the hand, were you, Mate?"

"Only if we don't take care of it, son," the older man replied, his brow furrowed. "It's clean, and it's closed for the moment. Hold pressure on this," he instructed him, showing how to keep the bandage he had formed closed. "And don't peek! I'll stitch it up when she gets back, and we'll know in a few days how serious it is."

Half an hour later, Sadrir returned with the shirts and sewing supplies, which she dropped off before going back down to ensure their dinner would be served on time. Making quick work of the stitches, the Mate appeared pleased with the results.

"I think you'll be fine," he announced, glancing around the circle of concerned faces as he finished. "Don't worry, guys. We'll know in a few days. The cut was clean and properly dressed. That's about all we can do at this point."

Holding the injured digit gingerly, Bally sighed. "I guess I need to be more careful next time."

"Aye," Rey agreed. "A sword isn't a toy. What were you doing to cut yourself like that?" he chided.

"I was just looking at it," the younger man defended, cutting his eyes over at the elf and feeling foolish at their afternoon of clanging them together. "I'm going to go lay down until we can eat."

Watching him exit, Ami thought about his elf friend and how much of their language he had learned. "Wouldn't it be nice if we could reverse my shell?" she observed randomly.

"How do you mean?" Piers inquired, cleaning up his mess and clearing off the table so it could be set for the meal.

"I mean, as it is, we can hear their words in our language, but what if we could use it to have their words come *out* in our language?"

"That would be weird," Rey observed, putting Bally's sword in his room as the old couple arrived to tend to their evening's needs.

"And damned useful," the first mate countered. "Bring it out and let's see if you can make it happen."

Pulling the stone out, the girl unlatched the cord and held the object in her hand, admiring the warmth. Turning to Animir, she beckoned him closer. Holding out her hand with the shell in her palm, she instructed, "Place your hand in mine. That's it," she praised as he slid his digits between hers, sandwiching the device. "Now, say something."

"What shall I say?" he replied.

Immediate laughter broke out from the three mortals, and Rey quipped, "That's a nice trick right there! We should have done it with Oldrilin last night."

"We didn't think of it last night." Amicia adjusted their grip. "But yes, this is nice. You can sit by me as we eat, and we'll put the shell between us. Whenever you need to speak, we can both place our hands on it and you can have your say."

He nodded, understanding fully and happy that the arrangement had been made. "They will bring the meal?" he asked, indicating the couple who had been making trips into the room while they tested her trinket.

Nodding, Amicia grinned. "Yes. It will only take a few minutes, and we can settle in for our dinner."

The old man dropped the wood onto the stack while his wife delivered the pitchers of water, and Piers observed, "Well then, let's get washed and ready to eat," dismissing them all to their quarters until the table had been set and their supper served.

A short time later, they regrouped, as the old couple had disappeared, and they could gather around the large table to dine. Oldrilin joined them for her broth and praised Ami for her discovery of how the merdoe could be used.

Baldwin also appeared, looking rested and somewhat better after the short nap. Taking his seat across from his friend, he beamed with his typical light-hearted demeanor. "Now we can really have a conversation."

Placing their hands side by side, the tips of the fingers on Ami's left hand and Animir's right pressed against the chalky white surface. "I'm happy to speak with you," the elf agreed, followed by another joyous round of soft laughter.

Smiling, Amicia declared, "Nothing can stop us if we refuse to give up."

"That's true." Piers raised his goblet in a toast. "To new friends."

Using his left hand to join the sentiment, Animir observed, "You have been most welcome among us. I am pleased to be seated at your table."

"Aye," Baldwin approved. "Too bad we can't stay here forever."

The group paused, if only for a moment, at his observation. Then, resuming his serving himself with his left hand, Animir quietly asked, "Are you planning on leaving soon?"

"We need to be gone before the snow falls," Piers replied. "Otherwise, we'll be trapped here all winter, and I dare say we wouldn't wish to impose on the Lady Cilithrand or her people for so long."

"I assure you my queen would be most displeased at your departure," the elf replied, turning his gaze to the girl seated next to him. "She is most fond of you, Lady Amicia."

Ami swallowed hard at the formality of his addressing her. Seeing the covert glances between the men, she faltered. "It was very kind of your queen to make such bold offers, but I belong with my friends. It is their wish to leave the Kingdom of Eriden, and I must aid them in that endeavor," she informed him noncommittally. She had no intention of leaving with them, but at that moment, she saw no need to split that hair, as getting away from Jerranyth would be their first concern.

"Offer?" the Mate asked in mid bite. "What offer?"

Glancing around, guilt washed over the girl's features. She should have shared what had taken place in the queen's palace right away. Now it appeared that she had been hiding something, as in fact she had. "The queen has offered to make me her princess and heir to her throne should I remain in the city of Jerranyth... as one of her subjects," the girl supplied, using her napkin on her lips after she did so.

"Really," Rey spat, hurt that she had lied to them. "And when were you going to tell us?"

"And more importantly, why would she make such an offer?" Piers snapped. "This was serious, Ami!" his voice grew loud as he poked the table with a stiff digit. "The very idea of it screams of treachery."

"I didn't accept the offer," Amicia replied angrily, then back-paddled, "I mean, I did, but I didn't actually mean it. When we are all ready to leave, I'm going with you," she assured. "I have no intention of crossing you, if that's what you wish to imply."

"Go where?" Animir came at her from the other side. "You can't leave Erlden. No one leaves but the dragons of the air."

"What do you mean 'dragons of the air'?" Piers cut in once more, having pushed his plate back in dismay. Demanding clarification, he suggested, "Surely there is a way out of here."

"I'm afraid that's the only way out," the elf supplied with a shrug. "The land is enchanted. You can't sail away, even if you have a ship, which I'm assuming that you don't. Vessels are sunk well before they reach our shores."

"Aye, by the dragons," Rey surmised, also dropping his fork and folding his hands in front of him to lean on.

"It doesn't matter, we're going to build one," Bally chimed in, still eating as if the conversation were perfectly normal.

His mouth open slightly in disbelief, the elf persisted, "The three of you. You will build a ship."

"Four," Ami clipped, dropping her cloth on the table and glaring at him. "I'm not a helpless elf maid. I'm capable of hard work as any man, and if we must build our own vessel, I am perfectly able to lend a hand."

Reynard grinned at her covertly, proud of her stamina, or what he had seen of it. Nodding, he agreed, "We'll find a way off and a way home. To the rim of the mortals, where we belong," he stated firmly before taking a swig of his wine.

"You're mad," Animir quibbled, trading his glare between them. "The queen will never let you leave. If she intends to have you as her heir, she would kill any who stood in her way." His lips pressed into a thin line, his grim warning hung in the air.

Studying him with clear green eyes, Ami's heart pounded heavily within her chest. "And will you tell her of our desire to depart?" She realized that if he said yes, that would leave them little choice as to what they must do next.

Blinking at her, she could see him arrive at the same conclusion. "I suggest we leave tonight," he stated calmly.

"Leave tonight!" Baldwin exclaimed, only then dropping his fork in surprise. "Are you coming with us?"

"Apparently, I am," Animir replied, not breaking his connection with the girl. "But we must hurry. I can get us out of the city, but only if we are unseen."

"Where will we go?" Bally insisted, confused as Rey and Piers left the table, their plates hardly touched. Bumping his finger against his chair when he tried to stand as well, he winced in pain, shaking it as unshed tears formed. "Son of a bitch!"

Swallowing, Ami didn't move. "Are you really going to help us or is this some kind of trick to get my friends killed?" Her eyes narrowed into thin slits. The queen had wanted her, and it would stand to reason her friends were expendable if they stood in the way of her achieving that goal.

"No trick," the elf shook his head slowly. "I promise, I will do all that I can to help you get away from here... on one condition. Take me with you."

"And why would we want to do that?" Piers demanded, returning from his room as he shoved his gear into the bag he had carried when they fled Riran.

"Because I'm no good at being an elf," Bally's friend confessed with a small pout. "I am tolerated among my people. I'm of the line of nobles, but I serve in the armory as a common serf. I am forbidden to ever marry, and my life holds no meaning within the walls of Jerranyth. Please, do not leave me here. My humiliation is not to be borne!"

"We'll take you," Amicia agreed, leaping to her feet while yanking at the ties of her dress. "Rey, help me out of this thing!" she shouted, stomping through the door to her bed chamber. Grabbing Bally's clothes from her table, she unfolded them and dropped them over the sweater on the back of the chair.

Arriving to help, Reynard pulled at the laces so they could remove the gown. Unable to loosen the knot, he picked up the girl's dagger and removed it from the metal sheath. "Hold still," he commanded, cutting the strings and helping her hoist the material over her head.

Pulling the shirt into place over her underclothes, she shoved her legs into the pants and worked them up. Then, each foot slithered into a wool sock, and she applied the boots, stomping her foot into them angrily. "I can't believe we're leaving like this," she hissed.

"Like what?" Rey demanded, helping her to pack her bag by dropping the dagger, brush, and mirror in the bottom.

"Just once!" she replied loudly, then softened her tone, "I'd like more than five minutes to pack before all hell breaks loose and I have to run."

Rey laughed in spite of himself. "Well, stop pissing off dragons and elves, and maybe you'll get a few more minutes to pack," he taunted.

"I'm going down after the caretakers," Piers informed her from the door of her room.

"What? Why?" she gasped, following him across to the stairs.

"They're going to know we left. We'll bring them up and lock them in a room. Don't worry, they'll be fine. Sadrir will discover them in the morning and let them out."

Breathing heavily, Ami agreed, "Good thinking. Go, and we'll be ready to leave when you get back."

With a quick pass around the suite, each made sure they had everything they would need, including the leftovers from their meal. Scrapping them into the napkins, Amicia added them to her pack, then announced, "Everyone, take a blanket from your bed and roll it as well. We'll tie them to carry for now, but they will come in handy if we see any snow out of that storm we saw building."

Dodging back into her room, she snatched the striker from its shelf below the lamp and shoved it into her bag, then set to work on her quilt. Pulling the strings out of the dress that Rey had cut, she used them to tie the bedding into a tight roll.

Noticing the merdoe still on the table, Baldwin grasped it firmly and offered it to the girl. "Don't forget this!"

"Right! I can't believe I almost left it," she gasped, thinking of Olirassa, who had given it to her as she replaced it around her neck and hid it between her breasts.

"Orb of truth, my ass," she seethed. She wasn't sure how the elf queen had done it, but she felt certain the siren had never had any intentions of harming her or her friends. *Now if we can just get out of here before the elves find us,* she mused, throwing her pack over her shoulder and waiting anxiously for the others.

TWENTY-EIGHT

Running in the Rain

"I SAID MOVE!" the Mate shouted, his sword drawn as he followed the two small elves who had cared for their suite up the stairs.

"Piers, please," Amicia whined, offering her hand to help the old woman up the last few steps. "They're coming as fast as they can. I'm sorry," she whispered, catching their prisoner's gaze.

"Over here," he ordered, ignoring her plea and placing the couple in his own quarters. Once they were inside, he closed the door and used a chair to wedge beneath the handle to prevent their escape.

Her eyes wide, Ami recalled the first time she had entered the room and realized that the hinges were on the wrong side. "Do you think they lock people in these rooms often?" she observed.

"Well, they're built for keeping people in rather than out," Rey observed, hoisting his filled pack onto his back. "Is everyone ready?" he asked as he positioned a second sack on his front, empty at the moment.

In a fit of genius, he had removed one of the feather pillows from its linen case. Cutting leg holes in the bottom, it made the perfect pouch for carrying around minia-ture mermaids. Using the rope ties, which normally secured the drapes, he had hung the sack from his shoulders, so he could carry Oldrilin but keep his arms free as he did so.

Ami held the bag open while he lifted the siren and placed her in her pouch. For once, she didn't argue and accepted being strapped to his chest without a word. Perhaps the knowledge they were leaving the elf city was enough to convince her to do as she was asked.

Glancing at the elf, Ami sighed. "I'm sorry, Animir. We can't risk letting you go home for anything."

"We must pass through the armory," he informed her. "All I will need is in there."

"Weapons," Rey surmised.

"Yes. A bow and many arrows that I can carry for myself," he agreed.

Nodding, Rey slapped him on the shoulder, officially welcoming him to their group. "Good man."

"He's actually talking pretty good, even without the magic trinket," Baldwin observed, joining the trio in the "ready to leave" category. He had gathered all that they came with, and his bag held the ropes, weapons and a few odds and ends, as it had before.

"Yes," Ami agreed, still slightly suspicious of that fact. Choosing not to voice her concerns, she followed along with the others as the Mate led them down stairs. On the ground floor, they paused in the entrance room to their spire.

Leaning against the arch, just inside the door, their leader peered anxiously up and down the path. "When do they put out the lamps?" he asked, briefly flicking his gaze at Animir.

"Soon," the elf replied, licking his lips. "The rain falls, most stay in. The lamp-lighter will put them out to conserve fuel."

On the far side of the community, down the slope, Piers could see lights disappearing slowly, one at a time. "Speak of the devil," he whispered. "He comes this way," he announced. "Everyone sit on the stairs and remain quiet. He will pass without ever knowing we are here."

Obeying his command, the group hovered on the stone steps, ready to fight if they must, but hoping to hide if they could. His feet scuffing along on the wet cobblestones, the elf approached, pausing at each lamp with a long wooden rod in hand. On the end of his staff was a brass cup that he used to snuff each flame. Practiced at his task, he only took a few seconds to extinguish each one and move on to the next.

Shivering in the damp air, Oldrilin's teeth chattered as she burrowed against Rey's chest. Taking pity on her, he unrolled his blanket and wrapped it around his shoulders, forming a tent over her to keep in the warmth.

"What's wrong?" Ami whispered when she noticed his doing so.

"Nothing," he replied, "she's cold. So I think it will keep her warmer. I don't think she's ever seen actual winter before. In their lagoon, it's always summer."

Nodding, Amicia smiled at his thoughtfulness and wished for a moment there would be someone who could carry her. The picture of such a thing cause her to giggle before she dismissed the thought and refocused on the task at hand.

Shifting to the other side of the entrance, Piers continued to observe the lamp-lighter, or in this case snuffer's progress. Once he had disappeared from sight, their leader commanded, "All right, Animir, you're up my friend. Through the armory, you said?"

"Yes, follow close," the elf instructed with a beckoning motion. Forming a single line, they did as they were told, each walking upright and calm so as to not draw attention in case they were spotted.

In the center of the group, Rey followed behind Ami and Bally, who took the spot right behind his friend. Behind him, he could hear the Mate's firm boot-clomps as he brought up the rear. Beneath the blanket he had wrapped around him, he could feel the siren strapped loosely to his chest, and felt thankful his device had held.

Opening his covering, he smiled down at her, noting that she had fallen asleep in the warm pocket, reminding him once again of a child rather than a woman. Folding his blanket around her snugly, he frowned up at the sky as drizzle dampened his hair and beard. "What a miserable night," he mumbled.

"We'll take it," Piers replied from behind. "More chance no one will be out to notice our departure."

Arriving at the fountain, the group ambled along, taking the southern path. The armory lay at the end of it, and they entered the dark building without having seen a soul yet. "Perfect," Animir breathed, his air frosting as he paused to allow his eyes to adjust to the dark. "Should we dare light a few lamps?"

"I think we can risk it," Piers agreed, then commanded, "Bally, you and Rey stay by the door. Anything moves up the path, you be sure to let us know well before they get here."

"Aye," the two younger men agreed in unison as Animir lit a few of the torches that added a soft glow to the chamber.

Moving quickly, he then pulled down a few of the bows, trying the strings until he found exactly the one he wanted. Then, he gathered arrows and placed them into a quiver with a sling that would hold them across his back. "Anyone else want one?" he asked when he was done.

"I'll take one." Ami followed his example and tried out a few until she found one that she could draw easily. When she had made her selection, the elf presented her with her pack of arrows, which he had prepared for her. Helping her slip them over her back, it rode on top of her pack and quilt in a large lump.

"You carrying enough?" Bally asked with a laugh as he joined them.

"You want to carry some of hers?" Piers demanded, punching the younger man in the chest.

"No, I just thought it was funny," the boy replied, rubbing his injury while avoiding catching his stitches on the frilly cloth of his new shirt.

"Well, don't," the older man growled. "Let's move!"

Putting out the lights, the group continued on, out through the forge. Soon, they came to a narrow trail that disappeared into the forest. "We go this way," Animir informed them, indicating the path.

"Where does it lead?" The Mate eyed the specified route warily. Heavy forest, their progress would be slow, and the wet ground would add to the danger of that route.

"Esterbrook, more or less," the elf supplied calmly. "Realm of the nymphs and satyrs, south and west of here."

"Oh," Amicia chimed in. "The queen said they are an enemy of the dragons. Surely we will find solace there."

"All right, we head for Esterbrook," Piers made the choice, assuming he would still be in command of the group even if they were following the elf. "We push as far as we can into the night and tomorrow and hope they don't know where we have gone when they wake up in the morning. With any luck, they'll think we've returned to Riran."

Following the elf through the narrow trail, the limbs of trees pushed in around them, catching on their packs and slowing them significantly. "Try not to break the limbs," Reynard suggested. "If we do, it will just leave a trail better for them to follow us."

"True," Ami agreed, slowing her pace and taking care when she became snagged on a branch.

Ahead of them, Animir kept moving, pushing forward as his mind raced. "*My Lady Cilithrand,*" he mentally called into the darkness.

"*I'm here,*" came her disembodied reply.

"*I have our guests,*" he informed her. "*What is your wish, my queen?*"

"*You are on the southern trail, leading into the dark forest before the meadow?*"

"*Yes, your highness.*"

"*Good. Take them through the Shadowlands and down to Esterbrook. There, await my further instruction.*"

Tromping through the dense woods, the group followed Piers, despite their exhaustion. They had left the elf city shortly before midnight and had yet to take a real break. Driven by fear of being caught, none of them dared to complain, but their leader could tell they were getting tired.

"I think we've pushed about as far as we can," Piers finally announced a few hours after sunrise the following morning. Gathering the group in a clearing in the trees, a selection of large rocks created a natural stone garden of seats, and he indicated them with an outstretched hand, "Everyone rest. I'll check the access to the brook over to the west. If we can get to it, we'll eat and have a good drink before we push on."

"Push on," Bally groaned once he disappeared. "The man is a sadist, I swear it."

"He just wants to be sure they don't catch up to us," Rey corrected, opening his blanket and helping Oldrilin to the ground. As soon as her feet were planted, she scurried away.

"Where's Ami?" Baldwin continued, noticing she had disappeared.

"Taking a piss," the other man supplied while loosening his load and dropping it onto a rock. Stretching, he groaned, then stepped into a group of brush to relieve himself as well. "Animir!" he called. "How far to this Esterbrook place?"

"A few days, maybe a week," the elf replied, his eyes watching around them tirelessly.

"I've got water," the Mate announced, rejoining them. His voice lighter than it had been since they fled the tower, he held up the two wine bottles from the night's dinner. "Amicia, you have what was left from the meal?"

"Aye." She grinned, adjusting her sweater around her shoulders against the chilled air. "I've got what there is, but it won't be much. And I took the goblets, so we can have a good drink at least."

"Anything is better than nothing. We'll try for some game and a fire before the sun sets," he agreed.

"I don't see any sun," Baldwin whined.

"Well, it's there," Piers snapped, on edge with the boy. "We're keeping a positive attitude, remember?" he demanded, glaring at the younger man intently.

Nodding, his voice cracked, "Yes, sir." He looked as if he might cry, with the skin around his eyes taking on a deep red hue as he blinked rapidly. From his seat on one of the rocks, he looked beaten with his hunched shoulders and drooping frame.

Sensing something wasn't right, Ami intervened. "Here, Rey. Give everyone a share," she said, handing him the rolled napkins that held the food. "And the cups are in my bag as well, for the water," she tacked on. Reaching for Bally, she offered more quietly as she knelt before him to peer up at his strained features. "What's the matter?"

"I'm tired," he replied, his lip trembling and actual tears forming and dampening his thick lashes before he swiped at them with the back of his hand.

"We're all tired, love," she soothed. Standing, she pulled his cheek against her stomach and rocked him gently, as if he were a small child in need of comfort. "It'll be ok," she whispered, leaning over so her head was closer to his and she could speak softly to him. "The Mate will see us through."

Lifting his arms, he hugged her against him, clinging to her as if he might be swept away into oblivion if he lost his grip. Accepting her petting, she pulled his hat off and ran her fingers over and through his shaggy hair.

"Feel better?" she asked after a few minutes of stroking.

"Much," he agreed with a loud sniff as he released her. Wiping his sleeve across his face, he forced a smile. "Thanks, sis," he teased.

"Any time." She giggled, happy she had been able to help. Turning to Rey, she accepted her small share of the rations and her goblet brimming with clear, sweet water. Taking a seat on a short flat rock, she sat the cup beside her and nibbled at her meal as she glanced around at the others, noting that they all appeared worse for wear.

Finishing his food, Piers emptied his glass and refilled it before he passed one of the bottles. "Have as much of the water as you like," he encouraged. "I'll refill these to carry. We may not have access next time we stop."

"That's good thinking," Ami praised with a stretch. "We should push forward, at least until dark, and maybe the path will get easier ahead."

"Maybe." The Mate accepted the empty jugs and set out through the trees as he had promised.

Shivering violently, Rey looked around at the dark overhang above them. "Is this place always so dreary?"

"Yes," Animir agreed. "The haunted woods."

"Haunted?" Ami's eyes darted between her companions. "I don't believe in spirits," she sneered. "If there's anything out there, I'm sure it's not a ghost, so forget it. We should repack and be ready to leave when he returns, as it is," she suggested.

"We're in a different land, love," Rey reminded her, still searching the treetops and leaves in earnest. "I swear this forest has eyes. I feel them watching us, be they spirits or some other creature."

"Ami's right. Just because dragons and sirens turned out to be real doesn't mean that we'll be meeting a phantom." Bally laughed anxiously, agreeing with the girl in a backhanded way as he repacked his gear as she had requested.

Studying his new friends, Animir didn't join in their chatter. He knew what lay within the trees and the danger they would face if luck were not with them. But silence was his ally, and he could not afford to reveal too much to the strangers in his land.

"We keep to the trail," Piers instructed, returning with their water supply and hoisting his pack. "We don't want to tempt fate by wandering off, regardless of what might or might not be out there."

"Aye," Rey reluctantly agreed, closing his blanket around his mermaid and preparing to set out once more.

TWENTY-NINE

Shadowlands

LYING BENEATH DARK TREES, Piers listened to the eerie silence of the forest around him. The humid air thick, it seemed to press down upon him. He had never heard a quiet like this, where no birds sang, wind rustled, or even bugs crawled. The breathing of his companions signaled that they slept, the faint passing of air disproportionately loud in the quiet.

Across the circle of bodies, Baldwin twitched, and Piers pushed himself up to observe him in the dim light. Listening to the boy pant, he sighed. Standing, his movements slow and purposeful, he crept towards him and knelt on the damp, black soil.

His arms lay across his chest, his injured hand stiff. Lifting it gently in an effort not to wake him, the Mate inspected the wound. Red and swollen, the skin puffed around the stitches. Infection had set in, and a fever had seized his young friend, but in the middle of nowhere, there was little he could do for him.

"It's bad, isn't it," Bally said in a hoarse whisper.

"It ain't good," his leader replied. "We need to get moving. Our only hope is to get you to Esterbrook while there's still time to do something about it."

Respecting the silence of the trees, he woke each member of their growing party in turn. Rising and rolling their bedding, they prepared to leave their small camp. They hadn't bothered with a fire. The temperature had been moderate since they left the slope of the mountain the day before, and with no food to cook, it wasn't worth the trouble.

"How is he?" Ami asked quietly, eyeing the other two men as Rey helped Bally prepare his pack.

"Worse," Piers whispered back. "He's got a fever, and I dare say he can travel maybe another day at best. If we don't make the meadows before tomorrow night, we'll lose him."

His words a knife cutting through her heart, Amicia wiped at her tears. She knew

179

he wouldn't lie to her; not about this. They had been through too much together, and he was preparing her to accept the inevitable. "Who's going to carry Bally's pack?" she asked, observing as he wrapped himself in his quilt rather than carrying it.

"I have his bag," Animir agreed somberly.

"I've got his sword and ax," Piers informed her. "He can focus on staying on his feet."

Glancing around at his friends, the young man's heart heavy, he sighed. They were looking out for him, but it brought little comfort. He was tired, he hurt, and he would lie there and not move if he could get away with it. It was a good thing they weren't going to let him do that.

Taking up their single-file march, Animir led the way, with Bally behind him. Rey currently carried Oldrilin, but she had gotten down to walk several times, and sat in her pouch with her back to his chest so that she could watch where they were going, which made her happy.

Ami and Piers brought up the rear. The girl's load heavy, she fought her own exhaustion but refused to ask for help. *Bally needs it more than I do,* she rationalized. Gripping her merdoe through her shirt, it felt warm through the thin material. *Please,* she silently prayed. *Please help us to make it. I couldn't bear to lose one of them now.*

They had been walking for the better part of the morning when the trail abruptly opened into a wide clearing about the size of the yard that had once been in front of Amicia's home. The trees surrounding it formed a barrier between it and the thicker woods. The ground exposed to the sky, the rays of the sun cut through the clouds in patches and shone down in golden pillars of light.

Stopping instinctively, the group turned in slow circles, admiring the odd difference in the feel of that place. "Well, this is new," the Mate observed aloud as the others silently took in the warm air and light.

"What the hell is that?" Rey asked, pointing at a large animal hovering in the shadows of the trees. Its eyes glowed a rich gold, and its breath could be heard as deep pants that floated across the space between them.

Turning their backs to one another, they formed a ring, with Bally in the center as he was in no condition to fight. Slowly drawing swords and bows, the four healthy group members prepared for a battle as the collection of creatures crept forward from all sides.

It's a wolf, Ami thought to herself, then frowned. *We killed a pack of wolves at Nalen two years ago. These things can't be wolves… they're the size of horses!*

Six in number, the beasts were large; all black, with smoky, grey undertones that accented their faces, chests, and tips of tails and ears. Their snouts long and sharp, their ears stood in stiff points, as if listening to the very heartbeats of their soon-to-be victims. Slinking towards them, their footfalls were silent, and had they not been spotted, they could have been upon them without a single indication of their existence beforehand.

Their teeth bared, growls broke the silence. Kneeling down, Rey slipped the ropes from his shoulders, and Lin climbed out of her sack, dragging it behind her as she joined Baldwin in the center of the small box of protection, for as long as it would last against the monstrous-sized beings.

"Stay where you are!" Piers commanded, raising his sword with his right hand and holding up the left as a signal to stop.

"Why have you entered our forest?" a snarl rumbled in reply.

Glancing at the elf, Amicia realized that only they two heard the words within the menacing vocals. "What are they?" she whispered, hoping their native group member could shed some light on their situation.

Shaking his head, the young man swallowed hard, his fear forming in small droplets of perspiration across his forehead. "They are the keepers of the dark forest. The Shadowlands," he replied. "Friends to few, if any, and most likely the end of us."

Her eyes wide, Amicia instantly recognized their situation would come to a head quickly if a truce could not be reached in short order. "Please!" she spoke up, stepping forward and breaking their ranks. Dropping to one knee, she bowed her head and stared at the large paws of the animal who had spoken. "We request safe passage through your lands."

Meeting her with a few short paces, the leader of the pack snarled at the men who moved to protect her. His breath hot against her skin, she shivered, but held her ground.

"Stay back," she commanded, laying her bow and pack of arrows on the dark earth next to her. "We're no match for them," she hissed. "Please," she said again, slowly raising her soft green eyes to meet the burning glare of the alpha's orange orbs.

"You speak our tongue," the monster growled. Sniffing noisily, his posture relaxed, and he pranced a circle around her as he inspected her smaller form, his long tail swishing as he moved. "You smell of mortal, of the rim. What say you? How come you to this land?"

"Shipwrecked," she offered meekly. "Abandoned by the tide and running for our lives. Dragons hunt us, and we barely escaped the elf city of Jerranyth a few nights ago. Our friend is taken with fever, and we only hope to make the meadows of the nymphs before it's too late."

Sitting on his haunches, his black and grey coat shown in the patches of light. "And have you a name, human?" His comrades followed suit, and all sat staring at the party. Their posture still tense and stiff, they waited for his command to attack if it would come.

"Amicia Spicer," she replied, standing. At her full height, she could look him square in the eye. "What sort of creature are you?" she dared to inquire.

"I am Uscan, head of the southern pack. We are called wolf, but I doubt your flimsy versions do us justice."

"Wolf," she breathed, "no, you are far too large. Are you certain you are related to them?"

"All life of the rim sprang from Eriden," he informed her. "There have been many adaptations and abominations to our species since leaving our sacred land. You are lesser beings to those of the Kingdom."

Regaining his voice, Animir spoke up, demanding, "Why speak you so unkind?"

"Truth is neither kind nor unkind, elf," he growled an angry reply. "Be silent, or earn your reward."

Clamping his jaw shut tightly, the latter glared at him. When Piers hissed, "What's going on?" Animir shook his head and whispered back, "She's talking to them. We wait."

"*Talking* to them?" Rey asked incredulously.

"Shh," Ami rebuked, then returned her focus to the giant wolf before her. "My apologies for my misunderstanding. Mortals of the rim have no knowledge of Eriden or the source of our ancestry. There are many other… myths… about the creation of our world and the origins of our animal and plant life," she explained, growing confident. "Please, forgive us," she bade with a bow of her head while placing her hand over her heart in a small curtsy.

"Nothing to forgive," Uscan agreed as he looked her up and down. "You are the leader of your pack?"

"I speak for my friends, yes," she offered with a small grin. "We have been trapped here many days. Piers was first mate on our vessel. He leads us," she explained, using an upturned hand to indicate the man in charge.

Seeing himself being presented, the Mate lowered his weapon and bowed at the hip. Never taking his eyes off the beast, he remained stiff, ready for an attack at any moment.

"You should rid yourself of the elf," the pack leader advised. "They are untrustworthy at best and conniving deceivers at worst."

"Animir is our friend. He helped us to flee the queen's grasp," Ami gasped. "We wouldn't think of parting with him."

Studying him and the others for a long moment, Uscan appeared to be considering their plight. "Very well," he finally said with a nod of his giant head. "We will deliver you to Esterbrook."

"Deliver us!" she breathed, panting slightly with fear and joy mixing in her gut. "You will show us the way?"

Barking an order to his pack, he laughed, "We will carry you. Each of you climb upon one of us, but hang on tightly. We wouldn't want to lose any of you along the way."

Lying before her, Uscan waited for her to take her place upon his back, as did the rest of his group. Turning to the others, she explained, "They're going to carry us to Esterbrook. Everyone needs to climb onto one of them and hang on so you don't fall off."

Glancing anxiously at Bally, Piers snapped, "He can't hang on! He's hurt and taken with fever, remember?"

"Then we can both ride on Uscan. I'll help make sure he doesn't tumble to the ground," she offered, closing the distance between them and grasping Baldwin by the arm to escort him to their benefactor. "Please, Piers. Let them help us," she begged, urging the younger man to climb on.

"Creatures of the forest should never be trusted," Animir stated defiantly, his hands forming fists as if he intended to punch the notion to ride out of her.

Ami cackled. "Funny, they said the same thing about you." She had gotten her charge loaded and swung onto the massive back behind him. Her hands running over the thick fur, it felt coarse when her fingers rubbed one way and yet soft when pushed the other.

Grasping a handful with one and sliding her arm around her companion, she stated firmly, "I'm taking Bally to Esterbrook. The rest of you can either get onto a wolf and come with us or get there the best you can."

"Wolf!" Rey shouted. "Are you blind? They're not wolves, these bastards are huge!"

"I don't have time to explain," Ami called back as Uscan got to his feet and trotted out of the clearing, headed west via a narrow path.

"Pick a ride," Piers commanded, hoisting his pack. Gathering Ami's things from where she had left them, he also placed them on his back and climbed onto one of the currently docile creatures. "We can't afford to split the group or to let them get away from us."

Obeying, Rey scooped up Oldrilin and placed her in front of him when he slid onto the thick fur. Grasping two fists full, he held on for dear life as the Mate and Animir did the same.

Trotting along after the leader, the rest of the pack caught up to him easily, and they picked their way expertly through the thick woods. Arriving at a brook late in the afternoon, they paused, allowing everyone to have a drink and refresh themselves in the cool, flowing water.

Catching Amicia, Piers demanded, "Care to explain what's going on now?"

"They're helping us," she replied. She had been talking to Uscan off and on as they moved and had learned a great deal, or at least his version of things. She was coming to understand that the truth was never an exact, tangible thing, and that the point of view of every creature altered its meaning.

"As you know, this is called the Shadowlands. He and the other wolves patrol the great forests of Eriden. This is the southern pack," she added indicating their new allies with a toss of her golden locks. "The dark forest here isn't home to much in the way of animals. The land was cursed after the great war centuries ago, and few dare to even enter, much less make it their home."

"Why are they helping us?" Rey asked in an accusing tone. "Animir obviously doesn't trust them."

"I don't have an answer for that," she admitted quietly. "I only know that they are, and Bally needs that help, so we will take it. If it has a price later, I'm willing to pay it for his sake."

Breathing deeply, Reynard glared at his friend. Leaning against a large rock next to the rippling water, he appeared pale. Still wrapped in his blanket, his stocking cap crooked on his head, he coughed violently before resting back against the stone and closing his eyes. "I hope we make it," he admitted quietly.

"Aye." The Mate refilled his wine bottles and returning them to his pack. "Are we ready to move?"

"Yes," Ami agreed, "Uscan's team will see us there."

Resuming their positions, the group continued as the trees and land changed on the other side of the stream. The woods grew less dense, with plants springing up on the forest floor. Small patches of open ground and meadows broke up the landscape further, and they were on the outskirts of a lush, green, open field as the sun set.

"Welcome to Esterbrook," Uscan informed her as they trotted forward in the growing darkness.

Before her, gentle hills rolled, with patches of trees and water in between. She could see the lay of the land from their slightly raised position, but nowhere could she pick out a fire, a building, or anything that resembled a town or community. "Do these nymphs live like the sirens? In a primitive culture without social order or structure?"

"They are as structured as any realm of Eriden. If you seek a city, you should have remained with the elves, for theirs is the grandest of the southern lands. We will take you to the sacred circle, where the nymphs and satyrs congregate, but from there you are on your own," Uscan replied.

"I understand." She sighed, tightening her grip on the young man before her. He had grown more relaxed with each mile, and she feared that he would lose consciousness any time. *Just get us there,* she mentally added, *and we'll do whatever we must to gain their trust and aid.*

THIRTY

Esterbrook

A FULL MOON had been rising as the sun sank into the west and hung at about one-quarter of the way across its arc as the pack of wolves trotted into a large clearing. On the ground, concentric circles formed by large white stones glowed in the luminescent cascade. Their steps unhurried, the group converged on the most center ring of the four, which spanned ten feet in diameter.

"Wow," Rey said quite loudly. "This place is amazing!"

With no living thing in sight, Amicia leaned forward, pressing her body against Baldwin as she did so. "Is this the place, Uscan?"

"Yes," he replied, coming to a stop and lying on his belly so they could climb down safely.

Sliding off first, Ami turned, expecting to help Bally do the same. Instead, she found him to be unconscious, his eyes closed and his face pale beneath the moon-glow. Giving him a firm shake to wake him, he fell backwards instead, languishing over their rescuer's back. "Shit," she muttered, fighting gravity to keep him from crashing to the ground. "Piers, I need you!" she screamed.

On the spot, he and Rey rushed forward. The mermaid had been sitting on the fur-covered seat on her own and bounced anxiously around them as the two men each claimed a side, lifting the boy off Uscan, who seemed relaxed and patient as they did so.

"Make a pallet," the Mate commanded.

Unrolling her bedroll quickly, Animir helped Amicia spread it onto the ground. "I couldn't wake him," she explained as she did so, tears swimming in her soft green orbs. "What should we do?"

"Where are the nymphs?" their leader asked, glaring at the elf and then the wolf. When no one responded, he began barking orders. "Fine. Gather some wood, and we will build a fire. I'm going to need something to boil some water in –"

"Here?" Animir cut him off. "This is a sacred place. You can't stack wood and build a fire where ever you like."

"The hell I can't," Piers shouted, covering Bally with his quilt. "This man is dying, elf. If we don't do something immediately, our chances of saving him drop to nothing!" A small, feminine hand fell on his shoulder, ending his tirade.

Twisting to face her while still kneeling next to his friend, the Mate held his jaw firm. Before him, standing at about four feet in height, a beautiful young woman with long silver hair smiled down at him. "Yes," he breathed. "Right," he agreed to an unspoken observation.

"Forget the fire," he corrected, his tongue flicking over his lips. "They will bring water and medicine for him. Cover him with another blanket to keep him warm."

Frowning at his odd behavior, Rey demanded, "What's going on?"

"She spoke to me," Piers informed him, unrolling his own pack and smoothing the new cover over his friend. "I could hear her in my thoughts."

"Hear –" the other man began, then halted, his mind racing. Glancing over at Oldrilin, who smiled at him, he recalled the time he had heard her speaking to him inside his head. "They're telepathic," he announced, the link suddenly clear.

"Oh my God!" Ami gasped. "Cilithrand said she couldn't read my mind, but in time we could possibly build the connection. I wonder how it works, exactly."

"Members of the same species are often connected by rights," Uscan informed them. He had been licking himself calmly but stopped for a stretch as he explained. "Those in the same family have an even greater chance. Mates and close friends can develop the ability over time. Part of the magic of Eriden is the depth of our connections to one another and the world around us."

Her mouth hanging open, Amicia processed the information. Glancing over at Animir, she could see the lines of worry forming in his forehead. "Dear God," she breathed.

"Are you going to translate, or do we have to guess what he said?" Rey suggested curtly.

"He said that members of the same species can talk to each other telepathically. Mates, family and friends may also be able to."

"And what about total strangers?" he pushed, pointing at the nymph who had returned with a wooden cup of healing elixir, followed by a second bearing green leafy material, which she pulled pieces from and applied to Baldwin's swollen hand.

"Maybe some creatures are better at it than others," she tacked on, still staring at Bally's young friend.

Following her gaze, Rey squirmed. "Does that mean this guy could be informing the elves where to find us? How far does it reach?" His voice rose as he realized the implications of such a talent.

"I don't know, Rey!" she snapped, tearing her eyes away and focusing on Bally. They had managed to rouse him, and she knelt beside him to help him sip the liquid, which smelled of some form of warm tea.

Glancing around at the gathering, he could see that their party had been joined by more of the small women, but a couple of males also came with them. Although all of the new additions were near the same height and build, their eyes, hair, and skin held an even wider variety than the mermaids had.

Staring up at the female who tended him, Bally gasped, "I'm delusional. This woman is green!"

"No, Bally." Piers chuckled as he crouched near the top of his head. Leaning forward to tussle his hair, he tacked on, "These are the nymphs, and so far I see every color of the rainbow here, near enough. More than even the sirens boasted in their fish forms."

Around them, nymphs and satyrs poured onto the circles. Taking seats or standing, they filled the wide rings made of stone. Their voices light and cheerful, they sounded like song birds, rather than the seductive tones of the siren. Joining their hands, they lined the rings in a swaying, undulating motion as some unseen energy force danced through them.

Rising slowly, Piers could feel the warmth flow through his body, like the buzz of a lightning storm out on the sea. Turning in a slow circle, he took them all in, reaching out to them through his thoughts. "They're praying for him," he whispered. "To mother earth, the wind and the trees. The very fabric of nature as it winds and binds us all."

"It tingles," Amicia observed, standing as well. Taking a few steps, she stood beside him, looking up into his strong features. "Piers," she called softly, placing her hand in his and giving him a squeeze.

Returning the pressure, he smiled down at her. "Bally's going to be ok. They have surrounded him with their protection, healing him from the inside out with their power."

Joining them, Rey shook his head slowly side to side. "This doesn't feel right. How do we know we can trust them? Trust anyone here?" he asked, staring at Animir.

Biting his lip, the elf couldn't hear the trio over the sound of the nymphs and their ritual chant, but he knew the look. If he didn't do something and quick, he would lose his position among them, and Cilithrand would kill him for it. Taking a few wide steps, he walked right up to them.

"Please," he gasped, placing his hand on his chest, flat against his heart. His mouth opening and closing a few times, he could not form the words.

"How can we trust you?" Ami spoke for the group.

"I brought you to the nymphs," he replied in a shaky voice.

"The wolves brought us to them," Rey countered with a heavy scowl.

"But I was," the elf insisted, stammering. "I help you. I swear on my life, I would never cross you, Lady Amicia."

Puckering his lips as he removed himself from her grasp with a step back, the Mate shifted his gaze, back and forth between Bally and Animir, sizing up what had occurred from the moment they arrived in Jerranyth. "You should confess, then. Tell us everything, and we will consider not spilling your blood upon this sacred soil."

Swallowing hard, Animir could see the rage in the older man's eyes. Knowing he suspected the elves of treachery, he could also see his salvation. "It was our job to make you happy," he agreed with a deep nod. "To keep you within the walls of our city."

"That's why you became friends with Bally," Rey accused, pointing at him with a stiff digit.

"Yes, he wanted a friend, and so I was assigned to be so. And that is why your siren was spared for you, as it was as you desired. And girls were sent to please you," he admitted in turn, flicking his gaze over at the first mate. "And you were given fine clothes and a hot bath to soothe you," he said more quietly to the girl.

"She could read my thoughts," Amicia gasped. "The whole time, nothing was secret!" The girl's mind flashed to her desire for those very things when she first planned her trip to the west, and she felt violated that those private desires had been used against her.

"She knows what lies within your heart," Animir informed them, a tear forming and spilling over onto his pale cheek. "The queen is a powerful witch. To live among her people means to obey her every command. To fail in her wishes holds the most dire of consequences."

Frowning, Piers suddenly leaned back and growled, "Is it just me, or is he speaking damn near perfect now?"

"Hey, he is," Rey agreed, placing his hands on his hips.

"It's not him," Uscan informed them, striding up to the group and raising his furry chin at their friend, who still lay on the ground. "Your comrade is almost healed."

"If it's not him, then how?" Ami asked in surprise, keeping their focus on the elf.

"You stand in one of the most sacred and powerful places in the Kingdom of Eriden," the wolf replied. "The essence of our world flows through you, and you have been joined to us."

"'Tis true," a nymph with dark ebony skin agreed, slipping her pudgy hand into Amicia's. "You are one with us. The spirit of all things lives within you."

"And we can understand all the creatures of this kingdom, as they can all speak to each other," Piers filled in, his eyes wide as he looked around again, listening to the voices of the nymphs. "How long will it last?"

"Hard to say," the girl replied, her teeth a beautiful, bright white when she smiled. "I am Zaendra, maid to the queen Preivia," she supplied with a small curtsy. "I have been sent to serve you."

Instantly suspicious, Rey inspected her from the top of her dark puffs of hair to her bare feet, then shook his head slowly. "I just want to go home. No more ships, no more strange people or customs. Just my parents' farm, even if I have to work for my older brother all the rest of my life."

Her face drawn into a heavy frown, Oldrilin slipped her tiny fingers into his. "Rey Daye sad."

"Aye." He shrugged, kneeling down and wrapping her hand completely. "I don't belong here, Lin. None of us do. I can't help feeling like the more we see here," he paused, sighing heavily. "The more we become a part of this place, the less our chances of ever getting away."

Placing her free hand on his shoulder, she patted him, her head cocked to the side as she studied his clear hazel orbs. Her lip forming a small pout, her chin crinkled as if she would cry.

Realizing his words had hurt her, he pulled her small frame to him into a firm hug. "I'm sorry, Lin. I know things have been turned upside down since we got here, but we will find a way to make things right. We'll get you back to the sirens and get ourselves home, one way or another. I swear it."

"Perhaps, but not tonight," the nymph with silvery-blue hair agreed. "For now, your friend must rest. We will spirit you into our homes among the meadows and forest for a rest," she informed them, lifting her hand to indicate the edges of their great gathering.

"That will be acceptable," the Mate agreed. "But we wish to remain together, if you don't mind."

"You do not trust us," she declared, her eyes narrowing into thin slits as she glared at the elf. "A wise precaution considering the company you keep. I am Preivia, queen of these lands. You have met my maid, Zaendra," she indicated the girl who still held Ami's hand. "Our homes are small, but I'm sure we can accommodate you."

Stumbling to his feet, Baldwin joined them on weak knees. "That was incredible," he shouted, shoving his hand out for inspection.

Grasping the appendage, Piers exposed the cut he had stitched before they fled the tower, but the threads had been removed. In their place, an ordinary cut remained with no sign of the infection. The wound was not completely gone, but it no longer threatened the boy, and would be mended in a matter of days, if that long. Clicking his tongue, he addressed the queen. "We don't need much. We'll sleep in the trees if we have to."

Smiling up at him, she waved her hand towards a large clump of trees to the east of them. "Then have your pick."

"Thank you." He hoisted his pack and called to the others, "Everyone stick together. I'm with Rey on this one. The sooner we get off this damned rock, the better."

"We will leave you then," Uscan called after them.

"You won't stay with us?" Amicia asked in surprise, raising a hand as if to pet his long snout as he stood before her.

"I'm afraid the Shadowlands awaits, princess," he growled gently, then said more quietly, "but ever should you need us, you may call to us again."

"Again?" she breathed, her heart skipping a beat. "I don't remember calling to you a first time," she said with a small, anxious laugh.

"But call you did," he replied sternly. "*Please help us to make it,*" he mocked her tone, and she could hear her own voice as she had whispered the prayer.

"You heard me," she gasped.

"Yes, and we came to you. And so we will again if ever you have need of us," he replied, turning his back to walk away.

Watching him go, Ami pulled on the string that held her merdoe. Freeing it from her shirt, she stared at the shimmering inner side beneath the glow of the full moon. *This thing is very powerful,* she surmised. *More than just a translator,* as she had once assumed. Tucking it back inside, she hoisted her pack, bow, and arrows and ran to catch up to the others as they marched into the line of trees and disappeared.

THIRTY-ONE

Blindsided

SEATED BEFORE HER MIRROR, Lady Cilithrand pulled the braids from her hair. Selecting a large flat brush, she ran it through her long, silky strands. Her mind reaching out, she searched for Animir.

She had done so several times over the last few days and knew that the human they called Baldwin lay near death. However, it would be of little consequence. *The girl, Amicia,* she thought with a smile. *She is the key to achieving my desires.*

Continuing to stroke her honey brown locks, the queen frowned at her reflection before her. Animir had been a faithful servant, but it troubled her that she could not reach him at that moment. Rising from her chair, she sauntered across the room, her long gown floating about her as she moved.

Lifting a glittering orb from its resting place on a table, she peered into it. She again smiled at how she had deceived Ami with a similar crystal. *The orb of truth,* she snickered. *Silly girl.* She had not realized how gullible mortals could be.

The queen had acquired half a dozen of the small, magical globes, as they were quite common in the Kingdom of Eriden, and virtually every magical family had one. However, they were simple to operate and even easier to manipulate by those who knew how. Inhaling sharply as an image came into focus, she glared at Animir as he lay sleeping beneath the trees with his companions in the glen.

"So, you made it to Esterbrook, but you did not see fit to inform me," she muttered angrily. "You'll pay for that."

"Cilithrand," a deep voice growled from outside her balcony, interrupting her plotting.

Glancing around at her empty suite, she breathed in deeply through her nose, then pushed the air out through a relaxed jaw to calm herself. Returning the orb to its small pedestal, she smoothed her hair and pursed her lips. Inspecting her appearance in her full-length mirror, she purposely made him wait before presenting herself on the stone extension of her quarters.

"Lamwen," she greeted Gwirwen's captain evenly.

"Which tower are they in?" he demanded, adjusting his footing on the narrow ledge on which he perched. A full-sized male, he stood fifteen feet high from the ground, which was about half his entire length, and his wings spanned almost thirty feet when he spread them.

The dragon had visited Jerranyth several times over the years, but he held no real love for the elves. His bright green skin and dark emerald accents shimmering as he twitched eagerly, he would make his work there quick.

"They've gone," she informed him flatly, her features betraying no emotion.

"What do you mean gone?" he hissed, smoke trickling out between his teeth. "You assured our king, Gwirwen, they would be here and ready to be taken." *Or killed.*

"As that was my intention," she assured, looking away and lifting her chin. "They have escaped. One of my weapons men is with them."

"You have a traitor," he coughed, displeased further with each revelation.

"He will be dealt with. In fact, you have my permission to kill him or punish him as you see fit," she replied with a gleam in her eye as she cut her gaze back to him.

"Very well," Lamwen agreed, again adjusting his footing and sending a few rocks plummeting to the empty path below. "Where have they gone?"

"You will find them at Esterbrook," she supplied, her lips curling into a thin smile.

"Esterbrook," he repeated with a deep laugh. "Of course. The nymphs hold great disdain at being made to bow before our new king. Our peace with them is fleeting, and we will take pleasure in making an example of them and those that harbor enemies of Eriden."

"As you should," Cilithrand agreed, turning and stepping calmly into her suite before closing the curtains to her balcony, essentially washing her hands of the humans and the dragon in one motion.

Leaping from his perch, Lamwen soared above the tops of the trees. Headed north, he landed on a snow-capped peak, where his two companions awaited their orders. "They've fled Jerranyth," he informed them curtly. "Either by escape or the queen has let them go. She's a conniving wench, and therefore it is difficult to say as to the how and why."

"We will hunt them?" Pardodan, a heavy-set dragon with blue and green scales asked calmly. Several feet shorter than the captain, he eagerly awaited his chance to prove himself useful as a protector of the kingdom before the king by the completion of this task.

"No need," Lamwen explained. "They've been taken in at Esterbrook."

"The nymphs." Vaudien, the third member of their hunting party laughed, his amethyst eyes glowing and accenting his deep purple and black skin. "They will pay for sheltering the fugitives."

"Indeed," Lamwen growled before leaping into the air. Taking a path south and west, the other two followed close behind, ready to do their master's bidding and close the matter for good.

Lying on her pallet beneath a small grove of trees, Amicia sighed deeply. In their exhaustion, the others had fallen into a peaceful slumber almost as soon as they had lain down, but not her. Pulling her merdoe from its hiding place, she rubbed the smooth inside and pondered the day's events.

Recalling how the wolves had shown up at the most opportune moment, she shuddered. *I called them,* she silently considered. She hadn't meant to, but it had happened just the same. Where knowing this might have brought her comfort, it did not. Realizing her ability frightened her.

I shouldn't use this thing anymore, she rationalized. Since the others had been infused with the magic of the land, there would be no need. *Maybe I should get rid of it, destroy it or something,* she mused.

Lightning flashed in a distant cloud. Glaring at it, she sighed. *I may have to wake the others before that gets here and we get soaked in a downpour.*

Staring at the storm, it approached quickly; too quickly. Her chest tight with fear, she shoved her shell between her breasts and leapt to her feet. "Piers!" she screamed, reaching him and shaking him fiercely. "Mate! The dragons are coming!"

"What?" he stammered, confused at his untimely awakening.

Next to him, Rey rolled over and demanded, "What dragons?"

"I don't know," she replied anxiously, pointing at the dark horizon. "The storm comes too fast to be natural."

The three men and the elf got to their feet, stretching and claiming their weapons. "Are we not going to run away?" she cried when she realized they weren't packing for a hasty exit.

"Not this time, love," the Mate informed her. "This time, we stand our ground." Glaring at the elf, he growled, "Are you with us, or should I end you now?" Raising his sword, he made his threat clear.

"Don't be stupid," Animir replied in a surly tone. "You will need all the aid you can get. Besides, I have not betrayed you, and my life will be at risk equal to your own."

Looking around, Rey whined, "Has anyone seen Oldrilin?"

All casting glances around them, they did not see the siren. Instead, they saw nymphs and satyrs pouring out of their burrows and beds among the treetops. In a massive ocean of bodies, they pressed in around the sacred rings but did not fill them in, keeping the inner three circles clear.

Joining them, Zaendra squealed, "You have brought the dragons back to the glen. For many moons have they left us in peace, but on the night of your arrival, they attack!"

"That was not our intention," Ami replied crossly, positioning her quiver across her back. She had taken a few practice shots with her new bow and had proven to be a poor shot, but she would stand with her friends and fight none-the-less.

Out in the meadow, Queen Preivia stood alone in the central ring as three large dragons landed around her. She appeared to be speaking to them. Frowning, Piers swore under his breath.

Cutting her eyes over at him, Ami asked, "What do you think?"

"I think without cover or a shield, we'll be burnt to a crisp in a matter of seconds," he replied tartly.

Images of burned cows sprang into her mind, and Amicia cursed as well. Gripping her bow tightly, she waited for the signal they would begin the battle.

But the signal did not come as she had expected. The power of the nymphs had been demonstrated earlier in the evening, and their cunning now came to light. In an instant, the queen disappeared, as if the blink of an eye had removed her.

In the same moment, a heavy flurry of rocks, logs and other debris rained down upon the trio still standing in the center of the sacred rings. Taking flight, their wings beat wildly, and flames spewed from their nostrils, scorching the lush, green field.

Her mouth open wide, Ami tore her eyes from the beasts and searched the edge of the tree line, where she could see large contraptions had been pushed out into the open space. Equipped with large buckets at the end of pivoting arms, she had never seen such a weapon.

"What are they?" she gasped, watching as a pair of satyrs cranked one of them into position, the long log pulled back. They triggered the latch once it was in place, and a roundish stone hurtled through the air, catching one of the flying demons upside the head as he gained altitude and wobbled for a moment before righting himself and joining his friends out of reach.

"Cannons of some sort." The Mate pointed at another contraption that had been fitted with a large arrow. "They've learned to forge."

"Yes," Animir agreed. "It is surprising to say the least."

Catching a whiff of uncertainty in his voice, Piers seized him by the front of his shirt and slammed him against a tree. "Something tells me you aren't surprised about this at all," he growled.

"I have no knowledge of this," the elf stammered. "Only to observe the weapons could not have been forged by the nymphs or the satyrs, who protect them. They have formed an ally, of this I am certain."

"The elves?" Rey asked, joining in the interrogation.

"The queen would never provide them with arms," Animir replied, his voice growing faint, "not unless it served her purpose."

"Served her purpose," Amicia repeated with a heavy frown. "She wants them to fight."

"Perhaps," the Mate agreed, releasing his prisoner and watching as the dragons swooped in for another run.

This time, the satyrs hit them with an even stronger volley, and the steel arrows ripped through the wing of the largest dragon, sending him crashing to the ground, where it lay perfectly still.

"They've killed it!" Amicia shouted, with a surprising mixture of anger and pain coursing through her veins as the satyrs continued to attack the defenseless creature, pummeling him with large stones and hunks of wood the size of a man's chest. Tears on her face, she slung her bow over her back and ran out into the sea of bodies. "Stop! Stop!" she shouted, pushing her way towards the center, where the helpless beast lay.

With their captain struck down, Pardodan and Vaudien flew higher, into the tumultuous clouds. They made a wide sweeping circle over the land, coasting on the currents of air as they evaluated their position. Inspecting the weapons, they knew they could set fire to the glen and wipe out all that hid within it, but at great cost to the kingdom as a whole.

"We need to confer with Gwirwen and the council," Vaudien observed. "The queen of Esterbrook reached an accord with Gwirwen soon after he came to power. They are allies of the dragons, and yet they have attacked us."

"Do we leave him?" Pardodan asked of his elder, unsure of their course.

Reaching out to his captain but only finding silence below, the elder snarled, "They were never so armed. We have been blindsided by their treachery, arming themselves so while under a truce with us. Lamwen does not respond to my calls, and I daresay we will lie beside him if we make another pass."

"Then we should seek the counsel of our king," Pardodan agreed.

Flying higher still, the pair headed north but would soon turn east as they crossed the whole of the kingdom. The dragons' cliffs lay on the opposite side of the continent, and therefore controlling this furthest point was of great interest to Gwirwen by treaty if possible, or by force if necessary. He would want to be kept appraised of any uprising that might be brewing, and the humans would be secondary of concerns, Vaudien felt sure.

Below, Lamwen lay on the ground, the concentric circles of the field radiating out from his lifeless form. Reaching him, the satyrs carried out a large net made of rope. Climbing over him as if he were a simple statue carved from rock, they covered him with it and staked it to the ground, shouting and cheering as they did so.

Arriving in the center, the group of outsiders paused while Amicia pushed closer, her cheeks damp with tears. Next to the beast, she could smell the blood as it oozed from his fresh wounds, the one on the side of his head coating the sacred ground with thick red blood. Her hand trembling, she reached to touch the leathery skin of his wing, the torn flap ragged and loose.

"Why did they run away?" Bally asked, staring at the two forms disappearing in the distance. "If the same species can talk to one another telepathically, why didn't they just call for help? They breathe fire. I'm sure they could have taken us."

"We have struck a peace with the dragons," Preivia explained, laying her hand on the snout of the creature before her. "A ruse to give us time to prepare. They dare not attack us openly. They have flown to inform the dragon council of our readiness to fight."

"But you attacked them," the Mate observed, glaring at the large lidded orbs. The dragon's breath hot, it blew over him as their prisoner huffed against his bonds. They had bound his snout by wrapping it with a thin rope so that it could not be opened, and he tapped the binding with a knuckle. "Will that thing hold him?"

"We should kill him now!" Rey spat, angrily clenching his fists around the handle of his sword.

"No!" Amicia screamed, leaving the broken wing and stumbling to stop him. Dropping her weapon, she lay against the neck of the creature, which stirred at her touch. "This dragon will not be harmed!" she commanded, as if she had the authority to do so.

The large, glassy eyes opened, and Lamwen shifted his head to have a better look at the flimsy female. Pulling against his bonds, he found that they were sound, and suspected that they had been reinforced by a magical spell or binding. Puffing a small blast of flame out of his nose, he forced his keepers back with the threat, but the girl did not move.

"I'm Amicia," she informed him in a shaky tone, backing away so he could see who spoke to him. Standing straight, she pressed her merdoe against her flesh through her shirt as she closed her eyes. *"I know you can hear me,"* she directed her thoughts towards him.

His emerald green orbs widened in surprise, but he did not reply. Instead, he lay still, patiently awaiting his fate.

"Please," she said aloud, her hand trembling as she stepped forward and placed her palm flat against his nose. A nostril on either side of the tiny hand, he could have blasted her with flames and roasted her on the spot.

Considering this, the girl's voice shook. "We mean you no harm," she pushed. "We have never meant any, at that. We only wish to go home," she finished quietly.

Closing his eyes, the dragon refused any rebuttal and lay panting against his prison.

Creeping forwards Piers seized her arm. "Come away, precious," he instructed. "This beast has no words for us mortals," he spat, wishing he could join Rey in his cry for blood. But Ami had spoken against it, and the dragon belonged to the nymphs at any rate.

Pulling her arm away, Amicia refused to leave him. "I won't go. Not until I know what you're going to do with him," she insisted, turning to face the queen.

"He will be judged fairly," Preivia assured her. "We are champions of life and do not seek to kill. Even our enemies are sacred to us."

Her face crinkled, and fresh tears stained the girl's cheeks, the queen's words resonating with her emotions. Walking back to the trees, Amicia refused to be comforted. The Mate held her tightly with one arm wrapped across her shoulders, preventing her from looking back.

Arriving at their bedrolls, he pushed her down upon her blanket. "Sleep," he ordered.

"How can I?" she sniveled.

Dropping down beside her, he wrapped her in his quilt and held her against his broad chest. Leaning back against the tree, he pinned her next to him and said more loudly, "Everyone get down and get quiet. The dragon is not ours, and it is up to the owner of this land to decide what will become of him."

THIRTY-TWO

Gone

AMICIA AWOKE TO BRIGHT LIGHT. Cracking her lids, she felt overly warm and coughed a few times as she sat up. Still next to Piers, he grinned up at her as she got to her feet.

"Well, that was cozy," he chortled, brandishing a salacious smile.

Looking down at herself, she flushed. She had slept next to him many nights when they were in Riran, and he had been stringing her along, toying with her emotions. "Yes it was, thank you," she replied stiffly, holding her harsh rebuke at bay.

Rubbing her face, she looked around, longing for a bit of water to remove the sleep from her eyes. Her gaze sweeping across the meadow, she gasped, "The dragon is gone!"

"What do you mean gone?" the man shouted, leaping to his feet.

Glaring at the group of nymphs that stood around the vacated trap, he muttered, "Well, shit." Marching across the open field, he couldn't wait to hear their excuse for freeing the beast.

"You, queenie," he snapped when he reached the gathering, "what's the meaning of letting him go?"

"As you said, the choice was mine to make," she informed him, her lips slowly curling, "and so it has been made. Lamwen will return to his realm unharmed."

"Unharmed," Rey sputtered, joining the group. "We should have killed him, after what they've done."

"This isn't their fight," Amicia countered, looking around at the men dolefully. When her gaze fell on Oldrilin, she gasped, "Oh, Lin. I'm so sorry."

"Aye." Reynard nodded angrily, his hands on his hips. "They killed our entire crew on the ship, and God only knows what's become of the sirens. He deserved to die," he spat bitterly.

"I find that hard to believe. No creature deserves to be murdered, even the guilty." Ami pouted with a heavy heart.

"You're wrong!" Rey shouted, throwing his arms into the air. "We could have sent them a message! We could have let them know we're not afraid. We could have shown them that we are not weak and that they should leave us alone or get what they've got coming to them!"

"We did send them a message," the girl replied softly. "A message of peace." Pivoting, her gaze wandered from face to face as men, elf, nymph, and satyr all stared at her. Squaring her shoulders, she said more confidently, "We've all suffered along this journey. Perhaps our act of compassion will be enough. Perhaps we can now search for a way home and be allowed to leave this wretched place."

The inhabitants of Esterbrook stared at her, and Oldrilin's lips sank into a heavy frown at her choice of words.

"I'm sorry," she gasped, pushing her hair out of her face and realizing how her declaration had sounded. "This is not a bad kingdom," she back paddled, wringing her hands anxiously. "It's not home, that's all. Please, forgive me."

Blinking at her calmly, Preivia reached for her trembling digits. "Amicia," she groveled. "You sweet princess. We understand your plight and your ill will towards our lands. But we cannot help you with this request."

Inhaling deeply, the smaller woman sighed as she dropped the connection and turned her back on her new friend. "We could wish you home to the rim of mortals with all our hearts, and yet the truth would still stand."

"And what truth is that?" Rey demanded, continuing his sulking at the turn of events.

"No one leaves the Kingdom of Eriden," she informed him quietly, looking over her shoulder to peek at his reaction. "The island is protected by a deep, ancient magic. Those who come here stay here. The only beasts who may leave are those capable of flight," she quietly added, confirming what Animir had said as they dined before fleeing Jerranyth.

"The dragons," Piers dropped with a grunt.

"Precisely," the nymph agreed. "So, unless you have a pair of wings tucked away beneath your clothes, I'm afraid that Eriden is your new home. The sooner you come to terms with that... and accept it... the better off you will be."

Books in the Dragon of Eriden Series
Whisper of Suffering
Journey of Darkness
Betrayal of Honor
Kingdom of Ruin
The Complete Set (All 4 Books in 1)

Maps of Eriden & The Rim of Mortals

Newrock

Domania

Palmeto

Rim of
Mortals

Myrrh

Nalen

Baycoast

Deernese

Characters by Race

Humans

Amicia Spicer is a young woman from Nalen discovering her true identity as the story unfolds. Her mother has revealed a secret about her origins upon her deathbed, and Ami is looking for the place she belongs in the world.

Reynard Daye is a young crewman aboard the Sea Serpent. He survives the destruction of the ship and joins the unlucky group of mortals as they crash upon the shores of Eriden.

Piers Massheby is the first mate aboard the Sea Serpent. He is a strong leader and guides the group through their perilous journey in search of a way home.

Baldwin Carter is the cabin boy on board the ship. He is mostly along for the ride, being young and inexperienced at handling the hardships that the group faces along the way.

Minor Human Characters:

Rupert Miller – Amicia Spicer's friend from Nalen, he expects that she will become his betrothed when her parents no longer need her.

Gus Spicer – Amicia's father.

Arely Spicer – Amicia's mother.

Shamus Smith – blacksmith in the desert city of Whitefair.

Geoffrey Tabard – trader from Whitefair.

Humphray Heron – trader from Whitefair.

Sirens

Olirassa is queen of the mermaids. She is the sovereign and protector of the city of Riran.

Oldrilin is Reynard Daye's caretaker in Riran. She becomes caught up in their escape and is swept away onto their adventure through Eriden. Her devotion to Rey is sincere, and she proves to be a valuable member of their group. She seems to have little magical ability but is able to transform into a large black fish.

Elves

Cilithrand is the queen of the elves. She resides in a magnificent palace in Jerranyth, located on the southern end of the elf lands, which consists of the lower end of the central mountains of Eriden.

Animir is an elf of higher class that has been outcast from his station. He no longer feels a part of his elf kin, and helps the group to escape Jerranyth, thereby joining them on their quest to find a way home. He had been banned from using his innate magical abilities, but with the freedom of the group, he explores his talents and regains his ability as a strong wielder of magic. A resourceful member of the group, they value his friendship and utility.

Minor Elf Characters:
    Sadrir – serves the group while they are in Jerranyth.
    Anerion – lead huntsman to Lady Cilithrand.
    Galiodien – Cilithrand's father and former king of the elves.
    Cothiel – female companion to Piers in Jerranyth.

Nymphs

Preivia is queen of the nymphs. She is the sovereign and protector of the city of Esterbrook and the surrounding areas known as the glen and the meadows.

Zaendra is an earth nymph. She is pleased to meet the group when they come into the glen and attaches herself to their company. Spending time with them while they reside in their cabin, she packs her things to leave with them at their departure, as she has always wanted to explore more of Eriden and sees this as her chance. She has some magical abilities and proves to be a valuable member of the group.

Wolves

Uscan is the alpha of the southern pack of grey wolves. His loyalties are often murky, but he holds an affinity for Amicia Spicer. He acts in her best interest both as a friend and advisor. As for the southern pack, they protect the Shadowlands, a cursed area of woods that acts as a natural barrier between the glen and the mountains of the elf lands.

Edeill is the alpha of the northern pack. His loyalties are also in question. His pack of great white wolves are the protectors of the northern woods, and they patrol a much larger area than their southern kin.

Minor Wolf Characters:
    Mirean – scout sent to Esterbrook for the southern pack.
    Aelalle – beta of the northern pack.

Wizards

Meena Gavaan is a wan, a female wizard, but unlike most, she was born with the ability to use magic, which is forbidden within their people. She has led a difficult life and faces tough choices throughout the story. She meets the group upon their arrival in the desert community of Whitefair and agrees to help them for a price. She leaves with them when they flee the oasis and travels with them on their journey, earning her place within the group with her special magical skill set and talent for using her powers in practical ways.

Minor Wizard Characters:
    Jaco Gavaan – Meena's deceased husband.
    Gradien Silversmith – magistrate of the wizard city of Whitefair, he is a powerful wizard, but also a bit of a scoundrel.
    Corvack – head of the security force in Whitefair.

Trolls

Yaodus is the king of the trolls. He is a powerful wielder of magic, which is rare but not unheard of among the trolls. He is distrustful of everyone outside of their community and takes his role of protector of his kind with the utmost of dedication. He is an unlikely ally of the group after Amicia convinces him of her worth, and his help is often the difference between life and death for the mortals and their friends.

Traok is Yaodus's eldest son. He is met several times, as he acts as the liaison between the group and the troll community on several occasions.

Dwarves

Baeweth is the king of the city of Rhong. As their sovereign, he is the protector of the growing city beneath the mountain. However, his family and people have endured a great deal in the last few hundred years. They have denounced the use of magic and are rebuilding after a daemon drove them from their previous home of Asomanee.

Hayt is the king's great nephew and heir to the throne. He holds no desire to ever be king and devises a way to win the trust of the group, then helps them escape rather than see them handed over to the dragons. He is a skilled engineer, and his abilities and knowledge prove useful to the group on their quest.

Minor Dwarf Characters:

Asyng – the king's sister and Hayt's grandmother, she is Baeweth's advisor.

Firen – Hayt's good friend and fellow engineer.

Vael – Another acquaintance of Hayt's, he is the guard on duty when the group prepares to escape.

Daemons

Kedoria is the queen of the daemons. Her loyalties to the elves are shaken when she is captured by Animir and recruited by Amicia. She commands the daemon forces, but they are only able to live in total darkness, which severely limits her utility within the group. She has a few named minions, but they are only briefly mentioned in the events of the story.

Gnomes

Thirac is the sovereign or king of the gnomes, also called the head of the elders. He is untrustworthy and holds little concern for the Kingdom of Eriden. Their people watch events unfold and record them in their tomes, which are stored in their great libraries hidden inside of the old trees of the marsh lands.

Sevoassi is the gnome the group encounters in the northern woods. He is a trickster who helps them escape the northern pack and gives Amicia a special red orb of unknown origin or purpose.

Minor Gnome Characters:

Ziyath (grumpy) – member of the order of the ossci, the highest and most powerful of the gnomes.

Mizath (happy) – member of the order of the ossci, the highest and most powerful of the gnomes.

Yimath – member of the order of the ossci, the highest and most powerful of the gnomes.

Dragons

Ziradon is Kaliwyn's father and rightful Supreme Dragon of Eriden. He is overthrown at the beginning of the story by Gwirwen, who imprisons him that he may suffer for the rest of his days. A powerful wielder of magic, he is seven hundred years of age. During his life, he has lost two wives and all of his sons. Princess Kaliwyn, his dragoness and heir to the throne, is all he has in the world.

Gwirwen is the current King of Eriden, but only because he was successful in taking over the throne. He is not as strong as Ziradon, and certainly not as wise. His poor choices lead to certain destruction, as the prophecy of the destroyer appears to be fulfilled by his doing.

Kaliwyn is the daughter of Ziradon and rightful heir to the throne of the Supreme Dragon of Eriden. Forced into the form of a mortal as a young dragoness, she is taken away to Nalen, where she is found and raised by human parents. She is not aware of her true self and must discover her dragon heart before it's too late.

Lamwen is the captain of the king's guard. He is assigned to protect the coast of the continent and leads the guard in that role. When the group makes it ashore, it is the guard's job to eliminate them. When their attempts prove unsuccessful, he is reassigned to spy on the group, where he learns of Amicia's identity. Becoming her friend and guardian, he is eventually welcomed by the travelers and becomes vital in their success.

Minor Dragon Characters:

Ziewen – female dragon, loyal to and eventually mated with Gwirwen.

Pardodan – loyal to Gwirwen, he longs to improve his rank in the king's guard.

Vaudien – loyal to Gwirwen, he takes Lamwen's place as captain of the king's guard when he is removed.

Kilawon – Kaliwyn's mother and Ziradon's late mate, who was murdered by Gwirwen.

Jarrowan – Lamwen's friend and supporter, he spends time with the group and even experiences human form for a few days.

Putwyn – a less than decisive member of Lamwen's followers who betrays him, then wishes to rejoin them. Most noted for helping the group escape the dragons by arranging for Baeweth to help them.

Onothwyn – a lesser member of the king's guard who helps to hunt the group.

About the Author

Anyone who knows me could tell you, I am a friendly kind of person, never met a stranger and take up conversations anywhere at any time. I work hard, and my mind never seems to shut down, as I wake up often in the middle of the night with ideas pouring out and demanding to be dealt with. Of course that means much of my books were written in the middle of the night.

I grew up and still live in the great state of Texas where everything is bigger, where we have warm weather and a central location. I love my state, my town, and my family, which includes my four sons, my significant other, and many friends as well.

I have thoroughly enjoyed writing this story and hope that you will love reading it just as much. And of course, there will be many more adventures to come.

You can follow Samantha Jacobey at:
Website: www.SamJacobey.com
Facebook: https://www.facebook.com/SamJacobey
Twitter: https://twitter.com/SamJacobey

Also by SAMANTHA JACOBEY

https://www.lavishpublishing.com/authors/samantha-jacobey/

A New Life Series

An epic adventure, TORI FARRELL's life IS one wild story... escaped from a biker gang and running from drug lords... used by the FBI and hoping to protect her present from her past... IT'S DARK - IT'S BRUTAL, and it's WORTH EVERY MINUTE OF IT!! (Mature Adult, 18+)

Irrevocable Series

From affluent beginnings, BAILEY DEWITT's life has become a broken mess... after her parents died unexpectedly, she didn't think it could get any worse. But when the arrogance of man catches up and puts the entire world into a dooms-day spiral, there will be only ONE PLACE she can run to - the ONE PLACE she wanted desperately to escape. (New Adult)

Teach Me to Prey

In this standalone thriller, JASON TRUITT and his friends have gotten their way for years. Deceit, sex, and foul play aren't normally covered in the curriculum, but they're doing whatever it takes to get under BECKY STEWART's skin. When one of the boys turns up dead, it's a race against time to save the others; a STUNNING STORY that will get your heart racing and leave you breathless by the end... (New Adult)

The Wicked Awakened

A Halloween novel; a five-hundred-year-old witch wants to turn SARAH MATTHEWS' body into her new home... A twisted tale involving a coven hell bent on seeing that she succeeds. Who will come out on top in this epic battle of wills? (Mature Adult, 18+)

The Binding

One cursed diary will change two strangers forever...Can Meri and Rider use her mother's old book to figure out why someone is after them? Or will the guilty party succeed, ripping the tome away before killing them and then slithering back into the darkness...

Also From Our Lavish Publishing Family

The Norn Novellas
A. Nicky Hjort
https://www.lavishpublishing.com/authors/nicky-hjort-1/

The Norn Novellas are all chapters in the epic saga of the youngest and most fickle of the four Norn Sisters. The same feisty immortal creature who must escape her inherent inner darkness to learn the meaning of life.

Each story takes a classic fairytale and spins it on its head, as we learn that maybe Norse Mythology was so much more than legend. And to think, you thought you knew those old tales so well.

Meet Za and find out what really happened...

When Tundra Turns to Ardnyt - Book 1: In the center of a magical world there grows a beautiful and terrible chasm of climbing plants. On one side of the Ivy Wall we find the hell-of-Tyndra, on the other, the heaven-of-Ardnyt. But legend has it that in the middle...lives a preternatural beast that imprisons and tortures the children from both sides.

When the war against time begins, Azza will have to cross over the Ivy Wall, something that has never been done before by a living being. But if she does make it through, she just might discover who she really is and how she became trapped in this alternate reality.

A fairytale at heart, this is the first chapter in the epic saga of the youngest and most fickle of the four Norn Sisters. The same feisty immortal creature who must escape her inherent inner darkness to learn the meaning of love.

A veritable palindrome from start to finish, the narrative of Where Tyndra Turns to Ardnyt journeys through duality to discover what shocking truths emerge when up becomes down, life becomes death, suffering becomes release, and the most unexpected endings become the most surprising beginnings.

Welcome to a place where forwards and backwards are exactly the same direction. Here Where Tyndra Turns to Ardnyt.

Where Ebon Sounds Like Ivory – book 2: Norse legend has it that the arms of the Yggdrasil tree—a sacred instrument of Odin—are ever-reaching, and its survival is necessary for life itself to continue.

During Winter's Solstice, when the search for her mortal mother begins, Za will have to cross over the Ebon Branch of the Dead—a feat that has supposedly never been survived intact. But if she does make it across and back home, she just might discover why she and the other three Norn Sisters of Fate came to be.

A fairytale at heart, this is the second chapter in the epic saga of the youngest and most fickle of the four Norn Sisters. The same feisty immortal creature who must discover her true origins to understand her inherent inner darkness. Only this way can she learn the meaning of unconditional sacrifice in the name of impenetrable love...when, as her destiny would have it, all the branches of such a powerful tree tremble treacherously in her tiny little hands.

A veritable unraveling of Snow White, the narrative of Where Ebon Sounds Like Ivory journeys through the most horrible of realms where shocking truths emerge. Here where death mimics life, obsession masquerades as devotion, and the most unexpected endings become the most surprising beginnings of a classic tale. One... you thought you knew so well.

Welcome to a place where the darkest of melodies births a miraculous tune of surrenderance. Here Where Ebon Sounds Like Ivory and Christmas, as we know it, begins.

Behind Blue Eyes Series
Sara J. Bernhardt
https://books2read.com/BlueEyesBeginner

A father's desire to save his child presents him with an unthinkable choice that leaves him darker than human, forced to roam through time alone as he searches for the place he belongs.

Adam Gold – Book 1: Fleeing the French invasion of Geneva Switzerland in the 1700s, Adam Gold books passage to America with his family. On the ship, Adam's daughter falls fatally ill. A mysterious man comes to Adam with a way to save his child by turning Adam into something darker than human.

The Medallion – Book 2: Adam Gold, an immortal with sweet eyes of blue, rushes through the centuries on a quest for reason and a thirst for revenge. To cope with his pain and regret, he sleeps away the years and awakes in a new era with a powerful, ancient vampire who sets her sights on him.

Golden Shackles – Book 3: When the ancient queen, Sekhmet snatches up Adam, he is faced with a terrifying decision. To help aid her in her vile plans or dare to stand against her.

Plus 3 more segments!

www.ingramcontent.com/pod-product-compliance
Lightning Source LLC
Chambersburg PA
CBHW060432180626
46817CB00007B/2780

* 9 7 8 1 9 4 4 9 8 5 5 5 4 *